Home OF HER Heart

Hearts of the War, Book 2
A Sweet World War II Romance

By *USA TODAY* Bestselling Author
SHANNA HATFIELD

Home of Her Heart

To those who possessed the bravery
to do the impossible,
and inspired a nation on to victory.

Books by Shanna Hatfield

FICTION

CONTEMPORARY

Love at the 20-Yard Line
Learnin' the Ropes
QR Code Killer
Rose
Taste of Tara

Grass Valley Cowboys
The Cowboy's Christmas Plan
The Cowboy's Spring Romance
The Cowboy's Summer Love
The Cowboy's Autumn Fall
The Cowboy's New Heart
The Cowboy's Last Goodbye

Holiday Brides
Valentine Bride

Rodeo Romance
The Christmas Cowboy
Wrestlin' Christmas
Capturing Christmas
Barreling Through Christmas

Silverton Sweethearts
The Coffee Girl
The Christmas Crusade
Untangling Christmas

Women of Tenacity
A Prelude
Heart of Clay
Country Boy vs. City Girl
Not His Type

HISTORICAL

Baker City Brides
Tad's Treasure
Crumpets and Cowpies
Thimbles and Thistles
Corsets and Cuffs
Bobbins and Boots

Hearts of the War
Garden of Her Heart
Home of Her Heart

Pendleton Petticoats
Dacey
Aundy
Caterina
Ilsa
Marnie
Lacy
Bertie
Millie
Dally

Hardman Holidays
The Christmas Bargain
The Christmas Token
The Christmas Calamity
The Christmas Vow
The Christmas Quandary

···✦ *Chapter One* ✦··

1941
Pendleton, Oregon
New Year's Eve

Feigned gaiety chimed in a cacophonous buzz around Staff Sergeant Klayne Campbell as he propped one lean, corded forearm against the fireplace mantel and surveyed the room with an expressionless gaze.

He raised a hobnail crystal cup of punch to his full lips and took a drink. The urge to spit out the syrupy concoction as it assaulted his taste buds nearly overtook him. He forced a swallow and stared into the cup. Overly sweet yet lacking any real flavor, at least plenty of ice floated in the crimson liquid.

Bodies crammed into the room for a New Year's Eve celebration left the space stuffy and uncomfortable. The hot chocolate or steaming cups of coffee the harried hostess offered guests failed to entice him. He had even less interest in the freely poured booze flowing in the room across the hall from the host.

The idea of picking up one of the colorful Christmas-themed magazines on a nearby table and waving it around to stir the air entered his mind, but he ignored it. He'd look ridiculous flapping a copy of *Good Housekeeping* in front of his face, especially with a little golden-haired girl decorating a Christmas tree on the cover.

It would have been a simple thing to move away from the cheerful, crackling fire, and find a cooler place to endure the party until he could escape. However, the corner where he stood gave him a vantage point from behind the drying branches of a Christmas tree to scrutinize everyone who entered the room.

Klayne wasn't sure how he'd allowed a group of his comrades to talk him into coming. He much preferred spending time alone. Tonight, though, he hadn't wanted to be stuck with only his dark thoughts for company.

When a handful of fellow members of the 17th Bombardment Group invited him to join them, he grabbed his cap and went along. Now, he wondered if he'd be better off back at their barracks where he could lose himself in a book. The novel he'd been reading, *The Keys of the Kingdom* by A.J. Cronin, about an unconventional Scottish Catholic priest struggling to establish a mission in China, had been quite engrossing.

His mind played over the plot as his piercing blue eyes flickered across the guests. Perhaps his maudlin musings were preferable to this crowd. It wasn't hard to see the majority of those in attendance were pretending to be happy and in a celebratory mood.

In truth, the majority of the country floundered in a sea of grief and devastation. Three weeks earlier, Japan had bombed Pearl Harbor, wreaking destruction and shocking a nation that had clung to peace instead of chasing war. Upon America's official entry into war with Japan and Germany, Klayne and his fellow U.S. Army Air Corp members knew it was only a matter of time before they were sent on a mission from their current base at Pendleton Field. He'd never heard of the Wild West town in northeastern Oregon before arriving in Pendleton back in the summer, after the Army air field opened.

The too-bright smiles and strained laughter of those attending this evening's gathering grated on Klayne's taut nerves. Rather than a festive, jubilant mood, he sensed an undercurrent of apprehension and despair among the partygoers. Life had rapidly changed from a struggle to overcome the challenges of moving beyond the Depression to grasping at every bit of hope and joy available because tomorrow had become such an uncertainty.

Notes tinkled from the piano in the opposite corner of the room and a dozen people belted out popular tunes mixed with Christmas carols. Klayne had spent Christmas day flying with a patrol along the West Coast, watching for signs of a Japanese attack. He'd only returned to Pendleton that afternoon.

Instead of convincing himself he might enjoy a party, he should have known better and stayed at the base.

A barely restrained cringe accompanied his next sip of punch. He held a bit of ice against the roof of his mouth and listened as the singers did a fair job of harmonizing on "O Come All Ye Faithful."

The scent of bayberry from the candles burning on the mantel beside him might have made him nostalgic, if he owned any pleasant holiday memories. He inhaled a bouquet of perfume from the women in the room, tainted by the underlying odor of alcohol. The aroma of food wafted to him as the hostess maneuvered through the room with a tray of meat-filled hand pies, still steaming from the oven.

Klayne was starving, but he didn't move from his hiding spot by the Christmas tree. He didn't belong at this party. He didn't belong anywhere. The military had provided the closest thing to a home and family he'd ever known. Even then, he didn't make friends, didn't form attachments. From experience, he knew it only ended in more heartache and loss.

Out of habit, his eyes again scanned the room. His gaze passed by the doorway then backtracked, settling on a dark-haired woman who strode in with a laughing blonde. The fair-haired woman was lovely and decidedly feminine, but didn't keep his interest.

From his undetectable position, he studied the brunette. The lights in the room glimmered off the hair she'd rolled away from her face and pinned in a cascade of curls at the back of her head. She exuded vibrancy and humor, a stark contrast to the haunted expressions of most in attendance. A ready smile brought out a dimple in her left cheek. He had no doubt that dimple, and the woman who owned it, left men befuddled for miles around.

The long red velvet evening gown she wore seemed similar in style and elegance to the dresses worn by many of the females in attendance at the party. But when she swung around to greet the hostess with a warm hug, her skirt flared out, revealing a pair of black and red cowboy boots. The sight tugged a grin from him, doubling his interest in this unusual woman.

His eyes traveled from her boot clad feet back up to her face and his heart skipped a beat, then another. The woman looked familiar. Indeed, she looked exactly like a girl who'd entranced Klayne during the famous Pendleton Round-Up back in September. The community encouraged the soldiers at the base to join in the annual event. Klayne had no interest in being packed elbow to elbow into bleachers among the cheering crowd, but the lure of witnessing the rodeo performance drew him there.

When a trick rider raced into the arena and performed a series of jaw-dropping stunts, Klayne hadn't been able to look away from her. He couldn't explain what or why, but something about that woman had drawn him unlike any other. A vibrant, lively spirit had practically oozed from her and filled the stadium at the rodeo with her presence.

Just like the woman now brought the room to life. If Klayne was given to fanciful thoughts, which he definitely was not, he would have said her entry into the room was like turning on the lights or switching from shades of gray to a rainbow of color.

One of the singers at the piano waved to her, trying to get her to join them, but the woman shook her head and looped her arm around her friend's shoulder. The two girls made their way over to a group of women speaking with a few men from Klayne's squadron.

Briefly, the woman greeted them, left the blonde with their friends, and made her way around the room, speaking to everyone. She'd just turned from addressing an older man she seemed to know well when she noticed him spying on her from around the Christmas tree.

Her head tilted to the right and she gave him a long, studying glance. When her gaze met his, something electric arced between them. Curious if she felt it too, he watched a slow smirk pop out the dimple in her cheek again. He'd never seen a woman smirk before and found it entirely fascinating as she walked across the room with purposeful strides.

The woman wasn't the prettiest he'd ever seen. Her nose was a bit too broad and slightly crooked, as if it had been broken in the past. Her chin was slightly too sharp, inarguably stubborn. Her hazel eyes were bright, lively, and inquisitive. But her lips, oh those tantalizing lips, were absolutely made for being kissed well and often.

Stunned, he realized something about her appealed to him more than any woman he'd ever met.

"What kind of man spies on a woman from behind a Christmas tree?" she asked, stopping in front of him and crossing her arms in front of her chest. Her face held a look of suspicious scrutiny.

Dumbfounded and caught in the act, Klayne lost the ability to speak.

The scornful look she'd given him melted into a warm smile. She laughed and placed a hand on his arm. "I'm teasing you, soldier. What's your name?"

He stared at her another moment before he looked down to his arm where her hand rested. It threatened to sear through the fabric of his shirt and brand his skin. Although he expected her to have soft hands with manicured nails, her hands were work-roughened, chapped, and with nails broken down to the quick. A scab covered the backs of two knuckles and a cut stretched along the length of her index finger.

"You're a quiet one, aren't you?" she asked, continuing to look at him as she dropped her hand.

"Most of the time, ma'am," he said, silently urging his tongue to regain function. "My name is Klayne. Sergeant Klayne Campbell."

"It's nice to meet you, Sergeant." She gave him a beaming smile and held out a hand to him. "I'm Delaney Danvers, but most of my friends just call me Dee."

"Miss Danvers, it's a pleasure to meet you." Klayne took her much smaller hand in his, astonished by the calluses on her palm and the strength in her grip. Whoever this girl was, she wasn't afraid of hard work. "Did you happen to provide a trick riding performance at the rodeo a few months ago?"

She shrugged, as though it was nothing. "I did. My dad and his friends talked me into doing it." Delaney leaned closer to him, as though she might confide a secret. "Did I look like an idiot? That costume gave me ten different kinds of fits."

Klayne swallowed down a laugh and shook his head, recalling the leather-fringed outfit she'd worn. "No, ma'am. You looked..." Before he voiced his thoughts, he snapped his mouth shut. He couldn't very well tell her she looked magnificent and dazzling, and had him on the edge of his seat the whole time she performed. The way she'd ridden her horse was poetic in its raw, wild beauty. The outfit in question made him wonder if she was a descendant of Annie Oakley or a heroine from the Old West. Each movement of the horse she rode caused the fringe to swing around her, leaving him spellbound. His gaze roved over her face again and he saw a glimmer in her eyes, as though she dared him to bombard her with idle flattery.

Her left eyebrow quirked slightly and she tipped her head to the right again. "How did I look, Sergeant?"

"Like a woman who has a great deal of knowledge about handling horses." His lips tipped up at the corners, almost into a smile. "You must possess an inordinate amount of control and strength to carry off those tricks, not to mention the bond of trust you obviously have with your horse."

A look of surprise flashed across her face, followed by one of delight. "That's one of the nicest things anyone has said to me. Thank you," she said, staring up into his face. She was slightly taller than the average woman, but still several inches shorter than his six-foot, two-inch height.

Firelight reflected in her intriguing eyes and cast an inviting amber glow around her. Klayne considered how it would feel to enfold her in his arms. He steadfastly avoided casual dalliances, but he couldn't help but wonder what it would be like to hold this woman close to his heart.

Maybe he'd even absorb a small measure of her vitality and exuberance. Would the skin of her arms feel as smooth as it looked? Would the velvet of her gown feel warm or cool to the touch as it glided over her decadent curves?

Chagrined by his thoughts, he set the cup of syrupy punch on the mantel and took a step back from her. To his amazement, she didn't seem eager to move on to speak to other guests at the party.

"I've never heard the name Klayne before. Is it a family name?"

He shook his head. "No." He grinned. "And your next question will be how I spell it, right? And then if people often mispronounce it?"

An affirmative nod met his questions.

"K-l-a-y-n-e. I tell people who struggle to pronounce it to remember Klayne on the plane."

"And are you Klayne on a plane?" She gave him a curious glance and swept a hand toward to his uniform. "Is that what you do at the base?"

"I'm on a flight crew." Klayne didn't feel the need to say more. In truth, that was all he felt at liberty to share.

"That sounds exciting and dangerous." She grinned at him. "Exactly the type of thing I'd love. Is it hard to learn to fly?"

"Depends," he said, holding back a smile.

"On what?"

"If you're scared of heights or plummeting from them."

Her laughter bubbled over him with encompassing warmth unlike anything he could recall. In that moment, he decided he'd be willing to do almost anything to experience it again.

She fanned a hand in front of her face and leaned away from the fireplace. "Whew. It's warm in here. I don't suppose you'd be willing to go for a walk outside?"

At his dubious expression, she moved nearer. "Sergeant Campbell, I promise I'm not up to anything. In spite of what you might think, I'm truly warm. Since I'm a good judge of character, I don't think you have any devious schemes in mind. I really would like to get a breath of fresh air. If Amy hadn't insisted I come with her to this party tonight, I'd be at home curled up with a good book, enjoying a peaceful evening."

Klayne had trouble picturing the vivacious woman sitting still long enough to enjoy reading, but he nodded his head and escorted her to the door. She pointed out her coat and he held it as she slipped her arms in the sleeves. Unable to stop himself, he gently lifted the bulky weight of her hair from inside her coat collar. For just a second, he fingered the silky strands before letting them go. The curls bounced against her back as she pulled gloves from the pockets of her coat. He took a deep breath, inhaling her luscious scent as he unearthed his coat from the pile by the door.

Together they walked out into the frigid evening air. Stars twinkled overhead while snow crunched beneath their feet. Frosty wisps of their breath curled around them as they strolled down the walk and out to the sidewalk.

Delaney turned to the right and Klayne fell into step beside her. Quietly, they strode to the end of the block and took another right. She cast a glimpse at him and then burrowed deeper into her coat. "Do you enjoy flying?"

"I do. It's something I've done for quite a while."

She continued studying him. "How long have you been in the military?"

"A dozen years, since I was seventeen," Klayne admitted. He bent down so his mouth was close to her scarf-covered ear. "But don't tell on me. I might have fudged on my age a bit back when I enlisted."

"Your secret is safe with me," she whispered, glancing up at him with an indulgent smile.

Klayne inhaled her soft, alluring scent and fought against falling into the captivating depths of her eyes. Out here, alone, under a velvety canopy of stars, he could sense her loneliness mingling with worry.

"Do you, um... have someone special in the Army?" He wished he hadn't asked the question when a sad look settled on her face. She must have a beau, or husband, in the military.

"Yeah, I do." She stared straight ahead. They'd walked half a block before she answered. "My brother, Mac, left Christmas Day for San Diego. He joined the Navy instead of waiting to be drafted." Her voice caught and she cleared her throat. "I'm praying he'll stay safe."

"Does he live here in Pendleton?" Klayne asked, reaching out to steady Delaney when her feet slid on a spot of ice. Even through the thick wool of her dark green coat, he liked the feel of her waist beneath his hand.

Delaney shot him a look of gratitude as she regained her balance and they continued on their way. "No. He moved to Portland many years ago, when he left for college. He met a girl there who was from the area and decided to stay when he talked her into marrying him." She grinned at him. "Carol is just a sweetheart and I love her dearly. They have one boy, Ryatt. He is a handful."

Klayne chuckled, picturing a boy with Delaney's smile and eyes sparking with life. "Ryatt is an unusual name."

"It is. Carol wanted to name him Wyatt, but Mac claims he misunderstood her and wrote Ryatt on the birth certificate. We all call him Ry. He'll be nine in February." Delaney's face softened. "That boy is just the cat's pajamas. He and I get along quite famously."

Klayne could only imagine. "Does your sister-in-law have family in Portland now?"

She shook her head, making her curls bounce in a way that forced Klayne to shove his hands deeper into his coat pockets to keep from fingering them again. The desire to bury his hands into the thick lushness of her hair was almost more than he could bear. Rapidly blinking to clear his thoughts, he focused on their conversation.

"No. Carol's folks are both gone and she didn't have any siblings." Delaney pointed to a café that was still open. "Hungry?"

Klayne nodded and pulled open the door, holding it as she preceded him inside. The place was empty except for one old-timer sitting at the counter, sipping coffee and eating a slice of pumpkin pie.

Delaney settled into a booth at the back and slipped off her coat. Klayne removed his then sat opposite her, grateful to get inside out of the freezing cold and for more time spent in her presence.

After the waitress took their orders and brought them both cups of hot coffee, Klayne held the cup between his hands and watched Delaney. She tucked an errant strand of hair behind her ear then sipped the hot, fragrant brew.

"Do you have siblings, other than your brother?" Klayne asked, suddenly wanting to know everything about her.

"No. Just Mac. He's ten years older than me. My mother passed away when I was twelve. Since then, it's been Mac, me, and Dad. We made a pretty good trio until Mac fell in love." She sighed and gave him a bittersweet smile. "Don't get me wrong, we love Carol and Ryatt to pieces, but it sure would have been dandy if they decided to live here instead of Portland."

"Do you see them often?"

Delaney shook her head. "No. Not as often as I'd like. They were here for Thanksgiving and Dad and I went to Portland for Christmas. Mac had to leave sooner than we expected. Dad decided to stay an extra week while Carol and Ryatt adjust to Mac's absence. Mac has an apple orchard southwest of Portland and we wanted to make sure the chores won't be more than Carol can handle. She'll have to hire someone in the spring to oversee the work through the harvest. Dad and I talked about me going to stay with her, but I'd sure miss being here, at home."

Klayne took a drink of the hot coffee, glad to replace the taste of the punch with something more aromatic and hearty. "Have you always lived in Pendleton?"

"You betcha." She leaned back in the booth with a look that made her appear comfortable with herself and with life. "My grandfather came here and bought a half-section of land. He planted wheat, made a good profit, and bought more land. Around the time dad came along, Grandpa started buying Hereford cattle. Now, we have about four thousand acres of wheat and five hundred head of cattle."

Klayne knew a little about ranching and farming, and the numbers sounded impressive to him. One thing he particularly enjoyed about being in Umatilla County was glancing down from a plane upon the rolling hills of golden wheat waving in the summer breeze. With blue sky stretching for what seemed like forever, it was an incredible sight to see.

"And you help out on the place?" he asked. From the rough condition of her hands, he assumed Delaney did more than her share of work. Her tanned face and toned arms made him think she spent a considerable amount of time outside.

She grinned. "Of course. I've been helping on Sage Hills Ranch since I was big enough to talk. Dad said I mastered riding before I did walking, although I never quite believed him."

Klayne couldn't help but smile, picturing a young Delaney with her dark hair in braids, little legs poking out to the sides as she rode an old mare.

The conversation ebbed as the waitress approached with their meals. Neither spoke as they tucked into the food. Delaney didn't pick at her meal, as so many women did, but ate a healthy portion before she sat back and dabbed at her mouth with a napkin.

"I needed that. I was busy in the barn with a sick cow all morning and skipped lunch. This afternoon, I got so caught up in bringing the ranch accounts up to date, I forgot all about the party tonight. Amy, that's my friend, the beautiful blond-haired imp I was with at the party, phoned to ask why I hadn't shown up at her place." She smirked again. "Let me tell you, I had to hustle to get ready and danged if I didn't tug on my boots instead of a pair of dress shoes."

She held out one leg and lifted the hem of her skirt just enough Klayne got a glimpse of the red and black boots.

"Perhaps you'll start a new fashion trend."

She quirked her eyebrow at him and shook her head. "That won't ever happen, but they sure are more comfortable than the ridiculous shoes most girls wear."

The waitress cleared away their plates, brought them each a piece of warm apple pie, and refilled their coffee cups before disappearing into the kitchen.

Klayne lost track of time as he listened to Delaney share about her family and friends. He asked just enough questions to keep her talking. Enthralled with her, with the sound of her voice, he could have spent the rest of his life right there with her.

Unfortunately, he had to be back at the base and ready to work the next morning. A peek at the clock on the wall above the order counter confirmed he'd monopolized her time for hours. In fact, the year wound to a close as the minutes neared midnight.

Delaney turned to look at the clock and gasped. "Oh, my stars! Amy will think I've been kidnapped or abandoned her, or some such nonsense. I better get back to the party right away."

She stood and started to yank on her coat, but Klayne took it from her, holding it as she jammed her arms into the sleeves. He repeated the action of lifting her hair from beneath the collar. When he did, his fingers skimmed across the satiny skin of her neck. She shivered in response.

Unclear if that was a good or bad thing, he stepped back, pulled on his coat, and left cash on the table to cover their meals along with a generous tip.

"I'll pay my share," Delaney said, pulling bills from the depths of her pocket.

Klayne folded her fingers back around the money and shook his head. "No. It's my treat. You saved me from suffocating in that stuffy house or dying from boredom."

Humor shimmered in her eyes. "I'm glad I could be of service."

He held the door as they stepped outside. The temperature had dropped even lower and they didn't dawdle as they walked. They were nearing the house where they met when chimes from a clock tower rang crisp and clear across the night, signaling the end of one year and the beginning of another.

"Oh, it's midnight," Delaney said, stopping and turning to face him. "Happy New Year!"

"Happy New Year to you, Miss Danvers." Klayne looked at her for a long moment before he abruptly tossed caution to the wind. Without asking permission, without a thought to the consequences, he pulled his hand from his pocket and slid it across her jaw, settling it on the back of her neck. His other hand wrapped around her waist and he pulled her close as his head dipped toward hers. The kiss he intended to impart should have been short and sweet, a friendly skimming of lips.

However, the kiss he gave her started with a slight brush of their cool lips, then something shifted between them. Klayne could no more have pulled away than he could have leaped up and grabbed onto the moon. Delaney's arms slid around his neck as her lips warmed beneath his.

He kissed her long, deep, and more passionately than he'd ever kissed another.

As the last chime rang out, he came to his senses and lifted his head, every bit as surprised as Delaney was by what he'd done. The moment he released her, her eyes popped open and the look she gave him held yearning mingled with astonishment.

"Wow, Sergeant Campbell! That's certainly an unforgettable way to usher in a new year." Her hand went to her throat and he watched as she struggled to slow her rapid breathing. "In fact, that is the most memorable Happy New Year wish I've ever received."

Klayne felt heat burn his cheeks despite the arctic air seeping into them. "I'm sorry, Miss Danvers. I didn't intend to… that's to say, I didn't mean… I didn't plan…"

She laughed, a sound that arrowed straight into his heart, and wrapped her arm around his. A light tug and they continued to the house where partygoers began to spill outside.

"It's okay," she said, leaning close to him. "You don't have to apologize for something I enjoyed so much. Just be careful you don't make a habit out of stealing kisses from unsuspecting girls and leaving them thoroughly discombobulated. If you do, I'll have to report you to the authorities."

Doing his best to appear repentant, he hid a grin and nodded solemnly. "Yes, ma'am."

Before he could say anything further, her friend Amy ran up to them. She dragged Delaney into the midst of their friends as they shared new year wishes and said farewells. Delaney cast one last, mesmerized look at him and offered a small wave before she slid behind the wheel of a vermillion red pickup.

Klayne expelled a sigh and strode over to where his group piled into a large sedan. The last thing he'd planned on this evening was falling in love.

★ *Chapter Two* ★

"If you don't get your head on straight, Sis, you're gonna end up missing a finger," Dill Danvers warned his daughter as he guided two large draft horses through the snow.

Delaney's head snapped up and she scowled at him. "I am not!"

Dill chuckled and waggled his hand, covered by a worn tanned leather glove, toward the twine she'd been slicing from around a bale of hay. "You pert near whacked through your thumb. What's got you so distracted? You've been acting loopy since I got home from Portland." The man continued to stare at Delaney as she tossed hay off the wagon to the hungry cattle awaiting their breakfast.

"My answer hasn't changed, Dad. You've asked that question half a dozen times in the last two weeks. I'm just worried about Mac. And then there's Carol and Ryatt. Are you sure they'll be okay? Do I need to go stay with them?" Delaney knew her sister-in-law had matters well in hand, but she felt a sudden need to run away from Pendleton and her foreign, puzzling emotions.

Then again, going to Portland would only remind her of Mac's absence. Part of her wanted to throw a temper tantrum Christmas Day as the family stood on the train platform in Portland to bid him goodbye. A ragtag band played off-key Christmas songs while members of the local chapter of the Daughters of the American Revolution passed out slices of fruitcake, cookies, and juice.

Carol cried enough tears for all of them, but Delaney wanted to join her. She put on a brave face and hugged her brother so tightly, they both had to catch their breath when she finally released him. After telling him to have a safe journey and to remember to write, she stepped back so Mac could hug his wife and child one last time.

Delaney hated war and the uncertain, fearful times that came with it. She didn't want to understand Mac's determination to do his part to defend their country, but she did. If she'd been born a male, she would have been fighting right alongside him. None of that changed the fact, though, that the brother she adored might never come home again.

A shake of her head dislodged the melancholy thoughts and drew her back to the feed wagon with cattle surrounding them.

Dill tipped his head toward her. "You can go stay with Carol and Ry if you want to, but they'll be fine. Mac left everything in good order and Carol really won't need help with anything until it's time to spray the fruit trees in the spring. Mac already lined up someone to take care of the orchard through the summer, so she's all set." Dill held the reins lightly in one hand, waggling his finger at her again. "There's something else bothering you. You can waltz all around it, but you can't hide the truth from me for long. If you tell me what it is, I'll quit hounding you." He grinned and took the reins in both hands.

Delaney's sigh rolled all the way up from her toes and twirled into a swirl of frost around her face when she expelled it. "Dad, why can't you just leave things be?"

"Because it's more fun trying to get a rise out of you, Sis."

A beleaguered sigh rose up from her chest. "Why must you call me Sis?"

"Because it's what I've called you since the day you were born. Your brother demanded to see his lil' sis and the name stuck. Get used to it."

Delaney wrinkled her nose in disgust and forked off more hay.

His eyebrow cocked upward, exactly like Delaney's so often did when she was humored or perturbed. "And stop changing the subject. I'll find out what's going on sooner or later. If you won't tell me anything, I guess I'll just have to call Amy and drag the story out of her."

Delaney pictured her friend spilling what little she knew about the New Year's Eve party to Dill over a cup of coffee and slice of gingerbread from the bakery Amy's parents owned. All Amy knew was that Delaney disappeared during the party and she found her outside with a good-looking soldier. When Amy plied her for more details, Delaney said she and Klayne went outside to talk because the house was too warm.

Amy didn't buy the story, but didn't press for more information.

Thoughts of Sergeant Klayne Campbell caused Delaney's cheeks to fill with heat. She recalled every detail of the time they spent together. The moment she'd walked into the party, she felt someone's eyes on her and turned to see Klayne half-hiding behind the Christmas tree in the corner. Looking both bored and wary, he leaned against the fireplace with one impressive arm propped on the mantel.

Even across the room, Delaney could sense the strength in his long, lean frame. The man had to be all wiry muscle. Cropped brown hair, thick with a tendency to curl on the ends, made her fingers itch to run through it. Blue eyes that pierced her with their intensity captured her attention before her gaze had wandered over his straight nose and square chin. Full lips beckoned and begged to be kissed.

Delaney didn't know what propelled her across the room to introduce herself, but she felt powerless to stay away from him.

His voice held a deep cadence that made her insides quiver. At first, she thought he was too reserved, too quiet, but then he smiled. It was like watching the sun burst through a stormy sky, brightening everything around it.

Up until that moment, Delaney would never have asked a man she didn't know to go outside for a walk with her. It was too forward, and potentially dangerous, but she'd asked him. He'd looked so uncomfortable and eager to escape, she wanted to help him. She also didn't want to miss the opportunity to get to know him better.

Instinctively, she knew she could trust him. He seemed like a gentleman, and he had been. Although some might argue the sizzling kiss they shared at the stroke of midnight nudged toward rakish, but Delaney didn't care. It was the single best kiss she'd ever received and she couldn't stop thinking about how much she'd enjoy another kiss, or dozens, from him.

The fact he attempted to apologize for getting caught up in the moment only made him seem special, different from the boys and men she knew.

Delaney might be bold and a little untamed, but she possessed a strong set of morals and planned to keep them. No one was going to talk her into doing something she didn't think was right, regardless of how handsome he might be.

At twenty-five, she figured she was past the marrying age, but didn't care. She'd never met anyone who stirred in her even the slightest interest in settling down with a husband. Then she'd met Klayne.

Something about the man, about his quiet, reserved ways, the wit he'd shared when she finally got him talking, and his gentleness made her want to know more. For the first time in her life, she thought about wedded bliss and babies, and spending her future with him.

Foolishly, she'd run off without giving him any personal information, like her phone number. However, he knew her name and the name of the ranch. All he had to do was ask around town and it wouldn't take long for someone to tell him how to find her.

Perhaps she'd merely served as a diversion on a night when those who are single feel particularly lonely.

Dill nudged her with his elbow and Delaney scowled at him. "Come on, Sis, spill the beans. Did you meet a fella?"

"Dad..." She drew out each letter until it sounded like an entire sentence. "Just leave it be. Please?"

"Okay, sweetheart. For now. Besides, we need to finish feeding these critters and get back to the barn. I'm about half-froze."

Delaney grinned and tossed off more hay. "Me, too. Last one back has to make hot chocolate."

"Deal."

Delaney jumped off the hay wagon, and ran over to the wagon on the other side of the pasture where two of the hired hands dumped off hay.

"Hey, Yank, go help Dad. We're having a contest to see who finishes first." Delaney grabbed a handhold and pulled herself onto the wagon.

"Sure, Dee." The gangly young man stepped down and jogged back to Dill's wagon.

"Are you always into some sort of tomfoolery?" asked Butch, a ranch hand who'd been around since her dad was a boy. She got the idea he'd started working on the ranch when he was in his early twenties and stayed. He never talked much about his past, but he was the closest thing she had to an uncle. Butch wasn't quite as spry as he used to be, but he could handle the big team of Belgians pulling the hay wagon better than anyone on the place.

She smiled at the older man and hefted a large forkful of hay. "According to you and Dad, I'm always neck-deep in some type of shenanigan."

Butch laughed and snapped the reins, encouraging the Belgians to increase speed. "Well, you typically are, Dee. What's the prize for the winners?"

"The loser has to make everyone hot chocolate." Delaney tossed off another large forkful of hay, grunting under the weight of it.

Butch glanced back at her and snapped the reins again. "Get to tossing faster, Girly. Your hot chocolate tastes like you mixed coffee dregs with turpentine."

Delaney laughed. "That's not nice. I only scorched it once and you all are never going to let me live it down. At any rate, Dad makes the best hot chocolate of anyone I know."

"Then get to hustlin' so we win!"

"Yes, sir!" Delaney put her back into it and hay flew off the wagon. She dared not look across the snow-covered expanse to see if Yank and her father were finished. One advantage she and Butch had was their proximity to the gate and barn.

Delaney used the side of her boot to scoot off the last bit of hay then slapped Butch on the shoulder. "Done. Let's go!"

Butch whistled and the Belgians broke into a trot. The hay wagon, which sported runners instead of wheels because of the snow, glided easily over the frozen crust on the ground.

Tilting back her head, Delaney closed her eyes and let the cool breeze stroke her face. The jingle of more harnesses drew her gaze over to where her dad raced his team of Clydesdales toward the gate. According to the story Mac shared, her dad and Butch had gone to an auction to buy a team of young work horses. They argued for two hours about which were better, Belgians or Clydesdales. Both men were so stubborn, they decided to purchase two teams and see which turned out to be the best. To this day, they still hadn't decided and the horses had been with them for fifteen years.

"Go, Butch, go!" Delaney encouraged, glancing back at her father and making a silly face.

As though they sensed the need to hurry, the Belgians picked up their pace and breezed through the gate heading for the barn.

Dill and Yank gained on them, but the Belgians pulled ahead at the last moment, arriving first at the barn.

Delaney waved her arms in the air then jumped down from the wagon, doing a few dance steps as she laughed. "We won! Again!"

Dill scowled at her as he set the brake and climbed down. "I'm sure you two cheated somehow."

"Oh, don't be a sore loser, boss," Butch said, grinning at Dill. "Just because my horses are better than yours," he taunted.

Dill glared at him. "I ought to fire you, old man."

"Go ahead. If you do that, you'll be left without a cook and someone to make sure the work gets done around here," Butch said, slowly climbing down from the feed wagon. He patted the rump of the horse closest to him then hobbled around to rub the neck of the other.

Before Delaney was born, Butch had been in a terrible auto accident that nearly killed him. While he recovered, Delaney's mother had taught him how to cook and had him help with the accounting side of the business.

When Mary Danvers passed away, Butch was the one who'd tried to teach Delaney how to cook and helped her learn to balance the ranch books. For years, her father had been so buried in his grief, he'd all but forgotten he still had a young daughter who needed him and a son who mourned the loss of a beloved mother. Eventually, Dill let go of his pain and took back his life. By then, Delaney was in high school and Mac was married.

Delaney sometimes wondered if her father's overwhelming grief wasn't what drove Mac to leave. She'd grown up assuming he'd take over the ranch, but he seemed to want to make his own way in the world.

Still, she hoped he'd someday return to the ranch with Carol and Ry. There was plenty of room for them all to live there.

Yank backed the feed wagons up to the haystack while two of the other ranch hands came over to help load hay, leaving the wagons ready for the next feeding.

"I'll start cookin' supper while you whip up a batch of hot chocolate," Butch said, ambling toward the bunkhouse. For the last dozen years, Delaney and her father joined the hands in the bunkhouse for supper. The rest of the time, they took turns making breakfast and lunch. Delaney wasn't an award-winning cook, but she did well enough to get by. Domestic skills had never held her interest like learning about farming and ranching. She'd much rather be outside breaking a horse, chasing cows, or building a fence than learning how to sew or clean.

She often wondered why her father hadn't hired a housekeeper, but anytime she suggested it, he told her it was good for the two of them to take care of the house without help. Sometimes the furniture grew a little dusty or the windows failed to sparkle before they got down to the task of caring for their home, but keeping the ranch running came first. It always came first.

Delaney wanted to bury herself in work, but for the next month, there wasn't a lot to be done. Other than feeding the cattle and riding horses, the chores were light due to the winter. Once the cows began to calve and spring work got underway, she'd be so busy she'd wish for a day of quiet. For now, though, she had too much time to get lost in her thoughts. And much to her dismay, they kept circling around to a soldier named Klayne.

In spite of the hours they'd talked, she still didn't know much about him. He'd enlisted young and mentioned flying with a crew, but she wasn't sure what he did. He seemed more like a loner than someone with many friends. He mentioned he liked to read, which surprised her. She pictured him as someone who was more of a doer than someone who read about others doing something. She supposed the same might be said about her, though.

At the back door, she and her dad stamped their feet, loosening the packed-on snow, before stepping inside what had once been a summer porch. Dill had enclosed it and made it into a laundry room for her mother not long after they wed. It made a good place to remove dirty coats and boots without traipsing a mess throughout the whole house.

Delaney had just kicked off her boots and hung her coat on a hook near the door when the jangle of the telephone rang from the kitchen. "I'll get it," she said, pushing open the door into the kitchen and hurrying over to lift the receiver from the phone on the wall.

"Sage Hill Ranch."

"Dee, it's Amy."

Delaney heard a hint of panic mixed with excitement in her friend's voice. "What's going on?"

"You need to come to town. Right now." Amy spoke in a whisper.

"What's wrong? Are you hurt? Are your folks okay?" Delaney asked. Dill stepped beside her and gave her a questioning glance, but she shrugged, still unsure of what Amy needed.

Amy laughed, setting her fears at rest. "Everyone is fine, but that cutie pie soldier you talked to the other night is here at the bakery. He just ordered a cinnamon roll and a cup of coffee. I can only keep him here for so long before he'll leave. Get a move on and come see him."

"I don't think so. It's best if I just…"

Amy interrupted her. "Oh, hush! Change out of whatever horrible thing you're wearing, wash off that rancid-smelling manure, and come to town. I'll see you in a bit."

Amy hung up and Delaney glared at the phone, wishing she could reach through it and throttle her best friend. Sometimes Amy thought she was far too clever for her own good.

"What's wrong with Amy?" Dill asked, pouring milk into a pan and setting it on the stove to heat for hot chocolate.

"She's bossy and loony," Delaney grumbled, washing her hands at the sink.

Dill grinned. "So are you. What's she want you to do?"

"She said she needs me to come to the bakery. Something about cinnamon rolls and coffee. I might as well go or she'll just bug me until I give in or pout if I don't."

"Bring home some of Myrtle's coffee cake. We'll have it for breakfast tomorrow," Dill said, grating a chocolate bar into the warming milk.

Delaney sighed. "Anything else you want from town?"

"Nope." Dill stirred sugar into the pan. "Sorry you'll miss the hot chocolate."

"Maybe I'll get a cup with Amy." Delaney spun around and raced up the back stairs, taking them two at a time. She wished she had time for a bath, but if she didn't hurry, she wouldn't make it to Pendleton before Klayne left the bakery.

She yanked off her overalls and flannel shirt, and the long wool underwear she wore under them in the bathroom. After taking a quick sponge bath, she hurried to her bedroom and flung open the closet. A frantic riffling through her clothes turned up a navy and green plaid skirt. She pulled it on, grabbed a cream cashmere sweater Mac and Carol had given her last year for Christmas, and then cinched her waist with a wide leather belt.

With deft fingers, she worked the braid she'd worn all day free and fluffed her hair. A few quick twists, and she pinned it up on her head, glad the waves from the braid kept her hair from looking flat. She swiped her eyelashes with a coat of mascara, spritzed on her favorite perfume, and touched her lips with lipstick. Hastily snatching up her green wool coat, she grabbed her handbag and a hat then clattered down the stairs.

"Anything else you need from Pendleton?" she asked as she tamped her feet into a pair of snow boots she saved to wear to town.

"Nope, just the coffee cake." Dill gave her a long look, both eyebrows shooting upward. "You look nice, Sis. Sure there isn't more to your trip than just meeting Amy?"

She grinned and tugged on her hat then shrugged into her coat. "I won't be gone long, Dad. See you later."

Her father would no doubt comment on her avoidance of his question, but she closed the door as he spoke, not interested in admitting why she was so anxious to get to town.

The red pickup she'd purchased three years ago started right up and she was soon on her way to Pendleton.

Within fifteen minutes, she pulled into a parking space a block away from the bakery and inhaled a deep breath. "This is absurd," she muttered to herself, but opened the door and rushed down the sidewalk toward Bellamy's Bakery.

She opened the door and stepped inside, greeted by the mouth-watering aromas of cinnamon, yeast, and chocolate with a hint of coffee.

Rather than her customary upbeat greeting, Amy stood behind the counter and unobtrusively pointed toward a corner table where Klayne sat with a cup in one hand and a book in the other.

Delaney walked over to the counter and smiled at her friend. "I'm surprised he's still here."

"Me, too," Amy said, clearly excited by his presence. "Once he finished the cinnamon roll, he pulled a book from his coat pocket and started reading. He's hardly moved in the last fifteen minutes.

"What should I do?" Delaney asked, trying to watch Klayne without staring outright.

"Just go say hello, like you happened upon him." Amy gave her a nudge that direction. "I'll bring you a cup of coffee."

"No, I want chocolate, please, and a macaroon. And Dad wants one of your mom's coffee cakes for breakfast tomorrow. Can you box one up? I'll grab it on my way out."

"Of course," Amy said, tipping her head toward Klayne. "Now, go on."

Delaney removed her coat and draped it over her arm, took a deep breath, then silently walked over to Klayne's table.

He glanced at her, dropped his gaze back to the book for a second, then his head popped up and he rose to his feet.

"Miss Danvers. What a surprise," he said. Stiff, he stood in front of her as though he considered snapping to attention. When she smiled at him, he grinned and relaxed his stance. "Are you spying on me?" he teased, referring to their initial conversation.

Delaney couldn't suppress her laughter. "No. My friend Amy's parents own this bakery. My dad was in the mood for coffee cake for breakfast, so here I am." Conveniently, she left out the part about Amy calling the house and demanding she rush into town while he was there. She also wouldn't mention that she broke multiple traffic laws as she sped to Pendleton.

"Would you care to join me for a minute, if you aren't in a hurry?" He motioned to a chair across the table from where he'd been sitting.

"I'd like that," Delaney said, taking a seat in the chair he held out for her. She draped her coat across the chair beside her and set down her handbag. Afraid her hair would look like a frizzy mess, she left her knit beret-style hat in place.

"Here you go," Amy said, approaching with a tray. She set steaming cups of hot chocolate in front of Delaney and Klayne then settled a plate full of assorted cookies between them. With a sly wink at Delaney, she spun around and left.

"Your friend seems nice," Klayne commented, settling his hands around the cup of hot chocolate.

"She has her moments," Delaney said. Amy's matchmaking efforts were annoying, but appreciated. Delaney might have been irritated with her friend if she wasn't so pleased to see Klayne again.

Attractive and commanding in his uniform, he looked even more handsome than she remembered when he smiled.

"This chocolate is good," he said, taking another drink of the sweet, warm liquid.

"It is good," Delaney agreed and leaned toward him, dropping her voice to a whisper. "But my dad's is better."

"You don't say." Klayne grinned at her and helped himself to an oatmeal cookie after Delaney took a chocolate covered macaroon. "Did your father make it home from Portland?"

Surprised he recalled her father had been with Carol and Ry the last time she'd seen him, she nodded her head. "He did make it home. My sister-in-law and my nephew seem to be getting along well."

"That's great news," he said, taking another drink of the chocolate. "Have you heard from your brother?"

"Yes!" She brightened as she thought of the letter they'd just received two days ago. She'd whooped so loudly when she collected the mail, Yank and Duffy both raced down the lane to see if something had happened. Jubilant to hear from Mac, she ran toward the two cowboys waving the letter over her head. Everyone on the place crowded into the kitchen as she read the letter. "Mac wrote us about going through training. It sounds horrible, but he says he's doing fine and learning something new every day."

Klayne leaned back and slowly nodded his head. "Getting used to life in the military can be challenging, but if your brother is anything like you, he'll do fine."

She tipped her head and gave him a studying glance. "Thank you, I think. You're either telling me

I'm tenacious and determined, or mule-headed and stubborn."

He grinned and lifted the cup of chocolate to his lips. "Maybe all of the above."

A scowl furrowed her brow before she broke into another smile. She lifted her cup and held it in her hands then pointed it toward his book. "What are you reading?"

"Nothing much," he said, sliding the book beneath his arm.

"Let me see," she said, wondering if he was reading one of those disgusting magazines with pictures of nearly naked women and hiding it in a book jacket.

His lips thinned and he shook his head. "It's classified."

Delaney set down her cup of chocolate and pretended to reach for a cookie before snatching the book away from him, holding it just out of his reach.

Shocked by what he read, she glanced from the book to Klayne before placing it back beside him.

"Why are you ashamed about that?" she asked, lifting her cup of hot chocolate again and taking a sip.

"Because grown men probably should read something more meaningful than Mrs. Wilder's book about her childhood years spent on the prairie." Klayne looked embarrassed as he stared at his hands, clenching the cup of hot chocolate between them.

Delaney reached over and settled her hand on top of his. "I think it's admirable you choose a variety of literature, Sergeant Campbell. It shows maturity and intellect. For the record, I greatly enjoyed her books, too."

He lifted his head and his gaze tangled with hers. She'd never seen a man with such beautiful, arresting eyes — the kind of eyes that could drive a girl to do something completely stupid and crazy.

Klayne smirked. "If the guys found out I was reading this, they'd never let me live it down. Some of them have a hard time making it through a Captain Marvel comic."

Delaney shook her head. "Oh, those poor fellas. They don't know what they're missing."

They spent a companionable hour talking about books, music, and movies.

"I don't mean to be forward, Miss Danvers, but I'm off duty tomorrow night." Klayne gave her a look full of hope. "Would you be interested in going to see a show with me?"

Even if she'd wanted to turn him down, which she didn't, the fortitude needed to tell him no was far beyond her ability to muster. Not when his company brought her so much pleasure. "I think that could be arranged. What time would you like to meet?"

"Would five be too early? We could have dinner then go to the show. Or see an earlier show and then have dinner afterward. Or we could just see the show." Klayne clamped his mouth shut, as though he'd said too much.

Delaney tossed him a saucy smile. "Dinner and a movie would be fine. I'll meet you at five at the theater." She scribbled an address on a paper napkin and handed it to him. Before she succumbed to the urge to lean across the table and kiss him, she stood and picked up her coat. Klayne hurried to hold it for her. The brush of his fingers across her neck, much as he had done the night of the New Year's Eve party, made her fight back a delicious shiver. The mere thought of his touch made goose bumps break out on her skin.

Chiding herself for her silliness, she worried she would turn into one of the ninnies chasing after anything in pants if she didn't get a better hold on her thoughts.

"Thank you for joining me, Miss Danvers," Klayne said, watching as she picked up her handbag. He walked with her over to the bakery counter. "May I escort you to your car?"

"Oh, that won't be necessary, Sergeant Campbell, but I do look forward to seeing you tomorrow. Go on and enjoy that book." She smiled at him and tilted her head toward the table they'd occupied.

He gave her a brief nod then returned to the table and resumed his seat.

Amy appeared behind the counter, grinning so broadly, her teeth might have fallen out if they'd been false. "Dee, this is so exciting!" she squealed.

Delaney frantically shook her head and glared at her friend. "Shush! He'll hear you."

Amy slid the boxed coffee cake across the counter and whispered, "He's so handsome."

"He is nice looking, but that's all I'm saying. What do I owe you?" Delaney asked, opening her handbag and taking out a coin purse.

"Oh, it's my treat." Amy craned her head to look at Klayne as he picked up his book and feigned reading it while casting glances at Delaney.

"You can't run a business giving away your food," Delaney said, holding the coin purse in her hand. "I want to pay."

"Just bring us a little beef next time you're in town. We'll call it a good trade."

Delaney rolled her eyes, but stuffed her coin purse back into her handbag. "That I can do."

Amy grinned and nodded in Klayne's direction. "So… what do you think?"

"I think you better get back to work and I need to go home, that's what I think." Delaney winked at her friend then reached out to squeeze her hand. "Thank you for calling me. I'm glad you insisted I come into town."

"My pleasure. What good is a best friend if they don't drag you into fun once in a while?"

"Indeed." Delaney cast one more look at Klayne and caught him watching her. She waved her fingers at him, made a funny face at Amy, and then rushed outside. The chilly winter air did little to cool her heated cheeks or dispel her wandering thoughts of the good-looking man inside. What would her father say when he found out she was falling in love with a soldier?

*** *Chapter Three* ***

"You aren't going anywhere until you fess up about what you did yesterday and who you're meetin' tonight," Dill demanded, blocking the doorway as Delaney tried to rush through it for her date with Klayne.

"Dad, I already told you. I went to the bakery yesterday. I even brought home the coffee cake you requested. Remember?" Delaney glowered at her father, hoping he'd move without further interrogation.

"I didn't forget. That cake tasted mighty fine with a cup of coffee this morning, but that isn't why you went to town. You had sparks dancing in your eyes like I've never seen. I want to know who put them there." Dill crossed his arms over his broad chest, letting her know he wasn't backing down.

A sigh of resignation rolled out of her and she glanced at the clock. If she didn't hurry she'd be late, and that would never do. "I met someone at the Millers' New Year's Eve party. And before you accuse me of having a secret beau, I haven't seen him since then. He was at the bakery yesterday afternoon so Amy called and insisted I come in to talk to him.

We spent an hour eating cookies and drinking hot chocolate, talking about books and music. He asked me to go to dinner with him tonight and a movie. If you don't stop this nonsense, I'll be late and that just won't do at all, Dad. Not at all."

Smug, Dill waggled a finger at her. "Now, was that so hard? Couldn't you just tell me that in the first place? Why all the secrecy? Who is this young man? Is he someone I know? From a family in the area?"

Subtly, Delaney maneuvered to the door. "No, Dad. I don't think he's from around here. He's um…" Her hand grasped the doorknob and gave it a turn. So close to making a getaway. "He's actually working at Pendleton Field."

"Oh? What's he do there?" Dill set his foot in front of the door, preventing her from pulling it open.

"He said he's on a flight crew, although I'm not sure what he does exactly. He's been in the army for a dozen years, he's twenty-nine, and really sweet. He's tall, polite, and he likes to read." Delaney blurted the details in a rush and yanked on the door, intent on escaping before her father could offer any comments. Only he braced a hand against the door, holding it part-way closed.

"A soldier? You're dating a soldier? Sis, you know I've warned you about them, about what those boys are after. What will happen when he leaves town and breaks your heart. Why, I thought you had better sense than to…"

She held up a hand to stop his tirade. "Dad, please listen to me. I'm not going to get my heart broken. We're just friends. That's it. We enjoy talking and…" Delaney thought about the New

Year's Eve kiss, but quickly tamped down that memory lest she accidentally divulge confidential information to her father.

Swiftly changing tactics, she looped her arm around Dill's and led him away from the door. "Dad, you raised me to be a smart girl, a careful girl, when it comes to matters of the heart and stupid boys. I promise I'll be careful around him. Sergeant Campbell really is very nice. He's been a perfect gentleman. Besides, you and Butch are always telling me I need to spend more time around young people. Isn't that what I'm doing by going out with him tonight? Don't you want me to have a little fun?"

Dill appeared conflicted as he ran a hand through his short, dark hair peppered with gray. "Fine, go have a wonderful evening, sweetheart, but you invite that young man to go to church with us Sunday. I want to meet him myself. And you better be home before the clock strikes twelve. There isn't a single good thing that happens after midnight."

She started to protest as she sidled to the door. "Dad, I don't think…"

He moved toward her but she tugged the door wide open. "I'll ask him. Bye, Dad. I won't be late!"

She hurried outside and nearly tripped over their dog as he lounged across the top porch step. "Moose, this is not the best place for you to take a nap."

The dog raised his big chestnut-colored head and cocked an ear at her. Her hand scratched over his head and down his back as she rushed past him. "Be good, Moose, and stay out of trouble."

He offered her a soft woof then returned to his nap.

Delaney climbed behind the wheel of the heavy, dark blue sedan that had been her mother's car. Her dad purchased it a few months before her mother passed away. For a long time, no one drove it. Eventually, Dill allowed Delaney to drive it. Now, she used it when she wanted to make a more ladylike appearance in town or if the roads were bad. The car was easier to handle than her truck. They'd had snow that morning and she didn't want to chance sliding off the road and missing her date with Klayne.

Yank had offered to warm up the car for her when she mentioned heading into town. As she slid into the toasty warmth of the front seat, she was grateful for his kindness. The young cowboy waved to her from the doorway of the barn and she mouthed "thank you" before putting the car in gear and heading to Pendleton.

From the moment she left the bakery yesterday, she'd been hard-pressed to think of anything beyond seeing Klayne this evening. She wondered if she could get him to smile again. When he did, it transformed his face from a stern soldier to an incredibly attractive man.

And those eyes! Gracious, but they were destined to make women swoon. Not that Delaney had ever swooned in her life, but his eyes were undeniably dreamy.

Consumed with her thoughts of him, the trip into town passed quickly. She parked the car near the movie theater. Klayne leaned against the brick exterior of the building, waiting for her. She waggled her fingers at him and he hurried over, offering her his hand before she could step out of the car.

"Evenin', Miss Danvers," he said, giving her an observant look, taking in the soft knit hat on her head to the snow boots on her feet.

Delaney's cheeks warmed beneath his perusal, but she hid her flustered state behind a bright smile.

"What movie are we going to see?" she asked, walking with him over to the ticket window.

"It looks like all that's playing is a scary film." Klayne pointed to a sign promoting a movie about a man who turned into a werewolf. "We can skip the movie and just go to dinner."

"No, I want to see it. Didn't it just come out last month?" Delaney started to take money from her handbag, but Klayne hurriedly purchased two tickets then guided her inside the lobby, out of the cold.

"Do you want popcorn?" he asked, glancing around to survey his surroundings.

"I think I better pass if we're going to eat dinner later." She motioned toward the concessions. "Don't let that stop you, though."

"I'll wait for dinner," he said, placing his hand on her elbow and walking with her inside the theater. When she started to head for a row half way to the front, Klayne redirected her to an unoccupied row in the back.

Curious if he felt safer with his back to the wall and no one behind him, she didn't say anything. Instead, she started to remove her coat. Klayne held it while she pulled her arms from the sleeves. She removed her hat and scarf, tucking them into the pockets with her gloves before she took a seat. Klayne seemed nervous as he sat beside her and surveyed the rows in front of him.

"I think we'll be safe here," she whispered, giving him a wry smile.

"Sorry. It's a habit to scan the room." Visibly he relaxed and settled into the seat. "Are you sure you don't need anything? Some candy?"

"No, thank you, Sergeant Campbell, but I appreciate you asking." Delaney brushed at imaginary lint on her skirt to have something to do with her hands. What she really wanted was to reach over and squeeze Klayne's upper arm to see if it felt as strong and solid as it appeared. In addition to looking virile and masculine, he smelled divine. Accustomed to the odors of cattle, horses, and the men who worked around them, it was an altogether wondrous thing to sit close to a man whose fragrance mingled spice, musk, and something ruggedly delicious she couldn't name.

She drew a deep breath then another before she noticed him watching her with an unreadable expression on his face.

"You know, Miss Danvers, I'd be quite pleased if you'd call me Klayne." The smile he gave her made him appear boyish and young, not so serious.

"I will if you keep on smiling like that," she teased, playfully bumping his arm with her shoulder.

For a moment, he looked surprised, but then he slowly nodded his head. "Being with you seems to put a smile on my face."

"I'm glad," Delaney said, primly folding her hands on her lap, like Carol had taught her. Despite the many protests she'd uttered over the years, she was grateful her sister-in-law had done her best to instill proper manners in Delaney. "If you want me to call you Klayne, though, you'll have to agree to call me Dee or Delaney."

He grinned. "Okay. It's a deal, Delaney."

The sound of him saying her name made a thrill shoot through her, but she forcibly ignored it and changed the subject. "So what does your family think of you being a soldier?"

A shrug rode his shoulders before he stiffened. "I have no idea. I've never met anyone in my family."

Delaney turned to him, confused. "You don't know your parents?"

"Or my grandparents," Klayne admitted. "I was left at an orphanage right after I was born."

Gently, she placed her hand over his as it rested on his thigh and offered a comforting squeeze. "I'm so sorry, Klayne. It must have been hard growing up without anyone."

"It was, but that's all in the past." He shifted uncomfortably on the seat, although he placed his other hand on top of hers, keeping it sandwiched with his. "Tell me more about your family. You mentioned your brother and his family. Do you have grandparents, extended family?"

"No. My mother was an only child. My father had two older brothers but they were both killed in the Great War. My grandparents all passed away before I was ten." Delaney questioned how they'd gotten on such a disheartening topic and decided to change it. "Do you like to go to the movies?"

"Sometimes. It depends on what's playing. Generally, if I go, it's by myself. Too many people chattering around me throughout the movie spoils it."

Delaney laughed softly. "I refuse to go to the movies with my brother for that very reason. He keeps up a running commentary that makes me want to stuff my handkerchief in his mouth."

Klayne chuckled. "I'd like to see that."

Before Delaney could further comment, the lights dimmed and images rolled across the screen. First there was a sneak peek at a movie releasing soon with Spencer Tracy and Katharine Hepburn, followed by promotion for a new film coming in February starring Ronald Reagan and Betty Field. Klayne sat forward and watched with interest when a newsreel showed bombs exploding in England and Nazi soldiers saluting Hitler.

Aware of the tense lines riding his shoulders, Delaney clasped Klayne's hand tightly with hers. She hated to watch the news about the war, terrified by the images she saw, scared about what might happen to her brother and others she cared about who would soon join the fighting.

Relieved when the movie began, Delaney sat back, ready to enjoy the film. Although horror movies didn't upset her, she used the excuse of being frightened to bury her face against Klayne's arm.

Klayne glanced down at her and grinned. The movie wasn't even half over and Delaney had spent most of the time with her face pressed against his sleeve, both hands wrapped around his upper arm.

He wouldn't complain one bit. In fact, it took a great deal of restraint on his part not to wrap his arms around her and hold her close.

After another fifteen minutes of listening to her gasp and hide her face, he swallowed a chuckle. It wasn't his intention to scare her spitless with the movie. He'd been surprised when she said she wanted to see it. His experience made him think she wouldn't enjoy it, but he certainly wasn't going to argue against sitting in a dark theater with her pressed against his side.

The scents of lemon and vanilla, blended with exotic notes, floated around him. He inhaled a deep breath, enchanted by the fragrance. It put him in mind of something oriental and feminine. The fragrance required confidence to wear, but fit perfectly on Delaney.

The complex, mysterious layers of the woman thoroughly intrigued him. The more he saw of her, the more time he spent with her, the more he wanted to get to know her. To work his way past each layer until he touched the heart of her.

However, it was foolhardy for him to even dream about a relationship with anyone. He had a feeling he'd be ordered into combat sooner rather than later and a female would only complicate matters.

Especially Delaney.

In spite of his head telling him to stay away from her, his heart wouldn't let him ignore her. Since the kiss they shared New Year's Eve, he couldn't get her out of his thoughts. Honestly, he didn't want to. The flavor of her mouth, so sweet and rich, stayed with him, as well as the feel of her in his arms. She fit against him as if they were poured from the same mold and had been split apart for all these years.

Such musings were ridiculous, but Klayne couldn't stop them. He felt powerless when it came to blocking Delaney from his mind. He'd replayed their conversations over and over, and dreamed of looking into her hazel eyes so full of life.

By chance, he'd run into her at the bakery. At least he'd thought it was by chance until he figured out her friend's parents owned the business. Amy must have telephoned Delaney and let her know he was there.

Regardless of her friend's scheming, Delaney had been as eager and happy to see him as he was her.

He glanced down as she watched the movie with wide eyes. Taking advantage of the reprieve of her clinging to his arm, he lifted it and placed it around her shoulders. Half expecting her to push him away or glower at him, she didn't even seem to notice until another scary scene filled the screen. She turned to him and burrowed against his chest.

Klayne smiled as he settled his hand on her back, rubbing it comfortingly. He bent down and placed his mouth close to her ear. "If you'd like to leave, we can. I don't want you to be traumatized."

"No. I'm having fun," she whispered. "Let's stay until the end."

Her hand rested on his chest, but she didn't lift her head. She merely turned it so she could see the screen. Klayne contemplated if her hand might burn through his jacket and shirt and brand his skin. The next time she grimaced and hid her face, he kissed the top of her head, breathing in her heady fragrance.

Unhurried, she raised her head until she could look into his eyes. Even in the muted light, he could see yearning flicker in hers. Without thinking about what he was doing, about what might happen, he cupped her chin, tilted it up, and grazed a soft kiss across her lips. Immediately, her hands slid up his shoulders and around his neck. The kiss deepened and rapidly gained heat as she pressed against him.

Klayne fought the inclination to haul her onto his lap, bury his hands in her hair, and lose himself in the sweet haven of her arms. Mindful they were in a theater full of people, many who knew her, he skimmed his lips across hers one last time and pulled back.

Eyes half-closed, she remained in a blissful daze. Finally, the fog cleared and she sat up, acting embarrassed as she tucked loose pins into her hair and moved so she sat with an uncompromising posture in her seat, gaze fastened straight ahead on the movie screen. Not so much as the hem of her skirt brushed close to his leg.

Klayne thought about reaching out to her, taking her hand in his, but he refrained. He didn't grow up learning how to act around women. The manners he acquired came from emulating happy couples he'd observed and from a commanding officer who instilled any number of life lessons in him, including the importance of cherishing women. He'd learned to hold open doors, help a lady remove her coat, make sure she was seated before taking a seat, and to stand when she rose.

Since Klayne had limited contact with females for the most part, he'd had to dredge up memories of everything he'd learned the moment he set eyes on Delaney. She made him want to treat her like a queen.

Now, he'd just bungled whatever hope he had of continuing their friendship until he left. The stubborn set to her chin and the board-stiff way she sat properly in her seat confirmed he'd crossed over a line. He hadn't meant to. One look in those lively hazel eyes, one glimpse of the bevy of emotions in them that matched his own, and he'd been unable to think straight.

The movie ended, the lights came back on, and still Delaney remained silent. Demurely, she pulled on her hat, wrapped the scarf around her neck, then began to slip on her coat. When Klayne tried to hold it for her, she turned to the side and jammed her arms in the sleeves.

He swallowed back a sigh and tugged on his coat then motioned for her to lead the way outside.

She didn't say a word until they stood on the sidewalk in front of the theater. At some point during the movie, it had started to snow. Big fluffy flakes drifted lazily from the night sky like confectioners' sugar slowly shaken through a sieve.

"Miss Danvers, I'm sorry. I shouldn't have... I didn't intend..." Klayne didn't know what to say. This was all so new to him. He had no idea what to say to a woman, this woman. Females were emotional, delightful, incredible-smelling, delicate things that generally terrified him.

A sticky situation like this was why he remained at his bunk reading instead of socializing. Trouble seemed to be the only thing he got for his efforts. Lambasting himself for kissing her during the movie, he held back his astonishment when Delaney placed a hand on his arm, drawing his gaze to her glove-covered fingers.

"I'm the one who should apologize, Sergeant. I shouldn't have gotten quite so carried away. You'd think I was in high school for all the decorum I exhibited." She tossed him a wary glance. "I'm not the kind of girl who goes around necking in public, just so you know. I might be a lot of things, but a..." She glanced around to make sure no one listened. Assured they were alone, she continued. "... a loose woman isn't one of them. I don't want you to get the wrong idea."

·*★ *Chapter Four* ★*·

Klayne barely subdued a grin. He had all kinds of ideas about the enchanting woman standing beside him. Snowflakes falling on her dark green coat and matching hat created a soft aura around her. When a snowflake landed on her eyelashes and she batted it away, he battled the urge to kiss her right there on the street.

"I know you aren't that kind of girl, Miss Danvers."

A relieved breath blew out of her, whirling into a frosty tendril floating between them. "May we please pretend I didn't act like a woman from Miss Clementine's place a few minutes ago? Can we go back to being friends? You'll call me Delaney, I'll call you Klayne, and this horrid stilted feeling will go away. Deal?"

She held a hand out to him and he took it, giving it a gentle shake. He wondered how a nice girl like her even knew a place like Miss Clementine's existed. Klayne hadn't frequented the brothel, but a few of the men he knew at the base availed themselves of the services offered. Klayne had helped two of the young men in his squadron get back to their bunks when they'd had too much to drink and too much fun there. He'd climbed up the "twenty-three steps to heaven," as many men referred to the second story business, to retrieve his comrades, but thought it was more like ascending steps to the gate of Purgatory.

Taking his thoughts firmly in hand, he smiled at the woman expectantly looking at him. "It's a deal, Delaney. Are you still up for dinner?" he asked, hoping she'd say yes.

"Absolutely. I'm about starved and I know just the place to go." She looped her arm around his and gave it a slight tug. Together, they strolled down the sidewalk.

Klayne soon found himself seated in an Italian restaurant where mouth-watering aromas filled the air and made his stomach growl.

Delaney grinned at him as she lifted her menu. "I've yet to eat anything here that isn't incredible. You are in for a treat."

Klayne glanced through the unfamiliar items on the menu and tried to recall if he'd ever eaten in an Italian restaurant. Sure he hadn't, he looked over at Delaney. "Why don't you order for both of us?"

Her left eyebrow shot upward as she lifted her gaze to his. "What do you like?"

"Everything. I'm not a picky eater. The only things I don't like are turnips, raw eggs, and okra."

"Well, I've never seen okra on any menu in town, you won't find turnips here, and all eggs are cooked, so you're safe." She took one last look at her menu then set it aside.

A waitress approached their table with a smile and a basket of warm bread. "Hey, Dee, what can I get you two?"

"Hi, Frieda." Delaney smiled at the young woman and pointed to an item on the menu Klayne couldn't see. "Two of those please."

She looked like she wanted to smack her friend when the waitress kept ogling him. After filling their water glasses, Frieda left, giving Klayne a parting glance over her shoulder.

"You seem to attract a lot of attention wherever you go," Delaney said. Her tone held a bit of impatience and annoyance.

Surely, she couldn't be jealous, could she? Klayne glanced around the restaurant then shrugged indifferently. He nudged the basket of bread toward her and watched as she poured olive oil in a dish then dipped the bread in it. Mimicking her actions, he broke off a piece of bread and dipped it in the oil before taking a bite. "That is really good."

"They've been making it that way for the last forty years. The owner's mother started this restaurant." Delaney could talk about neighbors and friends, businesses that had been in town for years. Perhaps it would distract her from the way several women continued to toss Klayne interested glances.

Delaney had never been the jealous type, mostly because she'd never found a man who held her interest for more than an hour or two. But observing women as they studied Klayne made her want to march over to their tables and snatch them all bald headed.

Mindful of her rising temper, she took a deep breath and slowly released it. "My dad asked me to invite you to join us for church this Sunday. We go to the Christian Church. It's not far from here."

Klayne gave her an apologetic look as he swiped another piece of bread through the oil on his bread plate. "I appreciate the invitation, but I'll be gone then."

"Gone?" Panic welled in her at the thought of never seeing Klayne again. As much as she hated to admit it, she had more than a passing interest in the man. Truthfully, she dreaded the day he'd leave Pendleton, even though she knew he would. With the country heading into war, soldiers like Klayne would be in the midst of it. "You mean... are you leaving for..." She couldn't quite bring herself to ask if he was heading somewhere dangerous overseas.

He reached across the table and settled his big, warm hand on top of hers as it nervously plucked at the tablecloth. "I'm on duty out of town for a while, starting Sunday. Maybe we could plan to do something when I get back."

Relieved he wasn't leaving for good, she nodded her head. "I'd like that very much."

The waitress delivered two plates full of steaming lasagna to their table and Klayne glanced at Delaney before cutting into his. "Lasagna? Is that right?"

"It's the best you'll ever taste." Delaney forked a bite and waited as Klayne sampled his. She could tell by the look on his face he enjoyed it, especially when he hurriedly cut another bite.

They spoke about the town and places Klayne had visited in Pendleton, which proved to be a short list.

"While you're stationed here, you have to go to the woolen mills. It's fascinating how they weave the colorful Indian blankets," Delaney said, taking another bite of her meal. Klayne had finished his already and eaten another piece of bread. She wondered how he stayed so trim and lean with as much food as he put away. Judging by his bulging muscles, he probably worked hard enough to burn off any calories he consumed.

She took one more bite then slid her plate toward him. "Want to finish mine? I'm trying to save room for dessert."

Klayne took her plate and ate the last few bites then leaned back. "What's your favorite dessert?"

"I love chocolate anything, but I am also quite fond of sweets with berries. It's like taking little bites of summer." Delaney waved at Frieda and the girl hurried over to the table. "May we please have two orders of zabaglione?"

"Sure, Dee. I'll be right back," Frieda said with a smile at Klayne then rushed into the kitchen. She soon returned carrying a custard cup in each hand then set them on the table. "Here you go."

After the waitress walked away, Klayne lifted a spoon and looked to Delaney. "What is this?"

"It's basically custard with berries on top. In the summer, the berries are fresh and so, so good. Right now, all they have are canned, but they are still good." Delaney waggled her spoon at Klayne's dish. "Go on. Try it. I promise you'll like it."

Klayne filled his spoon and took a bite. The creamy, smooth custard slid down his throat with a pleasing flavor and slight sweetness. The berries were the perfect contrast. He'd never tasted anything quite like it and was glad Delaney had chosen the custard to finish their meal.

"What do you think?" she asked, watching his face, attempting to gauge his reaction to one of her favorite desserts.

He feigned a lack of interest. "It's okay," he said, setting his spoon next to his plate.

Taken aback, she stared at him, flustered. "If you don't like it, we can order something else. I thought you said you aren't a picky eater. How can you honestly say that and not like this? It's amazing and silky, and so good."

"I know." Klayne grinned at her and picked up his spoon again, taking a big bite. "It's wonderful, Delaney. I'm just teasing you."

Her gaze narrowed and she scowled at him before taking another bite of her dessert. "You shouldn't tease about important things like dessert. Next time, you might not get any."

The fact she planned on there being a next time didn't escape his notice. He hoped there were many next times before he received orders to move on somewhere else. Tonight, with the smells of delicious food mingling with Delaney's unique, alluring scent, he didn't want to think about tomorrow. Instead, he wanted to focus on right now, on the woman who'd quickly taken over his heart.

Klayne knew it was nuts to fall for her, to continue to spend time with her. It would end in heartbreak, but he couldn't stop himself. The more time he spent with her, the more he wanted to be right beside her.

Yet, that would never be a possibility and Klayne knew it. Anxious to shift his thoughts elsewhere, he glanced down at the custard on his spoon. "What did you call this?"

"Zabaglione. They serve authentic Italian food here. Caterina, the original owner, came to Pendleton from New York. If you believe the local gossip, she was on the run from the mafia and got off the train here to keep from being dragged back to marry a horrid man. Her brother Tony came here, too. He ran an ice business for years before he sold it to his son-in-law. Now, he runs a photography studio. He's done that since 1900, I think."

Klayne offered her an impressed look. "That's a long time to take photographs."

"It sure is, but he's very good. If you ever want to have your photo taken, go see Mr. Campanelli."

"I don't think I need a photo, but if I do, I'll keep that in mind."

They finished their dessert and a second cup of coffee before Delaney glanced at her watch and sighed. "I suppose I better head home. I don't want Dad to worry."

"A worried father can't be a good thing," Klayne said in agreement. He wondered what it would be like to have someone care enough to worry about his well being. Then he wondered what it would be like to care about someone that much. To be a husband and a parent.

His gaze immediately fell to Delaney. Her arms glided into the sleeves of the coat he held as she tossed him a saucy grin. "Why, thank you, kind sir."

"You're welcome, milady." He bowed his head to her before he yanked on his coat. Delaney tried to pay the bill, but he hurriedly handed Frieda more than enough to cover it then ushered Delaney outside.

She huffed at him as a blast of arctic air circled around them. "Sergeant Campbell, I'm perfectly capable of paying for dinner, or, at the least, my own meal."

"I don't have a single doubt that you are perfectly capable, but it isn't going to happen while I'm around. This is a bona fide date tonight and therefore my treat."

She would have argued further, but the blizzard raging around them drew their attention. The snow that appeared picturesque earlier now seemed dangerous as it fell so heavy and thick, they could barely see ten feet in front of them. The wind howled between buildings, causing the snow to drift in the street and around parked cars.

"Oh, goodness," Delaney said, clearly displeased by the storm.

"Come on. Let's get you home." Klayne clasped her elbow in his hand and guided her toward her car.

"I think I better drive you home, unless you have a vehicle," Delaney said as she fished inside her handbag for her keys.

Klayne shook his head. "No, I don't have a vehicle. Some of the fellas gave me a ride, but I'll walk back."

Delaney gaped at him. "Walk? Are you daft? You can't walk in this!" She waved her hand around them for emphasis. "Do you have a death wish, you crazy man? It's a few miles to Pendleton Field and there is no way I'll allow you to walk in this weather."

Klayne thought about arguing with her, just to watch more sparks shoot from her expressive hazel eyes, but held his tongue. "Yes, ma'am."

In the few minutes it took them to reach her car, the snow nearly obliterated the ability to see their hands in front of their faces.

"You can't drive anywhere in this," Klayne said, stating what he felt to be a fact.

"I've driven in worse. I'll be fine. Besides, Dad will worry if I don't come home."

"Couldn't you stay with your friend from the bakery and call your Dad?" Klayne hated the idea of Delaney being alone on the road on a night like this.

"No. I wouldn't impose on them. They have a full house without any extras. Besides, a little snow won't keep me from getting home. Honest, Klayne, I'll make it with no problem."

"How about a hotel? I'll even pay for your room," he offered.

Both of her eyebrows shot up and she gave him a guarded look.

Palms out, Klayne held up his hands in front of him, as though he pushed back her racing thoughts. "I didn't mean I'd be there, too. I just meant if you don't have money for it, I'd be happy to pay to keep you from driving on these treacherous roads."

Her wariness melted into a soft smile. "Oh, that's sweet, but unnecessary. Thank you for a lovely, wonderful evening. I look forward to seeing you when you get back." She moved around to her driver's side door and started to brush the snow off the glass with her sleeve.

Klayne held back a primitive urge to throw her over his shoulder and carry her to the hotel he knew was located down a few blocks and around the corner. However, he had an idea cavedweller-like behavior wouldn't gain any favor with Delaney.

Gallantly, he opened her car door and held it for her. "Why don't you start it while I clean your windows? Do you have something I can use to scrape the snow off the windshield?"

Delaney started the car then dug under the seat, handing him a blue ice scraper with the name of a local service station emblazoned across the front of it along with the line "Have gun, will grease!"

Amused by the town's Wild West humor, Klayne took the scraper and stepped back. He gave Delaney a withering glare when she tried to join him and shut her door, trapping her and the warmth inside while he quickly scraped the windshield and side windows.

His fingers felt frozen by the time he opened the passenger door and slid onto the tan leather seat. Quickly, he closed the door, blocking out the snow and cold. The heat blowing through vents inside the car began thawing his cold-numbed hands and feet. "You're all set, Delaney. Let's go."

"So you are in agreement it's ridiculous for you to walk anywhere in this?" she asked, putting the car into gear and pulling away from the curb.

"No, ma'am. Not at all. But there is no way on earth I'm letting you drive home all alone in this mess. I'll ride with you out to the ranch and catch a ride back into town." Klayne expected her to offer a rebuttal or at least argue with him. The explosive anger that burst from her caught him off guard, though.

"You thick-headed numbskull!" she shouted, glaring at him. "You can't catch a ride back here from the ranch. The house is half a mile off the road and from there it's another mile to a main road. You might be able to find an idiot dumb enough to be out on a night like this, but I highly doubt it. I won't allow you to walk anywhere, and that's all there is to it."

He would have laughed at her bossy, commanding attitude if it wouldn't have further upset her. As it was, she could probably give a few of the generals he'd met a run for their money in leading with an iron fist.

If he decided to get out of the car and walk, there wasn't anything she could do about it. Short of running him over, he wasn't about to leave her alone, but he wouldn't mention that. Instead, he leaned back and settled against the leather seat. "How about we focus on getting you home first and worry about me later?"

"No! I'll take you to the base then I..." Delaney slammed on the brakes when she almost ran it into the back of another car she couldn't see through the blinding snow. The sedan slid to the right and she had to work to keep from hitting a parked car.

Visibly shaken, her breath came in short gasps and her wide eyes scanned what little she could see through the windshield.

"Are you sure there isn't somewhere in town you could stay?" Klayne asked again.

"I need to go home," Delaney said, gripping the steering wheel with tight fists.

"Then I'm going with you." She scowled and he gave her a mocking smile. "You can argue all you want, even take me to Pendleton Field, but I'm not staying there until you are safely home. Save some time and fuss, and let me go with you."

The glare she sent him might have terrified lesser men than Sergeant Klayne Campbell. He ignored her irritation and rubbed his hands together in an attempt to restore warmth.

Finally, she relented. "I'll allow you to accompany me if you promise you will not attempt to walk home in this blizzard."

Slowly, he tipped his head toward her. "I promise I won't walk anywhere while the weather is like this."

She gave him a curt nod then turned her focus back to driving. Klayne had a general idea of where she lived from the details she'd shared about the ranch, but he wasn't sure how far out of town she'd have to drive.

"What time do you have to report in the morning?" Delaney asked, breaking the silence that had settled around them.

"I don't have to be there until nine in the morning."

Rather than reply, she hunched over the steering wheel, arms stiff and back angled forward. Tempted to reach over and rub her tense shoulders, he had a feeling that might distract them both. The idea of insisting she allow him to drive crossed his mind, but Delaney was familiar with the road. Additionally, he figured she'd balk like a cantankerous mule if he attempted to take over her car. The thought of sparring with her held appeal, but they really did need to keep their attention on getting out of the storm. Klayne began to think he should have demanded she stay in town, whether she liked it or not, as snow blinded them to anything beyond a foot or so in front of the car.

Delaney was a good driver, even if she was nervous and edgy. When the car hit a patch of ice and spun in a half circle, she didn't panic. She managed to keep the car from sliding into the ditch by slowly turning the wheel. Her face paled to the color of the snow and her breath came in shallow gasps as she guided the car back onto the road.

"You're doing a great job, Delaney," he praised, placing a hand on her shoulder. If he had any idea where they were going, he would have taken over the wheel, but remained silent.

Finally, he started telling her a funny story, as a way to divert her worrying about the storm. As she listened to his tale, her shoulders relaxed and her grip on the steering wheel loosened.

Although all he could see was blowing, blustery white flakes, Delaney guided the car off the highway onto a side road. A short while later, she parked in front of a immense farmhouse that looked like something out of the dreams Klayne had when he was younger. He'd always wanted to live in a farmhouse with a big, boisterous, loving family. As an orphaned boy, he used to rip out house plans he found in discarded newspapers and save them, hoping and wishing someone would adopt him and take him to such a home.

"Come inside," she said, opening her car door and hurrying up the snow-covered walk to the porch.

Klayne followed. He'd thought about asking if he could drive her car to town and have one of the guys help him return it in the morning, but he wasn't sure he could find his way back to Pendleton in the snow. Since he didn't want to send himself to an early grave, walking was out of the question. The only other option was obeying Delaney's orders.

Before she opened the door, she smirked at him. "Told you I could get myself home."

"You did a fine job, Delaney. I didn't doubt your abilities, but I just wouldn't have felt right letting you make the drive on your own."

She grinned and opened the door. "Let's get inside. It's too cold to stay out here any longer."

Klayne stamped his feet on the mat in front of the door before following her inside. Homey aromas filled the air. The scents of bread and cinnamon, and a hint of lemon from furniture polish, blended with the fragrance of memories, laughter, and tears.

Awed, he remained on the rug just inside the door, afraid to mar the shiny surface of the hardwood around him with his wet boots.

"Don't just stand there. Let's go in by the fire," Delaney said, hurriedly removing her coat and scarf and hanging them on the hook of a hall tree to dry. She waited while Klayne removed his coat and hung it up, then slipped off his boots. He straightened as a big, barrel-chested man bustled down the hallway.

"Sis! It's about time you got home. I was ready to go out looking for you." He gave her a hug, and then noticed she had a guest. "And you brought home a friend." The man held out a work-roughened, scarred hand to Klayne. "Welcome to Sage Hills Ranch. I'm Dillard Danvers, but most everyone calls me Dill. You must be the young man who's had Delaney in such a tizzy."

"Dad!" Delaney rolled her eyes and tossed her father a dark scowl. She placed a hand on Klayne's arm, drawing him away from the door. "I want you to meet Sergeant Klayne Campbell. He insisted I shouldn't drive home alone in the storm, so now he's stuck here."

"That's alright. It's nice to meet you, Sergeant Campbell." Dill held out his hand to Klayne and gave him a friendly smile.

Klayne shook his hand. "I apologize for imposing on you, sir. My intentions were good, even if they left me stranded and at your daughter's mercy."

Dill chuckled. "And she can be a real tyrant." He ignored the daggers shooting from Delaney's eyes and motioned down the hall. "Come on back to the kitchen. We can whip up some hot chocolate and sit at the table. It's the warmest room in the house right now."

"Thank you, sir." Klayne waited for Delaney to lead the way then followed her father down the hall. "I can bunk down in the barn, sir, if you just point me in the right direction."

Dill shook his head and motioned to a cozy table for four in front of a bay window. "Go on and sit down while I stir up something hot to drink. I won't have you staying in the barn when we have plenty of room right here in the house. I do appreciate you keeping an eye on Dee, though. She's just as likely to fall head first into trouble as she is to stay out of it."

"Dad!" Delaney ground out between clenched teeth, each syllable bearing the weight of her annoyance.

Dill merely grinned and stirred shaved chocolate into the pan of warming milk.

"Is there anything I can do to help?" Klayne asked, standing in the kitchen, soaking in the cozy atmosphere as much as the warmth it offered.

Despite the way they seemed to clash, he sensed a great, abiding love between Delaney and her father. As though the two of them had an unspoken pact to face whatever challenges came their way together.

Klayne felt a pang of jealousy for the parents he never knew, the unconditional love he never experienced. After all these years, it surprised him he still felt such a sense of overwhelming loss when he witnessed a loving family. Although Delaney blustered and Dill goaded her, it was easy to see the affection and admiration the two held for each other.

"Just sit yourself down and I'll have this ready in a jiffy." Dill waggled bushy eyebrows at Delaney as she took down thick mugs from a cupboard. "If my daughter ever offers to make you hot chocolate, run the other direction. Our ranch foreman swears she tried to poison us all the last time she made it." Dill pulled a disgusted face and wrinkled his nose.

Klayne had to swallow back a laugh when Delaney shot a warning look his way.

"I didn't poison anybody. The one time I burned the hot chocolate was years and years ago. Why can't you all forget about it?"

"Because you get so worked up when we mention it, that's why," Dill said, winking at Klayne as he stirred the hot milk mixture.

Delaney ignored her father and set cookies on a plate then carried it over to the table. She set out three napkins and spoons then took a seat in the chair beside Klayne.

"Are you warm enough?" she asked, slipping her hand over his as it rested on his thigh. Surprised, he turned his hand over and clasped her cool fingers with his.

The small, private smile she gave him warmed him more than the comfortable kitchen where they sat.

Out of the corner of his eye, he studied her. Her shoulders still appeared stiff and she looked as though she had yet to relax after the nerve-racking drive home. If her father hadn't been standing on the other side of the kitchen, Klayne would have massaged her shoulders.

A whiff of her perfume tantalized his nose, and he decided that would be a bad idea. An incredibly bad idea.

Distance from the feisty girl was what he needed. And sleep. Exhaustion slowly sapped both his strength and his ability to stay alert.

Thankfully, Dill served the hot chocolate and carried the conversation as they drank it and nibbled on butter cookies.

As soon as they finished their drinks, Dill told Delaney to show Klayne to the guest room at the head of the stairs.

"Thank you, sir," Klayne said, as they all stood from the table. He held his hand out to the older man. "I appreciate your hospitality."

"My pleasure, son." Dill smiled. "Have a good night's rest. One of us will make sure you make it back to Pendleton Field before you get into trouble in the morning."

"I hate to put you out, sir. I can just walk. By morning…"

"The snow will be even deeper and probably just as cold," Dill cut in. "It'll be my pleasure to take you into town. I've been wanting to go see the base, and now I have an excuse."

"Yes, sir. Thank you, sir."

"You're welcome. Now go on with Sis and she can show you where to bunk tonight."

Klayne nodded and followed Delaney up a narrow set of stairs just off the kitchen.

"Dad wants to put you in the guest room next to his room." She led him down a hall and stopped at a door next to the front stairs. "This is it." The knob turned in her hand and she pushed open the door. She flicked on an overhead light that illuminated a comfortable room, even if it appeared a bit unused. A colorful quilt covered the bed and a bookcase and chair beneath the window beckoned a guest to sit and read. "Will this do?"

"It will be perfect. I really would be fine in the barn or sleeping on the sofa. I don't need any special treatment." Klayne admired the ruffled curtains at the windows and the braided rug on the floor. He liked that so many of the rooms inside the house had the original hardwood floors instead of being covered with carpet. It wasn't as warm in the winter, but he appreciated the gleam of the wood.

"We have plenty of space, so you might as well take advantage of it." She hurried across the room and took two quilts from a trunk at the foot of the bed. "With the door being closed, the room's chilly. You might need these extra quilts to stay warm."

Klayne had a few other ideas on ways to stay warm, but chased away the thoughts and nodded his head, accepting the quilts she held. "These will be great. Thank you. I really do appreciate you allowing me to stay, Delaney."

She backed toward the door, as though she was both hesitant and eager to escape. "Dad's room is right next door." A smile made the dimple pop out in her cheek. "My room is at the far end of the hall, which is why Dad put as many doors as possible between us. Have a good night, Klayne. Thanks for making sure I got home safely."

"You didn't need me along, but it made me feel better to make sure you got here." He grinned. "I had a nice time with you this evening."

Her face softened and her eyes brightened. "I had a wonderful time with you, too. Even if the movie was scary, I enjoyed it. Thank you for taking me and for dinner." She stood in the open doorway, looking uncertain. After a quick glance down the hallway, she stood on tiptoe and pulled his head down, giving him a quick kiss before rushing into the hall.

"Sleep tight, soldier!" she called.

He grinned and started to set down the quilts when she popped her head around the edge of the doorframe. "Bathroom is the third door down on the left. Good night!"

"Good night, Delaney," he said on a chuckle. Ready for sleep, he was stretched out in bed, breathing in the scents of sunshine and Dreft soap as he relaxed between the smooth, cool sheets.

Beneath a pile of thick quilts, head cradled by a plump feather pillow, Klayne drifted to sleep with visions of Delaney's smile filling his dreams.

✶✶✶★ *Chapter Five* ★✶✶✶

Klayne awakened all at once, as he usually did, and peered through the darkness enveloping him, trying to survey his surroundings. In the silvery-tinged shadows creeping through the windows from the snow-covered world outside, he could make out a dresser, trunk, bookcase, and chair in the room.

He recalled riding home with Delaney and sat up in bed, rubbing sleep from his eyes. It came as no surprise the country girl drove as well as if not better than he could. He probably shouldn't have insisted on accompanying her home in the storm, but he had been worried about her being stranded alone on the road at night. And he just wasn't ready to tell her goodbye.

However, he'd left himself in a bit of a predicament. He had to be back on base, ready to report by nine that morning or be in big trouble. Klayne had never once done anything to mar his service record and he sure didn't plan to now.

Quietly, he got up and dressed, then carefully made his bed. On silent feet, he made his way down the hall to the bathroom. The cold water he splashed on his face brought him fully awake. He squeezed a little Ipana toothpaste on his finger and brushed his teeth then finger combed his hair before stepping into the hall. As he crept past Delaney's door to the back stairs, he stared at it, tempted to peek inside. He'd bet every penny he had that she'd look just as beautiful sleeping as she did wide awake.

Before he opened the door to find out, he continued down the back stairs and into the kitchen. He realized he should have come down the stairs by the front door, since that's where he'd left his coat. He turned to go down the hallway when a light clicked on and he came face-to-face with Delaney.

Disapproval furrowed lines across her brow as she took a step closer to him, hands fisted on her hips. "Going somewhere, soldier?" she asked, clearly upset with his attempt to sneak out of the house.

"I need to get back to town. It stopped snowing, so I figure I can walk to the main road and catch a ride."

Delaney rolled her eyes, grabbed the sleeve of his shirt, and dragged him into the kitchen. The lights she turned on illuminated the welcoming atmosphere of the room.

She pointed to a chair at the table and opened a cupboard. The robe she wore tightened across her backside as she stretched to reach a tin of Folger's coffee grounds. With quick, efficient movements, she filled a red enamel pot with water. "Sit down while I make coffee. One of us will drive you into town. You can't walk in that snow. It'll be up to your knees in some places and you'll be frozen before you ever reach the road." She started the coffee then shot him a cool glare over the shoulder of her bright blue chenille robe. "I would have pegged you as being a lot smarter than a boneheaded dunce, Sergeant Campbell."

A teasing smile took the sting out of her words. Her smile slid into the smirk he found both adorable and alluring.

Klayne studied the heart pattern on the back of her robe. Smaller hearts encircled the hem that swayed around her dainty ankles as she heated the oven and whipped batter in a bowl. Knit slippers, the same color as her robe, covered her feet. Her thick hair had been subdued in a braid, which trailed over one shoulder. Stubborn locks escaped the confines and twirled along her neck and around her face, making him wish he could unravel the strands and run his hands through the soft tresses.

"Don't go to any work on my account," he said, moving behind her and inhaling the fragrance of her. If he lived to be a hundred, he'd never tire of that scent, something enticing and exotic that was all Delaney Danvers. His hands itched to bracket her waist and pull her back against his chest, but he resisted. "I don't mean to be a bother, Delaney."

She turned her head and grinned at him. "You aren't, Klayne. Don't give it another thought. Dad informed me it was a good thing you insisted I not drive home alone. According to him, you did good."

Klayne nodded and moved away from her before he surrendered to the unwitting temptation she presented.

"You can put me to work. I should do something to repay your kindness and hospitality," he said, glancing into the bowl as she stirred in a heaping spoon of cinnamon.

"I need to make breakfast anyway, so you might as well join us." Delaney greased a muffin tin and poured batter in the cups then slid the pan into the oven and rinsed her hands. "Dad will be down in a minute. If you promise not to run off, I'll hurry upstairs and change."

He gave her a rascally grin. "Don't feel like you have to just because I'm here. You look quite fetching in your robe with your hair all snarled like a rat's nest."

Delaney's hand shot up to her head and brushed over the tangled waves. "Oh!" She spun around and raced up the stairs. Humored by her rapid retreat from the room, he hoped she didn't think he really disparaged her appearance. On the contrary, had she lingered much longer in that soft robe that made her eyes even more vibrant, he might have given in to the urge to kiss her.

While she was upstairs, he found plates, cutlery, and mugs, setting the table for three. When he finished, he stood at the window by the table and stared out into the early morning darkness. He could see a light on in a building that looked like a cabin and assumed it must be the bunkhouse. A lone figure trudged through the snow to the barn. The door squeaked in protest as the cowboy opened it and disappeared inside. Soon light shone from the barn windows, too.

It appeared everyone at Sage Hills Ranch rose early. Since it was barely five, Klayne assumed he could sneak out of the house without disturbing anyone. Evidently, he needed a refresher course on rural life. It had been years since he'd milked a cow or gathered eggs, but he was tempted to go outside and ask if he could help. Delaney was right, though, when she said he wasn't dressed to traipse around in the snow, and that meant doing chores, too.

A stair creaked, drawing his gaze to the doorway as Dill walked into the room.

"Morning, Sergeant Campbell. Sleep okay?" Dill asked, pulling a suspender up over one brawny shoulder.

"I did, sir. Thank you for allowing me to spend the night."

Dill grinned. "I'm the one who should thank you for making sure my daughter arrived home safely, son. I don't know if you've noticed, but that girl can be a little headstrong."

Klayne chuckled. "I have made note of that, sir. That's part of what makes her different, special."

The rancher raised a bushy eyebrow and gave Klayne a studying glance as he tugged on a heavy sheepskin-lined chore coat. "I need to see to a few chores before breakfast. Just make yourself at home. Sis will be down in a minute."

"Thank you, sir." Klayne took a step toward the doorway. "May I offer my assistance, sir?"

Dill shook his head. "No. It won't take long to do this morning's chores. Besides, you'd ruin your snappy clothes out in the barn." The man yanked on a pair of boots, lit a lantern, and headed outside through the laundry room. Cold air whipped into the kitchen, making Klayne glad he could stay inside. He'd spent so much time in warmer winter climates, he hadn't yet adjusted to being somewhere it snowed and the temperatures hadn't topped the freezing point in days.

A shiver passed over him as he again glanced outside and watched a big dog playfully romp through the snow around Dill as he made his way to the barn.

"That's Moose," a soft voice said from behind him, startling him. He spun around and looked at Delaney as she tied a dark blue ribbon around the end of her braid. She dropped the heavy, gleaming rope and it slid down her back, reaching halfway to her waist. He took note of the jeans she wore with a thick blue and white flannel shirt. She looked ready for work on a busy ranch, which is exactly where they were.

"Moose?" he asked, forcing himself to take a step back before he kissed her rosy lips that turned up slightly at the corners. That slight upturn made her look like she was always ready to burst into a smile.

"Our dog's name is Moose." She pointed out the window to where the canine buried his face in the snow then lifted his head and shook it, as though he played a grand game.

"Moose, huh? What kind of dog is he?"

"A Rhodesian Ridgeback."

At his shocked look, she grinned. "One day a few years back, Dad went into town to meet the train. He'd ordered some parts for the tractor and they shipped them via railcar. Anyway, he'd loaded the parts and stopped to talk to some friends who were also picking up items at the depot. After the train pulled out, Dad started to leave but noticed a puppy wandering around the platform. The poor thing had feet that seemed twice as big as they should be, floppy ears, and his ribs poked out from being starved. Dad asked around, but no one claimed him, so he left word in the depot if someone came looking for a puppy to send them our way. But no one ever came looking for him. Dad thinks someone may have stowed him on the train to get rid of him or something along those lines. At any rate, we've got a big, gangly beast who loves to play and is an excellent guard dog. He can be a little stubborn, but he makes up for it with friendly affection. When my nephew comes to visit, Ry and Moose have the best time playing together."

"He looks like quite a dog." Klayne watched the dog romping in the snow in the light spilling from the house. "Do you have any problem with him treating the animals on the place like prey?"

She nodded. "Hunting is such a big part of that breed of dog. We worked with him a lot to ingrain what was okay for him to hunt and what was not. You'd be hard pressed to find a rabbit on the place, but he leaves the cattle, horses, pigs, chickens, and ducks alone." A grin brought out an intense sparkle in her eyes. "For the most part."

Klayne volunteered to cook eggs while Delaney fried crispy bacon. His mouth watered as she piled a plate full of the salty pieces and set it on the table.

Dill returned with a red nose and chilled hands, ready for a cup of hot coffee. He tucked something into the oven, washed his hands, and then motioned toward the table. After he asked a blessing, the three of them ate breakfast then Klayne helped wash and dry the dishes.

"Give me about ten minutes and I'll be ready to take you to town," Dill said, bundling up before he headed back outdoors.

"Are you coming, too?" Klayne asked, glancing to Delaney as she hung the damp dishtowel up to dry.

"Would you like me to go along?" She took an empty tin down from a pantry shelf and packed it full of butter cookies, giving him a coy glance from beneath her long, dark eyelashes.

"Nah. Why would a nice boy like me want to be seen with a wild girl like you?"

Her head snapped up and she glared at him a moment before she noticed the grin tugging at his full lips as he bit back a smile.

"Why, indeed, Sergeant? If you're going to be ornery, I won't give you these cookies." She held the tin to her chest, as though she protected a great treasure.

"Please, Delaney? I promise I'll behave. And to answer your question, I'd very much like you to go with us to Pendleton. But if you have responsibilities you need to see to this morning, I understand."

"I don't have anything to do that can't wait until I get back. It'll be fun to ride in freezing temperatures through the deep drifts of snow." She shot him a saucy smile. "I couldn't miss out on an opportunity like that."

Klayne shook his head. "You are crazy, Delaney Danvers."

She set the tin of cookies on the counter then wrapped her arms around his waist and leaned her head against his chest. "I am crazy, about you."

Stunned by her words, Klayne didn't know what to say. Unable to form a response, he folded his arms around her and kissed the top of her head.

They remained that way for a minute or two until Delaney pulled back. "Will you be warm enough on the way to town? If you need extra socks or warmer clothes to wear, you can borrow something of Dad's."

"I'll be fine," Klayne said. The warm car would keep him from freezing in his dress slacks and shirt with a nice jacket. At least he'd worn his heavy coat and had gloves and a scarf.

"Suit yourself." She shrugged and disappeared down the hall. Quickly returning with two thick bath towels, she removed bricks from the oven and wrapped them in the towels, leaving them on the counter. Hastily, she pulled on a dark blue sweater, and a heavy chore coat similar to the one Dill wore. A bulky navy blue scarf encircled her neck and she pulled on a white stocking cap that covered her ears. After yanking on a pair of leather gloves, she pulled bright red mittens over the top of them then pointed to the towel-wrapped bricks. "Let's take those out to Dad."

He lifted the bricks and followed her outside to where her father hitched a team of draft horses to a black sleigh decorated with gold and burgundy trim. It looked like something out of a Currier and Ives painting he'd once seen in a store window.

A grin split his face and he felt as giddy as a boy with two bits to spend on candy at the drugstore. "We're riding in this? All the way to town?"

Dill smiled at him as he adjusted a shiny silver buckle. "We sure are, son. There's more than a foot of new snow and with it drifted, the sleigh should be the easiest, fastest way to get to town. You two ready to go?"

"Yes, sir," Klayne said, handing Delaney the bricks as she tucked them onto the floor of the sleigh and covered them with a thick blanket to stay warm.

"I forgot your cookies," Delaney said, running back inside the house.

"And I forgot the bells," Dill said, heading to the barn.

Slowly, Klayne ran a hand along the high back of the horse nearest him. He'd almost reached the animal's pale yellow mane when Moose bounded over and stopped a few feet away, head tilted to the side as he studied him.

The dog had such deep, soulful eyes, Klayne felt drawn to them. With unhurried movements, he hunkered down, removed his glove, and held out his hand for the dog to sniff.

Moose took his time leaning forward and inhaling Klayne's scent. He took a second whiff before he inched closer and licked the back of Klayne's hand. "Hey, boy. Do I pass muster? What do you think?"

As though the canine understood him, Moose gave a soft woof and moved until he leaned against Klayne's side. Klayne rubbed the dog along his back and scratched behind his ears.

"See you made a new friend," Delaney said, walking over to him.

He smiled and continued rubbing the canine. "He's a great dog, Delaney."

"He is pretty great." She rubbed a mitten over the dog's face. "Normally, he doesn't take to strangers, so you really must be a good guy."

Klayne patted the dog's side. "What can I say? He's got great taste. Don't you boy?"

The dog woofed and raised his backend, wagging his tail, ready to play. Before Klayne could find something to toss for the dog to fetch, the tinkle of bells rang through the crisp morning air. Dill walked out of the barn carrying a leather strap with sleigh bells attached to it.

He fastened it to the harness of the horses then motioned to the sleigh. "Shall we get going?"

"Yep! We need to be sure Klayne is there before nine, Dad."

"Even with the drifts, it shouldn't take more than an hour and a half. We'll be there in plenty of time," Dill said, sliding onto the seat of the sleigh.

Delaney tucked the tin of cookies and a thermos beneath the seat then grinned at Klayne. He offered her a hand as she climbed onto the sleigh and sat down next to her dad. With effort, he folded his long legs into the limited space on the end of the seat. She pulled up a thick blanket then Dill reached behind him and settled a buffalo robe over the top of them.

"Where in the heck did you get this?" Klayne asked as he tucked the heavy robe in around his side.

The rancher wrapped the reins around his hands, released the brake, and clucked to the horses. The two draft horses leaned into the harness and the sleigh moved forward, gliding across the snow. "The sleigh or the old robe?" he asked.

"Both." Klayne couldn't stop his smile. He'd always wanted to ride in a sleigh and now he'd get to, all the way into Pendleton. The bricks kept his feet toasty warm, and he was grateful Delaney had placed them on the floor.

"My father purchased the sleigh the first winter he spent here in Pendleton. He was courting a lovely girl and thought this might help woo her."

"Did it?" Klayne asked Dill.

The man nodded. "Sure did. He married her that spring and they had forty happy years of marriage. My mother's family had this old buffalo robe. Her grandfather shot the buffalo and tanned the hide. We only use it when we take the sleigh out for a run, which is why it smells a little musty."

"But you don't notice it when you're outside," Delaney said, nestling into the warm covers between the two men.

Klayne wanted to reach out and adjust the robe around her, make sure she was warm enough, but he didn't. Not with Dill sitting on the other side of her.

On the way into town, Dill pointed out various farms and ranches, talked about families who had been in the area for a long time and those who were newcomers. "That's the Second Chance Ranch," he said, pointing to a pretty place as the sleigh whooshed past it. "Back in the early years of the century, Gideon McBride was the owner of a popular saloon in town. He met his wife when she led a temperance committee that was determined to shut down every saloon in town. Pendleton, and the county, voted in Prohibition back in 1908. Gideon married Millie and together they converted his saloon into a restaurant. One of their boys runs it now. If you have a chance, stop by McBride's Café. The family also owns several properties in town."

"A saloon owner and a temperance worker? That's quite a story," Klayne mused as they traveled closer to Pendleton. The watery light of predawn had given way to approaching daylight. From the lemony yellow streamers poking over the horizon, it looked as though it would be a beautiful day.

"Where did you grow up, Sergeant?" Dill asked, waving at a neighbor as he drove a feed wagon out to a pasture full of fat cattle. The red and black hides of the bovines stood out in stark contrast to the white landscape.

"Here and there," Klayne said, watching the cattle follow the feed wagon, eager for breakfast. "I was born in Oklahoma, but I've lived everywhere from California to Florida. I've spent some time in South America, too."

"Where in Oklahoma were you born?" Delaney gave him an odd look.

Klayne shrugged. "When I was eleven, I was in an orphanage in Kansas. Late one night, I snuck into the office, pried open the cabinet with files and found mine. No one would tell me about my past and I needed to know. From the few forms I found, I was left at an orphanage in the Oklahoma panhandle in 1912. I vaguely recall flat land and dirt, lots of dirt, but I don't remember how long I remained there. Through the years, I was in and out of various orphanages in several states." Klayne wouldn't share the rest of the details he'd discovered in that midnight raid of his personal files. No one needed to know the details surrounding his birth.

"Oh, that's terrible." Delaney slid her hand onto his thigh beneath the blankets and gave it a gentle pat before pulling it back.

Unsettled by her touch and sincerity, Klayne hid his reaction beneath a nonchalant shrug. "It wasn't so bad. I got to see a lot of this great nation of ours. Eventually, I made a good friend. He and I decided it would be smart to enlist and here I am."

Dill looked around Delaney to Klayne. "Have you been in Pendleton long?"

"I was here for the Round-Up, but left right after. We returned in late November." Klayne held back the fact he figured they'd soon leave Pendleton. America was desperate for a win, be it against the Japanese or the Germans. To accomplish that feat, more soldiers needed to be in the action.

"What do you think of Pendleton?" Dill asked as they glided along at a good clip. The bells chimed a pleasing melody with each step of the horses while the sleigh runners whooshed over the newly fallen snow. So far, they hadn't encountered a single vehicle. In fact, it appeared no one had dared attempt travel on the snow-covered road.

Klayne cocked his head to the side and smirked. "You've got a reservation full of Indians on one end of town and an insane asylum on the other. I can honestly say I've never been in a town quite like Pendleton."

Delaney scowled while Dill snickered. "It is unique, but it's home."

"Despite the town's Wild West reputation, I've found most of the residents to be quite friendly and welcoming. If I could pick a place to settle down in the future, I wouldn't mind staying here," Klayne said, waving a hand around them. "Well, at least when it isn't so cold and snowy."

"Shoot, son, this ain't nothing. You should have been here the winter of..." Dill kept them entertained with stories the remainder of the trip. As he guided the sleigh onto Pendleton Field, the sun turned the snow around them into glistening diamonds that made them all squint against the shimmering brightness.

Klayne glanced at his watch as Dill tugged on the reins, pulling the horses to a stop. He had a full hour before he had to report. With quick movements, he jumped down from the sleigh and tucked the blanket and robe around Delaney to keep any warmth from escaping. She gave him a look that heated him from the inside out.

"Thank you both for getting me back here with time to spare. I appreciate your help and kindness. Would you like to warm up before you head back?" Klayne reached out and shook Dill's hand then stepped back, wishing he could kiss Delaney. The cold had brightened the roses in her cheeks. Her fascinating hazel eyes sparked with a zest for life that held a magnetic pull. At least they did for him.

"Our pleasure, Sergeant, and thank you for offering to let us warm up. I think we're fine," Dill said. "Come out to the ranch anytime you like. You're always welcome."

Klayne dipped his head in appreciation and took another step back. "Thank you, sir. I might just do that." He glanced at Delaney. "Have a safe trip back to the ranch and thanks again."

Before he gave in to the urge to kiss her, he hustled toward his barracks so he could shower and change.

Dill snapped the lines and the horses leaned into the harness again. Delaney watched Klayne's departing form until her father nudged her with his elbow.

"You like him, don't you, Sis." He didn't ask it as a question, but rather offered it as a plain statement of fact.

"I do, Dad." Heavily, she sighed. "Heaven help me, but I do."

Dill hid a grin. "Well, I hate to say it, but I like him, too. He seems like a respectable, responsible young man. I won't say anything if you want to spend time with him while he's stationed here, but just keep in mind that boy will have to leave, most likely sooner than you'd like. Make sure he doesn't break your heart when he goes."

Mutely, Delaney nodded. Her heart was already too far gone after the handsome soldier to be anything but shattered when he left. But she couldn't and wouldn't think about that today. There'd be plenty enough time to worry about that later.

★ *Chapter Six* ★

An eighteen-hour pass fairly burned a hole in Klayne's pocket as his mind raced with plans. He hadn't seen Delaney since the morning after the big snow storm when she and her father gave him a ride back to town in the sleigh.

The whole event seemed rather dream-like now, like something he imagined. However, a few of the men in his squadron had seen him climb out of the sleigh and still razzed him about it from time to time.

He'd returned from flying with a patrol to discover the 17th Bombardment Group received an immediate transfer to a base in South Carolina. All planes, aircrews, and ground personnel would relocate to Columbia Army Air Base. No details were offered, other than the transfer would happen right away. His commanding officer approached him and asked if he'd be interested in volunteering for a special mission that was hazardous and top secret.

"The mission may be bad, Klayne," the captain said. "Odds are good half of you won't make it through."

"Understood, sir, but I'd still like to volunteer." Klayne wanted the opportunity to not only serve his country, but be part of something that sounded of great importance.

The officer nodded. "Good. I hoped we could count on you. I can't give you any details. You'll most likely find out the particulars once you get to Columbia."

Unable to explain the reason, Klayne was convinced returning from the mission would take a miracle. The thought of facing the end of his brief life without anyone who would grieve his absence left him shaken to his core.

Before he left town, Klayne had to see Delaney one last time. He'd made a request for a pass, for at least a few hours. His commanding officer didn't even bat an eyelash as he granted Klayne's request. It was the first time he'd ever asked for a special pass and might very well be the last.

When the officer handed him the signed document, he gave Klayne a stern look. "Be back here by no later than eight in the morning. Understood?"

"Understood, sir. Thank you, sir." Klayne hurried out the door and set a far-fetched dream into motion. It took five dollars and a promise to bring back something from the bakery the next morning to convince one of the young men with a car to let him borrow it.

Before heading out to the ranch, Klayne filled the car with gas, ran several errands, then stepped into a jewelry store with a window display full of red and white paper hearts along with a selection of Valentine's Day gifts. After paying for his purchase, he made his way out to the ranch.

The snow was packed on the road, but navigable. He enjoyed the drive, but not nearly as much as he had riding in the sleigh. It didn't take long before he drove up the Sage Hills Ranch lane and parked in front of the two-story farmhouse. He lingered for a moment at the end of the walk, studying the big yellow Victorian house. Dormers, gables, gingerbread trim, and the wraparound porch put him in mind of lazy summer days sipping cold lemonade, or at least how he envisioned a summer day on the ranch might be spent.

Tugging his thoughts to the matter at hand, he hurried down the walk and up the porch steps, but no one answered when he knocked on the door. He walked the length of the porch, gazing around, hoping to spy someone. Finally, he saw a familiar-looking figure riding a horse across the pasture. Delaney's dark hair bounced on her back with each step of the horse. The animal's breath created frosty puffs in the chilly afternoon air. Together, the duo presented a magnificent sight, one Klayne could have watched for hours.

Unfortunately, he didn't have a minute to waste. He tried to convince himself what he had planned was ludicrous, that Delaney would probably chase him off the place or sic Moose on him, but it didn't deter his need to give it a try. He stepped off the porch and headed toward the pasture. A warm, wiggly body bumped against his legs as soon as he stepped through the yard gate. He smiled and glanced down at the dog.

"Hey, Moose! How are you buddy?" Klayne patted the dog's head and gently thumped his side. "Are you staying out of trouble, boy? Huh?"

The dog waggled his entire hindquarters with excitement then fell into step beside Klayne as he continued on to the pasture.

Delaney turned the horse back in the way she'd come and noticed him. Her hand shot up over her head and she waved in greeting, urging the horse into a trot across the snow.

"Klayne!" she called as she neared the fence. "What on earth are you doing here?"

"Hi, Delaney!" He leaned against the fence, resting his arms on the top pole. Although he only had eyes for the woman riding the fine equine, he reached out and ran a hand along the neck of the horse. "I was hoping to catch you at home."

"I didn't realize you were back." She walked the horse toward the gate on one side of the fence while Klayne strode along the other.

"This is the first opportunity I've had to leave the base. I'm sorry I couldn't get in touch sooner."

Delaney offered him a sympathetic look. "I understand, Klayne. I really do."

He nodded and swallowed hard. She was even more beautiful and vibrant than he remembered. Everything about her oozed a zest for life, adventure, and fun. Would what he was about to ask her alter that? There wasn't anything in the world he'd do to change a thing about her.

Convinced his plans would only benefit her, he decided to forge ahead. "Do you have some time to talk, Delaney?"

"Sure. Just give me a few minutes to put Troy away. It won't take long."

Klayne opened the gate for her then closed it as she rode the horse to the barn. He and Moose caught up with her as she hefted the saddle from the back of the horse and carried it into the tack room.

Klayne breathed in the scents of leather, oil, and horses. He loved the aroma and took another deep breath, hoping to imprint it in his memory to take out later, when he'd need something pleasant to think about.

Moose stayed close, as though he sensed the finality in Klayne's visit. He kept one hand on the dog's head as he watched Delaney give her gelding a quick brushing then lead him into a stall and shut the door. She made sure Troy had water and feed before she brushed her hands on the seat of her jeans.

"Okay, I'm all yours," she said, starting to reach out to loop her arm around his. Suddenly, she jerked back. "Gosh, you look spiffy, Sergeant. Going somewhere special?"

Klayne grinned. "Maybe. That depends on you."

"Well…" Delaney glanced down at her chore coat and jeans covered in manure and horse hair. "I think I better clean up a bit first. Come on in the house and have a cup of coffee while I change."

She led him into the kitchen and pointed to where the red enameled coffee pot sat on the back of an old wood burning stove Delaney told him they used in the winter to keep the pipes from freezing. "The coffee should still be warm, or I could make a cup of tea if you'd rather."

"Coffee is fine, thank you." Klayne removed his hat and coat, setting them on a kitchen chair while Delaney shed her outerwear then dashed up the back stairs.

While she was gone, Klayne started to pour himself a cup of coffee then decided against it. Jittery and unsettled, he didn't need to further jangle his tightly strung nerves. He paced the floor, practicing the speech he'd decided upon when he'd first come up with his insane plan a few hours ago.

The sound of water running upstairs drew his gaze upward. An unbidden vision of Delaney taking a bath made him tug at his suddenly tight collar. Desperate for a distraction, he wandered down the hall, studying each photo hanging on the wall. Some were very old, darkened with age around the edges. In others, he recognized Dill. A few photos of a man who greatly resembled the rancher made him think the person in the photo was probably Delaney's grandfather.

In the front room, photos displayed across the top of an upright piano showed a little girl who had to be Delaney. In one photo, she gazed adoringly at an older boy who had her same eyes, smile, and stubborn chin. The boy couldn't be anyone other than her brother. There were photos of Mac with his wife, and then the two of them with a rascally looking little boy. Another image showed Mac's family with Delaney and Dill. All of them were smiling, full of more joy and happiness than Klayne had ever experienced.

A board creaked overhead and he headed back down the hall to the kitchen. He leaned against the doorframe, waiting for Delaney. It took only a few more minutes before she appeared. Her hair was damp, but she'd put on a lovely dress in a shade of peacock blue that brought out vibrant tones of blue and green in her expressive hazel eyes.

"Wow, Delaney. You look gorgeous," Klayne said, reaching out a hand to her. "I hope you didn't get cleaned up just for my benefit."

"Perhaps," she admitted, taking his hand then hesitating only a moment before she wrapped both arms around him in a welcoming hug.

He lifted her off her feet and kissed the top of her head, drinking deeply of her wonderful, enticing fragrance. "I missed you," he said in a husky whisper.

"I missed you, too. Let me get a good look at you." When she pushed against his chest, he set her down. She took a step back and tilted her head to the right, studying him from the top of his hair to the tips of his polished shoes. "I do believe you've gotten even better looking while you were gone. Have you been taking some sort of handsome treatments I should know about?"

Klayne chuckled. "No, ma'am."

"It really is good to see you, Klayne. I'd about given up on you coming back. Will you be here for a while?"

"No," he said with stark honesty. "That's what I wanted to talk to you about. Do you think we could sit down?"

A wary look passed across her face, but she quickly hid it behind a smile. "We can. Did you have a cup of coffee?"

"No, ma'am."

Delaney's left eyebrow quirked upward, but she didn't say anything. "How about a cup of hot chocolate?"

"According to your dad, it's not safe to drink any you make," he teased.

"I'll have you know I purchased a mix when I was in town the other day. All you have to do is add hot water and I've got a kettle of it already warm on the stove." Delaney took two mugs down from a cupboard and made hot chocolate, then filled a plate with oatmeal cookies. She handed Klayne a mug and motioned toward the doorway. "Let's go sit in the front room. It's more comfortable there."

She led the way to the room where Klayne had studied photos of her family and settled on one end of the sofa. Plagued with doubt and anxiety, he took a seat on the other end then accepted a cookie when she held the plate out to him.

"How have you been, Klayne? By the frown lines trying to permanently attach to your eyebrows, I'd have to guess something is bothering you," Delaney observed.

He'd almost forgotten her tendency of frankness. It was hard for him to concentrate with her scent ensnaring his senses. Her long, gleaming hair slowly dried into tempting waves he longed to run his fingers through, further distracting him.

As he gathered his thoughts, he took a drink of the hot chocolate. It wasn't as good as the chocolate her father made, but better than many cups he'd tasted.

"Is your dad around?" he asked, hoping to speak to Dill before he progressed with his plans.

"No. A water pipe burst in Carol's basement and she was having quite a time trying to clean things up. Dad left yesterday to go help her. He'll be back at the beginning of the week." Delaney gave him another long perusal then set down the mug she held. She took his hand in hers, gently holding it. "You don't seem quite like yourself, Klayne. Is something wrong?"

"No... I mean... well, it's um..." Determined, he set down the chocolate he still held in his other hand and sighed. He started to speak, couldn't get the words past his lips, and cleared his throat. He cast a quick glance at Delaney, touched by the concern on her face and the genuine affection he could read in her eyes.

With a hard swallow, he pushed out the words he'd been hesitant to speak. "I'm leaving, Delaney. New orders came in and I'm heading out soon. I just found out, but wanted to let you know."

"Oh, Klayne, I'm... I..." Tears glistened in her eyes. Rapidly, she blinked them away, but her voice sounded strained when she spoke. "I wish you didn't have to go."

"Me, too, but wishes won't change anything." He cleared his throat again. "Look, Delaney, I, um... I wanted to ask you something."

"I'm listening," she inched toward him, her gaze intently holding his.

For a moment, he allowed himself the indulgence of falling into the warmth of her eyes, of fantasizing about a life with her, before he jerked his thoughts back to reality. "I told you I'm an orphan. I've got no one, not a single person in the world who cares whether I live or die."

"That's not true!" she protested. Delaney slid so close her knee bumped against his. Possessively, she held his hand against her. Her pulse galloped beneath his fingers as they rested against the base of her throat. "I care, Klayne. Far more than you can know."

He brushed her cheek with his thumb, battling the urge to kiss her. But he wouldn't. Not until he somehow uttered what he'd come to the ranch to say. "Thank you, Delaney. I hoped you had more than just a brief, passing interest in me. In fact, I counted on the fact that we're friends."

Her gaze narrowed as she glared at him. "After those kisses we shared at the theater the last time I saw you, not to mention the one that nearly buckled my knees on New Year's Eve, we are more than friends, Klayne Campbell. And you know it!"

He grinned. "True. I do think of you as a friend and much more, because those were the best kisses I've ever had."

Pleased with his comment, she smiled at him with something in her eyes he hadn't dared hope to see. Slowly, he let his fingers trail across her jaw and along the slender column of her throat. Assailed with second thoughts, he wondered if perhaps he should stop this nonsense before he went any further. Regardless, something drove him to continue.

"What I came here to ask you today... what I need to talk to you about is kind of personal. If you'd rather not hear it, please just ask me to leave now."

"No, Klayne. Go on." She raised the hand she still held between both of hers and kissed his palm. "Tell me whatever you need to. I'll listen."

"Other than you, there isn't a person on this planet who cares what happens to me. If I died tomorrow, no one would really notice, not in any way that matters. I don't know if… that's to say, I'm not sure…" He stopped, hesitant to say too much. At the look of encouragement on her face, he continued. "When there's a strong chance a man will face death and death will come out the victor, he needs to set his affairs in order. I want to be able to leave something behind, even if it's only a little money to a friend I greatly value."

If he'd reached out and slapped her, Delaney couldn't have looked more stunned or hurt. "Klayne Campbell! You are not going to die. Are you always so fatalistic?" She glowered at him. "Where are you going that makes you believe you're going to die?"

"I don't know where I'm going, and I don't know exactly when. Even if I did, I couldn't tell you."

"I understand, Klayne, but don't go into this thinking you won't come out of it. That's not an attitude that will help you survive. You need to focus on reasons to make it through whatever lies ahead." Delaney looked like she wanted to smack him, but only tightened her grip on his hand. "Stop hemming and hawing around what you really want to say. Tell me what's going on in that head of yours."

Klayne stared at her, wondering if he'd ever meet another woman like Delaney Danvers. Somehow, he doubted it. In his opinion, she was one of a kind.

"I had a nice little speech all memorized, but if you don't want to hear it..." Klayne stood, grinning at her. He waggled a finger her direction and sidled toward the doorway. "Wait right here."

His footsteps echoed across the hardwood floors as he walked down the hall then hurriedly returned. He held a heart-shaped box of fancy chocolates in one hand and a small velvet box in the other.

He regained his seat next to her and held out the candy. "Since I'll be gone for Valentine's Day, I wanted you to have this. If I could be here, I'd make sure you knew, without question, that I want you for my sweetheart."

"That's so sweet, Klayne," Delaney said, taking the candy, opening the box, and selecting one before holding it out to him. He shook his head and she set the box on the table then bit into a rich caramel. "Oh, that's yummy. Thank you."

Involuntarily, his index finger traced the contour of her bottom lip and wiped away a bit of caramel clinging to the corner of her mouth. Her eyes darkened and her breathing grew shallow as she melded her gaze to his.

"Delaney, I..." He swallowed twice. "If something happens and I don't come back, I want you to be the beneficiary. It's not a lot, but it would give me peace of mind to know what little I have mattered to someone... to you."

Tears filled her eyes again. "I don't want you to talk like that, Klayne. You'll be fine. You'll come back and..."

He silenced her by placing a finger over her lips as he shook his head. "There is a very real possibility that I'm not coming back, Delaney. I'd hate to die knowing I haven't meant anything to anyone in my entire life."

"You mean so much to me, Klayne." Delaney threw herself into his arms and pressed her face against his neck. "I know it's crazy, but I'm in love with you."

Arms tightening around her, he murmured against the fragrant locks of her hair. "It's not crazy, Delaney. I've been in love with you from the moment you asked if I was spying on you from behind that crispy Christmas tree."

Her choppy laugh blew against his neck, heightening his awareness of her body held close to his. "Oh, Klayne, I love you, so much!"

For a moment, he couldn't speak. Not when the words he'd waited a lifetime to hear had just been spoken. No one warned him that love would strip his heart bare yet make it feel as though it might explode from being so unbelievably full.

Emotionally astounded at her confession of love, the miracle of it made him want to linger in the moment, bask in the glory of it, but he didn't have time. If he didn't get on with what he needed to say, he'd never get the words out. He kissed her forehead and pushed her back.

Before he changed his mind, he lifted the velvet ring box and pushed open the lid, revealing a round diamond deeply set into a wide white-gold band. Lover's knots embossed the circumference of the ring with the ends creating two hearts that surrounded the diamond.

"Oh, Klayne! It's gorgeous!" Delaney started to reach for the ring, then yanked her hand back and stared at him.

Klayne lifted the ring from the box and took her left hand in his, sliding the ring down her slender finger. He'd guessed well on the size because it fit perfectly. "I have no right to ask this Delaney Danvers, but would you marry me? Would you give me someone to leave behind, someone who'll remember me when I'm gone? I'm not asking for more than a marriage on paper so you'll receive the benefits when I'm dead. Honestly, that's all I'm asking of you. I don't expect a single thing from you, other than to give me the comfort of knowing I won't die completely forgotten."

***** *Chapter Seven* *****

Delaney gazed at the ring, holding it up so it caught the afternoon sun streaming in the window behind her. A sunbeam refracted in the diamond, sending splinters of luminescent light dancing on the wall near the fireplace. She released a long breath then pinned Klayne with an angry glare.

"How could you? How could you buy the most perfect ring I've ever clapped my eyes on and ask to marry me with such a pathetic, stupid, horrid proposal. No, I won't marry you just so you can go off and get yourself killed. Don't be an idiot!" The length of several heartbeats passed as she glared at him. His eager look of expectation wilted into one of wounded surprise.

Finally, she leaned forward and kissed his cheek, softening her harsh tone. "If you can come up with a better, more compelling, convincing reason for me to marry you, I might change my answer."

Immediately, Klayne dropped to one knee and took her hand in his, kissing the ring he'd slid onto her finger. "Delaney, from the moment I set eyes on you, you've captivated me. I've never met a woman like you. You're determined and stubborn and full of sass, but you're also exciting and beautiful, and so smart. You can fill a room with the vibrancy of your presence not to mention how thoroughly you fill my heart with your smile. Would you do me the great honor of becoming my wife? I love you and would do anything in my power to make you happy. I can't promise you anything at all, except my heart for as long as I live, which may very well be a short time into the future."

"That's much better," she said. Ever pragmatic and sensible, she nodded in agreement. "I'll take it." Delaney wrapped her arms around his neck and gave him a tight hug before pulling back. "Now, Sergeant Campbell, that's how you propose if you want a woman to say yes." She tugged on his hand. "Come on up here and properly kiss the girl you plan to wed."

Klayne swept her into his arms and settled back on the sofa with her across his lap. "Yes, ma'am."

He poured all the love he wanted to give her into that kiss and freely accepted what she offered in return. After several bone-melting kisses, they stopped to catch their breath. Delaney rested her forehead against his chin. "Wow, Klayne. That was... I don't have words for that, but I'd like to do it again."

"Me, too, sweetheart, but I think you should know two things before we proceed." Klayne kissed her nose and leaned back.

Curious, she gazed up at him. "And those two things are?"

"First, is that I truly do love you and think you're an amazing, incredible woman."

She blushed. "Thank you, kind sir. I love you, too. As my nephew might say, I think you're the bee's knees."

He grinned then sobered. "The second thing is that I really will only marry you on paper. I can't and won't ask more of you than that."

The elation she'd felt since he said he loved her slipped into annoyed frustration. "We'll discuss the particulars later. Do you have to be back at the base soon?"

"Nope, I've got all day to spend with you."

She grinned and pecked his cheek again. "Then let's make the most of it."

"I was hoping you'd say that." Klayne set her on her feet and stood. "I know it's sudden and we might not even be able to make it happen, but would you marry me today?"

Emotions flicked over her features, as though she processed his request. Surprise, consideration, doubt, then accord.

Resolute, she nodded. "Yes, I'll marry you. Just give me a few minutes to comb my hair and change and then I'll be ready to go." She moved toward the doorway. "It's too bad Dad isn't here. I hate to do this without him."

Klayne looked dismayed. "I planned to ask your father's permission and all that, but I hope you'll explain to him the extenuating circumstances."

Delaney waved a dismissive hand his direction. "Don't worry about it. Dad will understand. I'll be back in a jiffy. Would you please call the courthouse and see if Judge Rawlings is available today. If so, ask for an appointment to see him. He'll do the ceremony for us."

"I'll take care of it." Klayne headed toward the phone in the kitchen while Delaney raced upstairs.

He thought she'd looked beautiful before, but fifteen minutes later when she floated down the stairs wearing an airy white dress with her hair pinned up on her head, his mouth fell open in awed astonishment.

"Gosh, Delaney, you look... I don't even know words, honey. You're... enchanting and completely glorious." He strode over to her and watched twin blossoms turn her cheeks pink.

"I wore this dress to a summer party two years ago. It might not be the best thing to wear in the middle of the winter, but since it's white and elegant, it seemed like it would work for a wedding dress." Self-consciously, she brushed at the lace overlay of her skirt. Round, puffed shoulders gave way to gathered sleeves while white silk-covered buttons marched up the front of the bodice to a sweetheart neckline.

"You take my breath away," he said, brushing his lips over hers before enfolding her in a tender embrace. "Thank you for being willing to marry me."

"Thank you for asking." She pulled back and studied him. "Did you get an appointment with the judge?"

"I did," Klayne said, holding Delaney's coat as she slipped her arms in the sleeves. "We need to be there in thirty minutes."

"Then we better shake a leg," she said, grabbing his hand after he pulled on his coat and leading him back through the house to the front door.

It wasn't until they started down the porch steps that he noticed Delaney wore a pair of fashionable heels. She certainly couldn't walk through the snow in them, so he carried her out to his borrowed car, settling her on the front seat.

He closed the door, jogged around, and slid behind the wheel while she pinned a smart white hat on her head.

"I have some questions I'm going to ask and I want you to answer them," she said, giving him a look that said she wouldn't tolerate any evasive replies or nonsense.

"Ask away." He glanced her direction then shifted his gaze back to the road.

"Have you been married before?"

Taken aback by the question, he gave her an honest answer. "No. I haven't. I've never met a girl I liked that well."

"Good. And you don't have any children?"

Shocked, he whipped his head around and glowered at her. "No! Of course not! What kind of questions is that, for Pete's sake?"

"Well, I know sometimes men don't... especially those who... well, don't they um..." Delaney stammered. Abruptly, she changed the subject. "What's your middle name?"

"Thomas." He looked to her again. "What's yours?"

"Marie. It was my grandmother's name."

"Delaney Marie," Klayne said with an approving nod. "I like it."

"Thank you. I like it, too." She glanced out the window at snow covering the countryside then back at him. "Do you really not know anything about your parents?"

Klayne shrugged, hesitant to tell her what he did know, but compelled to share the truth. Since she had agreed to marry him, she deserved that much. "Remember I told you I broke into the office at the orphanage and read my file?"

"Yes."

"What I didn't tell you was that every orphanage I was in, they treated me like the lowest kind of scum. I didn't know why. Sometimes I'd try to be real good, obey every order and rule, but it was always the same whether I was angelic or acted like a little devil. They treated me like I was nothing."

"I'm so sorry." She placed her hand on his leg and gave it a gentle pat.

He wondered if she had any idea what her simple touch did to him, the fire it ignited in his veins. Purposely ignoring it, he continued. "The file I found that day had a list of orphanages where I'd lived and places I'd been picked up." He waggled his eyebrow and tossed her a rascally, boyish grin. "I escaped fairly regularly and made my way to a new town quite often. Anyway, I did find a record of my birth. I was born April 19, 1912, in Guymon, Oklahoma. My father's name was listed as C. Campbell with a question mark behind it. My mother's name was Francine Thomas."

Klayne sighed and stared out the window, watching horses in a fenced pasture run through the snow. "I took that slip of paper and saved it. When I was thirteen, I ran away from yet another orphanage and made my way to Guymon, determined to find one of my parents."

Delaney sat wide-eyed, waiting for him to continue. "Did you find them?"

"In a way," Klayne said, hating to divulge more, but felt compelled to tell her everything. This conversation would go down as the worst pre-wedding chat in the history of marriages. Then again, nothing about this marriage was typical. "I asked around town if anyone knew a Francine Thomas. I discovered that Francine was known as a… well, she was a…" Klayne glanced at Delaney. Despite her tendency to be bold and speak her mind, sweet innocence rested on her face as she waited for him to continue. He forced out the words. "She was like one of the girls at Miss Clementine's. She worked in a, um… well, she had a business in a nearby town. A drunken customer strangled her to death in 1913."

"Oh, golly, Klayne. That's horrible!"

"I went to the local newspaper office and read the article they'd published. The man who killed her was Carl Campbell. I can only assume he was my father." A short, derisive laugh escaped him. "It's no wonder all those people at the orphanages treated me like garbage. It's basically what I was, what I am. Born from a killer and a…"

"Don't say it!" Delaney clapped her hand over his mouth, then gave him an admonishing look. "I don't care who gave birth to you, it's who you are now that matters. You're a good, kind, honorable man. One I'm proud to know and pleased to love."

The words she said winged their way to his heart. Tenderly, he kissed her fingers. "And I'm proud to know you, Delaney. You're smart and lovely, sassy and silly, and perfectly wonderful."

Eager to know more about him, Delaney shifted the conversation. "How'd you end up in the army?"

"After I left Oklahoma, I ran into another kid with a story similar to mine. His name was Billy. We were close to the same age and both determined we wouldn't end up in another orphanage. Together, we rode the rails, worked whenever anyone would hire us, and made do the rest of the time."

Delaney's eyebrow hiked upward. "Made do? What's that mean?"

"Well, sometimes we were so hungry and desperate that we'd sneak into a henhouse after dark and steal a bunch of eggs. Since we didn't have a way to cook them, we'd just eat them raw."

She wrinkled her nose. "And that's why you said raw eggs are on the list of things you don't like to eat."

"Yep. I can't even stand the sight of a cooked egg with a runny yolk." He offered her an exaggerated grimace. "One winter, we hunkered down in an abandoned warehouse. There was a bin of turnips there. We assumed someone forgot to ship them, so we supplemented our meager diets with those. If I never eat another one, it will be too soon."

She laughed and lifted a hand in the air, as though making a solemn vow. "I promise I will never feed you turnips, okra, or raw eggs."

"Thank you. See, you already sound like a loving, devoted wife," he teased.

"I really will do my best, Klayne." Her eyes shimmered with emotion. "And I should probably admit that I have a terrible temper, I sometimes speak before I think, and I have opinions on everything."

He laughed. "Tell me something I don't already know."

She feigned affront, then wrapped her hands around his arm, giving it an affectionate squeeze. "How long did you and Billy stay together?"

"A long while. Billy and I worked our way to California. When we ran out of jobs there, we decided to try our hands at being cowboys. We made it as far as Kansas before we got kicked off a train we'd jumped and spent a few months working in the area on a ranch." He gave her a playful wink. "I'm not as hopeless with cattle and horses as you might think. Anyway, the rancher was kind and treated us well, but after the fall work was completed, he didn't have anything for us to do, so we decided to spend the winter someplace warm. We made it to Florida and spent a year working there doing odd jobs."

"Then what happened?"

"Billy and I had been down on our luck. We hadn't eaten a decent meal in weeks and were living on the streets. One day, we were walking past a building and saw a sign about joining the U.S. Army. With nothing better to do, we went inside and listened to what the man had to say. It took all of five minutes for us to decide anything had to be better than our current situation, so we enlisted. Turns out all those years of living in orphanages, following orders and feeling insignificant, made it easy for us to adjust to Army life. Billy and I both enjoyed it. We never went hungry, always had nice, warm clothes to wear, and a little money to jingle in our pockets."

"Is Billy here in Pendleton, too?" Delaney asked, looking forward to meeting someone Klayne clearly thought of quite highly.

Klayne grew quiet, shaking his head. "No. Billy died three years ago. The plane he was riding in crashed. Everyone died. Billy was the only real friend I've ever had and I miss him every day."

"Oh, Klayne, I'm so sorry. Losing him must have been like losing a brother." Delaney leaned her head against his shoulder and sighed. "If anything happened to Mac, I don't know what I'd do."

"Then we better hope he comes home safe to you and his little family," Klayne said, giving her an encouraging smile. He cleared his throat and lifted her left hand in his, caressing the backs of her fingers. "This is a terrible conversation to have on our way to get married."

Delaney laughed. "Well, it's certainly nothing like I pictured."

Klayne frowned. "I'm sorry, Delaney. I should have realized you probably would want flowers and a big wedding with a long dress, although that one is beautiful, and..."

She shook her head. "No, Klayne. When I thought about getting married, I always pictured it in our backyard with just those who mean the most to me there. I wouldn't know what to do with a big, fancy wedding." Her head settled back against his shoulder. "In fact, this seems just right."

"Thanks for being a good sport." He blew out a long breath. "I couldn't eat breakfast or lunch because I was so nervous, trying to think of the best way to ask you to do this." He cast a quick glimpse her way as they drove into the outskirts of Pendleton. "I appreciate you being willing to marry me, Delaney, even if it is in name only. It means the world to me to be able to leave something behind for someone who really cares."

She gave him an observant glance followed by a saucy grin. "I do care, Klayne. In fact, I probably would have said yes to your proposal even if all you'd done is said you loved me."

His eyes widened in astonishment as he turned down a street and parked near the courthouse. He jogged around the car and opened her door, giving her a hand as she climbed out. He held onto her fingers as they started down the sidewalk, then gave her an apologetic look and ran back to the car. From the backseat, he lifted a large brown paper sack and handed it to her with a sheepish grin.

She opened the bag and gasped, surprised to see a small bouquet of pink and red carnations.

"It's not much, but every bride should have a bouquet," he said as she glanced from the bouquet to him and back at the flowers.

"It's wonderful, Klayne. Thank you!" she wrapped her arms around his neck and give him a tight hug before twining their fingers together and tugging him across the street and up the steps of the imposing brick building.

Inside, she tossed away the bag that kept the cold air off the flowers, led them down a hall, and up another flight of steps.

At an open door halfway down another hall, she stepped inside.

"Hi, Betty. We have an appointment to see Judge Rawlings." Delaney spoke to a woman seated at an old oak desk that took up a large portion of the room. A foot-high stack of papers sat on one corner of her desk while a pile of file folders with slips of paper, notes, and photographs spilling out in disarray occupied the other corner.

The woman glanced up with a wooden smile. "I didn't realize the appointment was for you, Dee. How come no one knows about this young man of yours?"

Delaney turned to wink at Klayne although she spoke to the woman. "Would you want to share him?"

Betty gave Klayne a thorough perusal that left him feeling a bit ill at ease before she rose to her feet. "I certainly would not want to share him. In fact, you best keep this one under lock and key." She pointed to three chairs pushed against the wall by the door. "Have a seat. I'll see if the judge is ready for you."

Betty disappeared inside another office. Low murmurs made it clear she spoke to someone although their muffled words were indistinguishable. Only a minute passed before she breezed back inside the room and motioned for them to follow her.

"Where's your dad, Dee?" Betty asked, as they walked across the room.

"A pipe burst in Carol's basement, so Dad went to Portland to help her for a few days."

Betty's plucked eyebrows both neared her hairline as she gaped at Delaney. "You mean you're getting married while he's out of town."

Klayne didn't care for the woman's nosiness and he certainly didn't approve of the condescending way she glared at Delaney. "I'm afraid that's my fault. You see, I just couldn't wait one more day to make this lovely girl my wife and begged her to put me out of my misery."

Delaney hid her shock at his response to Betty by lifting the bouquet of carnations to her face and pretending to sniff them.

He settled his hand at the small of her back and ushered her inside the judge's chambers.

"Delaney Danvers! What in thunderation are you up to now, girl? Every time I turn around you're in one fine mess or another," Judge Kade Rawlings joked as he rose from his desk and stepped around it. Not quite seventy, the judge still had clear, arresting green eyes, a physique that made men half his age jealous, and a teasing smile that turned heads. Years spent as a deputy and then sheriff finally inspired him to go into another form of the law. He'd served Umatilla County as a judge for the last ten years with a firm hand and a jovial sense of humor.

"Judge Kade Rawlings, I'd like you to meet Sergeant Klayne Campbell, my soon-to-be husband, at least he will be if you'll marry us today," Delaney said, then turned to her fiancé. "Klayne, Judge Rawlings has known my family for a long time. His wife is the one who started the Italian restaurant we ate at the other night."

"The lasagna was the best I've ever eaten," Klayne said, holding out a hand to Kade. The man appeared to be a gentle giant. In spite of his broad frame and towering height, he had deep laugh lines and the kind of engaging smile that said he was always ready for an adventure. The two men shook hands and then grinned at Delaney.

Kade tipped his head toward Klayne. "So you want to marry this soldier. Have you completed all the paperwork?"

Delaney shook her head. "No, sir. We just decided today to wed because Klayne is leaving soon. I was hoping you could waive the waiting period and we could get on with things."

The judge frowned. "I can do that, but give me a reason why I shouldn't make you wait until your dad is back in town."

Tears filled Delaney's eyes and she took a step closer to Klayne, reaching down to clasp his hand in hers. "Please, Judge? If Dad were here, he'd give his blessing. He's met Klayne and likes him. If you don't believe me, you can phone Butch, but I can't promise he'll answer." She glanced at Klayne, then back at the judge. "Klayne is an orphan and just wants to leave someone behind. He's heading out on a mission soon and isn't sure about what might happen, about the future." She offered Klayne a caring smile then turned a pleading look to the judge. "Please, sir?"

Kade, who'd been orphaned at a young age, took sympathy on the couple and nodded his head. "Fine, but if Dill isn't happy about this, I want you to work that teary-eyed story on him."

Delaney grinned and returned to her typical vibrant self. "I'll do it!"

Kade chuckled, sat down at his desk, and picked up the phone. He held a brief one-sided conversation that ended with "right now and hurry it up!" before he hung up the receiver and opened a drawer in a filing cabinet behind him.

"Here's the form," he said, pulling it out and sliding it across the desk. "You two fill out that information and I'll be right back."

While the judge left the room, Delaney and Klayne each filled in the appropriate boxes on the form. He learned her birthday was in July and that she was five feet, six inches tall. He also learned unlike many girls, Delaney's penmanship was plain and serviceable, without any unnecessary flourishes or femininity.

Although he found her alluring and beautiful, Delaney was about the most no nonsense female he'd ever encountered. Even now, as she sat beside him in a lovely gown that might have been worn to a garden party at the governor's house, he pictured her with boots on her feet and her hair in a long braid down her back as she rode her horse in the pasture.

The sound of voices alerted them to the judge's return. He walked into the room with Delaney's friend Amy and a young man in a police officer's uniform.

"We'll need witnesses and I thought these two would do," Judge Rawlings said, grinning as Amy and Delaney embraced.

"I can't believe you almost got married without me," Amy chided as she brushed a tear from her eye. "You look lovely, Dee."

"Thank you, Amy," she said, clasping her friend's hand briefly. She reached out to shake the hand of the young man she'd known for years who happened to be Judge Rawlings' grandson. "Thank you for taking time to stand with us, Marc."

"My pleasure, Delaney. It's not every day Granddad demands I come witness a wedding." Marc grinned then cast an interested glance Amy's direction. The girl blushed then moved to stand beside Delaney as the judge signed the paperwork and motioned them all into place.

Everyone removed their coats, then Amy handed Delaney the bouquet of flowers. Covertly, Delaney slipped the ring off her finger and into Klayne's hand for the ceremony.

"Are we ready to proceed?" Kade asked, glancing from Klayne to Delaney.

"Yes, sir," Klayne said, no longer nervous, but unexpectedly joyful.

Rather than lead the couple in a traditional ceremony he'd performed dozens of times, the judge began asking questions. "Do you two like each other?"

Klayne raised a questioning eyebrow at Delaney, but nodded his head. "Yes, sir, we do."

"Do you respect each other?"

"Yes, sir," Delaney answered truthfully, albeit a bit confused.

The judge studied them both a moment. "Do you love each other?"

SHANNA HATFIELD

Klayne didn't hesitate to answer. "Yes, sir, I love her. How could I help it? She's one-of-a-kind."

The judge chuckled and looked to Delaney. She blushed, but answered the question. "I love him, too, with all my heart."

"That's good," Kade said with a smile. "Marriage isn't an easy thing. If you don't believe me, ask my wife. She's had to put up with me for more than forty years. There were times I thought she might bean me with one of her skillets. I'm certain there were days she wished the vegetables she furiously chopped at the restaurant had been some part of my anatomy, but you know what we've learned?" He paused for effect. "We learned that no matter how mad we might get, no matter how annoyed we might be with each other, at the end of the day, love prevails. Remember that. Love is the key. When Delaney is so stubborn and opinionated you'd like to throttle her, Klayne, think about how much you love her right now. And Dee, when Klayne is acting like an arrogant, overbearing, stupid man — because we men all have that ailment from time to time — recall the love swelling in your heart for him today. Marriage is frustrating and trying, it's challenging and downright hard some days, but it's the most wonderful, amazing, incredible thing you'll ever experience in your life. Don't enter into it lightly. Never forget to cherish and honor each other as well as the vows you make today."

Amy sniffled and Marc handed her a handkerchief.

Kade bit back a grin and continued. "Klayne and Delaney, the two of you have come to me today, signifying your desire to be formally united in marriage. Assured there are no legal, moral, or religious barriers that might hinder a proper union, please join your hands as we get on with the ceremony."

Klayne took both of Delaney's hands in his. Her hands were rough from work, but so small and delicate compared to his big paws. The slight tremor in her hands let him know she was nervous, although outwardly she appeared calm and collected.

The judge cleared his throat. "Klayne Thomas Campbell, do you promise to love and cherish Delaney, to honor and sustain her, to make her laugh and wipe away her tears, in sickness and in health, in poverty and wealth, and to be true to her in all things until death alone shall part you?"

A swell of emotion clogged his throat, but Klayne nodded and said, "Yes. I do so promise. I'll love, respect, cherish, protect, and honor Delaney to and with my very last breath."

"Perfect," Kade said, then turned to Delaney. "Delaney Marie Danvers, will you promise to love, cherish, and obey Klayne? Will you honor him, sustain him, in times of sickness and of health, of poverty and wealth, and to be true only unto him until death alone shall part you?"

Delaney cast a panicked look at Kade then at Klayne. "I... I, um..."

✳✳✶⭑ *Chapter Eight* ⭑✶✳✳

Every eye in the room shifted to Delaney as she scrambled to respond to the judge's question. Would she honor, cherish and obey Klayne? Would she take him as her lawfully wedded husband until death parted them? Especially when he thought that moment would happen sometime in the near future.

The enormity of what she was about to do hit her with the force of an oncoming train. Unable to speak, or even catch her breath, she struggled to cling to the last fraying threads of her composure.

Still holding onto her hands, Klayne gave them a light squeeze and looked at her imploringly, as though he willed her strength to continue.

It wasn't that she didn't care for Klayne. She loved him. Loved him with a completeness and openness, a soul-deep bond, she'd never come close to experiencing. Her affection for him wasn't what held her back from answering.

The real reason had very little to do with Klayne.

The fact her father was in Portland, Mac was at a Naval base, and Butch didn't even know she'd come into town gave her a moment of pause. Would the men in her life forgive her for a rushed wedding?

Would she be able to forgive herself for depriving them of the chance to see her wed?

Delaney raised her troubled gaze to Klayne's and stared into his eyes. Those blue eyes had captivated her, pierced her soul, the first time she'd looked into them, just as they did now. Did it really matter who was there to witness their vows?

The important thing was that she would belong to Klayne, even if it was only for a few months, if his morbid predictions proved true. With his defeatist views, Klayne might not realize Delaney had a habit of getting what she wanted. And what she wanted, more than anything, was to spend a long, happy life with him by her side.

Maybe this wasn't the wedding every girl fantasized of having, but the soldier standing next to her was better than anything she'd ever dreamed.

With a slight pressure to his hands, she smiled and shifted her gaze back to Kade. "I do so promise to love, honor, and cherish Klayne as long as we both shall live."

Kade raised a bushy eyebrow. "And obey? You forgot obey."

Delaney's gaze narrowed as she glared at the judge. "I didn't forget it, I was hoping no one would notice if I left that part out." She sighed then looked back to Klayne. "I rather like doing my own thing, but as your wife, I will do my best to obey you. Although our courtship has been brief, I love what I know of you, trust what I have yet to discover, and respect your integrity. Through all our years together, I have faith in your love for me and my love for you to see us through whatever joys and challenges life may bring. I offer myself to you with all my faults and strengths."

"And I gladly accept them," Klayne said, giving her a smile that made her knees quake.

Kade drew her attention back to the formalities of the ceremony. "Is there a ring?"

"Yes," Klayne said, holding out the band he'd slid on Delaney's hand earlier that afternoon.

The judge looked at it approvingly. "This ring is a symbol of the vows by which this man and woman have bound themselves to each other in the sight of God and these witnesses. Klayne please repeat after me."

Flawlessly, Klayne repeated the vow to Delaney. "I give you this ring as a symbol of my love. With all that I am, and all that I have, I will honor you, and forever love you."

He slid the ring on her finger and kissed it. Delaney blinked back tears while Amy snuffled.

Kade cleared his throat and concluded the ceremony. "Klayne and Delaney have given themselves to each other through these solemn vows, with the joining of hands and hearts, and the giving and receiving of this ring. By the power vested in me, I hereby pronounce them to be husband and wife. To these two whom God has joined together, let no one put asunder." The judge beamed at them. "You may now kiss your bride."

Klayne slid both hands along either side of Delaney's face and gave her a tender kiss, one that plucked at her heartstrings and made her want to melt against him.

The moment Klayne lifted his head, Amy pulled Delaney into a hug, sobbing and laughing all at the same time. Kade slapped Klayne on the back and introduced him to his grandson while Klayne fished money out of his wallet to pay for the license.

"Oh, Dee, this is the most exciting, incredible thing! I can't wait to tell everyone," Amy gushed.

"No, Amy. Please don't." Delaney would stitch her friend's lips together if that's what it took to keep her quiet. "I don't want anyone accidentally telling Dad before I have a chance to speak with him first. Please?" She looked at everyone in the room. "I beg of you, please keep this between us. It would break Dad's heart if he heard it somewhere before he makes it back to the ranch."

"We'll all keep quiet, Dee. Don't give it another thought," Kade said, waiting while everyone signed the marriage certificate. He stuck the papers that needed to be filed into a manila envelope and stamped it "Confidential." He gave Delaney a wink and dropped his voice to a whisper. "Don't worry about Betty. She knows I'll fire her faster than she can draw on those fake eyebrows if she so much as utters a single word about seeing you here."

Delaney held back a laugh as she hugged the judge. "Thank you, sir. I appreciate it so much."

"You're welcome, Dee. Now, you and this soldier get out of here and do something fun." Kade turned to Klayne. "I hear there's a sweetheart's dance tonight, if you can't find anything better to do. Although, as a newly wed couple, you might be able to think of one or two things to keep yourselves occupied."

Klayne settled his hand on Delaney's waist and nudged her toward the door. "I'll keep that in mind, sir. Thank you, again, for taking care of everything for us. Truly, we appreciate it."

"It's my pleasure, son. I know a thing or two about heading off to war. Keep yourself safe and come back to this girl. You must be something special to turn her head. She's had boys chasing after her since she was still in pigtails."

Delaney scowled at Kade then gave Amy one more parting hug. Klayne again thanked Marc for witnessing the ceremony then accepted Amy's boisterous hug. He held Delaney's coat and she slipped it on.

Before she changed her mind, Delaney pulled one carnation from the bouquet, then tossed the mound of flowers to her friend. "It's tradition!" she exclaimed then laughed at the shocked look on Amy's face before grabbing Klayne's hand and tugging him out the door.

Back on the street, they both glanced up as soft snowflakes began to fall. "Well, Mrs. Campbell, what would you like to do to celebrate our nuptials?" Klayne asked.

Unnerved by the fact she was now a married woman, she wasn't sure what she wanted to do. A group of girls walking by tossed Klayne several interested glances. Delaney fought down the urge to grasp his arm and shout out that he belonged to her.

Distracted. She needed to be distracted.

"How about an early supper?" She didn't wait for him to answer, but started walking down the street, hands stuffed into her coat pockets. Her thumb brushed over the metal of the ring encircling her left ring finger.

Married.

She was good and truly married, to a handsome, kind, intelligent, honorable man. The past few hours seemed surreal. Afraid if she closed her eyes it would all be a dream, she kept her focus straight ahead.

When she awoke that morning, she had not even the slightest inkling that before nightfall, she'd be Klayne's bride. If she'd known that, had any idea he was back in town, she wouldn't have spent all morning cleaning the barn, wrestling with a sick bull, and riding Troy.

Instead, she would have soaked in a tub of fragrant bubbles until her skin wrinkled up like a prune, then spent hours dressing in her finest clothes and styling her hair. As it was, she'd taken a slapdash shower and hurriedly washed her hair when Klayne arrived, then raced to change into the summer dress after she accepted his second proposal.

Head over heels in love with him, she eagerly married him. Only now that the deed was done, she considered the brashness of her actions. Frankly, she didn't know much about Klayne. In fact, the things she did know about him could be jotted onto a very short list.

Surreptitiously, she glanced over at him as he guided her around a patch of ice on the sidewalk. The worry gnawing at her stomach ceased and peace settled over her. She might not know much about the piddling little details one might like to know about a spouse, but the important things, the things about a man's character and heart, those she knew. Klayne was a good, solid man. One she could trust with her life and her heart. Never would he intentionally hurt her. Additionally, she had an idea he would move heaven and earth to keep her safe and protected.

He smiled down at her and kissed her cheek then held open the door to the Italian restaurant. "I assumed this was your destination," he said as she breezed inside.

"Yes. It seemed fitting to come here after Judge Rawlings performed our ceremony for us." Delaney waved at people she knew as the waitress showed them to a table. Thankfully, it was in a corner where they would have a little privacy. Klayne helped her remove her coat and Delaney glanced down at her gown, wondering if people would question why she wore it. With a mental shrug, she decided people could just wonder and gossip all they wanted. What she did wasn't any of their business anyway.

She and Klayne were soon enjoying plates of cheese-filled ravioli with slices of warm bread.

"This is delicious," Klayne said, lifting another piece of bread from the basket on the table.

"I've never eaten anything here that wasn't good," Delaney said, cutting a square of ravioli in half and watching wisps of fragrant steam float upward. She sniffed. "Sage and basil."

"Sage and basil?" Klayne asked, looking down at his half-eaten meal. "Is that what's in the ravioli?"

"I think so. I've been trying to pry the recipe out of them for years. Supposedly, it's a secret that will go to their graves."

Klayne chuckled and forked another bite. "Can't blame them for not wanting to share."

Delaney grinned and broke off a small piece of bread. "I suppose not." She glanced up when an older couple stopped by their table. Delaney hopped up and hugged the diminutive woman. "Mrs. Campanelli, it's so nice to see you."

"You as well, Delaney. Are you keeping busy at the ranch?" the woman asked.

"We are. Dad's in Portland right now helping Carol, but he'll be home in a few days." Delaney held a hand out to Klayne, who'd stood when she rose from the table. "Tony and Ilsa Campanelli, I'd like for you to meet Sergeant Klayne Campbell."

"It's a pleasure to meet you," Klayne said, shaking Tony's hand then Ilsa's.

"The pleasure is ours, young man," Tony said. "Thank you for your service to our country. I assume you're stationed here in Pendleton at the airfield."

"Yes, sir, at least for the moment." Klayne gave Delaney a look that made her stomach flutter.

"Delaney, dear, what on earth are you doing wearing a summer gown when it's only twenty degrees outside?" Ilsa asked, fingering the lace sleeve of Delaney's dress.

Delaney tipped her head toward Ilsa and glanced at Klayne. "Mrs. Campanelli is a famous fashion designer. Her gowns have traveled all around the world. And she made this one."

Klayne smiled at the petite woman who, despite her advancing years, remained a remarkable beauty. "Then I should thank you for making a gown that sets off Delaney's lovely features."

Ilsa beamed at him and Tony grinned. "So what are you kids up to?"

Delaney gave Klayne a conspiratorial look then leaned closer to the older couple. "Klayne and I just came from Kade's office where we got married."

She held out her hand and Ilsa examined the diamond ring. "Oh, Dee, we couldn't be happier for you. Will there be a reception later?"

Delaney shook her head. "No. If you both don't mind, we're trying to keep things quiet. The sudden wedding is because Klayne is leaving soon, but Dad doesn't know. I don't want anyone telling him before I have a chance to talk to him when he gets back."

"Understood," Tony said, placing a hand to his wife's back. "Congratulations on your nuptials and enjoy your evening."

"Thank you," Klayne said, politely inclining his head to them both.

The couple left and Klayne had seated Delaney when Tony reappeared. "I'd be happy to take a few photos, if you'd like."

"Oh, I hadn't even thought of a photograph, but that would be wonderful, Mr. Campanelli. We could come by…"

"Right after dinner?" Klayne interjected, not giving her a chance to suggest the following day.

She tossed her husband a curious look then turned her attention back to Tony.

The older man nodded his head. "That would be perfect. I'll get everything ready. Just come over to the studio when you finish up here."

Klayne shook his hand again. "Thank you so much, sir. We appreciate it."

"My pleasure." Tony strolled over to Ilsa as she waited at the door.

"That was kind of him to offer," Klayne said, eating the last bite of his ravioli.

"It was," Delaney said, feeling rushed to finish her meal. She didn't want to keep Mr. Campanelli waiting. "It might have been better to wait until tomorrow to go see him."

Klayne shook his head. "Oh, I think right now is perfect. You've got on your wedding dress and your cheeks are still pink from all the excitement. Besides, I think it's a good thing to capture the image on our wedding day. Not that I could ever forget the most important, wonderful day of my life, but it'll be nice to have a photograph of it."

Unable to argue with him when he said sweet things like that, she remained silent and forked a final bite of ravioli.

"Should we take dessert to Mr. Campanelli as a thank you for taking the photo?" Klayne asked as he paid the bill.

Delaney grinned. "No. Mr. Campanelli's sister is the one who started this restaurant. He gets all the wonderful Italian food he wants anytime he wants. His wife is a talented seamstress, but from the stories I heard, she practically burned down her dress shop before they wed when she attempted to bake bread. Her inability to cook is legendary."

Klayne chuckled and helped her on with her coat. "Are half the people in this town related to one another?"

Delaney shook her head. "Not half, maybe a third," she teased as they stepped outside and began walking down the street. The snow had stopped and stars glistened overhead. "Judge Rawlings is married to Caterina. Caterina is Mr. Campanelli's sister. Mrs. Campanelli's brother, Lars, and his wife started the first orphanage in the area. They still help there all they can, although they've turned over the management to one of the children they raised in the first group of orphans to live there. Mrs. Campanelli's sister, Aundy, and her husband also live in the area, on a farm near the orphanage. Their youngest son oversees it now. Their oldest son is a doctor here in town."

"Wow, that's a lot of family ties," Klayne said, trying to keep names and people straight. Delaney turned a corner and pointed to a shop door across the street.

Together, they walked inside Tony's photography studio. Klayne helped Delaney remove her coat, and then stared at the images on the walls. Some of them dated back to the first year Tony opened the studio, at the beginning of the century. Photographs of Indian mothers holding babies in beaded cradleboards hung beside images of wheat harvests and mule teams.

"Is that Mrs. Campanelli?" he asked, pointing to an image of a beautiful young woman standing beneath a lace parasol.

"Yes. Isn't she something?" Delaney asked, admiring the photo. Ilsa Campanelli was one of the most genteel, beautiful women she knew.

Tony stepped through a doorway and greeted them. "Come on back," he said.

Delaney led the way with Klayne right behind her. His nearness unsettled her, but she ignored it.

There would be time enough later to dwell on the feelings and emotions he stirred in her.

Much to Delaney's surprise, Ilsa arranged props in front of a screen. "This is going to be such fun," Ilsa said, motioning for them to step into place.

For the next twenty minutes, Ilsa and Tony worked as a team to position Delaney and Klayne in a variety of poses.

Delaney requested Tony take a few of Klayne by himself, and then Tony snapped a few of Delaney. The last photo he took of her, Klayne stood just to the left of Tony. When Delaney looked at him, he made the silliest face she'd ever seen and she burst out laughing. Her smile was infectious and that dimple danced tantalizingly in her cheek.

"That's the one," he whispered to Tony. Despite Tony and Ilsa insisting the photos would be a wedding gift, Klayne paid them.

"Thank you, again, for making time to do this for us," Klayne said as the couple walked them to the door.

"It's our pleasure," Tony said, thumping Klayne on the back as Ilsa gave Delaney a hug. "Now get out of here and enjoy your evening."

"We will. Thank you, sir."

Delaney looped her arm around Klayne's as they meandered back toward the car.

"Do you want to go anywhere? Do anything?" Klayne asked as they neared his borrowed transportation. "We could go to the movies. If you'd like, we could see about that dance Judge Rawlings mentioned."

"I'd rather just spend my time with you. Let's go home," Delaney said. The thought of Klayne being at the ranch with her sent an odd thrill chasing through her. In spite of the rushed, unexpected wedding, she couldn't deny how much she loved this man, how much she wanted to be with him. It felt right.

"I like the sound of that," he said, opening the car door and holding it for her as she slid onto the bench seat.

Klayne hurried around the car and started it. While they waited for the heater to kick in and begin blowing warm air, he pulled her into his arms and held her close. Music played on the radio and he hummed along as Bing Crosby crooned, "How Deep is the Ocean?"

Klayne softly sang the words in a smooth baritone voice. Astonished he could sing, she listened to the words that professed he loved her as deep as the ocean and as high as the sky. She wanted to wrap the pleasure of the moment around her to keep with her always.

Delaney breathed in his spicy scent and rested her head against his solid chest. Maybe she was wrong earlier. Home wasn't the ranch. From that moment on, it was in his arms.

In all her life, she'd never felt so secure, safe, cherished, and loved as she did when Klayne dropped a kiss on her forehead and cuddled her a little closer. This man, this elated feeling, was what she'd waited her whole lifetime to find.

Thoughts of Klayne leaving soon made her heart ache so badly she felt like she might suffocate, so she turned her attention to the evening ahead. Klayne might intend for this to be a wedding in name only, but Delaney had far different ideas.

"Let's go home," she repeated in a whisper. She looked up at her husband and willed him to be as in love with her as she was with him. The light flickering in his arresting blue eyes assured her of his affection every bit as much as the way he kissed her tenderly then put the car in gear.

She moved so he could drive, but sat close enough their thighs touched. Delaney felt heat sear through her with each bump in the road. By the time Klayne turned onto the Sage Hills Ranch lane, she wondered if she had a fever.

Klayne parked the car at the end of the walk and hurried around to open the passenger door. Delaney slid across the seat and he lifted her into his arms, carrying her down the walk and up the steps. He carefully maneuvered around Moose as the canine slept sprawled across the top porch step, snuffling in his sleep.

"That ridiculous dog," Delaney whispered, reaching down to open the door when Klayne bent his knees so she could reach the knob.

The door swung open and Klayne carried her inside. The house was dark, though warm, as he toed the door shut behind them.

Slowly, he set her down. He seemed hesitant to let go of her, but he finally took a step away from her when she reached out and flicked on a light.

"I appreciate you marrying me today, Delaney." He backed toward the door. "I can't thank you enough for what you did. It means the world to me." Another step back. "You'll receive some papers in the mail with information about becoming my beneficiary. I suppose I better go, though."

"Don't leave yet, Klayne." Delaney removed her coat and tossed it, along with her hat, on the newel post of the stairs. "You said you don't have to be back until tomorrow morning didn't you?"

Clearly hesitant to stay, he edged closer to the door. "I did say that, but I think it's best if I leave."

"Why would you want to do that, Sergeant Campbell?" Delaney moved in front of him and tugged off his coat and hat, dropping them on top of hers. She unbuttoned his dress jacket and guided it off his shoulders, letting her hands linger over the hard muscles of his arms as she pushed down the sleeves and brushed against him. She'd never been so intimately close to a man before and wasn't sure how to proceed. Nevertheless, of one thing she was certain — Klayne was not leaving her alone. Not on their wedding night.

Pure instinct kicked in as she removed his tie and began unbuttoning his shirt. "I'm pretty sure you'll have a much better time here this evening than you would back at Pendleton Field."

Klayne swallowed hard as an inner battle waged. She could see it in the lines around his eyes and the firm set of his jaw. Finally, he expelled a long breath then reached out and pulled her against him.

Sparks flickered in his eyes as he gazed down at her with such a look of hunger, she wondered if he intended to devour her. Slightly anxious by what she'd started in her attempt to seduce him, she considered if she was brave enough to see her bold actions through. Klayne was her husband, after all. A man she loved with all her heart.

Fingers trembling with anticipation and a little fear, she finished unbuttoning his shirt. Her cool hands slipped underneath the thin cotton of his undershirt. The heat radiating from his skin, along with the solid firmness of his abdomen, warmed her in seconds.

His breath blew across her neck as he placed a heated kiss to the pulse rapidly pounding in her throat. He lifted his head and the sparks in his eyes ignited into liquid fire. Intrigued, uncertain, and longing for something she couldn't explain and didn't fully understand, she couldn't tear her gaze away from his.

A sound of tortured misery escaped his throat on a low groan. "Delaney, you need to step away and show me to the door, right now. If you don't, if you wait one more minute, I won't be able to leave. Do you understand what I'm telling you, sweetheart? If you want me to leave, now is the time to tell me." He started to move away but she wouldn't let him, clasping her arms around his waist and holding on tight.

He held his arms out to his sides, not touching her. Even so, she felt a tremor pass through him as he fought to hold onto his control.

"Delaney Marie, if you don't turn me loose, I won't be held responsible for my actions. I know I promised you a marriage in name only, but you can only push a man so far before he lands beyond the edge of reason."

"I plan to hold you responsible for your actions, Klayne." She gave him a smirk as her hazel eyes darkened. "Fully and completely responsible." Her hands nudged off his shirt then slid up his arms.

One step closer and she obliterated any space lingering between them. "I don't want you to leave, Klayne. Not now, not ever. I love you so much." She pressed a quick kiss to his jaw. "I want you to love me, Klayne." A peck to his cheek. "Love me like I'll always belong to you."

The pleading in her gaze left him undone.

"I love you, Delaney. More than you can know." His lips and heart took full possession of her as he captured her mouth in a kiss full of more yearning and ardor than she imagined possible.

Languid and in a state of bliss unlike anything she'd ever dreamed, Delaney lost the ability to stand on her own.

Klayne bore her weight as she pressed against him, unable to get close enough. Suddenly, he swept her into his arms and started up the stairs. Delaney directed him to the guest room where he'd stayed the night of the big snow storm.

In the muted light from the slivers of moonbeams shining in the window, she enthusiastically surrendered to the tender yet undeniably passionate love of her beloved husband.

∗∗★ *Chapter Nine* ★∗∗

Stubbornly clinging to every precious minute of the few he had remaining with Delaney, Klayne denied rest for his exhausted mind and body.

He'd spent hours pouring out all the love he harbored in his heart not just for her, but for what she represented — someone to call his own, someone who thought he mattered and cared whether he lived or died.

After such a wondrous, phenomenal experience, he refused to surrender to something as commonplace as slumber. Instead, he turned onto his stomach, folded a pillow beneath his cheek, and watched her sleep.

In her arms, he'd finally discovered a place to belong, a place that was his and his alone. Through her sweet love, he'd found absolution from his past and hope for his future. Delaney had given him the home he'd always longed for and never knew how to find — the home of her heart.

Silver moonlight streaming in the window illuminated her face while the small lamp she'd left on in the hall cast a pale amber-hued glow around the room. Even in the murky shadows, he could see her eyelashes fan her cheeks and a slight smile ride the corners of her lips. He'd been right when he assumed she'd be just as pretty in sleep as she was awake. Silently studying her, he thought she looked so young and adorable, yet utterly tempting.

When he took a breath, he closed his eyes, memorizing her succulent scent. Whether he had one more day or fifty more years on this earth, he didn't want to forget a single thing about this miraculous night. For the very first time in his life, Klayne felt wanted, needed, and loved. So incredibly loved.

Delaney was the first person to say the words to him. *I love you.* Three simple words that had the most profound effect on him, rousing emotions he hadn't even realized he possessed. The affection, passion and devotion she'd so freely given him watered the parched soil of his heart. The seeds that had laid dormant there took nourishment from her love and blossomed into something beautiful and so very unexpected.

With his heart so full it felt like it might burst, Klayne reached out and fingered one of the silky locks of Delaney's hair. The dark tresses flowed in wild disarray over her pillow, and entangled around him. He loved the texture of her hair, the weight of it in his hands, the fragrance of it that put him in mind of exotic flowers with a hint of citrus.

He released the tendril of hair and indulged in tracing his fingers lightly down the exposed skin of her arm. It was so incredibly soft, smooth, and warm.

Unable to stop himself, he leaned over and skimmed a kiss across her lips.

"Mmm. Klayne," she muttered in her sleep and rolled toward him.

Delighted she thought of him even in her dreams, he slipped one arm beneath her shoulders and the other around her back, pulling her against him. She snuggled into the warmth of his chest, asleep. Desperate to taste her again, to revel in the sweetness of her, he pleasured her mouth with teasing kisses. When her lips parted, he kissed her deep and long.

Her eyes popped open. The fog in her gaze cleared away as joy and yearning took its place. Seductively, she smirked and brushed her hand across the muscles of his chest, twirling her fingers through the light brown hair growing there. "Hey, handsome, why aren't you asleep?"

The smirk heated his blood every bit as much as her touch, while the sultry tone of her voice made it impossible for him to think of anything beyond how much he loved her. He grinned and subtly moved closer. "How could I sleep, Laney, with you here beside me?"

"Laney?" she asked, pressing teasing kisses along his jawline and down his neck.

"I've decided that's what I'm going to call you when it's just us. You're Dee to your friends, Sis to your dad, but to me, you are Laney. Or I suppose I could call you Lady Lane. How about Larry, if I combine your first and middle name?

She laughed and the throaty sound of it cast what little sense and restraint he had left to the wind. He buried his hands in her hair and kissed her with a fierce possessiveness that left them both breathless.

When he lifted his head, she gulped in air and then mumbled, "Laney it is, soldier boy."

Later, as Delaney once again slept, Klayne took one more deep breath of her fragrance, imprinting it in his memories. Quietly, he slipped from the bed and yanked on his clothes. Downstairs, he found a piece of paper in the kitchen near the telephone. He wrote Delaney a note then carried it back upstairs, leaving it on his pillow along with a necklace he'd purchased for her when he'd bought the wedding ring.

Emotion clogged his throat as he bent down and kissed her forehead. Other than his friend Billy, he'd never had anyone to say goodbye to. Never had anyone who might miss him. Never felt such a desperate longing to stay.

The notion that Delaney wanted him there made him fight the urge to wake her up and tell her the full truth of why he insisted on marrying her yesterday. Waking her would only make their parting harder, though. Of that he had no doubt.

Conflicted, he hoped what he'd done, what they'd done, wouldn't cause her problems in the future. Until he was killed on the mission, she'd be bound by marriage to a man she barely knew. She couldn't date some nice local boy, fall in love, and live happily ever after, now that she'd become his wife. Whether he lived or died, she was stuck with him.

What have I done? he wondered. The immensity of the situation almost buckled his knees.

Instead of faltering, he braced one arm on the headboard, studying her for several long moments before he brushed a lock of hair away from her face and wondered if he'd ever again have the opportunity and privilege of spending a night in her arms.

Before he tossed aside his responsibilities and career to remain with her, Klayne grazed a kiss across her lips. She smiled and sighed happily. Her voice, when she spoke, was thick with sleep. "Love you, Klayne."

"I love you, too, sweetheart. So, so much," he whispered then straightened. The words bubbling up from his soul were easier to say when he didn't have to fear her reaction to them. His forefinger stroked across her hairline then along her cheek. "You are the first and only woman I'll ever love, Laney. What we just shared was better than anything I could have dreamed or imagined. Not because you're beautiful to look at and feel so good in my arms, but because you're lovely from the inside out and feel so good in my heart. Stay safe and please don't hate me. I'm going to miss you, my amazing wife."

Lest he change his mind and surrender to his need to climb back in the bed with her, he hurried outside into the darkness of predawn. Klayne arrived back at the base as the sky began to lighten. He returned the car to its rightful owner along with a dozen doughnuts he'd purchased the previous afternoon. Rather than answer questions about where he'd been or what he'd done, he offered another word of thanks then went to his bunk. Quickly gathering his things, he took a hot shower. He hated to do it, to wash away the faint lingering fragrance of his wife, but he had to get ready for the day ahead.

Hastily gulping a cup of strong, black coffee, he then reported for duty. In a whirlwind of activity, he found himself packing his things to leave that afternoon with those from his squadron. Those who weren't flying planes to Minneapolis for modifications or directly to the base in South Carolina would spend around five days traveling across the country via train.

With one last glance around his bunk to make sure he hadn't left anything behind, he rushed out the door. A messenger rushed up to him with a large envelope.

"Hey, Sarge. A gentleman dropped this off for you. Said it was urgent you received it." The young man handed him the envelope, snapped a salute and jogged off.

Klayne set down the duffle bag he carried and opened the envelope. Inside, he could see photographs Tony Campanelli had taken the previous evening of Klayne and Delaney, along with a note.

Flooded with a longing to go to his bride, Klayne closed the flap of the envelope, tucked it into his bag, and hurried to catch the ride to the depot.

He stood in line, watching the crowds. Indians with long, dark braids intermingled with teary-eyed women. Many wives and girlfriends gathered to say goodbye to the soldiers who boarded the train. Regret that he hadn't given Delaney the chance to bid him farewell pricked at his conscience, but he ignored it. Things were better the way he'd left them. He was sure of it.

Finally, Klayne boarded the train and took a seat next to one of the men from his squad. If Klayne had an interest in making friends, the man sitting next to him would have topped the list. Bob was a valued soldier and a good man. But the last thing Klayne thought he needed were more emotional attachments to cloud his judgment and rip his heart to shreds.

He'd vowed to never care for anyone again after Billy. Yet, all it had taken was one look from Delaney and he'd tossed aside his vow. Instantly, he'd fallen head over heels in love with the woman.

As the train left the station, Klayne had to grip the edge of the seat to keep from bolting down the aisle, out the door, and running back to Delaney. The note he left would have been read hours ago and she'd know he was gone.

Absently, he wondered if she'd despise him for what he'd done. For loving her so thoroughly then leaving like a coward while she slept. If he'd had to face her tears, he couldn't have left. He would have deserted the Army and run off to Mexico with her. Then again, she wouldn't abandon the ranch and he would never ask her to.

By some miracle, if he didn't die in battle, he hoped she'd speak to him when he one day returned home.

*** ★ *Chapter Ten* ★ ***

Delaney awakened in unhurried stages, not quite ready for a new day to begin. Oddly languid, she rolled onto her back and lazily stretched her arms and legs before slowly opening her eyes.

Surprised to find herself not in her bedroom, but the guest room, memories of the events of the previous afternoon and evening washed over her.

Heat burned her cheeks as she thought about the night she spent in Klayne's strong arms. She'd behaved so... wantonly. Or was that just the way a newlywed wife acted when she was madly in love with her handsome, charming husband.

Uncertain how to face him in the glaring light of day, she rolled her head to the side and found only an empty bed. Klayne's scent, a spicy masculine fragrance that even now made her stomach flutter in response to it, filled her nose as she moved onto her side and buried her face in his pillow.

She wondered where he'd gone. From the spears of light seeping in the window, she knew she was late rising. Had he already returned to the base? Under the assumption he'd go to Pendleton Field, do what he needed to do and return to her that night, she hadn't bothered to ask him when he'd be back or what time he needed to leave.

What if he'd already gone while she slept? Had he watched her sleep? Her face turned red just thinking of him studying her. In fairness, she'd studied him for the longest time as they rested in each other's arms. She wanted to be able to see him when she closed her eyes, to memorize every detail about him, knowing he'd leave soon. That was why she insisted on leaving the light on in the hall. It provided just enough illumination, she could see the warm light in his eyes and make note of the tiny scar above his lip that almost touched his nose. She committed to memory every freckle that dotted the back of his shoulders.

Klayne had been so sweet and gentle with his loving, yet he'd been consumed with a need for her. A need she not only recognized, but reciprocated.

Grateful her father was out of town and they had the house to themselves, Delaney slid her hand beneath the pillow and encountered something that crinkled. She turned on the bedside lamp then pulled out a sheet of paper, folded into thirds with her name scrawled across the front.

Wary of the note, of what it might mean, she unfolded the paper and read it.

Shocked and stunned, she blinked twice before she could read it again.

The third time she read it, she sat up straight in the bed, heedless to her state of undress, and experienced a great stabbing pain to her heart.

My Darling Wife,

The last thing in this world I'd ever want to do is hurt you, Delaney. In an effort to shelter you from the harsh reality of the way things really are, I chose not to tell you the entire truth yesterday. I let you believe that I'd be leaving Pendleton soon. While that isn't a lie, the fact is I'll be leaving today. I have a feeling where I'm heading is only a stop on the way to a bigger, grander mission, one I have yet to discover but have been assured some if not most of us will not survive.

My immediate departure is why I thought it best to keep our marriage one in name only. Please don't misunderstand, though. Last night was the best night of my entire life. Although I have often wished to find a woman who cared for me, could share a few scraps of her affection on this undeserving soldier, you, lovely Laney, amazed me by the generosity of your love. I am awed by the tenderness I've known the last several hours in the haven of your arms.

I should be ashamed of what transpired this last evening, of so eagerly accepting the love you so willingly offered, but I can't manage to summon a single regret. If I had only one memory to sustain me for the rest of my life, it would be of lying right here next to you, holding you in my arms as you slept so peacefully against my chest.

No matter what the very uncertain future might bring, I hope you'll remember this indisputable fact — I love you. I love you with all of my heart, my soul, my mind, and my body. I love you so completely, I can't even begin to fathom the miraculous possibilities of it. I love you more than I ever dreamed of loving anyone.

In case you think I'll forget you during this horrible war, let me assure you, there is no forgetting you, Delaney Marie Danvers Campbell. You are as unique, lovely, and rare as the exotic blooms your intoxicating fragrance brings to mind. From this day forward, you will be foremost in my mind and heart.

Thank you, beloved, for giving me something I've waited my entire life to find. You are the first person who ever said, "I love you," to me, and for that I'm eternally grateful. But it's more than that, far deeper than that. You've finally given me a home - the place I know I belong... right there in your heart.

It may be a long while before I have the chance to write to you. Please take good care of yourself, dear wife. Someday, I will return because I now have a reason beyond all reasons to survive. I have the love of a magnificent woman and that, sweetheart, is all the inspiration I need to make it through the weeks and months ahead.

Please express my apologies to Dill for not giving him a chance to grant his permission for our hasty wedding.

I'll keep your family, including your brother, in my prayers. Perhaps you'll keep me in yours, too. I'm sure I can use all the help I can get.

Don't cry any tears for me, Delaney. Just face each day with a smile, knowing somewhere out there is a man who loves you beyond all sense or reason, who would move mountains to be with you again.

I love you, my beautiful bride, with all that I am.
Yours forever,
Klayne

Delaney wasn't a woman generally given to bouts of hysteria or tears, but she broke down in heart wrenching sobs so uncontrollable, she soaked through the pillow she held against her face and had to use the sheet to mop away the tears.

She cried for the naïve dreams broken into shattered pieces around her. Somehow, she'd just known Klayne wouldn't leave her. He loved her. Wasn't that enough for him to be able to stay? She wanted him to be there, would have done anything to keep him with her. Perhaps he'd known she'd cry and beg him not to go, and that was why he snuck away while she slept.

They could have run away together, somewhere safe where he'd never be asked to leave her. Yet, even as she considered the possibility, she knew she couldn't have done it. The country needed Klayne more than she did.

Priding herself on her patriotism, Delaney had spent many hours in the last year and a half helping with the Bundles for Britain campaign. Although Amy knit scarves and sweaters to contribute, Delaney couldn't sit still long enough to do any handiwork. Instead, she gathered up clothes, blankets, shoes, and even some basic medical supplies to send to war-torn Britain.

She'd been among the first in town to volunteer to put up "Remember Pearl Harbor" signs and proudly wore a small Victory pin on her lapel whenever she went to Pendleton. She'd helped some of the women at church bake dozens and dozens of cookies for the soldiers stationed at Pendleton Field. Sage Hills Ranch had donated beef for community fundraisers to support the war efforts. Everyone at the ranch purchased war bonds every time they went to town.

The Danvers' household had been one full of patriotism and love of country from the moment her grandfather built it. How could she do any less than support her country and the brave soldiers who defended it?

Suddenly, her need to support the war effort seemed much more personal, far more urgent.

Tears abated, she sat up again and pulled Klayne's pillow to her, breathing deeply of his scent lingering on the case. When she turned her face to the side, she noticed a tiny, flat box tucked into the gap between the mattress and the headboard. Pulling it out, she opened the lid and read the brief note from Klayne.

The exquisite beauty of this made me think of you. I pray each time you wear it, you'll remember how much you are loved.

A gleaming silver chain joined in the front with a delicate filigreed heart from which a single, perfect tear-shaped pearl hung. Simplistic yet beautiful, Delaney sniffled as she lifted the necklace from the box.

"Foolish man. He probably spent a year's wages on the necklace and my wedding ring," she muttered and held out her left hand to admire the diamond on her finger. The band encircling her finger made everything seem starkly real.

Delaney returned the necklace to the box, grabbed the letter from Klayne, and bolted out of bed. She raced into her room, left the gift and note on her dresser, then rushed to shower. She dressed in one of her most flattering gowns, styled her hair so it waved and curled becomingly around her face, and fastened the necklace around her neck. Hastily grabbing her handbag, she dashed downstairs.

She may have been a weeping mess an hour earlier, but now she was mad. Klayne might think he was protecting her, sheltering her, but she deserved better than that. She needed more than that. He should have told her in the first place he was leaving today. The truth wouldn't have changed anything that happened, none of which she regretted. However, she would have at least been prepared to tell him goodbye, even if she didn't want to let him go.

After tugging on her snow boots and wool coat, she made her way out to the bunkhouse. The light was on in the barn and the men had no doubt been up for a few hours. She rapped once before opening the door.

Butch stood at the sink washing the breakfast dishes. He glanced over at her and lifted one bushy eyebrow. "What are you up to this morning, Girly?"

"I need to go into Pendleton, Butch. I'm not sure what time I'll be back. I just wanted to let you know and see if you needed any supplies."

"Nope, we're all set here." He gave her a long, knowing look. "Don't suppose your trip into town has anything to do with that soldier who was here last night?"

"As a matter of fact, it does." Delaney started out the door, but Butch's comments brought her up short.

"Your folks didn't raise you to act so slack with your morals. Just because your dad is gone doesn't mean it's okay to do something like let one of those pretty soldier boys sweet-talk their way into your bed. I may be old, but I ain't blind or stupid. I saw his car parked outside all night."

Delaney's entire face turned red as she spun around and loosed her temper on the old cowboy. "How dare you accuse me of... of being a..." She slammed her handbag down on the scarred surface of the big wooden dinner table and yanked off her glove, waggling her ring finger in Butch's face. "I married a very nice man yesterday. And yes, I did it without Dad knowing, but that was only because Klayne is leaving, right now, today. No matter what you thought I did, I didn't. Furthermore, you can just dang well keep this to yourself. I don't want anyone telling Dad before I have a chance to explain things to him. Klayne intended to ask Dad's permission, but as you know, that's impossible with him gone. Now, if you don't mind, I'm going to try to make it to Pendleton in time to say goodbye to my husband."

Butch's mouth had dropped open at the sight of the ring on her finger and continued to dangle in the air during her tirade. He snapped it closed as she grabbed her handbag and stormed out the door, fury fueling her steps all the way to the car. She started it and roared down their lane, much to the surprise of the cowboys in the barn and the chagrin of the man standing in the bunkhouse doorway watching her drive away.

Delaney's fury only increased when she arrived at Pendleton Field and asked to see Klayne.

"I'm sorry, ma'am, but Sergeant Campbell is not available for visitors today," a guard said.

She glared at the young man. "I'm not a visitor, I'm his wife. It's imperative I speak with him today."

The young man gave her a smug look and shook his head. "Now, ma'am, I know for a fact Sergeant Campbell isn't married. And he ain't one to dally with the women, either. I don't know what game you're playing, but you aren't gonna win. Unless you have some official business here, you'd best leave."

Infuriated to the point she could hardly see straight, Delaney drove down the road and waited an hour before trying again to see Klayne. A different young man acting as guard at the gate told her the same thing. It was then she noticed several women trying to get in and all of them turned away. The fact she wasn't alone in her plight didn't help her feel any better about the situation.

With each passing minute, she grew more and more desperate to see Klayne. She had no idea how to find him, even if she could sneak past the men guarding the gate.

Angry, hurt, and defeated, she drove into town. She parked her car with no idea of what she should do when she glanced up and noticed she'd driven to Tony Campanelli's photography studio.

Inspired with an idea, she rushed inside the studio, nearly knocking the bell above the door off its hook in her haste.

Tony walked into the reception area from the back, wiping his hands on a rag while the faint odor of chemicals filled the air.

"Well, Dee! What brings you back so soon? How's that new husband of yours?" Tony greeted her with a broad smile.

"Oh, Mr. Campanelli, I just found out Klayne has to leave today. I can't get anyone at the base to let me see him to say goodbye. I know it's a lot to ask, but I was wondering if you had time and wouldn't mind, could you print one of the photos you took for us last night and see that it's delivered? I'm hoping they'll at least give it to him before he leaves. I want him to have something... something to..." Tears clogged her throat and left her unable to speak.

Tony scowled. "It's a shame they won't let you in, but I'll do what I can. I was just working on some prints when you came in. While I finish, why don't you write that young man of yours a note? I can tuck it in with the prints. If there's anything else you want to include, just let me know. It'll take me about thirty minutes to finish."

"Thank you so, so much, Mr. Campanelli. I appreciate it more than you know," she said, banking her emotion and accepting the tablet of paper Tony slid across the counter to her.

He disappeared into the back and she heard the click of his darkroom door. She sat down in one of the chairs in the waiting area and tried to gather her scattered thoughts.

Her first inclination was to lambast Klayne for running off like a tail-tucked coward and not telling her goodbye in person. Her second was to whine and complain that life wasn't fair. Finally corralling her tumultuous emotions, she wrote him a letter that expressed her thoughts and, she hoped, the love she felt for him. She didn't hold back her disappointment, but she didn't beleaguer the point, either.

When she finished, she pulled a daintily embroidered handkerchief from her handbag, a gift from Carol, and tucked it inside the letter. She stuffed it into an envelope she found on the counter with Tony's business name imprinted in the corner.

With a glance at the clock, she realized Tony would be finished any minute. She'd hoped to run down the street and find something to send to Klayne. Her heartfelt letter would have to do.

Tony appeared and set a large envelope on the counter. "Write his name and the name of his squadron, if you know it, on there. I'll do my best to see he gets it before he leaves. I can't make any promises, but I'll try."

"I'm sure your best will achieve more than mine, sir," Delaney said, writing Klayne's name on the envelope and trying to remember if he'd mentioned a squadron. Vaguely recalling him talking about the bombardment group, she wrote that on the envelope and hoped it was correct. How had she married someone she knew so little about? Try as she might to regret it, to regret tying her life to Klayne's, she couldn't do it. Not when she felt consumed with love, and now concern, for him.

"Thank you, again, Mr. Campanelli. If there is ever anything I can do to repay your kindness, I hope you'll let me know."

Tony gave her a sly glance. "If you bake me one of those cakes with the coconut frosting, like you brought to church for the gathering we had after Thanksgiving, we'll call it even."

Delaney grinned. "Consider it done!" She picked up her gloves and handbag, moving toward the door. "I really do appreciate your help, Mr. Campanelli. With Dad out of town, I don't know what else to do."

"You're welcome, Dee. Try not to worry too much. I'm sure the boys are just headed for training somewhere."

She nodded and left, making her way back to the car. Feeling empty and lost, Delaney couldn't decide her next move. She had no desire to linger in town, yet she didn't want to go home. Normally, she would have gone to the bakery and visited with Amy, but she wasn't in the mood for her friend's cheerful presence.

The temperatures made it far too cold to sit in the car and pout, so Delaney started it and began the drive home. She was halfway there when she wondered if the soldiers would be leaving by train. If so, she might be able to catch Klayne at the depot. She turned the car around and sped to the station.

There were so many vehicles around, she had to park five blocks away then made her way over snow and ice covered streets to get there just in time to see Klayne step into a train car.

Although she rushed forward, he didn't see her. She jumped up and down, waving at him like a woman who'd lost her mind, but he took a seat on the far side of the train.

Intent on seeing him, on telling him goodbye, she started to board, but the porter barred her way. "No, ma'am, you aren't getting on this here train car. Now step on back. We are leaving."

"But my husband is on the train. I need to tell him goodbye!" Delaney lunged forward, but the man again pushed her back.

"I said no and I mean no. If you haven't told him goodbye yet, then maybe you'll do a better job of saying your farewells next time." The man hurried up the steps as the train began to creak and rock forward.

Delaney jumped up again, trying to see in the window, only to notice several men watching her. She frantically pointed in Klayne's direction, but the soldiers just laughed and waved.

Heartbroken, she buried her face in her hands and joined several other women in shedding tears as the soldiers rolled out of town.

···★ *Chapter Eleven* ★···

Klayne slogged his way to his tent at the Columbia Army Air Base, wishing, for many reasons, he'd never received orders to leave Oregon.

It might have been frozen and snowy there, but the relative comfort of the barracks seemed like luxury accommodations compared to the tents they camped in on a field of sloppy mud. The winter rains soaked into everything, leaving him perpetually cold and miserable.

On top of that, he missed Delaney with every breath his body drew in and released. He waited until after they arrived in South Carolina and settled into their meager accommodations before he opened the envelope from Tony Campanelli. He had no idea how the man had gotten it to him at the last minute, but he was grateful the photographer made the effort.

Suddenly nervous, Klayne wiped his hands on his trousers then slowly pulled three photographs from the envelope. The top image showed him and Delaney in a formal pose. He stood behind her with his hand lightly resting on the curve of her waist. They both faced the camera, looking happy and excited. The second photograph was of the two of them gazing at each other as they held hands. Anyone could see the smiles they exchanged held love and hope.

As much as he liked both of the photographs, it was the third image that made him sink onto his cot, heart hammering in his chest. Tony had captured Delaney laughing, dimple popping out in her cheek, while her eyes danced with humor and life. This photograph depicted the exact image of how he saw her when he closed his eyes.

For several long moments, he just stared at the photo, afraid to touch the image lest he accidentally mar it.

With a sigh that rolled up from his soul, he set aside the three photographs and stuck his hand back in the envelope. He drew out a small print of Delaney's laughing face, one that would fit inside a tiny space. Mr. Campanelli must have known how much Klayne would want and need that little photo. He carefully tucked it inside his leather wallet before removing a piece of paper and a small letter-sized envelope from the large manila envelope.

The note was from Mr. Campanelli. The missive thanked him for defending the country and encouraged him to keep safe.

Klayne opened the small envelope and Delaney's scent wafted around him. He picked up a delicate square of linen, embroidered with blue and yellow flowers in one corner, along with the initial D. Holding the handkerchief to his nose, he breathed deeply of the fragrance and closed his eyes, daydreaming of being back at the ranch in Delaney's arms. Assailed again with worries that he'd ruined her life by marrying her, he fervently hoped he was wrong.

He swallowed hard and drew his thoughts back to the present. Losing himself in his longings would only make the present more difficult to bear.

The letter didn't take long to read, but Klayne held it in his hands, studying Delaney's no-nonsense script, her frank words, and absorbing the fact she'd written him a letter even after she knew he was leaving. He read it again, pretending her voice spoke the words.

Dear Klayne,

Imagine my surprise when I awoke this morning to find you gone. What a dirty trick to pull on a girl, especially on one who is so completely and utterly in love with you.

How could you just leave me like that, without so much as a goodbye? I plan to have a very stern discussion with you about this matter when you come back. I expect a promise that you'll never, ever, in the next sixty or seventy years, do anything like it again. Got that, soldier?

I tried for hours to get in to see you, but apparently, you have quite a reputation of shunning women who claim to know you. The guards at the gate absolutely refused to listen to me when I tried to explain we wed yesterday. They laughed and sent me on my way, multiple times.

I'm not sure what guided me to Mr. Campanelli's studio. One minute I was driving around town, mad as a wet mule in a spring downpour, and the next I looked up and realized I was right outside his door.

He was kind enough to make these prints for you and promised to do his best to see you receive them. If you're reading this letter, then he succeeded!

I'm not an overly emotional girl, Klayne, but I have to tell you I cried more tears today than I have since my mother passed away. Why didn't you tell me the truth? At least then, I would have had the opportunity to tell you goodbye, to share one last kiss. (You have no idea how much I enjoy your kisses. None at all.)

Once I got over my tears and recovered from wanting to beat you senseless,

Klayne grinned and continued reading.

I just wanted to give you a hug and tell you I'll miss you.

As angry, annoyed, and downright irritated as I am at you, as much as I don't want you to leave, there are two things you should know.

The first is that I'm crazy for you and will love you no matter what. That's right, Sergeant Klayne Campbell, I love you, with all that I am. When you're free to go wherever you like, make sure you come straight to me, to the one place you'll always have a home — right here in my heart.

The second thing is that I'm proud of you. You're a fine, wonderful, gentle, caring man. And I know you're a good soldier. Only a man of your superb character would be willing to risk his life for his country on a mission he knows nothing about.

In the days ahead, don't ever forget who you are or that many people are praying for your safe return from wherever it is you must go.

Be safe, Klayne, and come back to me. Please.

I love you, forever and always.

Your angry but completely devoted wife,

Laney

Emotion thickened his throat and stung the backs of his eyes as he read the letter again, then studied the photographs. Delaney had made him laugh while taking him to task for not being forthright with her. If he had the chance to do it again, to see her again, he'd never be anything but one hundred percent honest with her, no matter the situation.

The fact that she said she loved him and wanted him to return buoyed his low spirits.

When the rain turned to ice on the tents and nearly froze the occupants inside, Delaney's promise to love him always and forever kept him warm. When the men griped about the conditions and speculated that they'd soon be dropping bombs on Germans, her reminder that he had a home to return to kept him going.

One day, word moved through the ranks that more volunteers were needed for a hazardous mission that would most likely claim many lives. "Some of you fellows are going to get killed," the captain said in warning. "How many of you will go?"

Klayne had already volunteered, back in Pendleton, but he stepped forward again, renewing his commitment to do whatever it took to help his country win the war. Sooner or later, he'd be drawn into combat, so he figured he might as well have a say in it.

From the moment the Japanese bombed Pearl Harbor, he, and many men just like him, had experienced a helpless, anxious-to-do-something feeling. Furious at the enemy and wanting to defend America, the anger and desire to take action gave him the drive he needed to push forward, even though he had no idea where the men of his squad were headed or when.

If Klayne died in battle, he hoped it would be doing something that would make Delaney proud. The idea of engaging in a secret dangerous mission seemed like it would fit the bill.

The beginning of March found Klayne and the twenty volunteer aircrews transferred to Eglin Field in Florida near Pensacola.

Ready to leave behind the miserable weather of South Carolina and eager to learn more about the mission, the men arrived to discover they had more than fifty hours of training before them and no further details of the mission. The only information they had was a reiteration that it was dangerous and some of them would die.

The officer in charge of forming a cohesive unit out of the volunteers from four different squadrons was popular amongst the soldiers, known for his aviation skills throughout the military.

Honored to work with him, Klayne and the others absorbed the seemingly endless training. The crews of each B-25 learned short-field takeoffs, daytime and nighttime bombing, and engaged in practice runs against imaginary attacking pursuits.

Each flight crew had five men including the pilot, co-pilot, navigator, bombardier, and gunner. Klayne's main responsibilities as a bombardier included sighting in the target and dropping bombs. He also had to coordinate with the pilot and the rest of the crew. In fact, when he took bombardier training, he had to memorize a long list of duties that rested on his shoulders. The responsibilities covered everything from taking over the navigator's duties should he be incapacitated to knowing how to load and fuse his own bombs.

With perfect vision, Klayne had excelled in his job, rarely missing a target. He'd flown on planes with the famous Norden bombsight. The seventy-five pound piece of equipment consisted of more than two thousand parts that helped accurately sight in targets. However, on the high-speed, low altitude practice flights Klayne and the others were training to execute, the expensive piece of equipment was useless.

He watched with interest as new bombsights made from scrap aluminum were installed on the modified B-25 planes. The sights supposedly cost less than thirty cents to make and worked far better in the low altitudes than the expensive alternative. The switch also alleviated the fear of the enemy capturing a Norden bombsight, even if Klayne still had no clue which enemy they would be bombing.

As he and his crew went on training flights over the coastal waters around the Florida panhandle where they were stationed, they speculated where the mission might take them. Some mentioned Japan while others were certain they'd attack Germany. A few even thought they might end up in South America.

Rather than join in the haphazard guessing, Klayne focused on honing his skills. During the training flights, he dropped concrete and sand-loaded practice bombs over remote areas.

Since Klayne was cross-trained as a nose gunner, he made note of the modifications to the B-25's armament. Top and bottom gun turrets had twin .50-caliber machine guns while a single .30-caliber machine gun was located in the nose of the plane. Half the time, the guns malfunctioned or the blast from the muzzle fired near the fuselage popped out rivets and ripped the plane's thin skin. Steel blast plates were installed and the belly guns removed to free up space for an additional gas tank. Workers replaced defective guns and repaired faulty parts. The crews practiced shooting at ground range, or strafing sea slicks on the gulf.

The tail of the plane was largely unprotected until one of the men devised the idea of cutting holes in the bomber's tail and inserting two black wooden poles that, to Klayne, closely resembled painted broomsticks. From a distance, they gave the appearance of twin .50-caliber machine guns.

Concerned by the discussions he overheard about maximizing fuel efficiency and removing unnecessary weight so each plane could carry additional fuel, Klayne assumed wherever they were flying would likely be a one-way mission with no place to land.

Their practice flights of taking off in short-distances, coupled with the training over water only served to solidify Klayne's suspicions they'd be out in the ocean on an aircraft carrier at some point during the mission.

As the days rolled by, a doctor administered shots for everything from typhoid and tetanus to yellow fever and bubonic plague. Klayne's friend Bob complained if the doc poked him one more time, he'd start leaking fluid through all the holes in his skin.

Between training and contemplating their futures, some of the soldiers fished, others wrote letters home. A few of the wives and families of the men arrived, staying in a hotel just down the road from the base.

Klayne often took the letter from Delaney along with the photographs from their wedding day and walked out to a secluded area. There, he could think about his brief time with her without being disturbed.

He'd return from those walks somber and withdrawn, but most of the men didn't notice. The majority of them already knew Klayne was a loner who kept mostly to himself. With the exception of Bob, he didn't often socialize, although he was always friendly and willing to lend a hand.

In the wee morning hours of March 24, orders came down to prepare to leave immediately. Half-awake and caught by surprise, the men rushed to gather their things. Encouraged to set their affairs in order and hurry to their planes, they received additional warnings to make no mention of their mission. Another opportunity to back out of the mission was extended to each man, but Klayne refused. "I'm in this until it's finished," he told his commanding officer.

After packing a canvas B-4 bag with items he deemed essential, Klayne tucked the rest of his belongings into his footlocker then sat down and penned a letter to his wife.

Every day for the past several weeks, he'd wanted to write her, but hadn't. He'd convinced himself it would be easier for her if he just disappeared from her life. Yet, as he sat down that morning and put pen to paper, he wished he'd kept in touch with her. The one letter he had from her showed signs of wear from being read so many times. He knew she would have written to him had he asked.

Now, it was too late to worry about it. From that moment forward until the mission was complete, he wouldn't be able to correspond with her at all.

He finished the letter, added it to the top of the footlocker of his belongings and shipped it off to her. While he was at it, he wrote a brief note to Mr. Campanelli, thanking him for the photographs and his kindness, assuring the man he would never know what a treasure the images had been to him.

Weeks ago, Klayne had made certain his financial affairs were in shape, with Delaney listed as a beneficiary if anything should happen to him.

As he hustled to leave, he sent up a prayer that he'd survive whatever awaited him.

Klayne stowed his bag and climbed into his crew's plane, sliding on his back down the bombardier's crawlway to the nose of the plane. The "greenhouse," a shell of light, durable plastic covering the bombardier's area of the nose, shielded him from the elements, but allowed him the best view. It also left him exposed if they happened to take frontal fire from the enemy.

Determined not to worry about that, at least not now, Klayne sat back and prepared to enjoy the cross-country trip from Florida to Sacramento where the planes would land at McClellan Field for final modifications and tune-ups.

The colonel in charge of the operation ordered the men to use the trip as another training exercise, encouraging them to test fuel consumption, and buzz the countryside, just as they might over enemy territory.

Excited for the adventure, Klayne and the crew had a memorable trip as the pilot hedge-hopped from Florida to Texas, where they stopped for the night. The pilot hugged the plane so close to the ground, Klayne could look up and see telegraph wires above them.

By unspoken agreement, the men decided since they might not live through the mission, to fly like they'd never flown before. They zoomed under bridges and terrorized herds of cattle. In Texas, they even chased a few cars off the road. As they landed in Sacramento, Klayne laughed as he watched the gunner from one of the other crews pull sagebrush from the bottom of his plane. Apparently, they weren't the only crew flying low and having fun on their trip from one coast to the other.

While final work was completed on the planes, the men used their free time to relax and get into mischief. Some went bowling, others dancing. A few of the men even tossed dollar bills out a hotel window to see what kind of commotion might ensue.

For the most part, Klayne observed the shenanigans without participating. His mind and heart were at a ranch in Pendleton. He wondered if the cows had all calved, if the snow had finally melted, and if Delaney had yet forgiven him.

Certain if he did survive the mission he'd never make it home in time for Delaney's birthday, he went shopping one evening and sent a gift to her in care of her friend Amy. He knew the girl would keep the gift a secret until Delaney's birthday.

The aircrews left McClellan Field for the Alameda U.S. Naval Air Station, arriving April 1. Klayne sucked in a gulp as they landed, gaping at the sight of an American aircraft carrier where their planes were being loaded.

He stood with the other men, watching as Navy sailors drained all but a few gallons of fuel from the B-25s. The planes were towed down the pier by a machine referred to as a donkey then lifted by crane onto the carrier's deck. Klayne, like many of the men on this mission, had never been on board a carrier or a Naval vessel.

Awed by the size of the carrier and the sudden flood of patriotism that washed over him, Klayne hid his feelings behind an indifferent look. Beside him, Bob animatedly discussed the proceedings as they boarded the carrier. Respectfully, they saluted the American flag and the officer of the deck before going to keep an eye on the planes. The carrier soon departed the pier, setting anchor in a berth for the night.

Late that afternoon, the men were given one last night of freedom. Klayne would have gladly remained at his bunk, but Bob wouldn't hear of it.

"Come on, old man, let's see what sort of trouble we can stir up before we head out," Bob said, giving Klayne a push onto the boat waiting to transport the soldiers back to land.

Many of them gravitated to a rooftop bar at a swanky hotel. While some downed whiskey like water, Klayne drank Coca Cola and brooded. Desperately, he wished he could spend just one more night with Delaney. He'd even settle for an hour. Just long enough to hear her laugh, see her eyes dance with the life and vibrancy he so closely associated with her.

Aware of his sullen mood, Bob thumped him on the shoulder. "Let's get some fresh air."

Klayne nodded and followed his friend outside. He'd decided weeks ago if he was going to die at the hand of an enemy, it wouldn't be quite as hard to face it with a friend at his side. He and Bob had gotten to know one another better. They'd been stationed together for more than a year. In that time, Klayne had learned many things about his friend, including the fact Bob had a wife and two beautiful little girls. He marveled that a man two years his junior had already settled down and started a family.

"How's Norene and the girls?" he asked as they strolled down the sidewalk with no destination in mind.

Bob grinned at him. "They're good. Norene said Chrissy can recite the entire alphabet and count to twelve. Amelia just got her first tooth." A wistful expression crossed his face and he sighed. "I sure hate not being able to see my girls and say goodbye in person."

Klayne patted his friend once on the back. Demonstrations of affection were as foreign to him as the enemy territory they'd be flying to. Except when it came to Delaney. With her, it seemed so easy and natural.

Curious if her brother was still stationed at San Diego, Klayne thought about placing a call to him, then just as quickly discarded the idea. What would he say to a man he'd never met and perhaps never would. It was entirely possible Mac had no idea Delaney had wed.

He cleared his throat and patted Bob on the shoulder again before dropping his hand. "I'm sorry, Bob. It must be doubly hard to face this thing, knowing you're leaving them behind. Did you at least get a chance to speak to them?"

"I did. Norene is staying with her mother near Phoenix, so I called when we stopped there to fuel up on the flight out from Eglin. I'm just glad I had the opportunity to spend a week with them at Thanksgiving."

"Me, too, Bob." Klayne looked out at the night, clear and bright with a big moon shining overhead. In the distance, they could see the ship at anchor with the B-25s silhouetted against the night sky.

For several long, quiet moments, they stared at the carrier and planes. "Where do you really think we're going, Klayne?" Bob asked.

Klayne shrugged then glanced around to make sure they were alone. Noticing a couple walking near them, he kept his voice low. "I don't know for certain, but I have a feeling it has a lot to do with avenging Pearl Harbor."

Bob nodded. "That's what I think, too. I guess we'll find out soon enough."

Forcing a cheerfulness he was far from feeling, Klayne pointed to a restaurant down the street. "If this is going to be our last meal, so to speak, what do you say we go order the biggest, best steaks that place has to offer. Then we should top it off with pie and plenty of ice cream."

"You're on!" Bob said, falling into step beside him. "Let's make it a contest. If I finish my steak before you do, you have to tell me what's in that envelope you take out and study every once in a while. You always look like you're a million miles away when you do."

Although Klayne had no intention of telling anyone, even Bob, about Delaney, he held out his hand. "It's a bet. And if I win, you have to pay for my dinner and I plan to eat until I pop."

Bob settled a hand on his shoulder and the two of them laughed as they walked across the street.

∗∗∗★ *Chapter Twelve* ★∗∗∗

The happy twitter of birdsong filled the air as Delaney rode a green broke horse around the corral by the barn. Mingled with the smells of the dirt in the enclosure and the distinctive aroma of the horse, she caught the welcome scents of spring.

The lilacs had not yet bloomed, but the flowers in the beds around the house were budding. The lawn started to turn green after shaking off the brown mantle of winter. Robins chirped along the fence and baby ducks huddled close to their protective mamas at the pond.

A rich, loamy fragrance wafted on the air.

As the world around her slowly came back to life after a cold, bitter winter, Delaney felt as though she, too, returned to the land of the living.

The first month after she married Klayne, she alternated between anxiety and anger at her absent husband. Maybe it was unrealistic, but she'd expected him to write to her, to let her know he was fine. He'd been gone two months, and she'd finally given up hope of hearing from him.

From the little he'd shared, she knew relationships weren't his forte. Perhaps, since he'd never been taught the fine art of communicating with a spouse, he just didn't realize a wife liked to know if her husband was alive and well from time to time.

Husband.

Delaney still hadn't gotten used to thinking of the handsome man she'd so brashly married as the person she'd spend her life loving. Oh, it wasn't the idea of loving him that threw her off. It was the fact they'd married and then he was gone the next morning. At times, he seemed more like a scrumptious dream that she'd abruptly awakened from.

Dill, in all his fatherly wisdom, had ranted and raved for two days about her marrying some fly-by-night soldier who'd never be around. Even though she knew her dad liked Klayne, it didn't keep him from threatening to shoot him on sight if he ever dared show up at Sage Hills Ranch.

The few times Delaney had tried calmly to discuss why she married Klayne and how much she loved him, her father's face turned red. He reiterated how stupid she'd been to tie herself to a man who would most likely never be seen there again.

Dill assumed Klayne concocted the story about shipping out the following day as a ruse to coerce Delaney into doing his bidding. He even went so far as to pay a visit to Judge Rawlings to confirm he legally married the couple then checked at the base to make sure Klayne was truly gone.

When Delaney found out what he'd done, she was understandably mortified. "Dad! How could you do something like that? It's embarrassing and just... rude! Do you really think so little of me or my judgment that you presume I'd marry some no-good drifter?"

Dill glared at her, but kept his mouth shut. From that moment on, it became an unspoken pact that neither of them would mention Klayne.

To keep from having to answer a myriad of questions from people in Pendleton about where he was and when he'd return, Delaney swore the handful of people who knew she'd wed to secrecy. Although some gave her curious glances, they all abided by her wishes.

Life on the ranch continued moving forward much as it always did. The difference was that they'd lost all their ranch hands except for Butch and another cowboy who was too old to be drafted.

Delaney bit the inside of her cheek until it bled when it came time to say goodbye to the cowboys who had worked so hard for them. She promised if they ever needed work, they'd always have a place at Sage Hills.

Yank was the hardest to watch leave. The young man was fun and full of teasing. He'd often brightened her days, especially in the last few months since she'd married Klayne.

"Take care of yourself," she said to the cheeky cowboy as she gave him a hug then handed him a basket full of food. "Write and let us know how you are from time to time."

"I will, Dee. You keep those old codgers out of trouble until I get back from winning this war." Yank gave her a broad grin then hurried out to the car waiting to take him to town.

With all the young men heading off to war, Delaney was hard pressed to find anyone to replace the cowboys who'd left the ranch. She had promises from four high school boys to work for her all summer, but until then, she and the three older cowboys struggled to keep up with the work.

Today was the first day she had a few extra minutes in what seemed like weeks. Instead of spending it inside, cleaning or tackling a pile of dirty clothes, she instead chose to ride a horse she'd started breaking weeks ago.

From her position on the back of the horse, the farm babies she could see made her smile. Calves cavorted in the pasture to her left while a handful of foals, legs long and spindly, raced around the pasture on the other side of the barn. There were little pink piglets down at the pigpen, fuzzy yellow chicks in the chicken coop, and even a litter of black and white kittens bedding down in an empty stall in the barn.

Spring was such a wonderful season of new hope and life. One Delaney generally enjoyed immensely. As she cantered the horse around the pen, it was hard not to celebrate the joy of such a pleasant spring day.

She'd just rounded the pen on Bandit when the toot of a car horn made the horse shy and hop a few steps before Delaney brought him under control.

She tied the horse to the middle pole of the fence before she climbed over it and walked to where the man who delivered their mail had parked near the back walk of the house. Generally, he left their mail in the box down on the road, so she wondered what brought him up to the house.

"Howdy!" he called, getting out of his car and opening the back door.

"Hello, Mr. Johnson. It's a beautiful day, isn't it?" she asked, smiling at the older man. He'd been carrying mail for as long as she could remember. Her dad mentioned one time that he thought the man had worked that same job for about forty years.

"It is a wonderful day, Dee." He hefted what appeared to be an Army issued footlocker and held it out to her. "This came for you and I thought I might as well deliver it instead of making you drive all the way into town to pick it up."

She smiled and reached for the trunk. "That's so kind of you, Mr. Johnson. Thank you."

"Well, I noticed it's from a base in Florida, so I thought it might be something from Mac. I know how eagerly you look forward to news from him."

Delaney knew for a fact Mac was on the West coast, not the East. She hid her curiosity about who sent the footlocker and grinned at the mail carrier as she started to take the trunk from him.

He pulled back and tipped his head toward the porch. "This is kinda heavy. Why don't I leave it on the porch for you? Dill can carry it inside later."

Through sheer determination, she managed not to take the man to task for assuming she would be too weak to lift the heavy footlocker. In fact, she was sure she'd have an easier time maneuvering it up the porch steps than he would.

As he huffed and puffed, laboring to lift the heavy trunk up the steps, she kept her hands in her pockets, afraid she might reach out and wrangle it away from him. When he set it down on the porch with a relieved sigh, she hid her smile.

"Would you like to come in for a glass of iced tea or a cookie, Mr. Johnson?" she asked.

"Oh, I better not, Dee. I'll be late getting finished with my route as it is." The man hurried back to his car and she strolled down the walk to see him off. After he slid behind the wheel, he waved out the window. "Tell Dill I said hello."

"I will, Mr. Johnson. Thanks again!" Delaney waved at the man and waited until he disappeared down the lane back to the road before racing up the porch steps and carrying the footlocker into the kitchen, setting it by the table.

The moment she opened it, a scent that had haunted her dreams every night since she met Klayne floated up to her.

"Klayne," she whispered, plopping down in a kitchen chair as her legs gave way beneath her. She stared at a letter on top, written in the same hand that had penned the note she'd found on her pillow the day he left her.

Uncertain what the letter might say, what the footlocker held, she decided she'd wait until that night to read it. If she became an emotional mess, she didn't want her father to witness it. He'd only remind her what a terrible decision she'd made and admonish her for not using better sense.

Sense had nothing to do with the reasons she married Klayne. Had her brain been functioning, she'd never have done more than offer him a polite hello at the New Year's Eve party.

Full blame for her current state could be directly attributed to her heart, traitorous thing that it was. She'd known falling for a soldier would leave her heartbroken, but she'd ignored everything except how much she loved Klayne.

And she did love him. With her whole heart.

In spite of his absence, and silence, she loved him more each day. Part of that stemmed from how proud she was of him for selflessly serving a country that needed him, even when he knew there was a woman who desperately wanted him by her side.

Delaney closed the lid and shoved the footlocker beneath the table, then went back out to work with the horse.

Thirty minutes later, when she'd been so distracted the horse tossed her off for the second time, she forced her attention back to her work.

Sore and tired when she wandered to the bunkhouse for dinner, Butch gave her a questioning look as he set biscuits and jam on the table. "Looks like you wrestled a bobcat, Girly. What happened?"

Delaney rolled her neck and shook her arms to loosen up her tight muscles as she walked over to the deep sink and washed her hands. "That new colt I've been working with tossed me off a few times."

Butch started to offer a comment, but she cut him off with a cool glare. "It's not his fault. I wasn't paying attention, that's all."

"That have anything to do with Lou Johnson bringing a package to the house earlier?"

Delaney shouldn't have been surprised Butch knew about the delivery. There were times she was sure he had eyes in the back of his head. Not ready to divulge any details, she shrugged.

"Was it from your young man?" Butch asked as he sliced a roast.

Delaney drained water from a pot of boiled potatoes then started mashing them. She hesitated to answer, but knew Butch would ask her dad about it later if he didn't get the information he wanted now.

She nodded. "It was from Klayne."

Butch waited for her to continue. When she remained silent, he bumped her arm with his elbow. "And? Did he say where he's at or why he hasn't written?"

"I don't know. I didn't read his letter."

Two shaggy eyebrows shot up toward Butch's receding hairline. "Well, why in the heck not? You've been waiting to hear from him since the day he left."

"I know. I just wanted to wait until later, in case, you know, I, um… in case it makes me…"

With more understanding than Delaney would have attributed to the old cowboy, he patted her shoulder. "It's okay, Dee. You read it whenever you want. If you need me to keep your dad out of your hair this evening, I think I could find something for him to do."

Delaney hugged the bowlegged cowboy and gave him a weak smile. "Thanks, Butch. What would I do without you?"

"Goodness only knows, but I hope to shout you never find out!"

She laughed at the line she'd heard more times than she could count and finished mashing the potatoes as her dad and Duffy strolled inside, ready for dinner.

After they ate, Delaney went out to work in the area where she planned to plant a huge garden, tilling up the soil. She and Butch always planted a large garden, but they decided to make it twice as big this year. Together, they'd discussed what to plant and where. Butch had even started some seeds, babying them along in the bunkhouse kitchen. In a few more weeks, they'd be ready to transfer to the nutrient-rich soil.

With each minute that passed, her attention centered less on the garden and more on the footlocker awaiting her inside the house.

Finally, she couldn't stand the waiting, the not knowing. She stowed the garden tools in the shed near the open-ended building where they parked the vehicles then hurried inside.

Still not quite ready to read what her husband had written, she snatched the trunk from beneath the table and carried it upstairs to her room.

A glance at the clock on the table by the bed assured her it was getting late, so she gathered her things and went to the bathroom where she took a quick shower and washed away the day's dirt and sweat.

Once she was clean and dressed in a soft cotton nightgown, she settled the footlocker on the bed, slipped beneath the covers and opened it again. Eyes closed, she breathed deeply of Klayne's scent.

Memories triggered by the fragrance made her almost feel like he was there, holding her again. She floated in the sweet bliss of those moments until she heard the clock downstairs chime the top of the hour. Reluctantly, she opened her eyes and lifted the envelope bearing her name from inside the footlocker.

Three pages of paper crinkled in her hands as she unfolded his letter and read what he'd written.

My Darling Wife,

I sometimes still find it hard to believe I was fortunate enough to not only meet you, but somehow convince you to marry me. No matter what you might think after my silence all these weeks, I do miss you, Laney. More than you can ever imagine. I convinced myself it would be easier on you (on us both) if I refrained from writing to you. In truth, they've kept us hopping and I haven't had much time for that sort of thing either, but that really isn't an excuse.

"It certainly isn't, soldier boy," Delaney spoke aloud then glanced toward the door to make sure her father hadn't heard her. She listened to the silence around her and concluded he was still outside.

Not a single day has gone by that I haven't thought of you and wished I was there beside you. Did I tell you I watched you sleep before I left that morning back in February? Well, I did. And don't wrinkle that adorable little nose of yours, thinking I'm being ridiculous.

You're gorgeous and stunning, even in your sleep. It was all I could do to keep my hands to myself, although, looking back, I don't think I did an altogether good job of that.

A blush seared her cheeks as she remembered every detail of that night.

The way you snore is cute, although at first I thought perhaps Moose had somehow snuck into the room and burrowed beneath the bed. Then I realized all the earth-shattering racket came from you. The way your lips puff out with each breath, like you're pouting, is particularly endearing.

"I don't snore! And I certainly don't sound like that mangy dog." Delaney huffed indignantly, although she smiled as she continued reading the letter.

Lately, I've heard a lot of talk about what the war will mean here on the home front. Rationing will go into full effect soon, so I wanted you to know to stock up on what you can while you can. You and your dad might already have this in place, but if you can add some hives for honey, it will be a good substitute for sugar. One summer, Billy and I helped a farmer harvest honey. Mmm, boy! That was one of the sweetest, tastiest experiences of my life (with the exception of our wedding night. It is hands down the sweetest and best of anything!).

I bet you're blushing right now, aren't you, Delaney?

"How could he know that?" she wondered, pleased that he in fact knew her better than she thought. She was also impressed with his advice. She and her dad had talked just last week about getting some hives. Dill agreed to seek the advice of a man he knew in Walla Walla who raised bees.

Joshing aside, I wanted to send you the things that I won't be needing, at least until this mission is over. As far as I can surmise, I'll be out of the country with whatever I can stuff in a B-4 bag. We just got orders to pull out this morning, so I'm rushing to finish this before I have to leave. No word has come down yet on where we are heading or exactly when (and I couldn't tell you even if I did know). We've been advised, repeatedly, it will be dangerous and some of those going won't make it back. I pray that we all do. Bear in mind that what we must do, we do for the good of our country regardless of our personal outcomes or safety.

I'll do my best to make you proud. I've never had anyone, other than Billy, who cared if I lived or died and I'm grateful every day for the precious gift of you.

By now, you should have received the paperwork that lists you as my sole beneficiary in the event I don't make it through this war. If you haven't, please speak with Colonel T. Smith at Pendleton Field. He can help you.

Thank you for asking Mr. Campanelli to get the photographs to me. They arrived without a second to spare, as I was leaving Pendleton Field. I forced myself not to look at them until we made it to our new location. If I had looked at them before I boarded the train in Pendleton, I'd never have been able to leave, especially not after I discovered your letter.

I've read it so many times, the paper might fall apart soon, but I keep it in my wallet, with me at all times. I also appreciate the gift of your handkerchief. If the other fellas got a whiff of it, or caught a gander of the girl I wed, they'd never let me live down the fact I married a tempting siren.

I hope your temper will have cooled sufficiently so as not to scorch the tough old hide right off me when I do see you again. I have much better plans in mind for when we are finally reunited.

"Indeed, Sergeant Campbell," Delaney muttered, touched by his efforts to tease her.

Perhaps by the time I return, Dill will have forgiven me for marrying his only daughter without asking permission. My guess is that he's plenty steamed about the whole thing. In fact, I bet you inherited that temper of yours from him. Am I right?

"You have no idea, husband of mine." She rolled her eyes before returning to the letter.

However, if I was in his shoes, I would be angry, too.

I'm sitting here, picturing spring at the ranch. I envision calves and foals running in the pastures, piglets with little curly tails rooting around in the mud, and everything green and fresh. Did I see a fruit orchard behind the house? If so, I'm sure the blossoms are breathtaking this time of year.

Do me a favor? Go stand outside and draw in a deep lungful of that pure, perfect air. As the scents of earth and flowers and sunshine fill you, think of me there, right beside you. I'd stand with one hand on the curve of your marvelous waist and the other around your shoulder as we lingered on the porch after supper.

Delaney sniffled and rubbed her nose on the edge of her sheet.

Make no mistake about it, I will fight through anything and everything to get back to you. There is nothing in this world I want more than to hold you in my arms again. If all I had in this lifetime was one more day to spend with you, I'd somehow make it enough. You are the most vibrant, amazing, enchanting woman I've ever met.

As absurd as it probably sounds, every day I've spent away from you only makes me love you that much more. I do love you, Delaney, with all my heart.

Keep us all in your prayers.

Until I can see you again, I remain faithfully yours.

Lovingly,

Klayne

Before she succumbed to the sobs welling inside her, Delaney went through the contents of Klayne's trunk. The heavy winter clothes she pulled out held the savory scent of him. She held his thick wool coat up to her face and breathed in the fragrance, breathed in the essence of him.

Eventually, she set the coat aside and removed civilian clothes, which included a pair of plain brown cowboy boots. The fact he owned a pair surprised her as much as the worn-down heels and scuffed toes, indicating they weren't just for show. An old shoebox with "Billy" written on the lid held letters and the last effects of Klayne's friend, including his identification tags. A photo of a young Klayne with a blond-haired boy, both smiling and looking as though they'd been into mischief, made her wish she could have known her husband's friend. If Klayne loved him, he must have been a good person.

She set aside Billy's box and continued exploring the contents of the footlocker. There were a few newspaper clippings about a drunken man going into a rage and killing a harlot at a brothel in Oklahoma. From what Klayne had shared, she knew the people mentioned were his parents.

No wonder Klayne struggled with relationships and attachments. He'd never had a mother's love, known the affection of parents or siblings in his formative years. He'd been shunned, tormented, and abused. She'd do well to remember his past when interacting with him in the future.

When he came home, came back to her, she planned to give him more love and affection than he'd ever imagined possible.

In a ratty wool sock that looked like mice had gnawed on the toe, she found a roll of money. Quickly tallying the bills, she came up with more than three thousand dollars. He'd scribbled a note and attached it to one of the bills with a paper clip.

"Never put all your eggs in one basket, or all your money in the bank!"

Sage advice, Delaney thought as she rolled the money together, and stuffed it back inside the sock.

Several books added weight to the footlocker. A few titles she recognized from books she herself had read. Others were authors new to her and she set those books aside, planning to read them when she had more time.

The last thing she pulled from the trunk was a large envelope tucked flat against the side. It looked as though it had been handled frequently. Inside were two of the photographs Tony had taken on her wedding day. Klayne looked so handsome in his uniform, and they both appeared so happy, so in love. She *had* been happier than she could remember in her life, until she awoke to find him gone.

Delaney had several prints Tony had made for her, but since the mere thought of Klayne sent her father into a blistering rage, she'd refrained from setting any of them out. They remained with her other treasured keepsakes in a small trunk in the back of her closet. In deference to her father's feelings, and for fear of losing it, she'd removed her wedding ring and left it in her jewelry box along with the beautiful pearl necklace.

Suddenly overcome with emotion, Delaney could no longer keep her tears at bay. She wept for the naïve girl she'd been, for the husband she missed, for the danger he'd put himself in. She ached for the childhood he'd never had and the love she longed to give him. She mourned the boy he'd befriended and those who would surely die in this horrible war.

Her father found her there, crying into her pillow with her wedding photo held in one hand and Klayne's coat in the other with the contents of the footlocker spread all around her.

"Aw, Sis," Dill said, sitting down on the edge of the bed and patting her on the shoulder. Delaney lifted a tear-stained face and he opened his arms to her. She sobbed against the soft, worn fabric of his cotton work shirt.

"Shh, baby girl. What's wrong? It can't be as bad as all that," he said, then glanced around realizing the footlocker must belong to Klayne. Concerned, he pushed her back and gave her a worried look. "Klayne's not... he wasn't killed in action, was he?"

Delaney mopped at her tears with her sheet and shook her head. "No. He's leaving on some secret mission and has no idea when he'll be back. He shipped his belongings here. And I just..." Her breath caught in her throat and she had to swallow back her tears. "I miss him so much, Dad. I know you think he's terrible, but he really is a good person."

"I know, sweetheart. If he wasn't, you would never have married him." Dill pulled her into a comforting hug, stroking his big hand over her mussed hair. "I'm sorry, Dee. I wasn't so much mad at Klayne as I am this war. With your brother off goodness only knows where, Carol trying to manage the farm and raise Ryatt alone, and your young man off to fight some unnamed enemy, it just made me mad that there has to be war and death and destruction before there can be peace."

"But, Dad, you said you'd shoot Klayne if he ever so much as thought about showing his face here. You said he was a cowardly, oily-tongued reprobate and..." Delaney sat up and stared at her father when he motioned for her to be silent.

"I know what I said, but you obviously love him, Sis. Put up your wedding pictures and talk about him if you want. You shouldn't have to pretend he doesn't exist. When he comes back to the ranch, we'll figure things out."

"Thank you, Daddy!" Delaney cried, throwing her arms around him again. When she pulled back this time, she held out the two wedding photos to him, since he hadn't seen the images Tony had taken.

"You do make a handsome couple," Dill said with a crooked grin. "You look so much like your mother, Sis. Just as spunky and lively, and full of sass."

Delaney grinned. "But my temper and stubbornness is all from you."

He pinched her cheek and rose from the bed. "And that smart mouth, too. I love you, baby girl. All I want is for you to be happy, and if this soldier makes you happy, then I hope he comes back to you."

"Me, too, Dad. Me, too."

∗∗∗★ *Chapter Thirteen* ★∗∗∗

A few weeks later, on a lovely mid-April day, Delaney's troubled thoughts kept her from concentrating on roguing the rye out of the wheat fields. The work was tedious and backbreaking, but had to be done to remove the rye that grew wild among the winter wheat.

She'd labored all morning in a field with Duffy and her father, but her thoughts were with Klayne and not her work.

The fourth time she accidentally pulled up wheat instead of rye, Dill scowled at her. "Sis, you're doing more harm than good at this point. I think you need a break. Go to the house, put on a nice dress, and take yourself into town to visit Amy. The rye will still be here tomorrow."

"But, Dad, we're already behind..."

Her father held up his hand and frowned. "I'm setting my foot down. Now, get out of here. Bring home a coffee cake for breakfast, and maybe some doughnuts if they have any left. We've got a crew of kids coming this weekend to help. Everything will be okay."

Delaney smiled, gave her father a quick hug, then walked to the house. Normally, a visit with Amy cheered her up, but Delaney couldn't shake the feeling that something was wrong.

They'd just heard from Mac that he was fine. Carol had sent a note all was well with her and Ryatt. The high school students her father hired would help them get the work schedule back on track.

That only left Klayne and his well-being in question. Delaney couldn't pinpoint what or why she felt such a terrible, immediate need to pray for his safekeeping, but she did.

Her thoughts lingered on him as she hurried to bathe and change into a dress. All the way to town, she contemplated where he could be and what sort of trouble might be plaguing him.

Rather than go straight to the bakery, Delaney parked her pickup halfway between the bakery and the church. Filled with hope that the bright sunshine and fresh air would help clear her mind, she strolled with unhurried steps to the church.

On the sidewalk in front of the familiar structure, she stood gazing up at the church building she'd attended all her life. Her parents had wed there. It was also where they'd held services when her grandparents and then her mother had died. It had been a place she'd laughed and cried, been convicted and repented.

Today, though, she sought solace.

The old oak door creaked as she pushed it open and walked into the cool interior of the entry. The scent of lemon oil and aged wood greeted her. The familiar scents were comforting as she moved into the sanctuary and trailed her fingers along the edges of the pews.

At the front of the church, she took a seat on a wooden bench, long ago worn smooth from pants and skirts brushing over it during services.

She set down her handbag, removed her hat and gloves, and rested in the quiet, letting the peace seep into her soul and calm her troubled mind. Time passed by as she let her thoughts drift and prayers ascend. Eventually, she pinned on her hat, smoothed gloves on her fingers, picked up the handbag, and headed back out into the warm spring day.

Amy glanced up in surprise when Delaney walked inside the bakery. "Oh, Dee! I haven't seen you in ages," she said, hurrying around the counter to give her a hug. "What are you doing in town today? I didn't know you ever left the ranch these days, except for church and supplies."

Delaney forced a smile and allowed Amy to guide her over to an empty table. "Dad practically threw me off the place. He told me I needed a break and insisted I bring home coffee cake and doughnuts, if you have any."

A laugh burst out of her friend. "What is it with your dad and coffee cake? I think he's our best customer."

"He really likes a slice of it with his coffee in the morning." Delaney glanced around, noticing the bakery seemed quiet, but then again, the afternoon was half-gone and they'd soon close for the day. "How have you been?"

Amy looked at some unknown spot over Delaney's shoulder. "Just fine."

"Oh, you aren't telling me something," Delaney said, leaning closer to her friend. "Out with it! What's going on?"

"Marc Rawlings asked me out again," Amy whispered, appearing quite pleased by the fact.

"Did you tell him yes?"

Amy nodded. "Of course! How could I tell a swell fella like him no. He's got those dreamy green eyes and broad shoulders and…"

Delaney giggled. "I think you're sweet on him."

Amy feigned insult, lifting her nose in the air, before grinning. "I do really like him, Dee. He's such a gentleman, and he's fun. I'm worried, though, that he'll leave soon. He's been talking about enlisting if he isn't drafted by the first of May."

"Oh, Amy. I'm sorry. It's so hard to think of all our young men off at war. I try to remind myself that what they are doing is something necessary and of great value to not only our country, but the other Allies."

"I know. Still, it doesn't make it any easier to let him go. Why, I just hate the thought of something happening to him. What if he's like Klayne and…" Amy snapped her mouth shut and shot Delaney and apologetic look. "I'm sorry, Dee. I know you don't like to talk about him."

"Actually, he's the reason I feel so unsettled today. I just can't get him off my mind. There's no reasonable way to explain it, but I have this niggling feeling that something happened, that something is wrong." Delaney reached across the table and squeezed Amy's hand. "Is that batty? I mean, we were only married such a short time before he left, but do you think it's possible to have a bond with him, one that says there's something very wrong?"

"Oh, Dee." Amy offered her a teary look filled with sympathy. "I don't think it matters how long you knew Klayne before you wed. The important thing is that you love each other. It's as plain as the nose on your face that he's crazy about you and I know you're in love with him. It seems reasonable to me that you'd feel a bond with him. After all, he is your husband."

Delaney took a deep breath, followed by another to stay the tears that wanted to flow out of her eyes and down her cheeks. She forced a smile and patted Amy's hand. "Let's talk about something else, something cheerful."

"Well, I heard that Clarence Mills told Ina…"

The remainder of the afternoon, Delaney did her best to focus on Amy's chatter. She even pulled on an apron and helped clean up once the bakery closed for the afternoon. Amy boxed up a coffee cake along with leftover doughnuts and two dozen cookies for Delaney to take home with her.

When she gathered her things to leave, Amy gave her a long hug. "Don't fret, Dee. Klayne will be fine. I just know it."

Amy didn't sound any more certain of Klayne's safety than Delaney felt, but she merely smiled at her friend and nodded. "I'm sure I'm just being a goose."

"A silly one at that," Amy teased, walking her outside. "See you at church Sunday?"

"We'll be there," Delaney said, waving once then hurrying back to her vehicle.

On the drive home, her thoughts once again turned to Klayne. Unsettled by the urgent need she felt to pray for him, she sent up dozens of heartfelt pleas for his safekeeping.

She parked the pickup, carried the sweets inside the kitchen, and then strolled over to the bunkhouse where she knew the men would be sitting down to eat supper.

"Dee!" Butch exclaimed as she walked inside. "We about gave up on you coming back. Dill thought maybe you decided to run away from home, but I reminded him you haven't done that since you were six."

"Seven," she said, taking a seat at the table and nodding at Duffy as he passed her a platter of fried chicken. "I was seven the last time I ran away and that was because Mac refused to take me with him to town. I wanted to get an ice cream at the drug store and he told me I couldn't go because he was meeting a girl. So I decided to run off."

Dill chuckled. "And you packed your little suitcase and made it all the way to the end of the lane before you got tired of lugging it. You sat down there for two hours, waiting for someone to fetch you." He winked at Delaney. "Your mama wanted to go get you five minutes after you left, but I told her to let you stew awhile. She was a nervous wreck by the time you finally got yourself back home. Of course, we kept an eye on you the whole time."

"You did?" Delaney stared at her father. "All I remember is waiting and waiting for someone to miss me and nobody did. I decided I'd stay down there all night, if that's what it took, but then I got hungry and had to come home."

"See," Butch chortled. "This girl will never miss out on a meal if she can help it."

Delaney lifted a piece of golden brown chicken in her fingers. "Darn tootin', especially if I don't have to cook it!"

The men all laughed. Delaney shared some of the news she gleaned from Amy about happenings in town. She avoided mentioning anything to do with the war, Klayne, or the horrible feeling she had in the pit of her stomach that something had happened to him.

The lively discussion about a meet your neighbor banquet, an A Cappella choir performance, and the Red Cross offering home nursing classes kept her mind off Klayne for a little while.

She helped Butch with the dishes while her dad and Duffy finished the evening chores. Exhausted from a day of worry, she went to bed early and fell into a fitful sleep.

In the wee hours of the morning, she awakened, drenched in sweat, heart pounding, sure that Klayne had been injured or killed. In a dream, she watched the plane he was on crash into the ocean repeatedly.

Unaware that she'd screamed in her sleep, she yelped in surprise when her Dad thudded into her room and flicked on a light. "Tarnation, Sis! Are you dying? Are you hurt? What's all the ruckus about?"

Her father observed the terror in her widened eyes and the shallowness to her rapid breathing. He sat on the edge of her bed and placed a steadying hand on her shoulder. "What happened, Delaney? What's wrong?"

She sighed and leaned back against the headboard, running a hand through her tangled hair. "All day, I had this feeling something is wrong with Klayne. Then I kept dreaming he was in a plane that crashed in the ocean. I watched it fall over and over again."

"Ah, Sis, I'm sorry," Dill said, giving her a fatherly hug then kissing her forehead. "Let me get you a drink of cool water then you settle back down and see if you can get some rest. You just look plumb done in."

"I feel done in, Dad. Like my heart's made of glass and it's about to break into a million pieces."

"Dang it, Dee. This is exactly why I…" His mouth snapped shut at her frosty glare. Without saying another word, he got her a glass of water and gave it to her, withholding his thoughts on her marrying a soldier.

She took a long drink from the glass then scooted back down in bed. Dill brushed a hand over her head and gave her a sad smile, one full of compassion. "I'm sorry, Sis, that you have to go through this. It's bad enough that Mac's getting ready to head into battle, but now you have the added worry of Klayne. For your sake, sweetheart, I hope he's well and safe."

"Me, too, Daddy," Delaney whispered. "Thank you."

Dill turned off the light and left the room. Delaney stared into the darkness for a long time. Finally, she got up and retrieved a scarf from

Klayne's footlocker. She held it to her face and breathed in his scent, praying he was alive.

The next time Delaney awakened, light filtered around the edges of her drapes, alerting her she'd slept in.

She started to jump out of bed, but was so woozy, she fell back and waited for the world to stop spinning around her.

When the dizziness passed, she slowly sat up and put her feet on the floor. She'd taken two steps across the room when her stomach revolted and she raced down the hall to the bathroom.

Weak and trembling after losing the contents of her stomach, she sat on the edge of the bathtub, holding her head in her hands and wondering what in the world was wrong with her.

Her heart still felt heavy, her mind inundated with worry for Klayne. With her stomach upset and chills racing over her clammy body, she wondered if perhaps she was battling a nasty bout of some stomach ailment. Perhaps a day of rest would be all she needed to feel better.

She staggered back to bed but couldn't sleep. Her thoughts continued spinning around Klayne and if he was safe. After taking a quick shower and dressing, she heard raised voices downstairs. Hurried steps carried her to the kitchen where her father, Butch, and Duffy hovered around the radio Dill had given her for her twentieth birthday. She'd loved the butterfly design on the front of it and left it on the counter by the bread box, listening to it when she spent time in the kitchen.

"What's going on?" she asked, stepping next to her dad.

"Shh!" Butch warned and pointed to the radio.

"In case you missed the earlier announcement, this news just in!" the reporter chirped in an excited tone. "The United States of America has taken the war to the heart of Japan. According to reports, they struck Tokyo along other cities in a daring daylight raid, dropping bombs and leaving a wide path of destruction. Japanese broadcasts say the insignia of the United States Army Air Force was visible on the planes. The bravery of the yet to be identified men will go down as the most daring air assault in history. Authorities in Japan claim to have shot down nine planes. We await confirmation on details. As soon as more information becomes available, we'll let you know. Now, tune in for…"

Delaney's legs turned to rubber and she would have toppled over right there on the kitchen floor if Butch hadn't noticed her swaying. "Grab her before she falls!"

Dill helped her over to a kitchen chair and fanned a dishtowel in front of her face while Butch got her a glass of water. "Drink this, Girly," he said, pushing the glass into her hands.

Fear unlike any she'd ever known seized her by the throat while her stomach roiled. She didn't know how or why she knew, but she had no doubt in her mind that Klayne was among the men who'd bombed Japan. What if his plane was one that had been shot down by the enemy?

"What's wrong, Sis?" Dill asked, hunkering down in front of her and pressing the back of his weathered hand to her forehead. "You don't have a fever. Are you ailing?"

She shook her head and forced herself to sip the water. "I'm fine, Dad."

"No, you aren't fine. Come on, tell us what's wrong. You seemed okay when you came downstairs." Dill stood and stared down at her, arms crossed over his broad chest.

"I was... it's just the radio report, the bombing, it... I think maybe..."

Dill's face paled and he plunked into the chair beside her, gaping at her. "You don't think... are you saying that he...?"

"What in tarnation are you two muttering?" Butch asked, glaring at them both.

Dill glanced at his daughter then turned back to his friend. "Delaney thinks Klayne was one of the men who bombed Tokyo."

"Klayne? That's the boy who, the one you..." Butch stammered. He'd promised not to mention her husband to anyone, and he hadn't. As much as it pained him to keep his mouth shut, he hadn't even said a word about the soldier to Dill.

Delaney sighed and looked from her father to Butch, then to Duffy. "For those who don't know, I married a soldier stationed at Pendleton Field back in February. That is information I prefer remain confidential," she said, staring at Duffy until the man nodded in agreement. "I don't know for a fact Klayne was involved in the raid, but I've just had this feeling something happened to him, something horrible. I can't shake it and after hearing the news on the radio, I feel some inexplicable certainty he's tied to the bombings. That's his job, a bombardier. He volunteered for a secret, dangerous mission. He didn't even know what it was, just that it would be hazardous. Chances of surviving it were slim, or so he said."

Dill placed a hand over Delaney's as it rested on the table. "I'm sure he'll be fine, Sis. Why, that boy might be somewhere safe and cozy right now. You can't know for certain he was involved in the raid."

"I know that, Dad. I know it's silly to be this worried about him, but my gut says he was there and something is terribly, horribly wrong." Delaney looked at the three men, waiting for one of them to assure her she was jumping to conclusions and panicking for no reason. When they remained oddly silent, she knew she couldn't sit there any longer with them waiting for her to fall apart.

She stood and moved toward the back door. "Come on. Don't we have work to see to?"

"We sure do, Girly," Butch said, giving Dill a look full of wary concern. Dill shrugged as he and Duffy followed him outside.

Delaney rode in the farm truck out to the wheat field with the three men to help pull out the rye by hand. By noon, her back hurt, sweat trickled down the sides of her face, and she was dying to sit next to the radio, listening for more news, but she kept working. Butch made sandwiches for them to eat, which they did, then got back to work.

Butch ambled back to the bunkhouse an hour before dinnertime to fix the meal. She walked into the bunkhouse with Duffy and her dad, ears tuned to the radio, anxious to hear another news report. When no new information was forthcoming, she returned outside, finished her evening chores, rode one of the geldings she was training, and even spent the last half hour before dark working in the garden.

Weary beyond endurance, she took a bath, soaking her tired muscles, and then climbed into bed. As sleep tugged her eyes closed, she sent up another prayer for Klayne.

The following morning, Delaney awakened herself calling out Klayne's name. She dreamed he was lost in a swirling darkness and she couldn't reach him. He called to her, begging her for help, but no matter how hard she tried, she couldn't find him.

Frightened, she allowed herself to cry for him, to pray for him, to plead for him to come home.

Delaney started to get up but was assaulted by another wave of dizziness. Rather than fight it, she waited for it to pass then carefully made her way to the bathroom. She managed to get dressed before her stomach turned on her.

When she finally made it outside, she veered far away from the bunkhouse where the smells of bacon and coffee lingered in the air, making her grimace.

"This is ridiculous," she muttered as she pulled on her gloves and made her way out to the wheat field.

The following three mornings she felt fine, but she spent the next week battling sickness each morning. She also battled against the despair settling over her. No solid details about the Tokyo raiders were reported. Every headline that mentioned the assault, every mention of Japan on the radio station drew her full attention, but she still had no idea who was involved and if Klayne was okay.

Whether he was involved or not, it was clear the bombs on Japan had accomplished two important tasks. The first was to prove to Japan's leaders they weren't beyond being attacked on their home front. From the reports she'd heard and the articles in the newspaper, the country had been in a panic after the bombing. Although the losses seemed minimal in the grand scheme of things, it was the psychological damage that created an American triumph, shattering the illusion Japan's leaders had created of them being untouchable by outside forces.

The second accomplishment was evident around them every day. American morale had been at an all-time low before the raid, but dropping those bombs had imbued the nation with hope, a renewed purpose, and a determination to win the war. News of the raid fanned the embers of patriotism into a bright flame that was spectacular to witness. However, she fretted the boost in morale came at a very high price, at least for the men on Klayne's mission.

Sage Hills Ranch was no different from the rest of the country. Although they'd done their part before America entered the conflict, Dill, Butch, Duffy, and Delaney worked doubly hard to do all they could to help the war effort. Butch saved boxes of tin cans, labels removed and smashed flat, that Dill delivered to a collection center. Those bits of tin would eventually be turned into ammunition. The old cowboy also saved every bit of fat to take to the butcher. From there, it was collected then processed into glycerin, needed for medical and surgical treatments. Every one of them was mindful of doing their part to help with the cause, but perhaps none as much as Delaney.

Each ounce of fat collected, each tin can recycled, and every war bond purchased made her feel like they were helping Klayne.

Despite all the work to keep her busy, Delaney continued to suffer from some unknown malady. She'd tried to hide her illness from her father, and did a good job of it, or so she thought.

One evening he gave her a knowing look and scowled. "If you don't haul yourself into Pendleton to the doctor tomorrow, I'll take you there myself. You don't do me any good when you spend half the day sick and the other half trying to hide the fact you are. Go find out what's wrong."

"Fine!" she hollered. "I'll go tomorrow."

"Fine!" he yelled, storming outside to finish a few chores. As spring progressed and they fell further behind on the farm work, the shorter all their tempers grew.

Butch had snapped at Duffy for not cleaning the mud off his boots before coming in for supper. Dill groused at Butch that the biscuits could be used as bricks.

Tired of their surliness, Delaney had called them all uncivilized brutes and marched back to the house. That's where her father caught up to her, demanding she seek the advice of their family physician.

The following morning, she waited for the sickness to pass before she bathed, styled her hair, and slipped into a nice dress. She felt feminine and pretty, instead of just another dirt-covered farmhand.

After gathering a few things to take into town with her, she waved at Butch as he sat outside on the bunkhouse porch, oiling bridles and harnesses. She climbed behind the wheel of her pickup and headed to Pendleton.

Delaney drove straight to the office of the doctor who had cared for her family since before she was born. As she walked inside, a Philco radio sitting on a cabinet behind the receptionist desk emitted the sounds of Artie Shaw playing "Begin the Beguine" while the scent of furniture polish blended with the odor of antiseptic.

"Hey, Dee. What are you doing here?" the receptionist asked, giving her a friendly smile.

"Hi, Susie. How's your mother doing? I heard she'd had quite a time of it with her arthritis this spring." Delaney truly did care about her neighbors and friends, but she wasn't in the mood for polite conversation. She wanted to see the doctor, find out what was wrong, and fix it as quickly as possible.

"Oh, Mama is much better. Doc has her doing some exercises that help, and being watchful about what she eats." Susie motioned to the empty waiting area. "If you're here to see the Doc, he's in with a patient right now, but it shouldn't be long."

"Thank you." Delaney was saved from making any further comments when the telephone jangled. Susie hurried to answer it while Delaney sat down on a wooden chair to wait.

She glanced around the office, taking in the robin's egg blue walls that appeared freshly painted. The walnut chair rail gleamed from a recent polish and the framed paintings on the walls all sparkled.

Doctor Nik Nash ran a tidy office, that was for certain. Unlike some children who were terrified of visiting the doctor, she'd always liked to see Doc Nik because he gave her Tootsie Rolls and told funny stories. His wife was as loopy about horses as Delaney and he had many photographs on the walls of his family with their horses.

When she was older, Delaney learned the doctor had been born into poverty to parents who worked as sheepherders in the southeastern corner of Oregon. They died in a blizzard, leaving him alone when he was just a boy. He eventually made his way to Pendleton where he was hired by Aundy Nash to watch over a herd of sheep she'd just purchased. Eventually, Aundy and her husband, Garrett, adopted Nik, sent him to college, and encouraged him to become a doctor. He returned to Pendleton back in 1910, armed with the latest medical knowledge and a desire to help the community with his skills. He'd been doing so ever since.

Now, as she impatiently sat in the waiting area, pondering what could possibly be wrong with her, the song playing on the radio drew her full attention. She listened as Glenn Miller played "Speaking of Heaven."

Pain stabbed her heart as she thought about Klayne singing it to her as she fell asleep in his arms. Memories of that night were better left tucked in the far reaches of her mind than explored. Goodness only knew when, or even if, she'd see him again.

Annoyed with herself for not thinking positively, she picked up a copy of Woman's Day magazine, admiring the image of five fuzzy yellow chicks against a background of blue on the cover. The lower corner of the magazine featured a scaled down version of a war bond poster. Delaney made a mental note to purchase more bonds while she was in town before opening the magazine and mindlessly flipping through the pages.

She'd tried three times to read an article before she gave up and slapped the magazine down on a piecrust-edged table.

Nervous and unsettled, she felt like life was spiraling out of control. Mac had sent a note that he was shipping out and didn't know when he'd be able to write again. Carol had sent an emotion-filled letter begging them to say prayers for Mac and asking if Delaney would like to spend the summer with her.

No matter how much Delaney might like to see her sister-in-law and nephew, she couldn't leave her father another hand short at the ranch. At least school would be out in two more weeks, and then they'd have extra help full-time instead of just on the weekends. The high school boys they'd hired couldn't get there a moment too soon.

A tangled jumble of thoughts cascaded through her head as she waited and worried. Finally, the doctor appeared at the doorway and grinned at her.

"Well, if it isn't Delaney Danvers, trick rider extraordinaire," Nik Nash said as he walked over to her and held out a hand.

She took it and rose to her feet. "Hi, Doc. I'd say if anyone has extraordinary talent at riding, it's your wife and daughter."

Nik laughed. "They are quite good at it, but Dally about twisted off my fingers in her excitement as we watched you perform at the Round-Up last fall."

Delaney smiled. "I'd be happy to share what I know with her, anytime."

"I'll pass that on." Nik motioned to the hallway. "Shall we figure out what's got you looking so pale-faced today?"

The doctor ran a series of tests, performed an examination, and asked what Delaney was sure had to be a hundred questions, several of which she found particularly embarrassing. He asked her to wait for him in his office then soon joined her, sitting across the desk from her as he delivered news that left her utterly dumbfounded.

She gaped at him, shocked. "I'm sure I misunderstood you. What... what did you just say?"

A laugh rolled out of him. "I said you're pregnant. If I estimate your due date correctly, you'll welcome a bundle of joy around the beginning of November."

"How could this happen?" she asked, glaring at the doctor, annoyed by the amused grin on his face as he sat across from her.

"I'm fairly certain you know exactly how it happened, Dee, but if you really want me to explain the birds and bees to you, I can." Nik's grin broadened as he leaned back in his chair. "You start with..."

Indignant, she huffed, cutting him off. "I'm well aware of the technicalities involved," she fumed. "I'm ... it's just that..." A sigh escaped her. "How can I be pregnant, Doc? I was only married for one day!"

Nik chuckled. "Apparently, it was quite a day, at that."

Heat burned up her neck and stained her cheeks bright pink as she narrowed her gaze and rose to her feet. "I don't see a single humorous thing about this, Doc. Not a single one. What am I supposed to do with a baby? We're down to just Duffy and Butch for hired help. Dad needs me able to work. Besides, I'm not sure a girl like me is cut out for motherhood. I hate staying in the house, can only sew a straight stitch under duress, and cook out of necessity, not pleasure."

"Well, maybe you should have thought about what might happen before you had that one memorable day with your husband." Nik teased, waggling eyebrows that were still surprisingly dark for his age. "You'll be a fine mother, Delaney. My wife worried the whole time she was expecting our first baby that she wouldn't do the job right. Like you, she's always preferred to ride and rope over cooking and sewing. However, she's a wonderful mother and I know you will be, too. You've got a loving spirit, a big heart, and a kind way about you."

Delaney absorbed his words. "Thank you."

Nik gave her an observant glance. "This husband of yours that I had no idea existed — who is he? Are you still married to him? Will I get to meet him someday?"

Tears stung Delaney's eyes. "My husband, whom only a handful of people have met, may not even be alive."

Nik's humor dissipated and he stood. "What do you mean, Dee? Did something happen?"

"I don't know anything for a fact, but I have reason to believe he was among the men who raided Tokyo. I've had this horrible feeling something happened to him over there." Delaney sank back down in the chair and fished a handkerchief from her handbag. She'd never been a girl who cried often, but the last few weeks, she felt like she might burst into tears every time she turned around. In light of the doctor's news, it made sense.

"Well, gosh, Dee, he's a real hero, then, if he was on that mission." Nik walked back around his desk and took a pamphlet from a filing cabinet then handed it to her. "I know you don't have any one close to give you advice about your condition or share ideas on what to expect, so read this booklet. I've found through the years, the information proves helpful in preparing mothers-to-be for their little arrival. My mother, wife, mother-in-law, and my aunts all contributed their thoughts on what was important for expectant women to know."

Delaney dabbed her tears, tucked the pamphlet into her handbag, and stood. "Thank you, Doc, for everything." She took a step toward the door then glanced back at him. "I didn't mean to sound like I don't want this baby. The shock of the news caught me by surprise, but I do want it. It might be the only thing I have left of Klayne." Her hand settled on her abdomen, as though she sheltered the tiny life growing there. "I'd appreciate it, though, if you didn't mention my marriage or this baby to anyone. I can't bear to have people ask me about him, not until I know what's become of him."

"I understand, Delaney. I wouldn't have said anything, anyway. I owe it to my patients to keep all their medical information private and confidential."

She nodded. "I appreciate that, Doc, and your help today." A small smile lifted the corners of her mouth. "Please give Mrs. Nash my regards."

"I will, Dee. Take good care of yourself. Get plenty of rest, drink lots of water, and eat as much fresh produce and lean meat as you can. This sickness you've been experiencing should go away soon. Some women suffer all nine months, others not at all. It's different for everyone, but many notice an improvement in the way they feel around the fourth month. Hang in there. And for goodness sakes, don't overdo on the ranch. You can't put in a day's work like a field hand. If you refuse to listen to me, I'll talk to Dill about what you can and can't do."

"I'll be careful," she said, hurrying to reassure him she took his advice to heart.

"Good," he said, pleased she listened to his warnings. "I also recommend you not ride, but if you are anything like my wife, you won't be able to follow that suggestion. I'll just tell you to stay away from anything that might buck you off."

"Understood," Delaney said, wondering who she could get to break the horses she'd started training. Butch could barely get a foot up in the stirrup and Duffy wasn't much better. Her dad had proclaimed himself too old to break horses a few years ago. Delaney had eagerly taken over the job, but now she'd have to put the training on hold or find someone willing to ride for her.

She turned back to Nik. "Say, you don't happen to know anyone who'd like a job training some three-year-old horses, do you?"

Nik lifted an eyebrow. "I might. What do you need?"

"Someone to come out and work with the horses I've started training. Maybe two or three times a week?"

"I'll see if I can round someone up and send them out."

"That would be wonderful, Doc. Thank you."

"You're welcome, Dee. Tell Dill I send my regards." Nik walked her to his office door and opened it. "And know that I'll be praying for your young man to make it home alive and well."

Emotion obliterated her ability to speak, so Delaney merely nodded her head and hurried out the door.

Back in her pickup, she sat staring into space, trying to come to terms with the fact that by Thanksgiving, she'd be a mother. She and Klayne would have a baby. Would he be excited by the news? Somehow, she knew he would be.

A vision of the two of them sitting on the porch with a dark-haired toddler playing by their feet cast her fears aside. Instead, she decided to focus on her hope for the future.

✶✶★ *Chapter Fourteen* ★✶✶

Klayne took a deep breath of salty air as he walked around the wooden flight deck of the carrier. He'd heard some of the sailors joke about the warship resembling a bathtub with a barn door on top, from the appearance the flight deck gave the boat.

The wind battered the rigging on the carrier island while waves slapped against the ship. Adding to the symphony of the sea were the bass notes of the warship pounding across the water with unrelenting determination.

He glanced up at the ship's stack where someone had painted "Remember Pearl Harbor" in big block letters.

Pearl Harbor was a horrific event he'd never forget. Even if he wasn't stationed there, he knew men who were. Men who'd gone to a watery grave when they were trapped inside one of the sinking ships. No red-blooded American would ever fail to remember that day.

After all the weeks of wondering and speculating where the mission he'd volunteered for would take him, now Klayne knew. When the colonel finally announced their destination, Klayne wasn't surprised they were headed right to the heart of the enemy. He and seventy-nine other men would fly to Tokyo, and other cities in the area, drop two thousand pounds of bombs from each plane, then do their best to keep from getting shot. If they survived, they were to fly to China and land on friendly airfields, refuel, then be on their way. They'd spent hours studying maps and charts, plotting routes, gauging instruments, attending lectures, and mentally preparing for the task before them.

The day of their planned take off quickly approached and Klayne wondered what he'd gotten himself into. Part of him felt a driving, almost primitive need to wreak as much devastation on Japan as they'd done to Pearl Harbor. The more rational part of him questioned if he'd make it out alive. He'd first volunteered to go because he didn't have anyone who cared if he lived or died. But now... now he had Delancy. Even Bob had become a close friend, one who would mourn Klayne's passing if something should happen to him. Klayne also knew the colonel leading the raid cared about each one of the men on the crews.

Klayne watched as a fleet oiler came alongside the carrier, topping off the tanks with more than two hundred thousand gallons of fuel. In addition to the carrier on which he rode, cruisers, destroyers, another carrier, and loaded fleet oilers accompanied them.

He'd marveled at the warship carrying the planes that was similar to a floating city. From the moment he'd boarded, he'd been treated well and lived better than he had most of his life.

A desalination plant on the ship made ocean water drinkable and provided fresh water for showers, galleys, and the boilers. Freezers, refrigerators, and pantries held an assortment of food. Many of the men in his group had gained weight, feasting three times a day on meals that included steak, chicken, fresh eggs, and green vegetables. A so-called mechanical cow churned dehydrated milk into ice cream, a treat Klayne certainly enjoyed.

The ship offered a team of doctors and corpsmen who could treat everything from a runny nose to an emergency surgery. Laundry services, a barbershop, and even a library were available for them to use. Sailors could pick up stamps and mail letters at the post office. The ship's store offered cigarettes, razors, toothpaste, or candy bars for purchase.

As he stood on the deck in the early morning light, Klayne took out the photo of Delaney he kept in his wallet and studied it. His index finger lightly traced across the dimple in her cheek.

"So, it is a girl," Bob said from beside him, startling Klayne so badly, he jumped nearly a foot straight up in the air.

"Dang it, Bob! You could get your scrawny neck wrung doing something like that," Klayne fumed. His heart settled back into its rightful place and slowed from a frenetic beat.

Bob laughed and snagged the photo from Klayne's fingers. He gave it a thorough glance then handed it back. "Who is she?"

Klayne wouldn't lie to his friend. "My wife."

Bob's jaw dropped and he gaped at Klayne. "Your wife!" He stared at him a long moment, hardly blinking. Finally, a smile broke out on his face and he thumped Klayne on the back. "How did an ugly ol' cuss like you convince a pretty girl like that to get married?"

Klayne gave the photo one last glance and placed it in his wallet. He pulled out the wedding photo he'd had to trim down to make fit in the small space. He handed it to Bob.

His friend whistled. "Well, give me the dope, man. How did you meet? When did you get married? What's her name?" Bob grinned as he studied the photograph. "You've been holding out on me all this time."

Klayne took the photo from Bob and slid it inside his wallet, tucking it back into his pocket. The two of them ambled across the deck, heading below for breakfast. "I met her New Year's Eve. Some of the fellas talked me into going to a party and she was there. I don't know what happened, but I just couldn't get her off my mind."

"And how come you didn't tell me about her sooner?" Bob asked as they made their way down a set of steps.

"I dunno. I guess it's all seemed like a crazy dream and I was afraid if I talked about it, I'd wake up and she'd be gone." Klayne respectfully tipped his head to a group of passing sailors as they headed toward the mess deck. "When I found out I was shipping out, I asked Delaney to marry me and she did, that very day. We left the following afternoon."

Bob gawked at him. "You mean you married this sweet girl and then left the next day? Why wasn't she at the train station to see you off? Loads of the wives and girlfriends were there."

Klayne looked a little embarrassed. "I failed to tell her about that. Early that morning, I left her a note and snuck out of the house while she was sleeping. I thought it would be easier on her that way, but the one letter she wrote to me after that set me straight on how I'd be doing things in the future."

Bob chuckled. "I can't wait to meet this girl. You said her name is Delaney?"

"Yep. Delaney Danvers. Her father owns a big wheat and cattle ranch near Pendleton. She works just as hard as the men, and man alive, you should see her ride. She was one of the trick riders at the Round-Up."

"You don't say." Bob gave Klayne another studying glance. "And you married her the day before we pulled out?"

"Yes. I just couldn't stand the thought of dying on this mission without leaving something behind, someone behind. If I'm gonna die on this trip, I want it to have a purpose greater than just serving my country. I wanted it to be protecting someone I love. You know what I mean?"

His friend grew solemn and settled a hand on his shoulder. "I do know, Klayne. I completely understand. I sure hope I don't die out there, but if I do, things are squared away with Norene and the girls. I'm glad you have Delaney. Or at least you might if you don't try sneaking out on her again."

Klayne smirked. "I think she'd probably hunt me down and shoot me if I did that."

Bob laughed. "I'll give her the gun."

The two men spent the remainder of the day with their crews, attending to what seemed like a hundred and one little details before their planned day of departure. At a meeting that day, they were given another opportunity to back out of the mission, but no one did.

That night, Klayne rested in his bunk, his mind going over every aspect of the mission. The first hurdle would be getting the plane into the air off the carrier. A missed takeoff meant a plunge into the Pacific Ocean. The other concern weighing heavily on him was having enough fuel to get them to the airfield where they were supposed to land in a friendly area of China, beyond the borders of what had been occupied by the Japanese. Even with the extra gas tanks they'd installed on all the planes, and cans of gas they'd carry with them, he wasn't sure they'd have enough fuel to make it.

He figured they had a fifty-fifty chance of getting the planes launched off the carrier. If they made it to Japan, he figured the odds were similar that the enemy would shoot them out of the air. By some miracle, if they made it all the way to China, he assumed another fifty-fifty chance existed they'd be captured. The probabilities seemed to be firmly stacked against survival.

His thoughts wandered to his B-4 bag, packed and ready to go with a pistol, knife, an extra clip of ammunition, a day's worth of C rations, a flashlight, a full canteen of water, a gas mask and a hand ax. He'd added several candy bars and cartons of cigarettes to his supplies. Even though he didn't smoke, he thought the cigarettes might come in handy to use for a trade or bribe.

The pistol they'd issued Klayne was in such bad shape, he joined several others in digging through a box of parts. The men carefully rebuilt their .45 weapons.

Additional supplies came from the doctor who would serve as a gunner on one of the crews. He packed a medical kit for each raider that included a pint of whiskey, supposedly for snakebites. The doctor had lectured them on drinking only boiled water and eating only cooked food once they arrived in China. Then he gave them all their final vaccinations.

Klayne grinned as he recalled one of the men muttering how the doctor thought all disease must have started in China for the way he went on and on about being careful to avoid getting cuts or any open wounds.

Like the rest of the men on this mission, Klayne felt edgy. He just wanted to get the raid over with. From the moment the colonel told them they'd be bombing Tokyo and a few surrounding cities, he'd felt relief that they were actually going to do something that would not only strike fear into the enemy, but also boost the spirits of those at home.

Thoughts of home made his heart ache with a longing to be back in Pendleton with his wife. Klayne closed his eyes and pictured Delaney riding her horse across a snowy pasture. Her enchanting scent filled his senses, lulling him into pleasant dreams.

The following morning, he rose early, as was his habit. He went up to the flight deck to check on the plane and found the gunner there, also taking a look at it. Together, they made their way below decks for breakfast, where Klayne took a seat next to Bob.

"If we keep eating like this, I'm going to need all new uniforms," Bob said, patting his stomach as he forked another mouthful of eggs and ham.

"It's sure been good grub," Klayne agreed. "I heard, though, that after a month or so, they run out of the fresh vegetables and meat, and things aren't quite so peachy."

"That makes sense," Bob said, buttering a biscuit. "I'm glad they still have plenty of good food now, though."

"Me, too." Klayne visited with Bob and the other men around them as they ate.

Klayne and Bob were on their way up to the flight deck when a muffled roar vibrated through the ship. Cries of battle stations immediately followed.

"What in the heck?" Bob asked, staying on Klayne's heels as the two men rushed for the top deck. The bitterly cold, stormy weather didn't faze them as they looked around to see if they were under attack. Other air crew members joined in the scramble and flung around questions, but no one had any answers. The ship shuddered and echoed with the sound of heavy gunfire.

On the flight deck, the men watched a nearby cruiser shoot another blast. In the distance, Klayne could see an enemy ship low in the water emitting a black plume of smoke while dive-bombers circled over it. The Japanese boat erupted in flames then slipped beneath the waves, but not before they'd sent out a transmission, warning Japan of the approaching armada of ships.

Amid the deep bursts of guns firing from a cruiser, the sea crashing against the ships, the wind howling fiercely, and the excited cheers of the men, Klayne heard someone yell, "Let's go!"

He and Bob raced back to their bunks to get their bags. Glad he'd left his packed and ready, Klayne quickly tucked in the last of his belongings and ran back to the flight deck.

Sailors slid across the wet surface to help the airmen yank off engine and gun turret covers. Others topped off fuel tanks. Klayne helped rock the plane back and forth to get the air bubbles out and make more room for the much-needed fuel.

While the gunner stowed five-gallon gas cans handed up through the rear hatch, Klayne helped lift them in. Keyed up on adrenalin and excitement to be heading out on the mission, the first bombing of Japan, Klayne felt ready, yet strangely unprepared. They were hundreds of miles from Tokyo, almost twice the distance they'd planned to fly. Would the fuel last long enough to get them to China? Would the Japanese be waiting for them, ready to shoot them all down before they had a chance to drop a single bomb?

A voice over the ship's speakers ordered, "Army pilots, man your planes!" Most of the men were already hastily preparing to embark on the journey.

Klayne tuned out the booming bark of commands from the carrier's island as he worked, but admired the way the Navy jumped in and took charge. Ropes were untied, wheel blocks whipped out of the way, and the little mechanical donkey moved planes into position for takeoff.

When the Navy finished, the planes were criss-crossed along the back end of the flight deck, two abreast, with the sixteenth plane's tail hanging off the carrier. Klayne couldn't fathom how the lead plane would have enough room to takeoff.

During the frantic preparations to launch the mission far ahead of the planned departure the following day, the carrier plowed forward into head winds, trying to take the planes just that much closer to the destination. Every gallon of fuel saved in flight could be the difference between life and death.

Klayne felt a hand grab his arm and turned to look at Bob. His friend looked him in the eye. "Whatever happens, it's been a pleasure to know you," the man said, shaking Klayne's hand. "If I don't make it out of this thing, make sure this letter reaches Norene." Bob handed him an envelope.

"You'll make it just fine, you sappy dunce." Klayne tucked the envelope inside his leather bomber's jacket. "And when we get on the other side of this, I'll even buy you dinner to celebrate."

"It's a deal. I'll order a big juicy steak, hot buttered rolls, mashed potatoes smothered in gravy, blueberry pie, and…" Bob sobered and gave Klayne a bear hug. "Be safe, my friend."

Klayne returned the hug then stepped back. "You, too, Bob. Thank you. And if something happens to me, please let my wife know how much I love her."

The man nodded once then jogged over to his B-25 and scrambled inside. Klayne climbed into his crew's plane, fighting back the feelings of claustrophobia that always swamped him when he entered the plane. He stood taller than many of the men on the mission; the average height for a pilot was around five-eight while the gunners averaged closer to five-four. The narrow, confined spaces didn't even allow room for him to stand upright once he was inside the plane.

He cast a glance to the skies overhead. The weather was fine for flying, but the sea was another matter. The storm-tossed waves rocked the carrier until it looked like a seesaw, bobbing down and up. If a wave hit a plane on takeoff, a crash seemed inevitable. The idea of landing in the churning seawater made Klayne's gut clench as the dangerous reality of the situation settled over him.

Instead of a raid over Tokyo under the cover of darkness, they'd have to drop the bombs in broad daylight. The pilot offered one last opportunity for the crew to back out, but none of them did.

Determined to see the mission through to the end, Klayne slid down the crawlway and settled into the bombardier's seat. He looked out the clear plastic cover at the B-25s lined up in front of him and the seawater gurgling over the end of the deck.

The lead plane, piloted by their colonel, revved its engines while the signal officer waved a checkered flag in circles. Sailors pulled away the wheel chocks holding the plane in place. The signal officer dropped the flag and the bomber roared down the flight deck. The plane's wheels hugged the white line that had been painted along the length of the deck. The B-25 charged to the end of the flight deck and disappeared.

Klayne held his breath then released it in a whoosh when the plane zoomed up and into the gray skies above the bow of the ship.

Sailors cheered in an ear-shattering celebration of success and encouragement unlike anything Klayne had ever heard.

The planes took off one after another, with scant minutes between each departure. In no time at all, Klayne found himself clutching the edge of his seat in nervous anticipation as the pilot of their plane revved the engines to a deafening roar.

The signal officer dropped to the deck and they stuttered forward down the runway, timed for the plane to lift off as the ship crested a wave. The bomber neared the left edge of the ship, but the pilot guided the plane back onto the white line as he picked up speed. One minute they were on the ship, the next in the air as a sheet of ocean spray waved them on their way.

All sixteen planes made it into the air, flying in a staggered string due west toward the Japanese coast.

If all went according to plan, the crew had more than two thousand miles of non-stop flying in front of them before they could land. Thoughts of the airfields in China, prepared for their arrival, impressed Klayne with how much planning had gone into the mission.

It wasn't until they were in the air that Klayne realized he'd failed to pack any food to eat beyond the candy bars he'd tucked into his bag. And his bag was buried in the back of the plane where he couldn't even reach it if he'd wanted to. He should have grabbed a thermos of coffee or water, or brought along sandwiches. He listened as the pilot used the inter-phone system to call down to him. "K.C., did you pack a lunch?"

"No, sir. I got so excited about getting everything else taken care of, I completely forgot." Klayne hoped he wasn't the only one stupid enough to leave without giving a thought to extra food.

"We did, too," the pilot said with a chuckle. "We'll starve together, I guess."

The plane skimmed above the swells of the ocean while the occupants remained silent for the most part, nerves taut, each man lost in his own thoughts. Klayne focused primarily on his responsibilities, playing over and over in his mind what he needed to do. He couldn't give any thought to Delaney because it would distract him to the point of driving him mad.

Instead, he visualized flying over their targets in Tokyo and dropping the bombs. Hours into the trip, Klayne felt antsy. The sun chased away the clouds as they drew closer to Japan. Then, in the distance, land rose ever so subtly above the surface of the water. Small boats anchored off the beach bobbed in the water like a child's toy in a bathtub as their plane thundered above them. White sands rapidly blended into rolling green fields.

Klayne didn't know what he expected, but the tidy farm fields, lush green grass, and fruit trees filled with blossoms wasn't how he pictured the land of the enemy. It was lovely, picturesque, and the first land he'd seen since they'd left California behind. Buildings soon filled the landscape and Klayne drew in a breath as they whizzed over a school. The low altitude at which the plane flew gave him an unobstructed view. Little ones stood outside, waving with big smiles on their faces.

The enormity of the task before him, before them all, settled on him with a crushing weight. Whatever happened was down to a matter of do or die. There was no going back, no changing their course of action.

The sight of a Japanese flag, a blood red circle contrasting sharply against a stark white background, flapping on a tall flagpole brought him back to the reason of their mission. The Japanese had taken something from America that could never be replaced. They'd attacked them, wreaked havoc on America, and tried to bring the nation to their knees.

Now, it was time for retribution.

Klayne wanted to balk at the idea of potentially injuring or killing innocent civilians with the bombings, but the colonel assured him it couldn't be helped. Loss of life was inevitable in this mission. Klayne just prayed the men on the B-25s wouldn't be among those who died today.

"Keep your eyes open," the pilot said, giving everyone a reminder to watch out for enemy planes as he flew through a valley heading toward Tokyo.

Suddenly, the sky seemed full of Zeros flying above them. Klayne leaned forward, waiting for incoming fire, but none happened. It was as though the enemy couldn't see them skimming just feet above the tops of an evergreen forest.

Nerves jangled, Klayne craned his neck and watched as the planes disappeared before he released a long, relieved breath. "That was close," he muttered. With every second and every mile, the mission became more and more real, as well as the possibility he wouldn't survive it.

After flying over a few small villages, they topped a hill and there, glistening like a smooth sheet of glass, was Tokyo Bay. The early afternoon sunlight reflected off the water, making it appear as ongoing as an ocean.

Klayne could see several large fires burning from the bombers who'd reached Tokyo before them. A smoky haze loomed over the northeastern section of the sprawling city.

The pilot pulled up, gaining altitude in preparation for dropping the bombs. Antiaircraft fire thundered around them as they zoomed past the Imperial Palace.

Klayne sighted in the first target as the pilot announced, "bomb bay doors open." He dropped the first five hundred pound bomb on a factory that covered almost half a city block with multiple chimneys looming against the sky. The bomb landed on the outer rim of the target, and hit, causing minimal damage.

With no time to worry about failing to maximize destruction opportunities, Klayne focused on the next target, another factory. The second bomb detonated atop a pile of coke, a fuel made from coal used in steel mills. The third bomb also landed on a factory. As they flew through the southern part of the city, he dropped the final bomb, an incendiary. The moment it hit the wind, the bomb separated, dropping dozens of small firebombs on a shipbuilding factory. The explosives scattered, igniting fires across the area.

Klayne glanced back and watched one of the five-hundred pound bombs explode. The factory walls puffed out, as though the building had filled with air, and then dissolved in a black cloud laced with red.

In a scant minute, they'd completed the task of dropping bombs on Tokyo.

The enemy had successfully traced their altitude, but they continued to miss hitting the plane as flak burst into explosions all around them. The pilot dove lower and picked up speed, anxious to get away. Klayne didn't draw a breath as they roared past the emperor's home and out of the city.

Although the enemy pursued them, the B-25 hugged so close to the ground, the Japanese planes gave up and turned back to the city.

Before long, their B-25 was once again over the water, heading south in an effort to confuse the Japanese on their actual destination.

The adrenaline coursing through his veins ebbed and left Klayne, along with the rest of the crew, worried about running out of fuel long before they reached China. A headwind sucked up precious stores of their fuel. They'd used all the auxiliary gas and were now drawing from the wing tanks.

The pilot slowed his speed and dropped altitude until the B-25 glided about twenty feet above the water. They followed a planned course until they were on the twenty-ninth parallel, heading for the airfield where they would land in China.

The men all complained of headaches, Klayne right along with them. He accepted one of the chocolate bars the gunner sent forward. Although he wasn't hungry, he nibbled on it, praying they'd make it to safety.

An occasional fishing boat or yacht broke up the monotonous surface of the sea below them. Late that afternoon, they flew over Japanese submarines refueling at a tanker. Klayne wished he had a bomb left to drop on them. As it was, he was glad they flew by seemingly unnoticed.

Unable to stay in his compartment a moment longer, he crawled up from the nose and stood behind the two pilots in the navigator's area, stretching his limbs and rolling his shoulders.

"I don't know about you all, but that was plumb scary," Klayne said. The others quickly agreed.

For a while, all five men seemed to feel a need to be together. Some of them smoked and the copilot carried on a conversation with the navigator as they continued toward China, watching as the weather deteriorated.

Soon, rain splattered the windshields. With the expectation of good weather all the way, the storm they encountered tightened their nerves like a newly strung strand of barbed wire.

Klayne returned to the nose, keeping an eye out for trouble and land. In a moment of self-indulgence, he took out the handkerchief Delaney had sent to him and sniffed her fragrance, comforted both by the scent and thoughts of his wife. Carefully tucking it inside his pocket, he returned to keeping watch. The sky darkened and the storm increased to the point they could hardly see in front of them.

The weather shifted and the wind they'd fought against turned into a tail wind that blew them closer to their destination.

Mid-evening, Klayne sighted land, an island with strange peaks rising up from it. They traveled onward and then there was a vision of surf breaking below them along a beach. The plane turned south, the men still hoping to make it to their planned landing. However, approaching the airfield in the dark, knowing it wouldn't be lit for fear of attracting the Japanese, would make it impossible to find.

The pilot gained altitude and flew on. In an unexpected moment, the storm abated just long enough Klayne could see a stretch of beach nearby. Solid land extended for miles. The pilot wanted to land on the beach, spend the night, then take off at first light to find the airfield.

Klayne knew it was probably a sound plan, since they were running low on fuel. His only concern was the Japanese finding them on the beach and taking them captive. The plane dropped closer to the beach and they all looked for logs, anything that might cause the plane to crash. Assured it was clear, Klayne removed the parachute he'd pulled on earlier and fastened a life vest in place.

One moment he watched the water draw closer as they prepared to land. In the next, the engines heaved a lusty cough and died. The plane sagged, caught the water, and flipped over with a deafening screech as metal crunched and bent.

Klayne awoke underwater, disoriented. *At least I'm not dead, yet*, he thought. It took him precious seconds to discern which direction was up and swim to the surface. He gulped in air and saw the beach ahead of him. The other members of the crew battled to make their way out of the wreckage, but they were all alive.

Slogging his way out of the water, he collapsed on the beach. A vision of Delaney, laughing with that dimple in her cheek, filled his thoughts as blackness overtook him.

The next time he came to, he was in a filthy little hut, his face pressed into the malodorous soil of the floor. His entire body ached and he couldn't open his eyes. His left arm and leg both felt as though they'd been squeezed by a vice. Riddled with pain, he groaned.

"It's okay, K.C. You'll be okay," the gunner assured him. Klayne passed out again and didn't regain true coherency for three days.

He awakened as warm water soaked dried blood away from his eyes, allowing him fully to open them for the first time since he collapsed on the beach. "Where am I?" he croaked, trying to glance around him. One eye felt cloudy, as if cotton fibers clung to his eyelashes. Despite his attempts to wipe it away, the vision impairment remained. His panic deepened when he glanced down to see his broken arm and mangled leg. A headache more painful than any he'd ever imagined enduring throbbed so badly, he would have been sick at his stomach if he'd eaten anything.

Instead, the darkness of pain-free oblivion welcomed him again. In that place, where his dreams kept the pain at bay, he thought of Delaney, of the life they might have had together. He envisioned the ranch, the fields of winter wheat ripened, ready for harvest, waving like ripples over a golden sea. He imagined cattle grazing in the pastures, their red and white coats standing out against verdant green grass and deep blue skies. He dreamed of holding his wife, of loving her with his heart wide open with no secrets or barriers between them. His arms ached for her, his hands longed to run along the silky contours of her skin, while his senses conjured her alluring scent.

If he survived this ordeal, he vowed to return to Pendleton and Delaney, to be the husband she deserved. To adore her so completely, she'd never have to question his loyalty or his love.

Uncertain if days or hours passed before he next awakened, he looked into the face of a young Chinese man. He introduced himself in English as a doctor. "Sergeant Campbell, I am Doctor Wang. I do not have the medical supplies necessary to treat your wounds, but I will take you and the others where you can receive the help you need. It is a long journey, the way will be difficult, but I am confident we will make it."

Unable to share the doctor's confidence, Klayne turned his head to the side and surveyed the rest of the crew. The pilot's leg was in worse shape than Klayne's, sliced open so that the bone was exposed. The co-pilot's injuries had already become infected. The navigator had two broken arms. Only the gunner managed to escape with nothing more than a knot on his head. Of the five of them, the gunner was the only one able to walk on his own.

The rest of them were so overwrought with pain, they could barely keep from slipping into madness. They hadn't received so much as an aspirin since the crash, due to their medical kits sinking along with their belongings.

Klayne held his breath until he passed out from the pain the following morning when the doctor arrived with Chinese men carrying sedan chairs. The wounded soldiers were loaded into them. The trip proved grueling and nearly unbearable, but somehow, they made it to the hospital.

A sigh of relief escaped him as he settled onto the thin mattress on an iron bed. After his wounds had been treated and he found some ease from the pain, Klayne listened as the gunner told him about their group barely escaping Japanese patrols. Vaguely, Klayne recalled being loaded into the bottom of a junk boat and drifting silently along the water, covered by a mat in suffocating heat. No wonder he'd passed out and remained oblivious. They'd gone from one village to another, finally coming upon someone who contacted the doctor.

Grateful to have survived long enough to receive medical care, Klayne just hoped he wouldn't die from the wounds he suspected were infected. From his inability to straighten his body, he assumed something was also wrong with his back. Fear gnawed at him that he might never walk again.

"What day is it?" he asked the gunner, trying to regain his bearings.

"Why, it's the twenty-fifth of April, Sarge."

Klayne slowly nodded. He'd spent his thirtieth birthday lying face-down in a boat, escaping the Japanese. Although he remembered nothing of the day itself, he would definitely never forget the circumstances surrounding it.

★★★ Chapter Fifteen ★★★

The days blurred into one long stretch of futile effort as Delaney fought to keep up with work on the ranch.

She spent an hour or two each morning nauseated then found herself in need of a nap each afternoon. Most of the time, she ignored it. But when she was so weary she couldn't keep her eyes open another moment, she snuck off to sleep for twenty to thirty minutes, just long enough to wake up even more tired.

The days dragged by and still no word came from Klayne. Struggling not to sink into despair, she sat at the table playing with her food rather than eating it one sunny May afternoon.

"Sis, you need to get your head back on straight. You've been acting strange for a while. I can't stand to see you like this," Dill said, glaring at her from across the table in the bunkhouse. "Go into town, visit with Amy, do a little shopping. Just get out of here. I think a change of scenery will do you good."

Stubborn and proud, she refused to tell her father she was expecting Klayne's baby. The lectures her father had already poured down on her about making a stupid, rash decision by marrying the soldier would seem like lofty praise compared to what he'd tell her now.

Delaney just couldn't bring herself to share the truth with him. She shook her head and pushed a potato around on her plate. "I can't, Dad. We barely finished the spring branding. Now, we need to..."

"Whatever it is, we'll take care of it for today," Butch said, glancing at Duffy for agreement. The cowboy hurried to bob his head up and down. Butch looked back at Delaney. "See, there's no reason for you to stick around here. Actually, it would be a big help if you could run by the store. I have a list of supplies we need. With those new ration books, I think I figured out how much we can get of each item on my list. I'm happy you two decided to bring in some hives for honey. With sugar at the top of the ration list, I'll sure be glad to have it for a sweetener."

Dill nodded in agreement. "I think it'll be a good investment, although I'm not looking forward to tending those bees."

"I'll do it, Dad. I'll see if I can find a book or something about taking care of them while I'm in town. The county extension office might have some information," Delaney said, wanting to feel useful, even if the men were booting her off the ranch for the day.

"That'd be great, Sis. Anything you could find out would be a help." Dill smiled at her then continued eating his lunch.

After the dishes were cleared away, Delaney returned to the house, dressed for town, and hurried out to her pickup. She drove into Pendleton with the windows rolled down, enjoying the fresh breeze and the scents wafting on the air. It smelled of springtime and home and sweet memories from her younger years.

When she pulled into town, she went directly to the county extension office and spoke with an agent who seemed knowledgeable about bees and honey production. He gave her a booklet that provided basic information and encouraged her to stop by if she had more questions.

From there, she went to the store and filled Butch's list, sparingly using stamps from the ration book. She set the groceries in her pickup then walked down the street to the bakery. Amy helped a customer, but smiled at her as she entered. As soon as she had the customer happily on his way, Amy rushed around the counter and gave Delaney a big hug.

"Oh, Dee, you look like the weight of the world is resting on your shoulders. Still no word from Klayne?"

Delaney shook her head. "Not a peep. I'm so worried about him, Amy. I just know something has happened to him."

"Think positive," Amy admonished, guiding her over to a table and taking a seat across from her. "I'm sure he's fine, wherever he's at. When he does come back, though, I plan to give him a piece of my mind."

Delaney worked up a smile at the thought of her friend standing up to Klayne Campbell. She had no doubt the girl would have him cowering in his boots before she finished with him. "You'll have to get in line behind me, Dad, and Butch."

Amy nodded and glanced at the clock. "I'm just about finished for the day. What do you say we go do something fun? I could use a little cheering up, too."

"Oh, Amy. Did Marc leave?" Delaney asked, reaching across the table to pat her friend's hand in a comforting gesture.

"Yes. Just this morning. He's off to basic training and who knows when he'll be back." Amy sighed then stood and held a hand out to Delaney. "Come on. It's too pretty outside for us to sit here and mope after men who don't even appreciate us. Let's go see a show. I heard there's a comedy playing this afternoon."

"I could use a good laugh," Delaney admitted, following Amy to the back room. Her friend removed her apron, washed her hands, tidied her hair, then slipped on her hat and gloves.

They both bid Amy's parents goodbye then walked outside into the bright sunshine.

"Did you see the letter in the paper from the Secretary of the Treasury?" Amy asked as the two of them strolled down the sidewalk.

Delaney nodded. "I did. How could you not purchase war bonds after reading it? I found the way he called purchasing bonds a tithe for liberty an interesting way of phrasing it."

"I did, too. I just think of those poor soldiers fighting without adequate weapons and want to spend every penny I have on war bonds." Amy waved to a group of girls they both knew. Delaney smiled and waved then tugged Amy inside a store selling war bonds. After they each made a purchase, they continued ambling toward the movie theater.

They were nearly there when a car full of soldiers drove by. One cheeky young man leaned his head out the window and whistled.

Delaney waved at them and smiled while Amy scowled and voiced her disapproval. "Why, they are getting positively uncivilized, whistling like that. What on earth are you encouraging them for?"

"I don't know. It's just since meeting Klayne, I feel a little more inclined to overlook a whistle or two because I know they don't mean anything by it. I think they're just blowing off a little steam," Delaney said, as the girls arrived at the theater.

They purchased tickets, popcorn, and bottles of cold soda pop before taking seats in the middle of the theater.

"I heard this movie is supposed to be fun," Amy said, munching her popcorn.

"I've yet to see one with Bob Hope I didn't like," Delaney whispered, settling back as the lights dimmed and a newsreel showed frightening scenes from the war. The glaring words of "Yanks Bomb Tokyo!" got her immediate attention. Images of a Naval carrier dipping through ocean waves flashed across the screen. It talked about a brave group of men launching an air raid against Japan by dropping bombs on Tokyo. Delaney dropped the popcorn when the camera panned over the raiders and there was Klayne, looking proud and determined as he stood with his comrades. The newsreel went on to show the planes taking off and some of the men being awarded medals from the Chinese government, but she didn't see Klayne among them. The announcer bragged that the planes departed on their mission from the magical place of Shangri-La. As the announcer prattled on about the magical land enchanting the soldiers on their successful mission, Delaney's face lost all color.

Unable to breathe, she rose to her feet and hurried out of the theater. Only when she was outside, leaning against the brick of the building did she draw in a breath.

"Dee?" Amy asked, hurrying to catch up to her. She placed a hand on her shoulder and gave her a concerned look. "Dee? What on earth is the matter?"

"Klayne was there," Delaney said, her voice low and raspy with emotion.

"What? Klayne was where?"

"On the raid. I saw him on the screen," Delaney said, numb with shock. "What if something happened to him? What if he's hurt? What if they…"

"Don't think about what might not be true, Dee." Amy took her hand and tugged her back in the direction of the bakery. "Come on. Let's get you something to drink and you can have a moment to get over the shock of this all."

Delaney tugged her hand away from Amy. "No. I need to find out where he's at. I won't get a moment's rest until I know he's alive. I just… I have to know, Amy."

"Okay. What do you want to do?" Amy asked, walking beside her as Delaney made her way to her pickup.

"I'll go to Pendleton Airfield and see if anyone there can give me any news." Delaney opened her door and slid behind the wheel while Amy scrambled up on the passenger side. "You don't have to come."

Amy smiled. "I'm here for you, Dee. Whatever you need. Now, let's go see what we can find out about your husband."

An hour later the girls returned to the bakery, frustrated and deflated. No one at the base would talk to them because not a single person they spoke with would believe Delaney was married to Klayne. Nothing in the paperwork they had on file mentioned her name, so they refused to say anything about the raid or who survived. By the end of the conversation, Delaney had the idea none of the men she talked to knew more information than the newsreel had provided.

"I'm sorry, Dee," Amy said, patting her hand. "I'm sure as soon as anyone is able, they'll get word to you about Klayne."

"I know you're right, Amy. Thanks for going with me," Delaney said, squeezing her friend's hand. "I appreciate your support."

"It's what I'm here for. Do you want to come in for a while?" Amy asked, opening the pickup door and sliding out.

"No, I think I better head home, but thank you, Amy."

Her friend nodded. "Anytime, Dee. If there is anything we can do, please let me know."

Delaney nodded. "I will. Thanks again."

Amy shut the pickup door and Delaney headed home, consumed by her thoughts and sickened by her concerns for Klayne. Perhaps all her worrying was for nothing. Maybe he'd survived the raid and was right now back on a base in the states. That thought calmed her considerably as she parked the pickup near the bunkhouse and grabbed a sack of groceries off the seat.

"Hey, Dee. I thought maybe you'd stay in town and eat supper with Amy," Butch said as she walked inside the bunkhouse. "You have more to carry in?"

She nodded and Duffy ambled out to bring in the rest.

Dill, who just walked in, took one look at her face and opened his arms to her. She rushed to her father and buried her face against the front of his dusty shirt, not caring if it got all over her dress.

"What's wrong, Sis?" he asked, giving her a tight squeeze before releasing her and taking a step back. "Did something happen in town?"

"I saw Klayne," she blurted as tears burned the back of her eyes.

Dill's hands curled into fists and he moved toward the door. "You mean that no-good low-life is back in town and didn't even let you know? Why, I'll teach him…"

Delaney settled a hand on his arm before he could march out the door. "No, Dad. He's not back."

At her father's confused look, she hurried to explain. "Amy and I went to see a movie. The newsreel was about the raid on Tokyo. It showed the men who went on the mission, and there was Klayne, larger than life on the screen." Delaney's voice caught and she brushed at a wayward tear that trailed down her cheek. "I'm worried, Dad. What if his plane was shot down? What if the Japanese took him captive? What if he's lying injured somewhere in some…"

Dill gave her a comforting hug as she fought to subdue her tears. "Don't jump to conclusions that likely didn't happen. That raid was weeks ago. By now, he's probably safe at a base, if not here, then one of the American bases overseas. The news I read in the paper said everyone was fine and no planes were lost."

"I know what it said, but I still have this feeling that something happened to him, Dad. Something horrible."

"You can't go around borrowing trouble, Sis. Why don't we go to the airfield tomorrow and see if we can find out anything from them?"

Delaney sighed and paced in front of the old table. "I tried that already. Amy went with me. The guards wouldn't even let us in the gate until Amy threatened to scream as though she was being murdered. The officer we spoke with was kind, but he said there is no record of Klayne being married and they can't give me any information because I'm not listed as his wife."

"Surely there's something that can be done," Dill said, watching his daughter prowl around the bunkhouse kitchen like a caged animal. "Just calm down and we'll figure it out."

"How can I calm down, Dad?" Delaney yelled. "My husband may very well be dead or dying and no one will tell me a blessed thing." Before Dill could offer her any words of comfort or advice, she ran out of the bunkhouse and inside the house. The slamming of the back door echoed to the three men as they stood in the doorway, watching her run away.

"I sure hope that young man of hers comes back, Dill. She really and truly loves him," Butch said, moving over to the stove where he took a casserole out of the oven.

"I hope he comes back, too," Dill said, sending up a prayer for the young man he'd only briefly met.

The next morning, Delaney wrote a letter to the man who had reportedly been in charge of the mission. She highly doubted her letter would reach him, but it made her feel better.

After that, she pulled on a pair of work gloves and headed out for a full day of work.

The teen boys they'd hired arrived and their help on the ranch made a noticeable difference in what was accomplished each day.

Delaney worked alongside the rest of the men while Butch took over all cooking duties. Even if Delaney had time to cook, which she didn't, the smell of coffee percolating or meat frying sent her rushing for the bathroom. Finally, the morning sickness that plagued her subsided, but her energy flagged every afternoon. Most days, she managed to sneak in a quick nap, although it took evasive measures on her part to keep her dad from discovering that fact.

One morning, two of the five boys they hired helped Dill sweep out the loft in a shed where they planned to store the freshly cut hay, once it dried enough to stack. The June day was warm and bright as they worked.

Delaney labored in the garden, watering plants and pulling weeds. She waved to her dad as he pushed remnants of last year's hay, dust, and who knew what else off the edge of the loft to the ground below. Part of it drifted over the grain drill that seeded the fields. Duffy had repaired a broken brace on it the previous evening and left it sitting there. One of the boys would scrub it clean before Duffy put it back in the equipment shed, ready to seed the next crop. The repair work they usually accomplished in the early spring had been delayed by the shortage of help, so the men worked on it whenever they had a chance. With the extra hands, they were finally catching up on the work that a month ago had seemed so endless.

Dill leaned on the broom handle and returned her wave before going back inside. Delaney resumed weeding and watering, and praying for Klayne. Constantly, her thoughts turned to him, wondering if he was well and safe. Questions about when he'd get in touch with her and if he'd come home kept her anxiety simmering.

As she tugged weeds from between the feathery tops of the carrots, she heard a yell and spun around.

Dill bounced off the top of the grain drill, hit the metal bars across the front, and caught the hitch with his foot before landing on the ground with a sickening thud.

⸳⸳⁕★ *Chapter Sixteen* ★⁕⸳⸳

"Dad!" Delaney screamed, racing toward him as the boys poured out of the barn and shed. Duffy jumped off a tractor he'd been fueling and Butch hurried out of the bunkhouse.

The two boys who'd been working in the shed reached Dill first, followed by Delaney. She dropped to her knees in the dust and touched her father, grateful his chest continued to rise and fall. Blood poured out of his nose and from a cut on his lip, but it was the wounds she couldn't see that worried her most. Both of his legs rested at unnatural angles and the ankle of his left foot appeared twisted to the side.

"Someone phone the hospital," she said, flapping her hand at the boys. One of them ran to the house.

"Do you think his back is broken?" Duffy asked as he knelt beside Delaney.

"I don't know," she whispered, yanking a handkerchief from her pocket and holding it beneath Dill's nose.

Butch reached them, assessed the situation, and took charge. "Tommy and John, go take the door off the tack room and hurry right back with it. Gordy and

Jason, run into the bunkhouse and grab the stack of blankets off the bed closest to the door.

The boys hurried to do his bidding, leaving Duffy and Butch to give each other silent looks over Delaney's head. Butch took a step closer and placed his hand on Delaney's shoulder. "Go get your pickup, Dee. Drive it right over here close so we can load your dad."

Numb, Delaney sat for a moment until Butch squeezed her shoulder. She bolted to her feet and raced to her pickup, starting it and turning around in the driveway.

She eased it close to where her dad sprawled in the dirt, his face a ghastly shade of white beneath the red blood smeared across his skin. The boys returned with the door and blankets. Butch padded the door with two folded blankets then working together they all carefully lifted Dill onto the makeshift stretcher.

"Heft him into the back of the pickup," Butch ordered. Delaney scrambled into the back and guided them as the men and boys hefted. The one who called the hospital said they could send someone out, but it would be at least half an hour.

"Go back in and tell them we're on our way," Butch said, sliding behind the wheel as Delaney sat next to her father in the bed of the pickup.

Duffy stayed behind to keep an eye on the boys. "Let us know as soon as you hear anything," he called as Butch ground the gears and hustled toward town.

The trip to Pendleton was the longest Delaney had ever taken. Time seemed to slow to a crawl as she did her best to cushion the bounces while Butch roared down the road. Staff poured out of the hospital when they arrived, moving Dill onto a stretcher and wheeling him inside.

A nurse cornered Delaney and started asking questions. She answered them then nervously paced back and forth, wishing someone would tell her what was happening.

She jumped up from the chair she'd been sitting in when Doctor Nash appeared in the waiting area.

"Doc! How's Dad?" she asked with a pleading look in her eyes. Nothing could happen to her father. He was all she had left in the world. With her mother gone all these years, she'd always relied on the steady presence of her father. Mac was at sea, no doubt heading into battle, and Klayne... Delaney choked back a sob as a thought of her husband's probable whereabouts flashed through her mind. "Will Dad be okay?"

"Let's sit down," Nik said, guiding Delaney to a nearby seat. "What happened to Dill?"

"He fell out of the hay loft on top of the grain drill. He hit the top of it facing down, bounced off the cross bar, then hit the hitch," Delaney said, trying to keep the emotion out of her voice. "The boys don't seem to know what happened. One moment he was sweeping out the loft, and the next he'd fallen."

Nik shook his head. "That explains his injuries. He busted both legs, Dee. The femur, that's the bone in your thigh..." Nik pointed to his leg to demonstrate where he meant. "Dill must have snapped them both when he hit the top of the drill. The good news is both breaks were clean. The bad news is it's going to take a while for those to heal, especially when he doesn't have a solid leg for support. He also broke his left ankle. It's going to require surgery. In addition, he has seven cracked ribs, one of which punctured a tiny hole in his lung."

Delaney's face paled and she felt woozy. Nik pushed on her back until she bent forward with her head between her knees. "Just breathe, Dee. Take in a deep breath."

She did.

"Now, take another."

She inhaled and released the breath, took another, then slowly raised her head. Calmer, she faced the doctor. "Is Dad going to be okay?"

"Eventually. The punctured lung can be dangerous, but you got him here quickly and we were able to treat it right away. Surgery on his ankle is next, then we'll set both of his legs. Oh, and he broke his nose, again. What's that? The fourth time?"

Delaney nodded. "Third, but who's counting?"

Nik grinned and patted her shoulder. "If you want to go home to rest, I can phone you when Dill is out of surgery."

"No, I'll stay. Butch is here, too. He went outside to get some air," Delaney said, wanting Nik to know she wasn't alone.

"That's good. As soon as we finish setting his legs, I'll give you an update on how he's doing."

Delaney bobbed her head in agreement, finding it hard to speak.

The doctor pointed toward a chair in the corner. "Make yourself comfortable and don't forget to take care of yourself. You know you have more than just your health to consider."

She nodded again and watched as he walked away. When Butch returned, she told him what the doctor said. The two of them waited for what seemed like hours. As afternoon edged toward evening, Butch went to find them something to eat. Delaney had no appetite, but she knew she needed to eat something for the sake of the baby.

With no one else in the waiting room, she settled her hand on her abdomen. So far, the tiny bump of the baby didn't show enough anyone had noticed.

Delaney knew she needed to tell her father, and she wanted to tell Amy, but she just couldn't find the words. Her father already had too many things on his mind, worrying about the crops and the cattle when they were having to make do without experienced help. The distance he'd put between them when he found out about Klayne devastated her. She couldn't imagine what her father would do when he found out she was expecting Klayne's baby.

"What a mess," she mumbled, leaning back in the chair and closing her eyes. The crinkle of a paper bag alerted her to someone's presence. She opened her eyes and watched as Butch sank onto a seat beside her. He took hamburgers out of the bag and passed one to her, along with a cold bottle of milk.

"Eat up, Girly. You'll need your strength," he said, taking a bite of the hamburger.

"Thanks, Butch." Before eating the hamburger, she took a long drink of the milk. Hungry, she ate every bite of her meal, then finished the milk.

She got up and walked around a while then resumed her seat. Butch appeared to be dozing with his face propped on one hand, elbow braced on the arm of the chair.

Delaney picked up a copy of a popular magazine. Surprised to see it was the current issue, she studied the image of Hedy Lamar on the cover. Vaguely recalling the actress had a new movie releasing soon, she supposed that was the reason for the cover story.

She flipped through the magazine, noticing a cigarette ad with pictures of uniformed soldiers. The ad said, "You want steady nerves when you're flying Uncle Sam's bombers across the ocean." The ad made her think of Klayne. She wondered if he smoked. Although it seemed everyone smoked these days, she detested the habit. His kisses tasted like spearmint gum, not the residue of cigarettes, but she supposed it was entirely possible he could smoke like a steam engine and she'd never know.

Annoyed by how little she knew about the man she married, perhaps she shouldn't have been so eager to say "I do." Yet, when she thought about how Klayne made her feel, how much she loved him, she was glad she had agreed to marry him before he left.

She just wanted him to come home. At the very least, she needed to know he was safe.

With a weary sigh, she continued flipping through the magazine. She glanced through an article about three things every woman could do to help the war effort. A photo showing a woman cleaning and servicing her sewing machine caused Delaney to roll her eyes. She'd have to brush the cobwebs off hers before she could clean it, and that would only be after she remembered where she'd stored it. She didn't have any particular talent at sewing and rarely had the time. If she needed something new, she ordered it from Ilsa Campanelli. If something needed to be patched, there was a widow woman in town who gladly did the work to make extra money.

Delaney perused an article about Yale at war then read the article about *Tortilla Flat*, the movie Hedy Lamar starred in, based on John Steinbeck's novel. Her eyes lingered over lovely drawings of birds, making her think of peaceful spring days.

Since she'd gone through the magazine so quickly, she turned back to the front and slowly thumbed her way through one page at a time. She'd just turned a page when a familiar face jumped out at her from a black and white photo.

"Thunderation!" she exclaimed, sounding just like her father.

Butch jumped and nearly toppled out of his chair then glared at her. "What's all the ruckus about? Is Dill okay?"

"Doc hasn't come back yet, but look at this," Delaney said, shoving the magazine into Butch's face. She tapped the image of her husband with her finger. "That's Klayne, Butch. Right there! That's Klayne!"

"Well, quit waggling the durn thing all over the place and let me get a gander," Butch said, taking the magazine in his hands. He studied the images of the young soldiers, his gaze coming back to rest on Klayne. "He's a fine-looking man, Delaney. Stands tall and proud, but what impresses me is the look in his eyes."

"What look is that?" she asked, curious.

"One of kindness," Butch said, handing the magazine back to her. "He looks like a good man, Girly."

"He is, Butch. He really is."

Another hour passed before the doctor appeared, letting them know Dill did well in surgery. Both of his legs were set, but he'd be in the hospital for a while, recovering.

"You two might as well go home and rest. Dill won't be awake for a while and he'll be so groggy, he won't know what's going on anyway. Come back in the morning and he should be ready for a visitor or two then."

"Thank you, Doc," Delaney said, giving the doctor a quick hug.

"My pleasure, although I should tell you I watched while one of the young whippersnappers did the surgery on Dill's ankle. He did a great job on it, too." Nik smiled and thumped Butch on the back. "Take this gal home and make sure you both get a good night's rest."

"I'll do it, Nik." Butch placed his hand on Delaney's arm, guiding her toward the doorway. "Thank you for taking good care of the boss."

Nik nodded then left.

Delaney and Butch returned to the pickup and made their way back to the ranch. They found all five of the boys still there, keeping busy as they waited for news.

"Dad is out of surgery and he'll recover, but it's going to be a long, slow process," Delaney said, explaining the extent of her father's injuries to the boys. "If you know anyone looking for work this summer, let me know. We could use another pair or two of hands since Dad won't be able to get out of bed."

"Would you hire a girl, Miss Delaney?" one of the boys inquired.

"If she can work hard, I sure would." Delaney grinned at Tommy. "You have someone in mind?"

"Yep, but I'll ask her first, to see if she's interested."

"Fair enough," Delaney said, motioning for the boys to leave. "You boys worked hard today and I appreciate all your help. Have a good evening."

"We will. Good night, Miss Delaney. We're awful glad Mr. Danvers will be okay," Tommy said.

Delaney nodded. "Me, too."

The next morning, she flipped on the radio in the kitchen as she nibbled a piece of dry toast. She listened to a man state the Battle of Midway continued, with the U. S. Navy fighting hard against the Japanese. Somehow, in all the trauma with her father's accident, she'd somehow missed the fact that the American Navy battled against the Japanese in the Pacific.

Absently, she wondered if Mac was anywhere near that area. How she wished he'd joined the Army instead of the Navy. Then again, she supposed fighting off a boat wasn't any worse than combating Germans on land.

With a quick prayer to keep the Allied men fighting there safe, and a longer plea for her brother's safekeeping, she flipped off the radio and hurried outside. At least she knew Klayne wasn't in the midst of that particular battle, since he was in the Army Air Force.

The next few days were filled with work, visits to the hospital to sit with her father, and more work.

Delaney had never been so tired in her entire life.

The third morning after Dill's accident, the boys that worked for them arrived with an extra car and three high school-aged girls.

"Miss Dee, we know you need more help and well…" said Tommy. He'd become the group's spokesperson, although as he talked, he swirled the toe of his scuffed work boot in the dirt. He took a breath and looked up at her, making eye contact. "This is my sister and my two cousins. They can work hard and know how to do things on a ranch."

"Do they?" Delaney asked, trying to hide her smile. The girls all looked to be about sixteen or so. They wore denim overalls with the legs rolled up, boots, and cotton work shirts. Delaney walked closer to the girls. "What are your names?"

The tallest girl bore a striking resemblance to Tommy and straightened a little taller. "My name is Louise, Miss Dee. I'm almost sixteen, can work as hard as my brother," she tossed a glance at Tommy, "and I'm not afraid to get my hands dirty."

"That's good," Delaney said, "because if you work here, your hands, your face, and most of the rest of you will be coated in dirt by the end of the day." She turned to the other two girls. "And you are?"

"I'm Jilly and this is Lina," the more outgoing of the two said. "We used to live on a farm until our dad decided he wanted to sell insurance and we moved to town."

"I see. And you both like to do farm work?" Delaney asked. Jilly enthusiastically nodded her head while Lina slowly shook hers. Delaney focused on the shy girl. "What do you like to do, Lina?"

"I like to clean house and cook. I'm good at doing laundry, and I don't mind working in the garden. Tommy said he thought you might need some help around the house, too." The timid girl glanced up at Delaney then dropped her gaze.

Delaney smiled at the girls. "You all three are hired. I'll see how you do today and we'll talk about wages at the end of the day. Does that sound fair?"

"Yes, ma'am!" they all three answered.

Delaney set the boys, Louise, and Jilly to work outside then returned to the house with Lina. She showed her where the washing machine was located, the rags and supplies she used for cleaning, and asked if the girl would water the garden before she started working on the chores inside.

"Yes, ma'am," Lina said, grinning shyly.

"Maybe you'd like to listen to the radio while you work," Delaney said, flipping on the radio and listening in surprise as the announcer relayed the news that the Battle of Midway was over and the Americans had triumphed.

"Despite the overwhelming odds, the American Navy has proven they are a force to be reckoned with. The battle is over folks, and victory is ours," the reporter proclaimed with excitement.

Spontaneously, Delaney executed a few dance steps around the kitchen, then gave Lina a hug. "That's such wonderful news!"

"It sure is, ma'am," Lina agreed.

Delaney patted the girl on the back then moved toward the door. "Just call me Miss Dee like the rest of them, Lina, and we'll get along fine."

"Yes, m.." Lina blushed. "Yes, Miss Dee."

"I'll check back in on you in a while."

That afternoon, a car drove up the lane and Nik Nash got out along with a beautiful blond-haired girl every bit as tall as him. She looked willowy and graceful, like Delaney pictured a fairy might appear.

"Dee! I've brought you a new hand with the horses," Nik said, motioning to the girl. "This is Charlotte. I went through medical school with her older brother. She is excellent at handling horses. Lottie has been bored almost to death since she arrived last week to spend the summer here. Maybe you can keep her busy?"

The girl blushed but reached out and shook Delaney's hand. "Nik may be exaggerating slightly, but I'd be happy to help with your horses if you need someone."

"I do need someone, Charlotte." Delaney looked over the girl and smiled. "How old are you?"

"Twenty-two. My fiancé enlisted in the Army and my folks thought it might be a good idea for me to get a change of scenery for the summer, so here I am. I'm hopeless in the house, can't cook to save my life, but I like to work outdoors."

Delaney laughed and turned to Nik. "Now, this is my kind of girl."

Nik chuckled. "I figured you two would get along well. Why don't I leave Charlotte here for a few hours so you can both see how things might work out? I can drop back by around five."

"That won't be necessary, Doc. I can drive her into town when I go to visit Dad this evening."

"Perfect," Nik said, backing toward his car. "Your father is coming along quite nicely. In spite of his insistence we let him come home, it will probably be another week or two before I feel comfortable moving him out here. Even then, he'll need constant care."

"I'll figure something out, Doc," Delaney said, wondering how she could run the ranch, care for her father, and take care of herself. She saw the doctor eyeing her, as though he gauged to see if she was following his orders to get plenty of rest.

He nodded and opened the car door. "If you need help, let me know."

"I will," she said. They both knew she wouldn't, though.

Delaney turned to Charlotte and motioned toward the corral next to the barn. "Want to give riding one of the horses a go?"

"You bet!" Charlotte said, falling into step beside her. "And please call me Lottie, Miss Dee. Everyone does."

"Lottie it is," Delaney said, leading the way over to the horses. An hour and a half later, she almost hurried into the house to call the doctor and praise him for sending her Lottie. The girl was a marvel with horses and had no trouble at all riding any of the horses. Delaney had her ride four different horses, of varying ages and temperaments. Lottie's gentle hand combined with her unyielding determination to bring the horses around to her way of thinking gave

Delaney confidence in the girl's abilities to handle the job.

As Lottie saddled one of the mares who hadn't been ridden for a while, Delaney lowered her voice. "Did Nik tell you why I need help with the horses?"

"All Nik said was that you have too many irons in the fire and need some help with the horses this summer. That's all I need to know." Lottie grinned at Delaney as she swung onto the back of the horse and patted the chestnut's neck. "I'd ride from dawn to dusk if someone would let me."

"You might come to regret those words," Delaney teased, as she moved away from the fence. "I'll be back in an hour to head into town."

"Thanks, Miss Dee. I'll be ready to go." Lottie loped off across the pasture and Delaney went to check on the work the boys did as they finished hauling in the first cutting of hay under the supervision of Duffy.

Assured they had things well in hand, she'd started toward the equipment shed but stopped when Lina ran outside, waving one of Dill's dirty shirts over her head. "Miss Dee! There's a telephone call for you. It's urgent!"

★ *Chapter Seventeen* ★

Delaney broke into a run and raced to the house, taking the back steps in a few leaps before charging through the laundry area and into the kitchen. She lifted the receiver and listened breathlessly to her sister-in-law sobbing on the other end of the line.

"Carol, I can't understand you. Take a deep breath and tell me what's wrong," Delaney said, imagining a hundred horrible scenarios that started with Ryatt and ended with Mac.

"It's Mac. He was in the Battle of Midway. I just received a telegram he's been injured. I don't know more than that, but I wanted to let you know." Carol snuffled into the phone.

Shocked, Delaney knew it wasn't the time to give in to her emotions. Carol needed someone to lean on.

"Let's think positive, honey. Mac is as tough as nails and you know it. He'll probably be back up and ready to fight again in no time at all." Delaney tried to keep her tone cheerful and upbeat while panic and worry seeped into her. "Do you need me to come there? Help with anything?"

Carol sniffled again. "No, Dee. You've got your hands full there. I'm sorry. I shouldn't have added more worries, but I..."

Delaney interrupted her. "No, Carol. We're here for you. Always. For anything. Call anytime you need us."

"Thanks, Dee." Carol sighed.

"You're welcome." Delaney could picture the woman wiping her cheeks and straightening her spine.

"How's Dill? Is he getting along okay?" Carol asked, clearly anxious to change the subject.

Delaney barely held back a derisive snort. "No, he's not. He's terrorizing the hospital staff, demanding someone, anyone, bring him home. The doctor said it will be a few more weeks before that can happen and then someone will need to be in the house to take care of him."

"Oh, gosh, Dee," Carol's voice sounded heavy with concern. "What are you going to do? Should Ry and I come spend the summer there?"

"No, Carol. We'll be fine," Delaney said, then hurried to add. "Unless you want to spend the summer here. You know we'd love to have you."

"I know, and we'd love to come, but I wouldn't feel right leaving our farm unattended. The neighbors have had some strange things happening at their place. You know the big farm Mr. and Mrs. Yamada owned? Well, once they had to report to the Assembly Center, a very nice young man purchased it. Ryatt's little friend Petey said he was a captain in the Army before his plane crashed and he almost died. I don't know all the particulars, but it looks like he'll keep the fruit stand open this summer."

"Oh, that's a great thing," Delaney said, knowing the fruit stand drew customers to the area, many of whom would see Mac's apple orchard and remember to come back in the fall to purchase apples. "Are you sure you two are doing okay on your own?"

"We're fine. Ryatt, bless his heart, thinks he's the man of the house with his daddy gone and tries hard to do his share." Carol's voice softened. "He's such a good boy, Dee. I don't know what I did to deserve him."

Delaney giggled. "You married my brother. He's such a handful, you got Ryatt as a reward."

Carol's smile carried across the phone lines. "Indeed. Ryatt can be a handful, too, but he's also a sweetheart."

"Just like his dad." Delaney's heart ached, thinking about her brother. Wherever he was, she hoped his injuries were minimal and he was safe. "Listen, Carol, I better run. Thank you for letting me know. I don't think I'll tell Dad right now. He needs to focus on getting well."

"Agreed. I'll let you know if I hear anything else."

"Thanks, Carol. Take care and tell Ry his Aunt Dee sends her love."

"Consider it done," Carol said, then disconnected the call.

Delaney thanked Lina for running out to get her then hurried to change her clothes. She rushed back downstairs, stopping to speak to the girl as she finished the last load of laundry. "Lina, you did a great job today. If you want to come back tomorrow, I could certainly use your help. Here's your wages."

She placed money in the girl's hand and watched her eyes widen with delight. "I'll be back, Miss Dee. Thank you!"

"See you tomorrow?"

"Yes, ma'am!" Lina said, then blushed.

In the coming weeks, Delaney would be more grateful for Lina's help, the help of all the kids they'd hired, than words could express.

While Lina kept the house spotless, the laundry washed and pressed, and the garden watered and weeded, the rest of them worked outside. Delaney pushed herself from dawn to dusk, but couldn't make it through the day without stopping for an afternoon nap. Since she couldn't very well sneak into the house with Lina there, she finally admitted the truth to the girl, showing her the picture of Klayne she'd found in the magazine, along with her wedding pictures. Lina promised not to tell a soul, and as far as Delaney knew she hadn't.

Jilly and Louise kept up with the boys and Delaney gave them the same wages. Those girls earned every penny, too. Three times a week, Lottie came to work with the horses. Sometimes, she'd stay late and help if they were in need of an extra hand.

Typically, Sage Hills Ranch had half a dozen cowboys working there year-round and added an additional six to eight during the busy summer months. Although some of the kids helping on the ranch were inexperienced, they worked hard and gave their best to whatever task Delaney asked them to do.

With Dill unable to do anything but gripe from his bed and the baby siphoning some of her strength, Delaney was surprised to find the ranch work wasn't suffering as she'd anticipated. The young people brought endless energy and loads of fun to work with them each day, something she both looked forward to and appreciated.

They'd made it part-way through the month of July without any problems, other than her dad's constant care. Lina took on part of those responsibilities. Much to everyone's surprise, Dill stopped grumbling and grousing anytime the girl stepped into his room to bring him a drink or something to eat. He actually smiled at her and exchanged pleasantries. Delaney could have whooped with joy to find Lina considered Dill as the grandfather she'd never had and didn't mind keeping an eye on him during the day.

To simplify his care, Delaney had moved all the furniture out of a room that had once been a study. With plenty of young legs and backs to run up and down the attic stairs, Delaney packed up everything she wanted to keep but wouldn't use and had the boys haul it to the attic. She discovered both Jilly and Lina were excellent seamstresses and set them to the task of making new curtains for the windows from the stacks of fabric her mother had purchased shortly before she passed away.

After Delaney and Louise cleaned the room and installed a new area rug, the boys set up an iron bed they found in the attic, along with a bedside table, a rocking chair, and a small desk. Delaney had Duffy run into town and bring home a new mattress and pillows, to ensure Dill would be as comfortable as they could make him. Until her father was fully recovered, Nik advised against him navigating the stairs.

For now, the small room was Dill's domain. The bed was positioned so he could look out the window and see part of the pasture and the barn. Twice a day, Butch went in to visit him and challenge him to a game of checkers to alleviate Dill's boredom.

Delaney worried her father would notice the rounding bump at her midsection, but so far, he'd not paid her any mind. It was only a matter of time before she'd have to tell him the truth, but she kept putting it off. She still hadn't told him about Mac, either.

She'd all but given up on hearing from Klayne. The pain that pinched her heart each time she thought of him confirmed in her mind that something was wrong with him, something horrible that kept him from reaching out to her.

With no time to dwell on the morbid possibilities, she focused her attention on the unending work of running the ranch.

Her birthday arrived and, much to her surprise, Lina baked a chocolate cake and Butch made ice cream. Amy showed up and handed Delaney a gift in a fancy wrapped box.

"What's this, Amy? You already gave me a gift. I love the gloves," Delaney said, holding the box and looking at her friend.

"Your husband mailed this box to me back in April. He sent a note, pleading with me to keep it a secret and give it to you for your birthday," Amy said, tapping the box with her finger. "I'm dying to know what it is. Open it!"

Delaney carefully removed the paper, setting it aside since it was too pretty to tear. She lifted a note taped to tissue paper hiding the contents of the box and read it.

Happy Birthday, my darling wife!

I'm sorry I can't be there with you today to celebrate, but I hope you enjoy these gifts. The top one is just for you because I think you'll enjoy it, especially in your Eastern Oregon heat. The bottom gift is, in truth, more for me. I can't wait to see you wear it when I return home.

Love you always, Delaney.

Have a special day!

Your devoted husband,

Klayne

Tears filled her eyes but she blinked them away and folded back the tissue. Her fingers traced over a pale blue summer dress with dainty flowers in the print. Lifting it from the box, she held it out and grinned. The style would hide her expanding figure and still look fashionable.

Pleased with the dress, she passed it to Amy then looked back in the box, curious what else Klayne had sent. She started to pull out a filmy, silky bit of fabric then realized it was a daring peignoir set. Embarrassment burned her cheeks as she placed the lid back on the box and set it beneath her chair.

If Klayne returned home anytime soon, he'd be surprised to find he'd left a pregnant wife behind, one who would most certainly not wear something so seductive as the negligee set he'd sent. However, thoughts of him wanting to see her in it drew out her smile.

Altogether, it was a pleasant birthday, even with her husband missing, her brother in a Navy hospital, and her father recovering from his injuries.

⋆⋆★ *Chapter Eighteen* ★⋆⋆

One hot, sunny July day, Delaney had just left the bunkhouse after lunch and started toward the house to take a nap when Lina ran outside, calling for her to hurry inside to answer a telephone call.

Fearful of what might have happened now, Delaney raced inside and snatched up the receiver Lina had left sitting on the old wooden stool they kept by the phone.

"Hello?" Delaney answered, slightly breathless.

"Is this Delaney Danvers?" a male voice inquired, one she didn't recognize.

"It is." Apprehension slithered down her spine, making her shiver despite the heat of the day.

"Miss Danvers, this is John Phillips. Our son, Petey, is best friends with your nephew, Ryatt."

"Oh, hello, Mr. Phillips. It was so nice to see your family at Christmas. How is Lucy? I suppose you've welcomed that sweet little bundle of joy you were expecting in late spring by now. I'm sure congratulations are in order," Delaney said, wondering why in the world Carol's neighbor would be calling her.

"Lucy is well, as is our baby girl. Thank you for inquiring about them. But that's not why I'm calling," John said, clearing this throat. "I don't know how to tell you this, other than to just spit it out, Miss Danvers. Carol received word this morning that your brother passed away from the wounds he sustained at the Battle of Midway. She came right over here to our place to leave Ryatt so she could go into town and see about making arrangements to bring his body home for burial. Carol mentioned plans to call you once she had more details. On the way to town..." The man's voice caught and he paused for the length of several heartbeats before he cleared his throat again and continued. "Carol missed a curve on the way into town and crashed. I was the first to reach her. She took my hand and said it was an accident, that she didn't want to leave behind her baby, meaning Ryatt. She died a few minutes later."

"Oh," Delaney gasped, plopping onto the stool since her legs would no longer hold her. Lina scurried over, giving Delaney a concerned glance. "I... This is..." Delaney couldn't think, couldn't breathe. In one fell swoop, she'd lost two people who meant the world to her. And poor Ryatt. How would her nephew go on without his parents? "Is Ryatt still with you?"

"He is, Miss Danvers. We're happy to have him here as long as necessary, but if you could come right away, I think it might be a good thing. Ryatt is doing his best to put on a brave front, but the boy is just overwhelmed by all that's happened, and with good reason."

"I'll be there as soon as I can. Would you put Ryatt on the phone, please?" Delaney took a calming breath. She had no idea what to say to her nephew, but needed to assure him everything would be fine.

"I'd be happy to put him on the phone, but he finally fell asleep. I sure hate to wake him," John said.

"No, let him rest. Just tell him I love him and I'll be there as soon as I can." Delaney looked up at the ceiling as tears burned the backs of her eyes, hoping to keep them at bay. "Thank you for calling, Mr. Phillips. I know how difficult it must have been. We appreciate you taking care of Ryatt for us."

"It's our pleasure to care for the boy, for as long as you need. Safe travels, Miss Danvers. I'm so sorry to be the one to tell you about Carol and Mac. They were both fine, fine people and we'll greatly miss them. We'll see you soon."

Delaney hung up the phone and sat there, staring at the floor for several minutes. Her mind replayed happy moments from her childhood spent tagging along with her brother. She pictured the joy radiating from Carol and Mac on their wedding day and the pride that nearly popped the buttons right off her brother's shirt the day Ryatt was born.

Gone.

Her beloved brother and sister-in-law were both gone. Just like that.

She began to wonder what she'd done to deserve such an endless chain of trouble. First Klayne disappeared, then the armed forces took her ranch hands. An unexpected pregnancy, her father's accident, and news that Mac had been wounded just piled up one problem on top of another.

But hearing someone say two people she loved so dearly were gone was almost more than she could bear. How could Mac and Carol be dead?

She'd just received a chatty letter from Carol last week, talking about how much fun Ryatt was having that summer with Petey Phillips.

"Are you okay, Miss Dee?" Lina asked, placing a hand on Delaney's arm, drawing her from her reverie.

"Not exactly, Lina." Delaney stood and inhaled slowly, knowing what she needed to do, but dreading it. "Would you please call the depot and reserve a ticket for me on the next train to Portland?"

"Yes, ma'am." Lina picked up the telephone and placed the call.

Delaney squared her shoulders and walked down the hall to her father's room. She found him staring out the window, watching as Lottie rode Troy away from the barn to go check the fences in the west pasture.

Dill glanced at her then pointed out the window. "That girl has a way with horses. She puts me in mind of you, the way she handles them so effortlessly."

"Thanks, Dad." Delaney sat down on the edge of the bed and took her father's hand in hers. "Daddy, there's something I need to tell you."

His gaze met hers and awareness glittered in his eyes. "It's Mac, isn't it?"

Delaney nodded. "Carol just received word this morning that he's gone. He was injured at the Battle of Midway, but there was hope he'd recover."

Dill swiped a hand over his face, but before his emotions got the best of him, Delaney hurried to finish delivering the bad news.

"Dad, there's something else. Carol was in a car wreck this morning on the way into town to see about bringing his body home. She..." Delaney's voice cracked and tears rolled down her cheeks. "She didn't make it, Dad. The neighbor said she died shortly after he found her. Ryatt is with the Phillips family right now, but I need to go to him."

Unable to speak through the pain squeezing his throat, her father reached out and pulled Delaney into a hug. No longer able to contain her grief, she sobbed against him. She cried for the adored brother she'd never tease or laugh with again. She mourned the sister-in-law who had loved her as she was and encouraged her to be independent and strong. And she grieved for her nephew who would grow up without his two devoted, loving parents. Burdened with soul-deep sorrow, thoughts of Klayne trickled in, compounding the horrible, throbbing ache in her heart.

"Why do bad things keep happening, Dad?" Delaney asked, in a choppy breath.

"I don't know, Sis, but there's a reason for everything, even if we can't see it and don't understand it at the time." Dill patted her shoulder then pushed her back, wiping away her tears with his palms.

"I will never understand how any good could come from ripping Mac and Carol away from Ryatt, from us. They were such good people, Dad, full of laughter and kindness. Why do people like them get snatched from us while terrible people exist?"

"It's not for us to decide who lives and dies, honey. You know that. Don't let bitterness overtake your reason," Dill cautioned.

Delaney stood, clenching angry fists at her sides. "Like you haven't been consumed with bitterness since your accident? All you've done is gripe and complain and..." At the look on her father's face, she snapped her mouth closed. "I'm sorry, Dad. It's just this... I can't bear it. I can't bear to lose them both, especially with Klayne..."

"I know, Sis. I know. It's okay. Everything will be okay." Dill took a cleansing breath and reached for a handkerchief on the bedside table. He blew his nose, wiped away the tears he'd shed, and faced his daughter. "You need to get to Portland right away. Ryatt needs you now more than ever. Send one of the boys to find Duffy, and Lina out to get Butch. I'll talk to them while you go pack."

Delaney nodded and returned to the kitchen, asking Lina to get Butch and send Tommy to find Duffy. With heavy steps, she went upstairs, took a shower and washed her hair, then packed a suitcase. She attempted to dress in a lightweight summer suit she'd worn two summers ago on a trip she'd taken with Amy and three other girls to the coast.

The skirt was so tight, she couldn't get the top to button, so she fastened it with a safety pin and covered the waist with the blouse and the jacket.

After pinning on a hat, gathering a pair of gloves, and snapping her suitcase closed, she carried the case downstairs and left it at the door. She went back to see her father, kissed his cheek and told him she'd take care of everything.

"I'm sorry all the burdens are falling on your shoulders, Delaney. If I could lift one of them, I would."

"I know, Dad. I'll most likely be gone three or four days, depending on how long it takes to make arrangements for Carol's service." Delaney moved to the door and looked back at him. "If you think of it, have Lina, Louise, and Jilly clean one of the bedrooms for Ryatt."

Dill nodded. "I think we should put him in Mac's old room. The boy might feel closer to his folks that way."

The lump of emotion prevented her ability to speak, so Delaney hurried from the room and back to the kitchen. Duffy and Butch met her on the porch steps. By the look on her face, they both knew something was wrong.

"What is it, Girly?" Butch asked, settling a hand on her arm.

"Mac and Carol are both gone," she said, pushing the words past the enormous, jagged knife of pain that twisted and turned in her heart with each relaying of the words.

"Gone? You don't mean..." Butch looked at her incredulously. "What happened?"

"Mac died from wounds he received at the Battle of Midway. Carol found out this morning and was on her way to town to see to arrangements for his burial when she ran off the road and crashed into a tree. She died soon after."

"And the boy? Is Ryatt okay?" Butch asked, concerned.

"He's at a neighbor's house. I'm leaving right now to go there, but need a ride into Pendleton to the train depot.

"I'll take you, Dee," Duffy said, spinning around and hurrying over to the building where they parked the vehicles.

"Bring that boy home safely, Dee. We'll all help take care of him," Butch said, giving her a hug then carrying her suitcase out to the pickup Duffy drove up to the end of the yard.

"Thank you, Butch, and please keep an eye on Dad while I'm gone."

"I will, Girly. You can count on all of us," Butch said, setting her suitcase in the back then closing the door once she slid inside.

Delaney waved to him. The kids spilled out of the barn and buildings to wave goodbye.

Four days later, Delaney stood in the cemetery as cold rain drizzled from a sky the color of worn concrete. Ryatt leaned against her, soundlessly mourning his parents. She'd managed to arrange to have Carol buried beside her parents. Mac's body had not yet arrived, but would soon join his wife's in the tidy little cemetery.

Now, as her sister-in-law's body was laid to rest, Delaney wanted to shout that it wasn't fair, wasn't right, for a woman so kind and sweet and loving as Carol to have her life cut short. Especially when she left behind a son who needed his mother.

Battling her tears and her emotions, Delaney held them in check as the pastor concluded the service. She turned to those who had come to pay their respects, to mourn the passing of a dear woman, and offered them a gentle smile. "Thank you all for being here today. Ryatt and I appreciate your presence and prayers more than you can know."

With a nod to the crowd, she ushered Ryatt toward the car she'd hired to take them to the depot to catch the afternoon train back to Pendleton.

Ryatt's little red-haired friend Petey followed. The boy flung his arms around her nephew, giving him a tight hug. From the moment she'd arrived at the Phillips' home, Petey had done his best to draw Ryatt out of the hollow shell he'd climbed into. However, his efforts were to no avail.

Ryatt had run to Delaney, clinging to her as he cried. In the days she'd been there, he'd hardly said anything, hardly eaten anything, so mired in his grief, he barely functioned.

Even now, as Petey promised to never forget him and to always be his best friend, Ryatt gave the boy a half-hearted hug.

Delaney bent over and hugged the feisty little rascal. She'd known Petey Phillips since he was just a tiny thing, and the boy was full of spunk. "Thank you for being such a good friend to Ryatt, Petey. You are always welcome to visit him at the ranch. Don't forget that."

"I won't." Petey's lower lip quivered as Delaney gave him a parting hug then nudged Ryatt, numb and silent, into the car. Before they pulled away, Ryatt turned and lifted his hand, pressing it against the glass in a final farewell to his best friend.

On the long train ride home, Delaney thought about the whirlwind of the last few days. She'd packed up everything of Ryatt's and things belonging to Carol and Mac she thought he might want, either now or someday in the future. Arrangements were made to ship it all to the ranch.

John and Lucy Phillips had been such a help to her, offering to do anything they could to assist her. Lucy had taken her aside and asked Delaney when she was due. Surprised the woman had seen past her efforts to hide her pregnancy, Delaney told her the truth about Klayne and the baby. Lucy gave her a hug and invited her to write if she needed any help or advice in the coming months.

Relieved to have someone she could confide in, Delaney thanked her and returned her focus to packing up what had been her brother's entire life into boxes and shipping crates.

With John's help, she'd contacted a realtor about selling the farm, and discussed the possibility of renting it until a buyer was located. For the remainder of the summer and through the harvest, the man Mac had hired to oversee it would continue, reporting to Delaney.

As Ryatt sagged against her, succumbing to his exhaustion, she settled a hand around the boy, drawing him against her. She wished she could take away his pain, make everything happy and carefree for him again, but it wasn't to be. Delaney hated the war, hated that it had robbed her of Mac and Carol, leaving her nephew orphaned. The thought of an orphan brought Klayne to mind. The familiar ache pushed the air from her lungs, making her blink to hold her tears at bay.

She placed her hand to the slight mound of her stomach and felt the baby kick. The days were limited that she could keep hiding her condition from her father and the others. Instead of being a coward, she should have told them the truth in the first place. Now, she tried to think of the best way to tell them she was expecting Klayne's baby.

Whether it was from the heat beating down on the train, the stuffy atmosphere inside the car, the grief dragging her down, or the weariness of body and mind that had plagued her for weeks, Delaney suddenly felt ill. With no time to gently set Ryatt aside, she leaped to her feet and rushed toward the restroom.

The remainder of the trip, she ran back and forth to the restroom, further distressing Ryatt.

An hour from Pendleton, he threw himself against her, holding her so tight, she thought he might crack a rib. He turned his face up to her, eyes glistening with tears, and pleaded in a raspy voice. "Don't die, Aunt Dee! I need you!"

"Oh, baby," Delaney said, wrapping both arms around him and rocking him from side to side. "I'm not going to die, Ry. I promise. I'm just a little under the weather, that's all. Don't worry, sweetie. We'll be home soon."

"I want to go back to my home. I want Mom and Dad to be there," Ryatt sobbed.

Delaney did her best to soothe him, ignoring her own discomforts as they neared Pendleton. She'd wired ahead to let Duffy know when to meet the train. As soon as they stepped down to the platform, he was there, hat in hand as he greeted them.

Ryatt remained silent, clinging to her hand as Duffy gathered their bags and led the way to the pickup.

"Would you like to stop and get an ice cream or a soda pop?" Delaney asked Ryatt. The boy shook his head and leaned against her, as though he lacked the will and strength to stand on his own.

At the ranch, Delaney slid out of the pickup and reached in for Ryatt, but Duffy shook his head. "I'll get him, Dee."

When he started to lift Ryatt, the boy bucked against him and scrambled out the door after his aunt, eyes wide with terror at the thought of being separated from her.

Delaney settled a hand on her nephew's back and guided him up the steps and inside the house. After she removed her hat and gloves, she led Ryatt down the hall to her father's room. "We're back, Dad," Delaney said, stepping inside the improvised bedroom.

"I'm mighty glad to see you both," Dill said, smiling at Ryatt and patting a spot on the mattress. "Come sit over here, Ry, and tell Grandpa all about your trip."

Ryatt continued to linger at the door with Delaney, as though he couldn't bear to let her go for even a minute.

"It's okay, Ry. You go ahead and sit with Grandpa while I go change my clothes." Delaney gave him a little push forward. The boy stepped across the room, but turned back to her with a look that made her think of a beaten dog she'd once seen pawing through garbage in town.

Her heart constricted with pain and she backed out of the room. Upstairs, she changed her clothes, then went to the bathroom and splashed her face with cool water. Glad her sick spell had passed, she studied her face in the mirror. Twin splotches of bright red looked like badly applied rouge against the pale hue of her face. Dark circles attested to her lack of sleep while sorrow haunted the depths of her eyes.

What had happened to the smiling, happy girl who hadn't a care in the world?

Everything in her world had tilted off kilter the day she met Klayne Campbell. Despite the truth, despite the sensible part of her brain yelling at her to be reasonable, she shifted every single thing that had gone wrong in the past six months onto his shoulders. Regardless of where he was or if he'd ever return, his shoulders were broad enough to bear the blame.

****★ *Chapter Nineteen* ★***

Klayne had no idea how or where they'd come from, but one of the other plane crews arrived at the hospital. He almost cried when he recognized the doctor who'd served as a gunner so he could come along on the mission.

"You boys are sure a sight for sore eyes," he said, grinning as the five men crowded around the beds where he and the others convalesced. Not a one of them was injured, although they all looked dirty and tired.

Try as he might, Klayne hadn't been able to stand upright and he knew it had nothing to do with his broken leg or arm. The Chinese doctor assured him he'd be fine, but Klayne was starting to doubt the man's cheerful assurance. Although the Chinese medical staff did their best, Klayne was relieved to see Doc. Maybe now, he'd find out what was really wrong and begin to heal.

While the pilot and crew shared their harrowing story of crashing in the water and barely escaping a Japanese patrol, Doc disappeared. A short while later, he returned after he'd bathed, shaved, and changed into clean clothes.

Unhurriedly, he examined each member of Klayne's crew, even studying the bump on the gunner's head and declaring him fine.

Doc spent the most time with the pilot, who was clearly in distress from his leg wound. When he came back around to Klayne, the man looked at his arm and leg again then shined a light in Klayne's foggy eye. After he removed a bandage around Klayne's head, applied medicine to the wound, and rebandaged it, he gave him a studying glance.

"Can you give it to me straight, Doc?" he asked, wanting to know the prognosis, but at the same time hesitant to hear the truth.

The doctor carefully sat on the edge of Klayne's bed. "The breaks in your arm and leg were clean. They did a good job setting them, and you should heal fine. I'd prefer you have them in a cast, but this is better than nothing." Doc touched the edge of the sling holding Klayne's arm immobile. "I think the reason you can't stand up straight is that you strained your back when you shot out of the plane into the water. Basically, you were like a cannonball fired out of the nose of the plane as it crashed. With time and plenty of rest, that problem should resolve itself, but you'll have to be patient. I can't promise you won't have pain in it from time to time in the years to come, but I think it's more likely you won't notice issues."

Klayne nodded then asked the question that had really been bothering him. "What about my eye, Doc. They'll boot me out if I can't do my job and being able to see is definitely a big part of it. That's my sighting eye."

Doc rested his elbows on his knees and gave Klayne a long look. "The cut down your face went right over your eye, Klayne. It damaged the cornea. Your vision may improve as the scratches heal. However, one of them is very deep and you'll most likely always have blurry vision because of it."

Klayne didn't know which bit of news to digest first, the fact he had cuts on his face, or the fact he'd never see properly out of the eye again. His career with the military was effectively over. A bombardier who couldn't sight was useless.

"What cuts on my face?" he finally asked, reaching up and, for the first time noticing a bandage wrapped around his head. He could feel scabs from his eyebrow all the way down to his jaw.

Doc pulled his hand away and shook his head. "You need to leave those alone and let them heal. It looks as though the doctor here gave them a good cleansing. I don't see any signs of infection, which is a blessing, all things considered."

"I haven't looked at my face since the morning we left the ship." Klayne started to reach up again, but dropped his hand to his lap. "Can I look in a mirror, Doc?"

The doctor stood and hesitated by the side of Klayne's bed. "Let's wait a few days, Klayne. There's no rush."

"Please, Doc? I need to see." Klayne felt an almost desperate urgency to see what had happened to his face. It's not that he was vain, but he knew he was good-looking, knew Delaney found him inordinately attractive. What if she couldn't stand to look at him? What if he was grotesquely disfigured? "Please?"

The doctor motioned to a nearby nurse who produced a small mirror. Klayne couldn't see his whole face in it, even holding it out away from him, but what he did see caused him to suck in a gulp. He had no idea what was behind the bandage wrapped around his forehead, but from his eyebrow all the way down to his jaw a series of jagged, angry scabs gave testament to his wounds. Some cuts were deep, others shallow, one even dipped across his eyelid. Bruises covered both eyes, and a chunk of his lip was missing from one corner. He looked like some sort of macabre madman.

How had he not even noticed the wounds to his face? He supposed the pain from his broken limbs and the strain on his back made him oblivious to the other injuries.

Mindful of the rising look of disgust on Klayne's face, Doc took the mirror away and handed it back to a nurse. "It will all heal, Klayne. That little spot on your lip will fill in. You won't even notice it soon. The scabs will give way to scars that will heal. Most of them aren't deep and may not even leave a scar behind. Keep positive and focus on healing."

Klayne nodded, although all he could think about at the moment was what Delaney would say when she saw him again. In the course of a few days, he felt like he'd aged thirty years. What if he could never stand up straight again. What if the scars on his face looked as bad as the scab-covered wounds? What if he went completely blind in that eye? What if...

"Just stop it," he muttered to himself and took a calming breath. Until his wounds healed and he could return to Delaney a whole man, he wouldn't return at all. And if that day never came, she could just think he'd died in the raid, one more casualty of the war.

The following day, the gunner from Klayne's bunch and the other crew with the exception of the doctor, left the hospital, promising to let others know they had survived. They planned to make their way to a designated rendezvous area where they could get on a plane bound for home.

Klayne didn't look in another mirror during the remainder of the time he spent at the small hospital. The injured men of his crew had been there nearly three weeks when word came that Japanese were approaching the area. Early the next morning, Klayne and the other men were loaded onto sedan chairs and carried out of the city. Doc fussed over the pilot who was still recovering from surgery on his leg.

A full month had passed since the Tokyo raid. As Klayne rode uncomfortably in the chair, he noticed the wild, beautiful land in which they traveled. Sometimes there were paths, other times nothing but tangled jungle, but onward they went. They traveled through villages where they were greeted warmly, given strange and foreign food, and offered small gifts. Finally, they reached a village that had an old bus. The men were loaded in it and they continued on their journey.

Despite their shouts of terror, the driver seemed only interested in honking his horn and careening around corners and winding paths as fast as the old bus could rumble. The airport they eventually reached had been blown up by the Japanese, as was the next airport they journeyed to. With each passing mile, hope of getting out of China alive diminished. The doctor did find a supply of iodine, though, and dabbed the wounded men from head to toe, covering every scratch, bite, sore, and cut with it.

Klayne was surprised the next morning when they went out to load onto the bus and discovered a newer model Ford station wagon waiting instead. After the car took them as far as a water crossing, they boarded a ferry and drifted down a stream, making their way to another airport that had also been destroyed. After two more days of travel, the men made it to a train station. They boarded the train and continued their travels. The men arrived at a hostel where word was relayed to military forces to send a plane for them. Several days passed, each one bringing a greater sense of desperation to escape China before the Japanese captured them or they died from their wounds.

Finally, a plane arrived for them. When it did, Klayne's crew reunited with three other men from the raid who had flown in to rescue them.

The emotional reunion gave way to the men sharing what they knew about each crew, including the details that two of the sixteen crews had been taken prisoner by the Japanese. As far as the men knew, not a single plane had survived, all crashing in the ocean or in China.

Klayne's heart sank at this news, imagining the horrors visited upon the men who had been captured, especially if the Japanese discovered they had been the raiders who dropped the bombs on Tokyo and the surrounding cities.

On the fifth day of June, Klayne grew lightheaded as they flew over the hump of the

Himalayas and landed in one of the new American bases in India.

He'd just limped his way to a room for the night and settled onto the bed when a noise in the hall drew his interest.

All of the sudden his door burst open and Bob strolled in, wearing a broad smile. "Klayne, old man, the lengths you'll go to in order to get out of work are impressive!"

Klayne grinned and reached out a hand to his friend. Bob shook it, then gave him a bear hug. "What are you doing here, Bob? I figured you'd be back in the States."

"No. I've been working around here, bombing the Japanese transports when they come over." Bob took a step back and studied Klayne. "It's a good thing you're married. Girls are going to go wild for those rugged scars on your face. Makes you seem even more dangerous and untamed."

Klayne snorted in disbelief. "I look like some sort of crazed ghoul, but I don't want to talk about that. Have you heard from Norene and the girls?"

Bob nodded and patted his pocket. "Just got a letter today. They're doing great. Norene decided to stay with her mother for now, since I have no idea when I'll be back. The girls enjoy being around their grandma, so it's a good situation for everyone." Bob gave him a knowing look. "What about you? Have you written to Delaney and let her know you're okay?"

"No. I don't want her to know anything until I'm well. She's better off without me, particularly like this," Klayne said with disgust. "I'd be a burden to her, not a help. And the last thing she needs is one more thing to take care of on the ranch. I figure by now, she's probably lost most of her help to either the draft or enlistment."

"All the more reason for you to write to her. The poor girl is probably sick with worry, Klayne. It's only right to let her know you made it through and are heading home."

Mindful that Bob would only argue with him, Klayne changed the subject. The two men talked for several hours until Klayne could no longer keep his eyes open.

"Rest well, old man. I'll stop by to see you in the morning." Bob smiled as he walked out of Klayne's room.

The next morning, Bob ate breakfast with him then had to hurry to leave for his next mission. Before he left, he handed Klayne a letter. "If something happens to me, make sure Norene gets that. I have to assume the last one I wrote is probably at the bottom of the China Sea."

"Yep, but you know you're going to make it home to your girls so I won't have to deliver this," Klayne said, tucking the letter into his meager belongings. He'd collected a few things since the crash, gifts from villagers, including a tea set from a couple who somehow finagled out of him the truth about his married state. They insisted he take the tea set as a gift to his wife.

"Take care of yourself, Klayne, and tell Delaney not to let you off easy when you do make it home. When this war is over, I want all of us to get together. Maybe take a trip to the Oregon coast."

"I'd like that, Bob. You know where to find me. Be safe, my friend." Klayne gave Bob a warm handshake then patted his arm, hoping the man knew how much he valued his friendship.

Bob nodded, offering an unspoken confirmation that he understood then walked out the door.

Klayne's thoughts dwelled on Delaney after Bob departed. He hadn't been much of a husband to her in the months they'd been married. Bob was right. He had a lot of making up to do, when and if he ever made it home to her.

He continued to think about making amends as he flew from India to Baghdad, on to Cairo, Nigeria, Trinidad, and then Puerto Rico before landing in Washington D.C.

The injured men were taken directly to a military hospital. Klayne's arm and leg were properly reset and cast. The bandage on his head was removed and the wound treated, but he tamped down his urge to look in a mirror.

The colonel, now a general, who led their raid appeared and shook their hands, thanking them for a job well done and for their sacrifices.

For reasons Klayne couldn't explain, he felt antsy to be closer to Pendleton. Now that he was back on American soil, he wanted to go home. Even if he wasn't ready to face Delaney, he wanted to be nearer to her than clear across the country.

To his knowledge, no one, with the exception of Bob and the officer who'd filed his paperwork including her as a beneficiary, knew he'd married. He planned to keep it that way.

Near the end of June, the general decorated twenty-five of the soldiers who'd gone on the raid in a ceremony, awarded each one of them a Distinguished Flying Cross "in recognition of heroism and extraordinary achievement while participating in the Raid on Tokyo."

A week and a half later, the general came to the hospital and presented awards to those there. In spite of the fact some of the men were in casts and wearing pajamas, he proudly pinned on their medals. The Chinese government also sent awards to them through the military attaché at the Chinese Embassy in Washington.

Klayne didn't feel deserving of any awards or honor. He'd merely been doing his job. On top of that, they'd crashed their plane and their presence in China on their flight to escape had resulted in Japanese retaliation in nearly every village they'd visited.

The deaths of all those innocent people hung heavily on Klayne's heart.

Not long after that, Klayne and the rest of the men received promotions. He was pleased to move into the rank of Master Sergeant. He spoke at length with the general about his inability to continue working as a bombardier due to the problem with his vision which, as of yet, showed no signs of improvement.

"General, I know I've asked before, but do you think I could transfer to a hospital closer to home? Please?" Klayne pleaded with the general one afternoon when he stopped by to see how they all were recuperating.

"What's at home you're so eager to get back to, Sergeant?" the general asked, giving him an interested look.

"Well, it's just that…" Klayne looked around to make sure no one was listening. "I left a wife in Pendleton and I'd sure like to be closer to her."

"I see. How long have you been married?"

Klayne forced himself to hold the general's penetrating gaze. "We married in early February, sir."

The general couldn't hide his surprised look, but quickly replaced it with a passive expression. "I see," he repeated, then left.

The next morning, Klayne had just eaten breakfast when he received word he was being transferred that afternoon to a veteran's hospital in Portland.

With a shout of glee, he packed his few belongings and eagerly made the long, painful journey across the country.

He settled into the hospital with minimal difficulty, fueled by the thought he was at least in the same state as Delaney.

One feisty little nurse, who looked more like a pinup girl than someone trained in a medical profession, pushed him to the limits of his physical endurance. He heard other men griping about Nurse Billie being a hard taskmaster, but she got results.

Results were what he needed to make it back to his wife.

*⋆⋆★ *Chapter Twenty* ★⋆⋆*

Delaney wiped the sweat from her brow with the arm of her cotton shirt and settled the old dirt-encrusted hat back on her head. She looked ahead as the self-propelled combine she drove cut the golden sheaves of wheat, sucked it in, and separated the kernels of grain from the chaff.

Her back ached so badly, she could hardly stand it, but she ignored the pain and focused on the job at hand. By now, there was no hiding her pregnancy. She'd explained to all the young people in her employ that her husband had gone on a raid over Japan and disappeared. After the girls hugged her and dabbed at tears of sympathy, the boys had called Klayne a hero. They all wanted to see the photos and news clippings she had of him.

In spite of her heart and head telling her she was being ridiculous, she couldn't help but feel a hot, boiling anger every time she thought of him. There were days she wished she'd never gone to that New Year's Eve party, never met Klayne. Other days, her heart swelled with gratitude that she'd married him, loved him, for even such a short time. Because if nothing else came out of their very brief union, she would cherish the baby he'd given her.

The baby was the only bright spot Delaney could find some days. The previous week, the ranch had suffered another blow when they received word Yank, one of their favorite cowboys, had gone missing and was assumed dead during the Battle of Guadalcanal.

The men and Delaney mourned the news about Yank and prayed for the safety of their former ranch hands.

Uncertain how much more death, injury, or devastation she could take, Delaney tried to bury herself in work. Butch and Duffy had both thrown fits when she informed them she planned to drive one of the combines during their wheat harvest.

"You can't drive any equipment in your condition, Girly!" Butch had shouted.

Delaney had scowled at him and pulled on her gloves. "I can and I will, and there isn't a single person on this ranch who is going to stop me!"

Although Duffy and Butch continued to argue against her active participation in the wheat harvest, Delaney couldn't see how riding on a tractor seat would cause any harm to the baby. Just to help the men rest easier, she even asked Doctor Nash for permission and grudgingly received it.

As she finished a row of wheat and turned the combine to make another swath through the field, she glanced overhead. The September sunshine was as hot as if it were mid-July, beating down with relentless vigor. She would have wished for a breeze or clouds, but the sunny day was perfect for bringing in the wheat. If the weather held, they only had two more days before they'd be finished cutting almost four thousand acres of wheat.

Delaney was glad she'd talked her dad into buying three self-propelled combines the previous year. The machines made it possible for one person to cut a little more than fifty acres in a day. With three of them going, along with their old harvesters, they averaged almost five hundred acres of wheat a day.

After the days of working in the harvest, Delaney itched constantly from all the chaff. The sun had toasted her skin a deep golden brown from hours spent working outside. Her feet had swollen so much, she'd resorted to wearing an old pair of Butch's boots. Each movement she made of her heavy body left her tired. So very tired.

Perhaps once they finished the wheat harvest, she'd spend a day or two doing nothing but resting. Delaney couldn't even recall the last time she'd sat down and read a book for pleasure.

She'd read plenty this past summer, but it was mostly about caring for bees, equipment manuals, and scanning newspaper and magazine articles for any news that might mention her husband.

In the evenings, when she was so sleepy her eyes would barely stay open, she'd prop herself up in bed and read about helping a child through mourning. She had no idea what to do with her nephew beyond love him. The boy spent the first few weeks at the ranch withdrawn and glassy-eyed. He barely spoke, trudging through each day in a grief-induced fog.

Dill had tried to help Ryatt, having the boy spend time with him, telling his grandson stories and showing him photo albums. The pictures of his parents seemed to upset him more instead of alleviating his problems. Uncertain what else to do, Delaney finally led Ryatt outside and asked Lottie to take him for a ride.

From that moment on, Ryatt started to improve. He loved being around the horses, loved riding them, so Delaney let him ride every day. Gradually, Ryatt began to rejoin the land of the living, smiling and laughing again. The day he sat down after supper and replied to his friend Petey's numerous letters, Delaney wanted to cheer in triumph.

Now, Ryatt rode in a truck with Tommy as the young man drove wheat into town. There, it was weighed, graded, and added to the stores of wheat that would ship via railcar to a port in Portland before being loaded onto a ship. Ryatt's job was to help clean the grain out of the truck bed and make sure no grain spilled from the truck as they bumped across the field. Like a happy chipmunk, he chattered nonstop.

Delaney waved at him as she reached the end of the row and turned around before stopping. Golden grains of wheat shot into the back of Tommy's truck after he parked next to the combine. Ryatt jumped out and scrambled onto the combine, bringing Delaney a welcome treat.

"Look, Aunt Dee!" Ryatt said, handing her a bottle of Coca-Cola that hadn't yet grown warm. "Tommy and I got you a pop."

"Thank you, Ry," Delaney said, taking the glass bottle from her nephew and prying off the cap. She took a long drink then grinned at him. "Boy, that hit the spot. How did you two know I was dying of thirst?"

Ryatt grinned. "Tommy said you have one of the hottest, dirtiest jobs. I used my own nickel and everything!"

"You did?" Delaney would have reached out and mussed the boy's hair, but she didn't want to embarrass him in front of Tommy. For whatever reason, Ryatt looked up to the young man and often tried to emulate his actions. It was a good thing Tommy was a dependable, upright teen.

"Guess what else?" Ryatt asked, leaning against her as they watched grain fill the truck in a steady golden stream.

"I'll never guess so I suppose you'll have to tell me." Delaney took another swig of the cold drink, relishing the bubbly liquid gliding down her parched throat.

"Grandpa is sitting on the porch!" Ryatt excitedly wiggled beside her.

She placed a hand around his shoulders to make sure he didn't bump into something he shouldn't or fall into the front feeder. "How did he get there?" she asked, pleased her father was outside. The doctor had encouraged him to start walking with the help of crutches, but moving was painful for Dill and a very slow process that frustrated him.

"Lina said he walked out there all by himself. Ain't it swell, Aunt Dee?"

"It is swell, sweetheart." Delaney grinned at the boy and couldn't resist gently tugging down the brim of the old cowboy hat he wore that had once belonged to his father. "You know what else is swell?"

"No, what?" Ryatt pushed his hat back up, grinning at his aunt.

"You." Delaney wrapped him in a hug and kissed his dirty cheek, then tickled him, making him squirm and giggle. As she held onto him, the baby began kicking and Ryatt stilled, his eyes dropping to her overall-covered belly.

"She likes to hear me," he said, placing a hand on his aunt's rounded stomach. He leaned down and raised his voice. "Hi, baby! It's Ryatt. I can't wait to meet you. My friend Petey has a baby named Alice, but we call her The Princess. I bet you'll be a princess, too."

The baby kicked in response and Ryatt giggled again. "Gee, Aunt Dee, she's going to be a real royal-stepper. Just like you."

Delaney hugged the boy again then drank all but one gulp of the soda. She handed the bottle to him with a wink. "Think you can finish that for me?"

"You betcha I can!" Ryatt tipped back the bottle and drank the rest, then hopped down and climbed back in the truck. "See you at supper, Aunt Dee."

"Yep. I'll see you then, Ry. Keep Tommy out of trouble this afternoon."

Tommy grinned and rolled his eyes at Delaney as he put the truck in gear and pulled away from the combine.

Delaney made two more rounds through the field before the baby pressing on her bladder forced her to leave her work. Fortunately, they were in a field close to the house, so she went there. While she was in the bathroom, she took time to splash her face with cool water, comb the snarls out of her hair and braid it again. She brushed her teeth to dislodge the taste of dust and wheat chaff.

In the kitchen, Lina handed her a glass of water with a few pieces of ice floating in it along with two warm-from-the-oven chocolate drop cookies. Delaney drank the water and hurriedly ate the cookies.

"What would I do without your help, Lina?" Delaney asked, giving the girl's shoulders a squeeze as she made her way toward the door.

"Have a dirty house, filthy clothes, and no one to keep an eye on Dill?" Lina giggled. "Keeping your dad out of trouble is a full time occupation."

Delaney laughed. "It certainly is."

Lina, who had been so bashful those first few days at the ranch, soon relaxed and was as quick to tease and laugh as any of the other young people. She and Dill got along famously, a fact that pleased Delaney to no end. She had no idea what she'd do when school started again the following week. A few of the kids promised they could help on the weekends, but Delaney knew they'd be busy with school and other responsibilities. She'd keep them working as long as they wanted to come to the ranch, but the days of having extra hired hands were limited.

Musing over what she'd do without her kids, she thought of the young people who'd labored so hard for her over the summer months. Every single one of them had given their best to the job, done more than they'd been asked, and lifted her spirits during what had to be the worst summer of her entire life.

Delaney returned to the combine and climbed back on the machine. Each time she climbed up, she was sure she wouldn't make it with the weight of the baby throwing her off balance, but miraculously she pulled herself up and settled onto the seat.

An hour later, she and the others working the field finished and moved on to the next one. Butch brought out jugs of icy cold tea and a platter of doughnuts dusted with some of their precious supply of sugar.

Too tired to climb down from the combine again, Delaney had Ryatt bring her a doughnut and glass of tea. He sat beside her as they enjoyed the treat then he scampered off to get in the truck with Tommy as work resumed.

They were making a final pass before supper when Delaney looked toward the end of the field and saw a soldier standing there, leaning heavily on a cane.

Unable to catch her breath or her thoughts, Delaney finished her row and shut off the machine, her gaze riveted to the man as he limped toward her on the uneven ground. The buttons on his uniform gleamed in the bright afternoon sunlight. In spite of his obvious injury, he kept his posture formal and stiff, as though he was afraid of the reception he'd receive.

Her heart screamed at her to run to her husband while her head debated if it was really him. Convinced her mind played tricks on her, she hesitated to believe Klayne had finally come home.

Clumsily, she climbed off the combine and started his direction. The brim of his hat cast his face into a shadow, hiding his features, but she knew it was her long lost husband.

A few feet of distance separated them as they sized each other up, not having set eyes on one another for more than seven months. Klayne was much thinner than she remembered, although he still appeared strong with broad shoulders that could carry all the heavily burdened weight in her world. Almost shyly, he tipped his head back until she could see beneath the brim.

She sucked in a gasp. Whatever happened to Klayne hadn't left him unscathed. A deep, jagged scar ran from his left eyebrow across his eyelid and continued along his cheek right down to his jaw. Smaller, lighter scars marked where wounds had covered that side of his face.

Without thought to her actions, she stepped forward and swept the hat from his head, taking in the angry, red scar running parallel to his hairline. Someone or something had attempted to scalp him. Thank goodness, the effort had failed, because his brown hair shone in tempting waves in the sunlight.

Of its own volition, her hand traced the scars with a light touch, wishing she could make them vanish, not because of how they looked, but because of the pain they must have brought him.

"Klayne…" Emotion swelled in her throat and obliterated her ability to speak. Anger, relief, elation, dismay, joy, and despair warred within her at the sight of him.

His scent penetrated the smells of dust, sweat, and wheat around her. She breathed deeply of his familiar, masculine fragrance, wanting to wrap it around her like a barrier against the world.

She gazed up at him, forced herself to look into his eyes, and noticed the scar across his left eye. It marred that piercing blue orb that had first captured her attention. Relief filled her when she glanced at his right eye and found it as perfect as ever. Wariness battled with anticipation in the depths, as though he waited for her to welcome him home, grant her approval for his presence.

Shocked by his sudden appearance and the wounds he'd sustained, she took a step back, gaping at him. His uneven gait and the cane in his hand made it clear his leg had been injured. He held his left arm stiffly, as though it ached.

Despite the scars on his face, Klayne was far more handsome than she remembered. Rather than detract from his good looks, the scars gave him a dangerous, incredibly rugged appearance. The girls had been daffy for him before, but she had no doubt they'd find him even more attractive now.

What would a man like him want with a puffed up, pregnant wife who could barely waddle? Hot, tired, and filthy, Delaney knew she smelled like hard work mingled with a bit of despair.

Months had passed since the last time she felt pretty. Between her expanding waistline and the unending list of work on the ranch, she'd given up looking feminine. The only time she fixed her hair or put on a dress was for church, and she'd even stopped attending it regularly.

Additionally, she'd lost control of her emotions weeks ago. Tears sprang up unbidden over the silliest things and lingered ever so close to the surface.

Awkward and bloated, she wanted to duck her head and hide from this gorgeous man who'd broken her heart with his silence even more so than his absence.

For months, she'd done her best to believe he was alive, to dream of the day he'd return to her, open his arms, and profess his undying devotion.

Yet, now that he was here, fury surged through her for all the days and nights of torment she'd endured, imagining hundreds of horrible things that might have happened to him. He'd left her, all alone, to deal with the loss of her ranch hands, the injury of her father, the death of her brother and sister-in-law, and a completely unexpected pregnancy. She'd been the one who'd had to shoulder the weight of too many responsibilities and burdens, not him.

Unable to hold onto the thin thread of reason binding her to the last bit of self-control she possessed, she reached up and slapped Klayne across the face so hard, his head snapped back.

Stunned by what she'd done, a torrent of guilt and anguish flooded over her. If Klayne had been reluctant to reach out to her before, he certainly wouldn't want her now.

Tears burst from her and she raced toward the house, or at least as best as she could holding her big belly and wearing Butch's clodhopper boots.

So much for giving Klayne a warm welcome home.

★ *Chapter Twenty-One* ★

Klayne arrived in Pendleton, more uncertain about seeing Delaney with every second that ticked by. When he inquired at the depot office about getting a ride out to the ranch, an older gentleman volunteered to drive him, since he lived near Sage Hills Ranch.

As the man pulled up the lane, Klayne admired the harvested wheat fields, the cattle in the distance, and the big barn standing out against the deep blue of the sky.

The man stopped at the end of the walk in front of the house and grinned at Klayne. "Here you are."

Klayne stared at the house as he answered. "I'm obliged for the ride, Mr. McBride."

"My pleasure, Sergeant," the man said, touching the brim of his hat. "Thank you for your service to our country, young man."

Klayne nodded and slid out of the car then took his suitcase and bag from the backseat. He waved once as the neighbor left then turned to stare at the buttery-yellow farmhouse. It was as wonderful as he remembered, not just a vision from a dream. Flowers bloomed in pots along the porch and in beds surrounding the house. Someone had recently mowed the lawn and not a weed was in sight.

Unlike before when he felt like an outsider, an interloper on the ranch, he now had a reason and a right to be there. To make it his home. Well, he would if the woman he loved beyond reason still wanted him.

And that was a very big if.

Fear made his legs rubbery as he walked up the porch steps, and set down his suitcase and bag. Klayne knocked on the door and waited. He knocked a second time and the door swung open. A young, shy girl wearing a calico apron glanced up at him.

"Hello," she said, not quite meeting his gaze which was fine with him.

"Is Delaney Danvers here?"

"No, sir. She's out in the wheat field. You can find her on the combine, but they'll be in for supper soon." The girl flushed a deep shade of red but pointed to a distant wheat field where Klayne could see equipment stirring up a golden haze of dust. "Are you Sergeant Campbell?"

Klayne turned his attention back to the girl standing in the doorway. He wondered when and where Delaney had hired her. She looked too young to be out of school. "I am. If no one minds, I'll walk out to see her," he said.

The girl shrugged although she couldn't help observing his every move as he left his suitcase and bag at the door then limped out to the field.

Years had passed since he'd seen wheat harvested. He stood at the edge of the field and watched his wife drive a combine. Her hair was in a dusty braid, trailing over one shoulder. She wore a cotton shirt and a pair of overalls that looked too big for her slender frame.

Klayne needed a minute to gather his composure before he approached her. When he did, he wanted to drop the cane in his hand, wrap her in his arms, and lose himself in her love.

Delaney was prettier than he remembered. Even through the dust streaking her cheeks, she appeared beautiful. In spite of the scents that attested to the hard work she'd done that day, he caught a hint of her, the fragrance that was all Delaney. It had eased his darkest moments and filled his dreams when he had nothing but pain for company.

For a moment, he thought she was happy to see him. Her hand had brushed so tenderly over the scars on his face. Then she'd slapped him so hard he bit his tongue. Before he could speak or reach out to her, she burst into tears and ran off.

Klayne stood perfectly still, watching his wife run away. His very pregnant wife. The shock of seeing her quadrupled the second he realized she was expecting a baby.

For a brief moment, he questioned if she'd been faithful to him. After all, they'd been married less than twenty-four hours before he left town. Had Delaney taken up with someone else in his absence? Had she allowed another man to fill the empty place he left behind in her arms and bed?

Without even asking, he knew the answer. Not a single reason existed to demand who she'd been with or what had happened because he knew all too well who'd left her with child and vanished from her life.

The blame rested solely on his shoulders.

Assailed with guilt over what he'd done — marrying her, loving her, and leaving her — Klayne thought about going back to Pendleton without facing her.

He'd had such wonderful dreams of Delaney running to him when he returned to the ranch. He pictured her rushing to him, arms open wide, declaring her unending love.

Instead, she'd slapped his face and scurried off, but not before he read the emotion on her face as plainly as if she'd written it in big block letters for all to see. Of course, she'd been surprised to see him, but that gave way to pleasure, then shock, as she took in his scars. Pity might have flashed across her face, but first her legendary temper got the best of her. The explosion of tears accompanying her look of anguish and guilt was unexpected, though.

The realistic part of his brain that warned him he'd have to work to win Delaney's heart a second time wasn't a bit astonished by the slap she'd delivered. Klayne deserved it and a lot more. Essentially, he'd abandoned her since February. He could have written her from China. He could have mailed her dozens of letters in the past few months while he recuperated in Portland.

But he hadn't.

Until he could walk up to her and take her in his arms, he hadn't wanted her to know where he was or what he was doing. He didn't want her to think of him as an invalid who'd had to spend months dependent on others to care for his every need. Not until he could stand on his own two feet did he give any thought to letting her know his whereabouts. Even then, rather than telling her he was in Portland at the hospital, he kept quiet. Every day that he regained strength and healed from his wounds he counted as one day closer to coming home to his wife.

Now, she'd been the one to run away from him.

He couldn't help but question if she'd been repulsed by the scars on his face. The entire time he was in the hospital, he refused to look in a mirror. Fear of his monstrous appearance held him back. He refused to get a haircut or shave, using the tenderness of the scars as an excuse to hide behind a growth of bushy hair.

Nurse Billie Brighton discovered he had a wife one day when she caught him sniffing Delaney's handkerchief. The fragrance had long since disappeared, but he liked to pretend it still held a faint hint of her scent.

The nurse took him to task for not contacting his wife, but he held firm in his decision to keep Delaney from seeing him in such a state. Nurse Billie did help him heal as quickly as humanly possible, pushing him to exercise his limbs, eat healthy meals, and gain strength.

As his release date neared, she harangued him until he promised the moment he left the hospital to get a haircut and a shave. Even then, he couldn't force himself to look in the mirror, imagining how hideous he looked.

It wasn't until that very morning as he dressed and hurried to catch the train heading to Pendleton that he took a quick glance at his image. It was the first time he'd seen his reflection since he was in the hospital in China.

To him, the scars looked jagged, raw, and horrid, especially the cloudy streak through his eye. He settled his hat at an angle to shadow the left side of his face and kept his head tipped down, shielding people from the view of his scars.

Yet, he knew the scars weren't the reason his wife ran away from him. With a nod to those who were slowly drawing near, Klayne turned and limped to the house.

By the time he reached the back door where Delaney had escaped inside, Dill stood in the doorway, propped up by two crutches with both legs encased in casts from hip to ankle.

"Sergeant Campbell," Dill said in a flat voice.

"Sir," Klayne said, removing his hat and holding it in one hand as he stood on the back step. A bump from behind almost sent him sprawling, but he used his cane to catch his weight. When he regained his balance, he looked down at Moose. The dog's tongue lolled out of his mouth in what could have been a smile. Moose wagged his entire back end, as though he alone would serve as Klayne's welcoming committee.

"Hey, Moose. How are you, buddy?" He rubbed his hand over the dog's head and along his back, grateful for a scrap of affection, even if it came from the excited canine.

Moose offered a friendly woof and leaned against Klayne's leg, his tail beating out a steady rhythm.

Klayne looked up and found Dill giving him a long, studying glance. Reluctantly, the man turned just enough so Klayne could enter the house. Apparently, the dog's approval carried more weight than he realized.

The two men limped into the kitchen where the girl Klayne had spoken with earlier poured lemonade into glasses.

Dill tilted his head toward the girl. "This is Lina. She's helped around the house this summer. Delaney says Lina is the only reason the clothes and house are clean and I'm not in the insane asylum. Lina, this is Sergeant Campbell, Delaney's husband."

Lina blushed again and dipped her head with a timid smile. "I recognized you from your wedding photos. Welcome home, sir."

"Thank you, Lina." Klayne said, pleased the girl and the dog seemed happy he was back. He looked to Dill. "If you don't mind my asking, sir, what happened?"

"I fell out of the hayloft and landed on the grain drill. I wouldn't recommend it." Dill eased himself down to a kitchen chair and stretched out both legs. "I broke two legs, half a dozen ribs, had a punctured lung and I don't remember what all else Doc said was wrong with me. I spent half the summer in the hospital and the rest of it confined to bed. They've only let me be up on crutches recently." The rancher gave Klayne another long look. "I reckon you know a thing or two about healing from injuries."

Klayne kept his expression impassive. "I do, sir."

Dill raised an eyebrow. "Where have you been since the raid on Tokyo? Delaney was convinced you were part of it. When the government finally released the names of the raiders, it turned out she was right."

"I was injured that night, sir, when our plane crashed. It took several weeks to make it out of China and back to the states. I spent a month at a hospital in Washington D.C., and two more at a hospital in Portland. Yesterday, the doctor there released me." Klayne forced himself to meet Dill's gaze. "I came back to my wife as soon as I could."

The older man didn't move, didn't even blink, as he continued glaring at him. "I don't know why you decided not to write my daughter, and it isn't any of my business, but you shattered her heart. It's going to take more than a few words of apology to fix what's broken."

Klayne nodded. "I know, sir. I'm sorry, sir." He swallowed hard. "Had I known she was... that a baby..." Overcome by the thought that he would soon be a father, he took a moment to draw in a deep breath before continuing. "The choices I made seemed best at the time, but I see very clearly how wrong I was. I can only hope Delaney gives me a second chance."

"I pray, for your sake and hers, but most especially for my grandchild, that she does, too." With great effort Dill lumbered to a standing position, propped up on his crutches. Klayne stood, balancing himself with his cane. To his amazement, Dill reached out a hand toward him. He took it and received the man's hearty handshake. "All that aside, I want to thank you for serving our country, Klayne. The bravery of the men who went on that raid is something people will long remember. I can only imagine how hard the last several months have been on you. I'm grateful for what you've all done to not

313

only boost the morale of our nation, but also make those Japs think twice about attacking us."

Klayne almost smiled. "Thank you, sir."

Dill started to say something but the back door swung open and Ryatt ran inside. "Grandpa! Me and Tommy just got back from town and guess what I saw! There was a…" Ryatt drew up beside Dill and stared in awe at Klayne. "Wow! You're a real soldier!"

"You must be Ryatt," Klayne said, grinning at the youngster.

The boy bobbed his head up and down, sending his light brown hair flopping over his forehead and into hazel eyes very similar to his aunt's. Ryatt hurried to push the hair out of his way as he continued staring at Klayne. "Who are you?"

"I'm the man who married your aunt," Klayne said, continuing to smile at the boy.

"The one who bombed the Japs?" Ryatt asked, his face animated and eager to hear more.

"The very same." Klayne dug in his pocket and pulled out a jawbreaker, tossing it to the child.

"Gee, thanks, mister." Ryatt popped the candy into his mouth and tucked it into his cheek.

Klayne thought about reaching out to ruffle the lad's hair, but refrained. "How about you call me Klayne?"

"Golly, that'd be swell." The boy looked to his grandfather. "Where's Aunt Dee, Grandpa?"

Rather than answer, Dill pointed a crutch toward the door. "Go tell Butch we'll need an extra plate at supper tonight for Sergeant Campbell."

"Okay!" Ryatt turned for the door then stopped and glanced at Klayne. "It's nice to meet you, Klayne."

"It's nice to meet you, too, Ryatt."

Klayne watched him run outside then glanced at Dill. "Are his folks visiting? Is Mac home on leave?"

A pained expression crossed Dill's face and Klayne wished he hadn't asked about Delaney's brother. "Mac's gone. Carol, too. My son died from wounds he received at the Battle of Midway. Carol was so distraught when she received the news, she missed a curve in the road and crashed into a tree. I was still in bad shape then, so Delaney had to go to Portland and see to everything on her own. Ryatt... well, that poor boy..." Dill blinked away the moisture in his eyes. "It took some time for him to get back to acting like himself. Delaney's been worried about how he'll do when school begins next week. It was hard for him to leave behind his best friend, although those two boys write more letters than a lovesick girl with her first crush."

"I'm so sorry, sir. I had no idea about..." The enormity of all that had transpired in the last several months hit Klayne like a punch to the gut. Without showing a hint of his emotions, he tried to compartmentalize them and found he couldn't. What had Delaney been through since he left? What had she endured? He ticked off a list of what he knew.

Marriage to a man she barely knew who abruptly disappeared the day after their wedding. The wedding night, a glorious night Klayne would never forget, resulted in a completely unexpected pregnancy. The death of her brother and sister-in-law, both of whom she loved dearly. Stepping into the role of parent to her traumatized nephew. Dill's injuries. And, from the faces of the young men and women he'd seen outside, the necessity to replace her ranch hands with kids.

How had she handled it all and survived with her sanity intact?

Dill must have sensed his thoughts. He tipped his head toward the stairs. "Go on up and talk to her, Klayne. She's mad and hurt, but she's glad to see you, even if she hasn't exactly shown it. Her... condition, makes her emotions simmer on high most of the time. We've all been on the receiving end of her temper as she draws closer to her due date." Dill grinned. "For reasons I can't explain and don't really want to know, my daughter is still head over heels in love with you. At least she sure seems to be, when she isn't ranting about filling you full of bird shot if you dare set foot on the place again."

Klayne caught the man's teasing grin and offered one in return. "Heaven knows I don't know why she cares about me. I'm sure I deserve the bird shot and a lot worse," he said, then turned toward the back steps. "Thank you, sir."

"Go on," Dill urged then sat at the table with a painful groan.

As Klayne started up the steps, he heard Dill ask Lina to bring him a glass of lemonade and some of the cookies she'd baked that afternoon. At the top of the stairs, Klayne took a moment to muster his courage before stopping in front of the door he knew was Delaney's. Muffled sobs seeping from the room pinched his heart.

Klayne didn't know a lot about women and even less about one who was expecting a baby, but he considered Dill's warning about the pregnancy stirring her emotions. Unsure what to do, he finally reached down and twisted the knob. The door opened and he pushed it back then moved inside.

Delaney didn't bother to see who had come in. "Butch, I don't care what you have to say, just leave me alone. After all this time of wanting Klayne home, I slapped him. He'll never speak to me again. I already know I'm an idiot and don't need a lecture from you, or whatever command Dad ordered you to give me. Please, just go away."

"I can't do that, Delaney. Not when all I've thought about since I left in February is getting back here to you." Klayne took a step closer to her. The sound of his voice startled her and she bolted upright, glaring at him with tear tracks on her cheeks and droplets clinging to her eyelashes. He fished a pristine white handkerchief from his pocket and made his way to the bed, gingerly lowering himself beside her. "Don't cry. Please?"

"Klayne!" she whispered, looking at him as though he might be an apparition. For a long moment, they stared at each other, drinking in the sight of one another. Then she threw herself into his arms and hugged him tightly as her tears soaked his shirt.

"It's okay, Delaney. It's all okay now," he said, wrapping his arms around her and holding her close. As he held her, the baby kicked and Klayne jerked back in surprise, staring at her belly.

Delaney misread his reaction. Instead of seeing his interest in the baby and concern for her health, she assumed it was repulsion. She stiffened and moved away from him. "If you don't like the way I look, Klayne Campbell, you've no one but yourself to blame."

She stood and would have stormed from the room, except Klayne caught her hand and refused to let go. With effort, he rose to his feet then stepped in front of her, blocking her escape. He let go of the cane and it fell to the floor with a thud. His hand traced over the soft curve of her cheek.

Trying to gauge Delaney's thoughts and feelings was like riding on a runaway train, squealing around curves with metal grinding and no idea when or if he might crash, but there was no place he'd rather be.

Unyielding, she pulled back from him again and scowled. "Don't play nice with me, Sergeant Campbell. You let me think you were dead or being tortured somewhere for months. Months! You can't just waltz back in here and pretend you never left, pretend you..." Her voice cracked. "... love me."

Klayne took her arms in his hands and held on, refusing to let go, although his grip was gentle. "I'm not pretending, Delaney Marie. I do love you, with all my heart. I'm sorry I didn't write. At first, I couldn't, and then I just didn't. I was afraid if you knew what had happened, how I looked, you'd..." He stopped and stared down at her, losing himself in those hazel eyes so full of life, and right now brimming with anger and pain. "I was afraid you'd regret marrying me."

She sighed and some of the hostility melted out of her. "I don't regret marrying you, at least not right at this moment." A little of the Delaney he remembered sparked in her eyes and lingered in the hint of her smile. "I'm just mad and hurt you didn't trust me enough to not be a shallow nincompoop. Do you really think those little scars mean anything to me? You could have returned missing limbs and it wouldn't have made a difference in how I feel about you."

Encouraged by her words, Klayne took a step closer, but she took one back. "Just because I'm not giving you a black eye doesn't mean I'm ready to forgive you. You abandoned me, Klayne, right when I needed you the most. I understood about the mission and the secrecy, but once it was finished, you should have let me know you'd survived. You had no right to hide from me."

Chagrin rode his features. "I know, Delaney, but I..."

She held up a hand to silence him. "You can tell me all about what happened later. Right now, I need some time to absorb the fact that you are safe and you are here." A curious look crossed her features. "You are staying, aren't you? Are they sending you somewhere else? On another mission?"

Klayne shook his head. "No, I don't think so. The Army won't have much use for a bombardier who's lost the ability to sight his targets."

Delaney squeezed his hand and offered him a sympathetic glance. "I'm sorry, Klayne. Truly, I am. It's just... I don't..." Tears glistened in her eyes. "Please, give me a time to adjust to the suddenness of this."

He bent down and picked up his cane then backed toward the door. "Take all the time you need, Delaney. I'm not going anywhere."

Klayne returned downstairs and walked with Dill and Lina over to the bunkhouse where he found himself sitting between two of the high school girls Delaney hired to work on the place. Delaney hurried in just before Dill asked them all to bow their heads as he offered a prayer of thanks for the meal and for Klayne's safe return.

Throughout the meal, Klayne cast glances at his wife as she sat across from him and felt a sense of gratification when he caught her watching him a few times.

Everyone spoke about the wheat harvest, talking animatedly about finishing soon. Dill informed Klayne the harvest was late that year, due to the long, cold winter and a wet, cool spring.

Eventually, one of the boys asked Klayne about the raid he flew over Japan. Apparently, they all were aware of what he'd done, just not where he'd been since then.

"Did you really drop bombs on Tokyo?" the young man asked.

Slowly, Klayne nodded. "We did. Sixteen bombers flew that day, each with five-man crews and two thousand pounds of bombs."

"Wow!" Ryatt said, his eyes wide.

"Did you really take off from a place named Shangri-La?" One of the cheeky girls sitting next to him asked.

He grinned. "Of course. Isn't that what you read in the newspaper?"

Dill chuckled then turned to the girl who asked the question. "Sometimes the military can't share details, even after a mission, Jilly."

The girl nodded and gave Klayne another admiring glance before one of the boys asked another question. "What happened to the rest of the planes?"

"I'll tell you, but you all have to swear you won't repeat a word you hear."

Everyone nodded solemnly.

Klayne glanced around the faces before he continued. "Fifteen of the planes crash landed in China and on the water. One of the planes ended up in Russia. They didn't have enough fuel to make it to China, so they flew there. I know they landed safely, but I'm not sure where those men are right now."

"And the fifteen planes that crashed? Were many injured?" Delaney asked. Klayne noted the concern and sincerity in her gaze as she looked across the table at him.

He nodded. "One died during the crash. A few were banged up pretty good, others had minor injuries. All but one of the men on my plane suffered extensive injuries. Two of them will remain in the hospital for a good long while yet."

"Gosh, that sounds horrible," Jilly said.

"It was horrible," Klayne agreed.

"What about you, Sergeant? How badly were you injured?" Delaney inquired. Her eyes traveled from the scar near his hairline down his face.

Klayne wanted to duck his head and hide from her intense scrutiny, but he sat up straight and kept an impassive expression on his face. "Our pilot knew we didn't have much fuel left as we neared China. The night was dark, stormy, and we were a long way from where we were supposed to land. Even if we'd been close, we probably couldn't have found the airfield because they kept the lights out since the Japanese were so close. Anyway, the weather broke just enough we could see what appeared to be a smooth beach ahead. The pilot buzzed closer, to check for anything that might wreck us if we landed on the sand. We didn't see anything, so we were exchanging our parachutes for life vests when both engines spluttered and quit. Just like that." Klayne snapped his fingers, making Lina jump.

The boys laughed and Klayne continued with the story. "I was in the process of crawling out of the nose of the plane back into the navigator's area when we crashed. The force shot me back down that crawlway and through the glass nose of the plane like I was fired out of a cannon. On my unexpected exit from the plane, a few ragged edges of metal tried to scalp me while some equipment twisted my left arm and leg into a new shape and bent my back so far out of place I couldn't stand upright for more than two months. I don't remember crawling onto the beach or much of what happened until I woke up in a Chinese hospital a few days later. With the Japanese sniffing out our trail, we stayed there a few weeks before heading out again and eventually making it back to America through a route that took us around the world."

"I'm sorry, Klayne," Delaney said, reaching across the table and placing her hand over his.

Afraid she'd pull back if he turned over his hand and clasped hers, he gave a nod of acknowledgement and answered more questions from the young people sitting around him.

As soon as the dishes were cleared from the table, Klayne asked one of the boys for a ride into town. Before he left, Delaney hurried over to him, wrapped him in a tight hug, and whispered, "I'm so glad you survived and came back to me." She disappeared inside the barn before he could articulate a response or draw her closer.

Relieved the kids in the car didn't ask him a bunch of personal questions on the way to town, they dropped him off at Pendleton Field. Tommy, the boy Ryatt seemed quite attached to, offered to give him a ride out to the ranch tomorrow if he needed it.

Klayne thanked him and told him he'd call in the morning if he did.

After speaking with the commanding officer, Klayne felt a measure of relief that he'd still have a job and it would keep him right there in Pendleton, as a training officer. Whether Delaney liked it or not, he planned on sticking around and finding a way back into her arms and her heart.

★ *Chapter Twenty-Two* ★

A month after his return to the ranch, Klayne was so frustrated with his wife, he wanted to punch his fist through the barn wall.

Every step he took forward in their relationship, she pulled back three. Most of the time she acted cool, distant, and reserved. More often than he liked, he'd find her looking at him with seething anger simmering in her eyes, as though the very sight of him infuriated her.

She hadn't welcomed him back to Sage Hills, and certainly not into her heart or bed, but he couldn't leave.

The moments when she smiled, laughed, or teased him — when she forgot how much she pretended to despise him — kept him from packing up and leaving. In truth, those little scraps of her affection were all that sustained him during those hard, trying days.

With enough time and patience, Klayne held a small measure of confidence Delaney would come around and realize she still loved him. He could see it in her eyes, hear it in her voice when she said his name, but for reasons he couldn't understand, she wouldn't admit it.

A man who spent the first thirty years of his life primarily alone and unloved didn't expect a lot. Still, her indifference wounded him far deeper than anyone would ever know.

His road to recovery had been painful, some days excruciatingly so, but he'd clung to the promise of her love through it all.

Just when he thought he'd finally know what it was like to love and be loved, she withheld from him the one thing he wanted most. It would have been easy to walk away, to give up and move on. Then she'd do something unexpected, something sweet and caring that turned his heart into a syrupy mess, reaffirming his belief that she really did care for him.

Unfortunately, the sporadic kindness made it hard for him to find solid footing as he attempted to carve out a place where he fit in on the ranch.

Determined to greet the day with a more optimistic attitude, Klayne rose early, made the bed in the guest room where Delaney had insisted he stay, and went downstairs. He grabbed a cookie from the jar on the counter Lina had filled when she was there on Saturday to work, and headed outside.

The autumn day was warm and the air held a spicy, tangy scent. A dozen apple trees in the orchard still needed to be picked, but for the most part, the produce had all been harvested and canned.

Delaney's friend Amy had arrived one morning with a car full of women who helped make jam, juice, and canned dozens of jars full of vegetables and fruit. The root cellar, as Dill referred to the storage area dug into a mound of ground behind the house, had shelves full of glistening jars of food and bins piled with apples, potatoes, onions, and other produce that would see them through the winter months.

Klayne had known what it was like to be hungry and cold without anywhere to go, so he basked in the knowledge he'd have an abundance of food, a warm place to live, and plenty of work to keep him occupied. As of December 1, he'd go back on active duty and begin training young soldiers how to sight in bombs with accuracy. Even though he could no longer accurately sight, he had the experience and skill to teach others. Until he began work at the base, his commanding officer told him to continue regaining his strength and mobility.

Annoyed by the obstacles of using his cane on the ranch, Klayne had abandoned it a week after he arrived at Sage Hills. Sometimes he lost his balance and had to catch himself before he fell, but for the most part, he managed.

As Klayne made his way to the barn that golden October morning, he admired the changing colors of the landscape. Where greens and blues had dominated during the summer, now oranges, reds and browns began to creep in, painting the world in jeweled-hues of a different variety.

In the barn, he turned on the radio, took two buckets down from pegs in the wall and set about milking the cows. He hummed along to tunes he knew as he worked, his forehead pressed against the warm hide of the cow he milked.

When the song "Bewitched, Bothered, Bewildered," began playing, Klayne stopped a moment and stared at the radio. The lyrics so accurately expressed his current situation, he felt as though it had been written specifically for him. The singer crooned of losing his heart to a cold woman. Being around Delaney these last few weeks put Klayne in mind of the below freezing temperatures he'd endured during the winter.

Yet in the midst of the frosty tension she placed between them, there were moments of exquisite tenderness.

Last Saturday, she'd declared they must have a birthday party for him since he'd spent his lost and wounded in China. All the young people who worked for them came and Delaney served a moist cake topped with a delicious coconut icing. Much to his surprise, she wore the pearl necklace he'd left for her the morning after their wedding.

After the various gifts were opened, she presented him with a scrapbook that contained every article she'd been able to find that mentioned him or the men he'd flown with on the raid to Japan. Touched by the gift, he'd kissed her cheek and she'd leaned into him before Ryatt claimed her attention. Those sweet moments, brief as they were, fueled his hope for the future.

Klayne finished milking the cows and gathered the eggs, taking both to the bunkhouse where Butch cooked breakfast. After greeting the crusty old cowboy, Klayne made his way to the house with a small bucket of milk.

In the kitchen, he strained it into a pitcher and stored it in the refrigerator before rinsing the bucket and his hands. He'd just turned to take the bucket back outside when he found Delaney leaning against the doorjamb, watching him.

"Mornin', Delaney." He smiled at her, wondering what sort of mood she'd be in this morning. Even Butch had commented about the swings in her temperament being as unpredictable and wild as a cross-eyed batter in a ballgame. He let his gaze rove over her, taking in the dark braid that snaked over one shoulder, a blouse that brought out the roses in her cheeks, and a belly that seemed to expand on a daily basis. He wanted, so badly, to put his hands on it, to feel his baby move within her, but he resisted the urge.

"That's a pretty blouse," he said, admiring the floral print that appeared quite becoming on his wife.

Delaney glanced down and pushed away from the wall. "Thank you, Klayne. You're always so kind to offer a compliment or encouragement. I want you to know I appreciate it." He watched her swallow hard before she looked up at him. "In spite of everything, I'm glad you're here."

Much to his delight, she came to him and wrapped her arms around his trim waist, giving him a tight hug. "I'm so glad you made it home," she whispered.

Klayne set down the bucket in his hands and returned the hug, resting his cheek on top of her head. Her alluring scent filled his nose and made him wish she'd be this agreeable to his proximity and affections all the time. Not ready to push his luck, he simply hugged her and waited for her to make a move. From experience, she'd stiffen, act self-conscious, and pull away from him.

This time, though, she hugged him a little tighter then reached up and pulled his head down toward hers until their lips touched in a light kiss.

Mindful of her being as easy to spook as an untamed horse, he let her take charge of the kiss. When it deepened and the passion he remembered, had spent months dreaming of, sparked between them, he pulled her closer and lost himself in her love.

Neither one of them noticed Ryatt run into the kitchen or the boy's shocked expression at finding them in a heated embrace.

"Get away from Aunt Dee!" Ryatt shouted, charging into Klayne's side and knocking him off balance.

Klayne grasped the edge of the counter to keep from falling to the floor. Ryatt swatted at him, but Delaney grabbed the boy from behind, pulling him back.

"Ryatt! Stop that, this instant. You know Klayne's my husband. It's okay for him to kiss me," Delaney said, trying to calm the youngster. "He wasn't hurting me. Everything is fine, Ry."

"I don't want you to like him, Aunt Dee. You can't like him!" Ryatt yelled and ran outside.

Tears rolled down Delaney's cheeks and she brushed them away. Klayne followed her into the laundry room where she slipped her feet into the old loafers she'd taken to wearing when her feet were too swollen to fit in anything else.

"I'll go after him, Delaney. You stay here," Klayne said, opening the door.

Delaney set a hand on his arm, pulling him to a stop. "No. I'll go. It's my fault he's upset. I shouldn't have... you just looked." She sighed. "I enjoyed kissing you, Klayne, but I... I shouldn't..." Without offering any further explanation, she hurried outside to find the boy.

Klayne couldn't blame Ryatt for not trusting him. The child took his cues from Delaney. When she was cool and distant, Ryatt was, too. The days she treated Klayne like a close friend, Ryatt tagged after him like a besotted pup. Delaney's emotions, which jumped all over a broad spectrum, were confusing and hard for everyone. Navigating them had to be doubly hard for a boy who'd so recently lost both parents. Aware that Delaney couldn't help it, it sure didn't make for trouble-free days at the ranch.

An hour later, Klayne watched as Delaney walked Ryatt down their lane to catch the school bus. The boy had seemed withdrawn and quiet through breakfast, even when Butch and Duffy tried to tease him back into a good humor.

Concerned, Klayne just hoped once the baby arrived Delaney would return to her old self, Ryatt would settle down, and the road ahead wouldn't be quite so rocky.

The sewing machine whirred as Delaney worked to hem a pile of white flannel into diapers. She'd been so busy since she found out she was expecting, she hadn't spent any time actually getting ready for the arrival of her little one. Her and Klayne's little one.

The day she'd looked up and saw him at the edge of the field, she felt her prayers had been answered. All she'd wanted from the moment she woke up and found him gone back in February was for him to come home again.

In the quiet hours when she couldn't sleep or when her hands were busy at a task that left her thoughts free, she'd done nothing but dream of the life they would build together. So many grand visions for the future filled her thoughts and took root in her heart.

A longing to go to Klayne, to confess how much she loved him, needed him, nagged at her incessantly, but she ignored it. Some days, all she wanted was to sit next to him, rest her head on his strong shoulder, and let him help carry the load of her burdens. In those moments, she put more distance between them, widening the chasm she'd carved between the two of them.

The man had the patience of a saint. He'd not once acted upset or hurt by her anger or indifference. He'd accepted the boundaries she set and treated her with polite respect and kindness.

Delaney didn't deserve his kindness. She certainly didn't deserve his love. He'd explained why she hadn't heard from him for months, and the reasonable part of her understood.

However, the rest of her railed against his abandonment and the terrifying notion that he'd do it again. Fears of him leaving her, leaving her with a baby to raise on her own, kept her from admitting the truth to him. Not a day went by that she didn't give thanks for her husband, for his safekeeping, and for his steady presence at the ranch. Despite all the challenges hurled at him, Klayne met each one with a calm, confident demeanor that even Dill had commented was a help to them all.

Convinced he couldn't love her with her bloated, distended body and tumultuous emotions, Delaney decided after the baby came she'd have plenty of time to make things right with Klayne. The doctor assured her the roiling emotions she currently experienced should settle down a few weeks after the baby's arrival.

Clinging to the hope she'd still have a marriage to salvage then, Delaney focused her attention on preparing for the baby. She'd spent the last two days sewing receiving blankets and simple kimonos for the baby to wear.

Dill mentioned at breakfast there was a trunk in the attic with baby things in it and Klayne offered to go up and find it later.

As she snipped the thread on another finished diaper, the phone jangled in the kitchen. Delaney rose to her feet and waddled down the hall, picking it up on the fourth ring.

"Sage Hills Ranch."

"Mrs. Campbell?" a nasally voice inquired.

"Yes, this is Mrs. Campbell." Delaney hoped no more trouble was about to arrive at their door. She'd had about all she could endure for a lifetime, let alone the past several months.

"This is Mrs. Jenner, the principal at Ryatt's school." The woman sounded snobbish and imperial.

Delaney recalled meeting the pinch-faced educator the day she enrolled Ryatt in school. The woman had irked her then every bit as much as she did now with her better-than-everyone attitude.

"Mrs. Jenner, how may I help you this morning?"

"Is Ryatt unwell, Mrs. Campbell?" Mrs. Jenner asked.

Delaney frowned. "He's perfectly fine, or at least he was when he got on the bus."

She could almost hear the censure when the woman spoke. "Ryatt is not in his class. His teacher said he didn't arrive this morning. Are you certain he isn't at home, perhaps playing hooky?"

Delaney wanted to reach through the phone and shake the woman. "I walked him to the bus and watched him climb on it this morning. There is no possibility he missed it. Are you telling me, Mrs. Jenner, that you've lost my nephew?"

The woman spluttered. "Of course not. We do not lose children. Children may, in the course of their conniving high jinks, run off, but we most assuredly do not lose children."

"You're certain he isn't at class? At school?" Delaney asked, her mind whirring as she considered all the possibilities of why Ryatt was missing. Each idea made her more upset and worried.

"He is not in class or at school. Two of his classmates said he never came inside this morning. It is a shame children like that..."

Delaney slammed down the phone, grabbed her handbag and rushed outside. She'd taken three steps before she realized she didn't have on any shoes and backtracked inside to shove her feet into the old loafers. She made a quick trip to the bathroom, then hustled out the back door. Her father sat on the porch, reading a book in the morning sunshine, a blanket covering his lap and keeping him warm.

"Ryatt didn't go to class this morning. I'm going to find him," Delaney blurted as she wobbled down the steps and made her way out to the family sedan. She hadn't been able to drive her pickup since shortly after Klayne arrived home. Between having to climb up into it and trying to get her rounded belly behind the wheel, she'd taken to driving the car when she needed to go into town.

"Take Klayne with you." Dill pointed toward the shop where Klayne could be seen tinkering on an engine through the open door.

She glanced toward her husband, shook her head, and continued on to the car.

"Klayne!" Dill yelled at the top of his lungs.

The soldier snapped to attention and barreled out of the shop. He caught sight of Delaney hurrying toward the car in her rocking gait and Dill motioning for him to join her.

In a few long steps, he reached the car and held open the driver's side door for her. "Mind if I ride along?"

Her gaze narrowed as she slid behind the wheel. "Suit yourself."

Before she could start the car and leave without him, he hustled in the passenger side.

Throughout his years as a boy wandering aimlessly around the country then as a soldier tasked with dangerous missions, Klayne had experienced more than his share of terrifying rides.

None compared to the way Delaney roared into town. Heedless to national speed limits, rations on gasoline, or restrictions on rubber, she made the trip to Pendleton in six minutes flat. She'd cut two corners, scared the daylights out of the milkman, and nearly toppled a section of fence in the process. He'd closed his eyes when she skidded into town, frightening four drivers at a busy intersection.

The experience brought back memories of riding on the bus in China with the lunatic driver.

Klayne had braced one hand against the dashboard and the other on the door, wondering how much damage he'd sustain if he were forced to jump out of the careening car. Not that he would exit it with Delaney and his baby inside.

Even if she didn't want to talk about the precious little life that was a result of their intense, undeniable love, pride swelled in him each time he looked at her. Together, they'd created something, someone, who he prayed would be the best of them both, be better than both of them.

"Is there a fire we're going to?" he asked as she honked the horn, ran a stop sign and took a corner on three wheels. Impressed with her ability to keep the car on the road, he clenched the dashboard with a tighter grip.

"The principal called. Ryatt didn't show up at school. I put him on the bus this morning. What if he ran off, Klayne? What if he…" Tears brimmed in her eyes, as they so frequently did these days and she pressed her lips together to hold back a sob. If something happened to Ryatt she'd never forgive herself. He was all she had left of two people she'd loved and adored.

"Okay," Klayne said, cringing as Delaney barely missed hitting at car in an intersection and continued zooming down the street. He was surprised she hadn't been pulled over for endangering lives with her reckless driving.

A relieved sigh escaped him as she slammed on the brakes in front of the school and parked with one tire on the front lawn. Before Klayne could get out to help her, she was already waddling toward the door.

He had to hurry to catch up to her, open the door, and follow her to the office.

A round-faced woman with a ready smile glanced at them as they walked inside. The smile melted off her face and she offered them a sympathetic look. "Oh, Dee! I just can't believe Ryatt would disappear like that. We've questioned the students in his class as well as those who rode the bus with him. They all say he got off the bus here at school but no one recalls seeing him after that. He must have slipped away then."

"Thank you, Mrs. Johnson." Delaney took the woman's outstretched hand and held it in her own as she glanced around. "So he hasn't returned?"

The woman clucked her tongue and appeared quite distressed. "I'm sorry, dear, but no one has seen him."

"We'll find him," Delaney said, releasing the woman's hand, then clasping Klayne's. She needed his strength and support right then, even if she refused to admit it. She turned and headed to the car.

"If you were Ryatt, where would you go?" Delaney asked, knowing Klayne had plenty of experience from years of escaping orphanages and foster homes.

"The first place I always headed was the train depot. I'd hop on a train and ride it until I got caught."

She cast a horrified look his way and he held up his hands in a placating motion. "I'm sure Ryatt isn't planning on leaving town, though. Unless..." He remained silent for a moment. "Do you think he'd try to make his way back to Portland?"

"He might. He's been talking about missing Petey and the farm," Delaney said, leaning her head against the top of the steering wheel. The large, warm hand of her husband settled on her back and rubbed in comforting circles. "I just can't imagine he'd do that, though.

"Is there a place around here that's special to him?" Klayne asked.

Delaney raised her head and stared at him, sifting through her thoughts. "There's one place. Mac took him there a few times..." She started the car, bumped over the curb as she turned around and raced through town.

Just to be sure Ryatt wasn't trying to make his way to Portland, they stopped at the depot. The ticket agent assured Delaney no little boys had come in looking for a ticket and he'd keep an eye out for him in case he did wander in.

While she inquired inside the depot, Klayne walked along the tracks, looking for places where someone might jump onto a train car undetected. He found two bums hiding in a little culvert and ignored their whispered curses for him to leave them alone as he passed on by. Ryatt had no experience in stealing onto a train and he doubted the boy would try.

Convinced Ryatt wasn't there, he guided Delaney back to the car.

She sped out of town driving west for a mile or so then headed south. "A few times when Mac, Carol, and Ryatt were visiting, Mac took them for a ride up in the hills. They'd pack a picnic lunch and make a day of it." Delaney slowed and turned onto a dirt road. The car jounced and swayed as she drove over ruts and washouts. At one point, Klayne's head bounced off the roof of the car when she hit a large hole filled with powdery dirt. Before the car could stall, she zoomed through the hole and continued following the trail upward.

She gasped as the baby kicked in protest of the rough ride. Pain sliced across her abdomen, but she ignored it and kept both hands on the wheel. A trickle of sweat rolled across her forehead and into her right eye.

Klayne brushed it away and settled his hand on her shoulder. "Are you okay, Delaney? You look a little pale. Do you want me to drive? Do you want to turn back?"

She shook her head. "No. I'm fine. The only thing that matters right now is finding Ryatt." The glare she tossed at Klayne dared him to argue. Wise man that he was, he remained silent.

Delaney finally topped a hill and drove around a large outcropping of rocks then stopped the car. On a large boulder, alone, a little figure sat with knees drawn up to his chin as he looked out at the valley below them.

"Give me a minute with him," Delaney said, placing a hand on Klayne's arm. "Please?"

"Go ahead," he said, getting out of the car and leaning against the door.

She felt his eyes following her as she picked her way across the rocky ground and sat down next to her nephew. "Ryatt, what on earth are you doing out here and how did you even find this place?"

"Dad used to bring us here. Remember?" Ryatt said, turning his head so his cheek rested on his upraised knees. "I just... I needed to feel close to him and Mom today."

Delaney settled her hand on his back, not knowing what to say. How did one comfort a child who had lost his whole world? "I do remember, Ry. You had some fun times here."

They sat in silence for a few minutes before Delaney patted the boy's back. "Ry, it's not okay for you to run away from school. The teacher was worried, the principal was worried." Ryatt gave her a disbelieving look. "Okay, Mrs. Jenner was concerned by your absence. But I was scared sick something had happened to you. I can't lose you, Ryatt. You're all I have left of two of the best people I ever knew. You'd break my heart if you left."

Ryatt sat up and pointed toward the car. "But you have him." He glared at Klayne.

"I thought you liked Klayne, sweetie," Delaney said, pulling Ryatt into a hug made awkward by her protruding belly.

"I do like him. He's funny and nice, and he never hollers if I mess stuff up. He's a good guy, Aunt Dee. Petey would say he's a straight arrow, a real hero, and

I'd have to agree. If you had to marry someone, he's the right fella for the job."

Delaney hid a smile. "Then what's the problem? Why did you get so upset when you saw us this morning? I know you used to see your mom and dad kiss."

Ryatt shrugged, refusing to answer.

"Come on, Ry. You can tell me anything," Delaney encouraged, turning his face so he looked up at her.

Tears welled in his eyes and he snuffled, then brushed his sleeve beneath his nose, as though he could scrub away his emotions.

"What is it, baby? What's wrong?" Delaney drew him closer and removed his cap, feathering her fingers through his tousled hair.

"I don't want you to die, Aunt Dee! I don't want you to die!" Ryatt burst into gut-wrenching sobs that caused Klayne to cover the distance between them in a few strides. He sat down on the other side of the distraught child and gave Delaney a confused glance, uncertain what to do to make things better for her or the boy.

"I won't let anything happen to your aunt, Ryatt. Honest I won't," Klayne said, placing a hand on the child's slim shoulder.

"But it will! You'll both die, just like my mama and daddy!" Ryatt pushed against Delaney and would have run off, but Klayne grabbed him around the waist and pulled him onto his lap. The boy struggled against him for only a minute before his tense body sagged and he clung to the big man, sobbing out the grief he'd quietly tucked away since his parents died.

"We won't die, Ryatt. We won't," Delaney said, crying right along with her nephew. "Why do you think we're going to die?"

"That's what happens when you love someone so much, like Mom loved Dad. You love Klayne like that. He's a soldier. All soldiers die in the war. And when he dies, you'll die, too, just like Mom." Ryatt gasped for a breath and looked to his aunt, tears rolling down his cheeks. "I don't want you to die, Aunt Dee. I don't want Klayne to die! I hate war!"

"Shh, shh," Klayne said, rocking the boy back and forth, unsure what to do to calm or comfort him. He had no experience with children, but he recalled many times he'd wished there had been someone to hold him as he held the grieving child, someone to wipe away his tears and assure him all would be well. "Ryatt, look at me," Klayne ordered.

Ryatt sniffled and finally raised his gaze to Klayne's. Klayne smiled at him and brushed the mussed hair away from the boy's face then wiped away the tears from his cheeks. "Listen to me, son. I'll be going back to active duty soon, but because of the wounds I received, I'll stay right here in Pendleton, training others to do the job I no longer can. I'm not going back into battle and I'm not going to die. You have my solemn promise that I'll do everything in my power to keep your aunt safe. Do you think I'd break a promise?"

The boy shook his head and snuffled. "No. I could take your word right to the bank."

Klayne smiled again. "I'm glad you think so." He moved so Ryatt sat upright on his knee. "You know, Ry, you were right when you said I love your aunt

Delaney so much I'd die for her, die protecting her. But I promise I'll do everything I can to keep us all safe. Can you promise me something, though?"

Ryatt looked up at him with adoration and trust, curious.

"Will you promise to never run away again?" Klayne smirked at Delaney. "If you do and I have to ride with your aunt driving like a crazy woman, I might die of fright right there in the car."

Ryatt's eyes widened then he grinned. "I promise!"

Delaney released a choppy laugh. "My driving wasn't that scary."

Klayne winked at Ryatt. "I'll tell it to the world, it most certainly was. I bet you can find indents in the dashboard where I clung for dear life."

"I'm gonna go look!" Ryatt jumped off his lap and ran over to the car while Klayne helped Delaney to her feet.

"Thank you for that, for being so good with him," Delaney whispered as they watched Ryatt open the car door and examine the dashboard.

"He's my nephew, too. The poor little guy just needed to let out some of his grief and worries." He gave her a pointed look. "He might not be the only one."

Delaney sighed and turned away from Klayne, glancing out over the valley below them. "I forget how beautiful it us up here."

Klayne slid his arms around her, his clasped hands resting just above the mound of her stomach, and stepped close behind her. "It is a beautiful place. I can see why your brother liked coming up here.

Maybe in the spring, we could bring Ryatt and the baby here for a picnic."

"He'd like that," Delaney said, leaning against Klayne, absorbing his strength. Without success, she tried to recall all the many reasons she'd pushed him away, but couldn't think of one. Perhaps it was time to tear down the walls she'd built around her heart in his absence and let him in. Or at least, open the door a crack.

"We better get back to the ranch. Dill will be worried, too," Klayne finally said. He pressed a kiss to the top of her head then moved back. When she turned to face him, he merely took her hand in his and led her to the car.

Klayne assisted her in the passenger side. "If you don't mind, I'll drive home. Another ride like that one and I'll look like old Marvin Tooley."

Ryatt giggled as Delaney slid onto the seat next to the boy. Klayne closed her passenger door then took his position behind the wheel.

Klayne looked from Ryatt to Delaney. "Is it true Mr. Tooley is over a hundred years old?"

"No one knows for sure, but Dad said he was a cranky old coot when he was a boy." Delaney gave Ryatt a reproving look. "And don't you dare tell anyone I said that."

Ryatt rolled his eyes. "I won't, Aunt Dee." He took Delaney's left hand and Klayne's right hand and placed them together. "Thank you for coming to find me."

"Just remember, no more running away," Klayne warned. He kissed the back of Delaney's hand then started the car. "It's okay if you need to cry sometimes, Ryatt, and it's okay to be sad and miss your parents. You don't have to bottle all that up inside and wait for it to explode."

"Like when you shake a bottle of pop? Me and Petey did that one time at his house. The cap flew off and broke a plate his mother had hanging on the wall. Good golly, it was something to see with Dr. Pepper foaming all over the kitchen floor. We thought we were in for it, but Petey's dad came in and said he wouldn't miss the ugly plate at all, but he did make us mop the floor." Ryatt glanced up at his aunt. "Me and Petey saved up our money and bought his mom a new plate, a pretty one with roses painted on it."

"That's my good boy," Delaney said, ruffling his hair before setting the cap back on his head.

She glanced over at Klayne and smiled, mouthing, "Thank you," to him.

In spite of the rough start, perhaps this family still had a chance.

∗∗∗★ *Chapter Twenty-Three* ★∗∗∗

Delaney sent Ryatt up to get ready for bed after he finished his homework. Klayne had helped him with his history lesson while Delaney hand-stitched a tiny little sleeve into a dress for the baby.

Klayne hadn't questioned why she seemed so convinced it would be a girl, but he enjoyed watching her create the tiny pink garment.

Now that harvest was over and the cattle they had out in the hills had been rounded up and brought in closer to the home place, she seemed intent on preparing for the baby. The one time he'd asked about when to expect it to arrive, she'd tersely answered it was due in November and stalked off.

Perhaps the softening in her attitude he'd sensed recently would provide the opportunity for him to attempt, again, to get to know his wife better.

In truth, Klayne was growing weary of trying, but he wasn't one willing to give up without a fight. Every inch forward he'd gained with his wife had been a battle of wills, determination, and just plain stubbornness.

As he went over details of the Civil War with Ryatt, Klayne kept glancing over at Delaney's long fingers, no longer slender, but swollen from her pregnancy. They still looked elegant to him even in their rough, work-reddened state. She appeared lost in her thoughts as she stitched delicate rosebuds across the front of a little dress.

Klayne had never seen something so small, so sweet, and wondered about the baby who would fit into such a bitty little garment.

"Is that right, Klayne?" Ryatt asked, staring up at him with an eager look on his face.

"Yep, you got that last one right, Ry. Good job," Klayne said, reaching out to ruffle the boy's hair.

"Finish your milk and cookies then head up to get your bath," Delaney said, smiling at Ryatt.

"Yes, ma'am," Ryatt said. He stuffed the last bite into his mouth of a new type of cookie Amy's folks recently started carrying in their bakery. Several soldiers stationed in Pendleton had requested the cookie that had bits of chocolate and chopped nuts in a sweet vanilla dough. Amy said the cookies were rapidly growing in popularity and had sent home a few dozen with Delaney and Klayne when they took Ryatt in for a treat on their way home that morning.

Klayne helped himself to another cookie as Ryatt gathered his homework into the bag he carried to school.

The boy glugged the last of his milk then ran up the stairs, seeming lighter in spirit and heart than he'd been since the loss of his parents.

Klayne glanced around, expecting Dill to make his way into the kitchen, but the house remained quiet other than the sound of Ryatt running water upstairs.

"Where's your dad?" he asked, turning to look at Delaney.

"He said the worry of the day wore him out. He went to bed about half an hour ago." Delaney held out the dress she'd embellished and wrinkled her nose.

"What's wrong?" Klayne asked, rising and moving to stand behind her chair.

"I'm not particularly talented when it comes to sewing. It's mostly because I wouldn't sit still long enough to learn."

Klayne wiped his hands along the sides of his jeans and reached out to the feel the soft cotton fabric in his fingers. "I think it's perfect."

Delaney tipped back her head and glanced up at him. "You're kind to say that. It's far from perfect, but if I don't get a few garments made, this baby of ours will wind up without a thing to wear."

Klayne released the fabric and bent down, kissing Delaney's cheek. "I highly doubt that. Tomorrow, I'll go up to the attic and see if I can find that trunk your dad mentioned. Do you need a crib or anything for the baby?"

"Everything we need should be up in the attic. I thought I'd turn the room across the hall from yours into a nursery. I just painted it last year and no one uses it now. It was the room Mac and Carol always..." Her voice faded and she blinked to dispel the tears threatening to trickle down her cheeks.

Aware of her emotional struggle, Klayne backed toward the stairs. "I'll go check on Ryatt. Do you need anything?"

She sucked in a breath. "No, Klayne. I'm fine. I want to finish this, then I'll head off to bed."

By the time he made it upstairs, Ryatt was in his room, buttoning his pajama top. "Ready for bed, Ry?"

"Yep. I'll tell it to the world, but I'm plumb tuckered out," the boy said and climbed into his bed. Just as quickly, he climbed back out and dropped to his knees beside it, hands clasped together beneath his chin.

From past evenings, Klayne knew this part of the bedtime routine. He took a seat on the edge of Ryatt's mattresses and listened as the boy said his prayers.

"Thank you, Lord, for Grandpa, and Aunt Dee, for Butch and Duffy and the others who help with our work. Thanks for Amy and her parents for making good things to eat at the bakery and for giving me extra cookies. Thank you for Petey and his family, even Princess Alice. Thank you for Moose, he's the best dog in the world, and our wonderful horses. And thank you for Klayne, for sending him here to love me and Aunt Dee. We need someone good like him to love us and keep us safe. Please help Aunt Dee to like him all the time and not be mad or sad anymore. Amen."

Klayne's throat threatened to close with emotions. He swallowed hard and smiled at the youngster as Ryatt scrambled back into his bed and slid between the sheets. With practice, Klayne was learning the bedtime rituals of a normal childhood. He tugged up the covers and tucked them around Ryatt. When the boy begged for a story, he told him about one of the escapades he and Billy got into, although he changed their names and used it as a lesson about why young boys should listen to their elders and not run off on their own.

At the end of the story, Ryatt sat up and threw his arms around Klayne, tightly squeezing him. "Thanks for coming to find me, Klayne. I'm sorry I ran away and scared Aunt Dee. I didn't mean to be bad."

"We know that, Ryatt. Just don't do anything like that again." Klayne cupped the back of the boy's head with one hand and his stubborn little chin with the other. "I'll always be here for you, Ry. Don't ever forget that. If you need something, even if it's just to talk about a problem, you can come to me anytime."

Ryatt pulled back and grinned. "Petey's right, you're a real good egg, Klayne."

He tweaked the boy's nose before Ryatt settled back beneath the covers. "I'm glad I'm not a rotten egg," Klayne teased, rising from the bed. "They smell terrible and taste even worse." He made a funny face that caused the boy to laugh. Klayne ran a hand over Ryatt's wild hair. "I love you, Ryatt. Your aunt and I both do."

"Love you, too, Klayne. G'night." Ryatt shut sleepy eyes as Klayne turned off the lamp and then closed the door so only a sliver of yellow glowed inside from the light in the hall.

Klayne went into the bathroom and readied for bed. On his way downstairs to get a drink of water, the sound of sobs drew him to Delaney's room.

Conflicted, he stood outside her door. What if she pushed him away again? What if his presence only increased her distress? What if she needed him?

Unable to leave her alone, he tapped once and opened her door. She was in bed, resting on her side with a soggy handkerchief in one hand and the sheet clenched in her other.

"What's wrong, Delaney?" he asked, crossing the room in a few long strides. "Are you hurt? Did something happen?" With effort, he knelt by her bed and took her clenched fist in his, bringing the back of her hand to his lips.

"I'm fine, Klayne. I'm just..." She gulped a deep breath, then another. "If something had happened to Ryatt today, I would have died. I can't lose him. It would be like losing Mac and Carol all over again, only worse."

"I know, honey. I know." Klayne brushed the hair away from her face, much as he'd done for Ryatt earlier. "We found him and everything is fine now. Everything will be okay."

"No, it won't!" Delaney looked at him with fear in her eyes. "How can anything ever be right again when I've been so awful to you? You must think I hate you, but I don't. I'm just scared... scared of losing you, too."

"You aren't going to lose me, Delaney. I'm right here." Klayne stood with effort, suppressing a groan, then sat on the bed. Cautiously, he reached out and drew Delaney against his chest, enfolding her in his arms. He placed her hand over his heart. "Feel that? Feel my heart beat strong and steady? Each beat is just for you. When I wanted to give up, when I thought death would be easier than the pain I had to endure, I focused on my memories of you. I fought my way back here because I couldn't bear the thought of never seeing you again, never hearing your laughter, or tasting your kisses. The one thing that kept me hanging on was the hope of coming home to you. I love you, Delaney, with all my heart."

"I don't deserve your love or your grace, Klayne," she said in a voice choppy with emotion. "I'm sorry I've been so hurtful to you, so horrible and cruel and spiteful and..."

He silenced her with a quick kiss. "I know, Delaney. Don't give it another thought." Doctor Nash had sworn to keep his secret, but Klayne had gone to visit him one day just to find out what Delaney's pregnancy entailed. The man assured him many women experienced emotions very similar to Delaney's, especially toward the end of their pregnancy. Klayne had worried about it plenty, but tried not to show it. The doctor's assertion that she didn't really loathe him made him feel marginally better and gave him the reassurance he needed to wait patiently for her to open her heart to him again.

The sheet fluttered as the baby kicked, drawing Klayne's interest. Desperate to feel it, he gingerly lowered his hand until it rested on Delaney's stomach.

"Don't touch me, Klayne. Please?" she begged, flinching at his touch.

"Why?" he asked. His hand rested lightly on her stomach, waiting for the baby to kick again.

"Because I'm so hideous and ugly," Delaney whispered and ducked her head in shame. "The wife you left behind is far different than the one you returned to. I'm sure you hated coming home to an angry bloated hippo."

"You're the most beautiful woman I've ever seen," Klayne said in a husky voice, kissing her cheek, then the exposed skin on her shoulder. "There is nothing about this wonderful little life growing inside you that is hideous or ugly, wife. She's a reminder of how much I love you. How much you once loved me."

Tears glistened in her eyes. "I still love you, Klayne, with all my heart. It's just that... I'm..."

He raised both eyebrows, waiting for her to continue. Self-consciously, she tried to pull his hand away from her stomach, but he left it on the curve of her belly and splayed out his fingers. As a reward for his efforts, the baby kicked and he felt the tiny jolt. Amazed, he stared at Delaney with such a look of wonder, she smiled.

Resigned to sharing the baby and her body with her husband, she lifted his fingers in hers. "Move your hand over here. This is where she likes to kick when I'm trying to go to sleep." Delaney guided his hand over to her left side and held it in place with her hand over the top of his. The baby kicked two more times and once he was sure he felt a fist pressing against Delaney's flesh.

Deliberate in his movements, he tugged up the hem of her nightgown until he could see her skin in the light shining in the open door from the hallway. Delaney yanked at the fabric of her gown and grasped for the sheet, but he refused to allow her to hide from him. He pushed the nightgown up higher, flicked the sheet away, then bent down and kissed her belly. Gently, his big hand stroked over the mound created by the baby. "Why do you think it's a girl?" he asked.

Delaney smirked, the same smile that had tantalized him when he'd first met her. "Because you deserve to have a daughter just like me."

"Heaven help us both," Klayne teased, skimming a kiss across her lips although his hand continued to rub over her skin, exploring the contours of his wife. She felt nothing, yet everything, like he remembered.

She laughed and settled against him. "Stay with me tonight, Klayne. Please? I don't want to be alone anymore."

"You'll never have to be alone again," he assured her, moving so he rested next to her, taking her in his arms. "Just don't push me away again. My heart can't take it."

Delaney snuggled into his solid chest. "No more, soldier boy. Your place is right here, beside me."

Leisurely, he caressed her, holding her tenderly in his arms. "I missed you so much, Laney. More than you'll ever know. There were days when the only thing that pulled me through was thinking of seeing you again, of being with you like this."

"Oh, Klayne," she whispered, tears stinging her eyes. "I missed you, too. In spite of what you might think, I love you so much."

"And I love you." He cleared his throat then gazed at her indecisively.

"What is it?" she asked, reading the questions on his face and concern in his eyes. "What's wrong?"

"I wrote something for you," he said, as though he feared sharing it with her. "Something you might think is silly."

She moved her head so she could see him better. "What is it? A poem?"

"Of sorts. You probably don't remember, but the day we wed, we were walking down the street and I asked if you wanted to do something, go to the movies or a dance. You said there was nothing you wanted more than just to spend time with me."

"I remember," Delaney whispered, flooded with memories of that day that seemed like a lifetime ago.

Uncertain and somewhat shyly, he shared the words he'd written for her from his heart.

It might rain or it might shine
There may be clouds
At any time...

A blizzard might rage and blow
The flowers may bloom
But this I know...

No matter what,
No matter when,
I'd leave it all behind
Just to spend the day with you.

"You wrote that, Klayne?" she asked, peering into his handsome, beloved face.

"I wrote it for you, Delaney. There isn't anything I wouldn't do just to spend time with you. When I wasn't certain I'd survive, all I pleaded for was the chance to see you one more time, to spend just one more hour with you."

Tears trickled down her cheeks. "You don't have to worry any more, Klayne. There's no place I'd rather be than right here with you."

His thumbs brushed away her tears before his lips claimed hers in a kiss that left no doubt about the depths of his love and devotion.

✶✶✶ *Chapter Twenty-Four* ✶✶✶

In the days following Ryatt's disappearance from school, Klayne was happier than he'd ever been. Delaney moved her things into the guest room with him, since the bed was larger and the room had more space.

Together, they went up to the attic and found two trunks full of baby clothes and blankets that had belonged to Mac and Delaney, along with a crib, cradle, highchair, and baby carriage.

"This baby is going to have more stuff than she'll ever be able to use," Klayne said as he glued a loose spindle on the crib.

"Perhaps, but babies in general seem to need quite a bit of stuff, as you put it," Delaney said, as she ran a dust cloth over the furniture in the baby's room for the fifth time.

Klayne noticed she'd been spending a lot of time in the room, adjusting this and straightening that, as though the baby would care. It amused him to watch her fidget with the furnishings in the room. Fussing over little details seemed so at odds with her character, what he knew of her.

For the first few months, the baby would sleep in the cradle he'd already repaired and polished to a high shine, but he wanted everything to be perfect for the little one's arrival. As he replaced the lid on the glue and stepped back, Klayne glanced around the room, proud of how nice it looked. Delaney had done an excellent job creating a little haven for their baby.

In fact, to him it seemed the ranch had become a haven for them all.

Ryatt was doing well, both in school and at home. He'd made friends with a little boy named Grady Hill. Twice he'd gone to the Hill home after school to play and one Saturday, Grady came out to the ranch to spend the day.

Dill maneuvered around with ease on his crutches and grew more jovial as his pain lessened.

Klayne noticed his own strength and stamina improving each day. The clean air, wholesome food, and hard work on the ranch helped. However, he credited a large part of his drastic improvement to finally coming home to the place he belonged — in Delaney's heart.

He reached out to her and pulled her against his chest as they looked around the room. The pale yellow walls, the same color of freshly churned butter that matched the shade on the exterior of the house, appeared cheerful and welcoming. The cherry wood furniture gleamed and shone in the autumn sunlight streaming through windows covered by yellow gingham curtains sewn by Lina.

Although the room could be used for a boy or a girl, something about it seemed feminine to Klayne. He couldn't say what, exactly, other than Delaney was convinced she was having a girl. Ryatt continually referred to the baby as "she" or "my princess." In truth, Klayne didn't care if it was a boy or a girl. He just wanted it to be healthy.

He'd only had a little more than a month to adjust to the idea of becoming a father. The thought both frightened and thrilled him. He feared his lack of parents and unpleasant childhood might somehow affect his ability to be a good parent. Yet, he knew with unwavering certainty that he'd move heaven and earth to keep his family safe and make them feel loved.

The very notion of having a family of his own was such a foreign, unexpected, thoroughly wonderful realization to him. He had a family, a real family. Delaney and the baby, Ryatt, Dill, and even Butch and Duffy were among those he included.

It all started with a beautiful girl who captured his interest and his heart from his hiding place behind a half-dead Christmas tree.

"I love you, Laney," Klayne murmured into his wife's hair as he continued to hold her. His hands rested on her stomach, anticipating the moment the baby might kick again. Since Delaney had invited him into her bed and back into her heart, he couldn't get enough of touching her, being with her.

She acted embarrassed every time he grazed his hands over her skin, muttering about looking like a water buffalo or an elephant. But he loved the feel of her, of her warm, smooth skin, the hardness of her stomach as it harbored the growing life within, the scent of her that he'd clung to in some of the darkest moments of his life. He loved this woman — his woman — with a ferocity, possessiveness, and indescribable tenderness he'd never imagined feeling, not for anyone.

Delaney turned and looped her wrists behind his neck, smiling coyly at him. "I love you, soldier boy." She leaned against him, pulling his head down for a kiss.

Their lips had barely connected when the baby kicked so hard, Klayne grinned. "Are you sure this isn't going to be a boy? With a kick like that, he could be a great football player."

"If I could raise my foot higher than an inch off the floor, I'd show you how well a girl can kick!" Delaney stepped back and wrapped her hands around his arm, leaning against his side. "I don't really care if it is a boy or girl, but for some reason, Ryatt thinks he needs a princess of his own."

"Well, I've already got my princess, or maybe she's a queen," Klayne said, bending just enough to kiss Delaney's temple. "I don't care either, as long as the baby is in good health and happy."

Delaney sighed contentedly. "The room looks nice, doesn't it?"

"It does, honey. I'm proud of the work you've done to make a very special place to welcome our baby."

Another sigh rolled out of her. "I love hearing you say 'our baby.' For months, I had to think in terms of her being only mine, but I'd much rather share her with you."

Klayne hugged her close. "I'm glad you're willing to share. The one thing you have not shared, though, is what you want to name this child of ours."

Delaney tipped back her head and looked at him. "I know I should have a long list of names I like, but I really haven't come up with any that I'm particularly fond of. You want to take a stab at it?"

Surprised she wanted him to think of names for the baby, Klayne nodded. "I'd be happy to. Hmm. How about Dillette if it's a girl or Sassafras for a boy?" he teased.

Delaney narrowed her gaze and lightly smacked his arm. "I take that back. You clearly aren't capable of thinking of a proper name for this child."

She turned to leave the room, but Klayne lunged at her, playfully growling as he enfolded her in a hug from behind.

The sound of her laughter winged straight to his heart. "You are even crazier than me, Klayne Campbell, and that is no small feat."

"I know, but you love me anyway." He pressed a warm kiss to her neck and she wilted against him.

"Klayne, I love you so much," she whispered, turning in his arms and kissing him with such passion, he was momentarily caught off guard. Before he could take control of the kiss or deepen it, she pulled away and hurried down the hall.

He let her go, needing a moment to gather his thoughts and composure. When he least expected it, Delaney would shower him with affection and pour out words of love that were like a balm to his weary soul. He still hadn't grown accustomed to it.

For a man who'd thought himself beyond the ability to be loved, beyond the need for it, each time she said "I love you," the words and the emotion they carried fulfilled long ago abandoned dreams and sent his heart soaring.

No one ever told him how the love of a good woman would completely alter not just his thoughts, but his entire life.

Delaney's love definitely changed everything.

Klayne awakened with a start, uncertain what had drawn him from his slumber. For a minute, he thought he was back in China, fleeing the Japanese, but he opened his eyes and took in the shadowy shapes of the furniture in the bedroom at Sage Hills Ranch.

He reached out and felt Delaney's arm, assured she was there with him. When he first returned to the ranch, he thought it odd how Ryatt clung to her, needed to be close to her. Now, though, he understood perfectly what the boy had sought. Something about being near Delaney brought him comfort and soothed his spirit.

Quietly rolling onto his back, Klayne listened to the silence around him. All seemed fine, then he heard it again, a soft moan. He sat up and leaned over his wife, listening as she moaned again. Subconsciously, her hands gripped the sides of her stomach.

Afraid to wake her, but worried about her distress, he remained watchful until she relaxed and rolled onto her side, returning to serene slumber.

Unsettled, Klayne couldn't go back to sleep. He would have gotten up and gone downstairs, but he couldn't bear to leave Delaney. Instead, he settled himself behind her, angling his body around hers as though he could shield her from whatever disturbed her sleep.

Jumbled thoughts coursed through his head, thinking of his past, his future, his hopes and dreams. Finally, his eyes closed and he slept. When he awoke, he was alone in the bed. Rather than jump right up and start his day, he allowed himself to linger a minute, inhaling the scent of Delaney on the pillow beneath his cheek.

Never, in his wildest dreams, would he have imagined life being as good and sweet as it had been the last few weeks. The moments when he held Delaney in his arms made time stand still. Peace, unlike anything he'd ever known, filled him, and love surrounded him. Her love gave him purpose and made him feel like a brand new man, one who could accomplish anything as long as she was beside him.

With one more deep breath of her fragrance, he rolled out of bed and began his day. Later that morning, Delaney asked if he'd drive to Walla Walla to pick up several supplies there, then fill a grocery list in Pendleton.

"Butch needs some things, too. It would be such a help if you could go, Klayne. Do you mind?" Delaney asked, smiling at him as she scrubbed the stove until it shone.

He had no idea what they could possibly need from Walla Walla, but would do as she asked. "Is there anything special you want from town? Anything not on the list?" he asked, slipping on a jacket and pulling the new cowboy hat Delaney had given him last week down on his head. He'd owned a battered hat years ago, but he'd worn it until it was beyond redemption.

She looked at him over her shoulder as she rinsed out a rag in the sink. "I'd love a 3 Musketeers candy bar, if you happen to come across one. Oh, and if you think about it, you might drop by the school and pick up Ry on your way home. I think he'd be pleased if you did."

"Those are simple requests to fill, my darling wife." Klayne give her a loud smack on her cheek then gently swatted her bottom. "I'll be back before supper."

The warm smile she gave him almost made him turn back around to give her a real kiss, but he instead grinned and left.

The trip to Walla Walla was uneventful. He wondered why Delaney had sent him there. He thought most of the things he picked up on her list could have been purchased in Pendleton. Besides, the trip used an unnecessary portion of their tightly rationed gasoline and wore on the tire rubber.

Regardless, he enjoyed driving past the rolling fields, now barren of wheat, and humming along to the radio.

He purchased a hamburger and Coca-Cola for his lunch, browsed through a few shops, exploring the town, then headed to Pendleton. A few minutes before school released for the day, he parked out front, waiting for Ryatt.

Children spilled out the doors, laughing, running, some yelling. A few stopped to play in the orange and gold leaves scattered across the ground while others raced toward home in the crisp October air.

He opened the pickup door and waved as Ryatt ran out with the Hill boy. The two of them raced over to Klayne.

"Hey, boys. How was school?" he asked, settling a hand on Ryatt's shoulder.

"It was fun, Klayne. We had a spelling bee today and Grady got first place," Ryatt said, grinning at his friend.

"That's great, Grady. Congratulations." Klayne nodded to the boy.

"Thanks, Mr. Campbell." Grady looked from Klayne to the pickup behind him. "Whatcha doing today?"

Klayne smiled at the boy. "Butch and my wife both needed supplies. We thought Ryatt might like to skip riding the bus today."

"Boy, would I. That bus is the most everlastingly horrid thing on wheels," Ryatt said, shaking his head. "I'll tell it to the world, but roller skates on a washboard would have to be a smoother ride."

"You don't say." Klayne bit back a grin and motioned to the pickup. "Would you like a ride home, Grady?"

"Yes, sir!" Grady said, following Ry as the two boys scrambled into the pickup.

Klayne slid behind the wheel and drove them both to the bakery where the boys enjoyed milk and cookies, served by Amy.

"How's Dee?" Amy asked. She boxed up a dozen cookies and a coffee cake for him to take home.

"Very well, although she's cleaned the house from top to bottom and back again. I'm worried she might overdo, but I can't convince her to sit and rest."

Amy scoffed. "I'd wish you luck with that, but it's impossible to get her to sit still."

"I've noticed," Klayne said, paying Amy for the baked goods and the boys' after school snack. "The blanket you made for the baby is pretty. Ryatt and Delaney are convinced it will be a girl."

"And you have any doubt in your mind that Delaney won't get what she wants?" Amy asked, handing him the bakery box full of sweets.

"No, ma'am, I do not." He grinned. "I'm living proof of that."

Amy laughed and waved as Klayne left with the boys. He took Grady home then circled back to the heart of town where he and Ryatt went to the grocers and filled the shopping list. The store had a good selection of candy, partly because so many of the soldiers stationed at Pendleton Airfield were in town. He allowed Ryatt to choose three varieties, then added a 3 Musketeers bar to his pile of purchases.

"Klayne?" Ryatt asked as they loaded the groceries in the back of the pickup.

"What is it, Ry?" he opened the pickup door for the boy to climb in, but he just stood staring up at him.

"Do you think we could find something for Aunt Dee? Something pretty? I heard her tell you yesterday she couldn't even win a beauty contest against a deformed rhino. I think she needs something to cheer her up."

Klayne patted Ryatt on the shoulder and nudged him away from the pickup then shut the door. "That's a great idea, son. Let's go see what we can find."

An hour later, they climbed in the pickup, pleased with their purchases, and headed home.

"What do you think Butch will make for supper tonight?" Klayne asked. It was an odd arrangement, to eat nearly all their meals at the bunkhouse, but Delaney didn't enjoy cooking, at least not often, and Butch did. The old cowboy did a fair job at it too, turning out hearty meals that Klayne appreciated.

"Maybe he'll make baked noodles with cheese again." Ryatt licked his lips in anticipation, making Klayne laugh.

"I don't know, you about ate yourself sick on them the last time," the man teased the boy.

Ryatt scowled at Klayne, then broke into a grin. "But they're so good, Klayne. Why, I betcha my life no one makes baked noodles better'n Butch."

"They are good, Ry." Klayne would have reached over and ruffled the boy's hair, but a strange car parked in front of the house made him wonder who'd come to visit.

As they stepped out of the pickup, the sound of a woman's scream from an open upstairs window made Klayne vault down the walk, across the porch steps and slam inside the house in a blink.

Before he could clamber up the stairs, Dill hurried as fast as his crutches would carry him into the entry from the front room. "It's okay, Klayne. Doc Nash is with her."

Klayne's eyes pivoted from the top of the stairs to his father-in-law. "What's wrong with her?"

Dill chuckled and rolled his eyes. "In case you haven't noticed or somehow have forgotten, she's having a baby."

Stunned, Klayne gaped at the old rancher. "But it's not due until November. I thought she meant closer to Thanksgiving."

Much to his dismay, Dill laughed again. "Son, babies have a way of arriving when they're ready, and apparently, this one was ready today. I realize you might not know much about babies and such, but they do take nine months to arrive. Even you should be able to do the math from when you married my girl."

Klayne felt heat sear up his neck as he glared at Dill. "When did she go into labor?"

Dill shifted on his crutches and glanced out the door to where Butch and Duffy were trying to keep Ryatt from running inside. "Sometime during the night. She didn't want to worry you. That's why she sent you off on errands all day."

Klayne frowned. "I knew there wasn't any purpose to the trip to Walla Walla. I should have stayed here."

"Women are funny, mysterious creatures, Klayne, and when they head into labor..." Dill shook his head. "I can't make head or tails out of anything Sis has done today, and I won't even try. Doc has been here about an hour. Last time he came downstairs, he said it wouldn't be long."

Another anguished, pain-filled sound drifted down from upstairs. Klayne turned to rush up the steps, but a yell from Ryatt drew his attention to the boy. He broke away from the two cowboys outside and rushed into the house.

Klayne grabbed him before he could run upstairs, but Ryatt fought against him like a wild thing, desperate to get to Delaney.

Finally, Klayne carried him outside and sat down on the top porch step, holding the youngster against his chest while Ryatt bucked and squirmed to be set free.

"Ryatt! Listen to me! I promised you I'd take care of you and your aunt and I will. She's having the baby. That's all. I want you to calm down and pay attention to what I say."

To his credit, the boy's movements slowed then stilled and he looked up at Klayne.

"That's better." Klayne set him on his knee and braced a hand against Ryatt's back. "Bringing a baby into the world is a big, hard, painful thing. Your aunt will do just fine, but she might need to holler a time or two getting the job done. I don't want you to be scared. The doctor is here, and I'm here, and your grandpa is here. We're all gonna make sure she's safe, and you, too. Okay?"

Ryatt nodded then hugged Klayne. "Don't let her die, Uncle Klayne. Please?"

"I won't, Ry. Now, can you keep your grandpa company while I check on your aunt Dee?"

The boy nodded again.

Klayne set him on his feet and together they walked inside the house. Ryatt stood by his grandfather and watched with wary eyes as Klayne made his way up the steps. The door to Delaney's old bedroom was closed, so Klayne turned the knob and pushed it open.

Delaney strained against a contraction, hands clenched around the iron spindles of the headboard.

The doctor cast him a quick glance then turned his attention back to delivering the baby.

"You shouldn't be here." Delaney panted, giving Klayne a pain-dazed look of disapproval.

"There's no other place I should be, Delaney," Klayne said. He discarded his jacket and hat on the way to the bed. He stood beside it and wiped the sweat from her brow then tensed as her body tightened and another contraction rolled over her.

"You're doing fine, Dee," the doctor assured her. "When you feel the need to push, do it." Nik glanced up at Klayne and subtly tipped his head toward Delaney.

Klayne pried her fingers loose from the headboard and moved behind her. He supported her back against his chest and placed his hands so she could grip them. "Why did you send me away?"

"I figured you'd fuss over me and drive me nuts long before this baby decided to get down to the business of entering the world," Delaney said before another pain seized her. She swallowed back a scream and clenched Klayne's hands, nearly crushing his fingers.

"Push, Dee. Give it a good push," Nik encouraged.

Delaney pushed then rested against Klayne, limp and exhausted. If he could have traded places with her, he would have. He'd have done anything to spare her pain.

She leaned her head against his shoulder and looked up at him. "This is all your fault, you know," she said, offering him a weak smile.

He kissed her nose and grinned. "Not entirely."

The doctor chuckled. "Perhaps I need to give you both a lesson in the birds and bees."

Just as Delaney was about to offer a comment, another pain made her grip Klayne's hands so tightly he thought she might break all his fingers.

With a triumphant shout from her, the baby arrived.

"It's a little princess!" Nik announced.

"A girl, a precious baby girl," Klayne said, awed by the sight of his daughter as the doctor held her. From his position behind Delaney, he could see dark hair and a tiny hand waving in the air. Unable to breathe until the baby released a gusty cry, Klayne drew in a relieved gulp.

He shifted, allowing Delaney to sit up a little more so she could see the baby, too. "She's beautiful, Laney. Just like her mother."

Delaney squeezed his hand, tenderly this time. "Doc, I think you better examine my husband. He obviously needs a pair of glasses."

"Oh, don't be so ornery to the boy, Dee. Despite that scar on his eye, he sees very well, especially for one so smitten with his wife." Nik grinned and laid the baby on Delaney's chest.

She and Klayne counted every toe then examined each perfect hand, fashioned with long, slender fingers. He marveled at the tiny little nails that looked almost unreal in their wondrous construction. These were hands meant to create beauty in a world that no longer seemed quite so harsh and ugly.

While Delaney rested, the doctor showed Klayne how to give the baby a bath and instructed him in the proper way to hold one so little, supporting her head and back. When he'd managed to get a diaper pinned on and a soft kimono pulled over her head, he wrapped her in a blanket and carried her back to Delaney.

"She's the sweetest, most wonderful baby in the world," Klayne whispered as he handed his daughter to his wife.

"She is wonderful," Delaney said, cuddling the baby close and brushing a feathery kiss across her forehead. "But she needs a name." She looked up at Klayne with the beginnings of a playful spark in her engaging hazel eyes. "Please tell me you picked out something better than Ethel or Mathilda."

Klayne offered her a lopsided smile, unable to fathom how his heart could hold all the love bubbling up there for this woman and their child. "Hope. I'd like to name her Caroline Hope Campbell, if you don't mind. I thought Caroline, for Mac's wife, might be a good way to honor someone I know you loved. And Hope because that's what this baby has given us all."

Delaney's eyes brimmed with tears and she nodded. "You did good, soldier boy. Caroline Hope it is." She kissed the baby's forehead again. "Baby Hope, you have the most incredible daddy. I hope someday you marry a man just as wonderful as him."

Klayne looked at her like she was his most cherished treasure. Before he could say anything, though, Ryatt's voice carried up the steps. "Is she here? Did our princess arrive?"

Delaney smiled, the dimple deep in her cheek, while Klayne and the doctor chuckled.

"How about I introduce our princess to the family?" Klayne asked, carefully taking the baby from Delaney. He kissed her temple then walked out the door.

As he left the room, Delaney watched him go, considering all that had happened since she met Klayne. She'd survived some of the hardest, darkest days of her life, but also some of the happiest and best. No matter how it had happened, she wouldn't have traded a single minute, not when they'd brought her to this sweet, unforgettable moment. A moment filled with joy and so much love her heart ached with the fullness of it.

Against all odds, her husband had returned to her, had claimed his rightful place in her heart and her life. She and Klayne had mended their fences, made plans for the future, and rested in the knowledge that no matter what might come, they'd face it together. They would celebrate their triumphs and work through their challenges because they loved one another with an abiding, lasting love.

And because they had Hope.

✶✶✶★ *Chapter Twenty-Five* ★✶✶✶

April 1943

Delaney shifted Hope as she carried the baby out to the wheat field. Ryatt and Moose engaged in a game of tag beside them as they walked along a familiar path, worn from age.

In spite of the devastation of the ongoing war, new life sprang up all around them as spring arrived at Sage Hills Ranch.

Calves played on the far hill while foals bucked and jumped in the pasture by the barn. Grass that had been brown and crisp after the winter snows melted took on a lush, verdant green hue following warm days and spring rains. Tulips and daffodils balanced on slender stems, providing bursts of color in an ever-brightening landscape.

Eager to breathe in the sweet scent of spring, Delaney strolled out into the field, admiring bearded heads of wheat that would grow full and golden by summer's end. Ryatt and the dog followed in her footsteps to keep from tramping down any of the crop.

Delaney stopped and closed her eyes, tipped back her head and let the land fill her senses. In spite of the challenges, life was so sweet and blessed. Far richer than she'd dared to dream.

The baby wriggled and babbled in her arms. Delaney opened her eyes and smiled as Hope reached for a figure in the distance.

Klayne stood at the edge of the field and waved to them. He cut such a fine figure in his uniform, one Delaney didn't think she'd ever tire of seeing. Her husband enjoyed his work training soldiers at Pendleton Airfield, and she was grateful every day he came home to her each night.

"Come on, Moose. Uncle Klayne's here!" Ryatt said, excitedly retracing his steps with the dog woofing right behind him.

Delaney lifted the baby's little hand and waved it at Klayne. In the months since she'd opened her heart to him, she'd discovered home wasn't the ranch, the house where she'd grown up, or the town of Pendleton.

Home would forever be the place she held in Klayne's heart.

With a contented sigh, she lifted the baby higher in her arms. "Come on, Hope. Let's go home."

Lazy Daisy Cake

When I was a newly married, clueless girl, one of my aunts shared a recipe for an easy cake that I've made many times over the years. Imagine my surprise when I discovered it's been popular with brides both young and old for generations!

Lazy Daisy Cake:
4 eggs
2 cups granulated sugar
2 teaspoons vanilla
2 cups flour
2 teaspoons baking powder
½ teaspoon salt
1 cup milk
2 tablespoons butter
Topping:
6 tablespoons butter
6 tablespoons brown sugar
4 tablespoons heavy cream
1 cup shredded, sweetened coconut

Preheat oven to 350 degrees.
Beat eggs lightly and add granulated sugar slowly, until batter is pale yellow. Add vanilla. In a separate bowl, sift together dry ingredients. Heat milk and butter together until butter is melted (the easiest way is in the microwave). Fold dry ingredients into the batter then pour in milk mixture and beat well until thoroughly blended.

Grease a 9 x 13 inch pan (or a 10-inch cast iron skillet works, too) and pour in batter and bake for approximately 40 minutes, until cake is golden and a toothpick inserted in the center comes out clean.

For the topping, heat butter, brown sugar and cream in a saucepan, stirring to keep it from sticking to the pan. Bring to a boil. Add coconut and stir then spread on top of baked cake. Broil for three or four minutes, until coconut topping is golden and bubbling.

Serve with whipped cream or ice cream for extra deliciousness.

Author's Note

When I was writing *Garden of Her Heart*, I considered the other books I planned to write in the Hearts of the War series. As soon as I wrote about Ryatt Danvers losing his parents, I knew the story of his aunt Dee had to be next in the series.

In truth, I started to write the beginning of the story with Delaney bringing Ryatt home after the funeral service. As usual, my characters had other plans. So much of Delaney and Klayne's story happened months before that tragic event and needed to be shared with you.

We knew from *Garden of Her Heart* that Delaney was someone held in high esteem by Ryatt and his little friend Petey. As I pictured her and her big, dynamic personality, I imagined the type of man who would be a good balance to her.

Enter quiet, unassuming Klayne. A man without family or any roots. A man who is kind, gentle, and generous, but has never been given the opportunity to share that with anyone. For me, Klayne was an easy character to like and admire, despite his faults. For fun, I looked up the name Klayne and discovered those with this name supposedly have an urge for independence that causes them to find the "ties that bind" restricting. So perfect for his character, don't you think?

In the story, Klayne was one of eighty brave men who took on an impossible mission with courage and determination.

The basis for the mission he went on to bomb Japan came from what I read about the Doolittle Raiders. Actually, the idea for that came from a friend of our Lil Miss. She came home from school one day, excited that a friend told her about some men from Pendleton, Oregon, who were famous during World War II and suggested I look into the Doolittle Raid.

(Thank you, Bradey! What a fabulous suggestion!)

According to Captain Cavedweller, I dove into the research so deeply, he wasn't sure I'd ever resurface. The more I read about the men involved in the raid, the more I wanted to know about them.

Essentially, the bombing of Pearl Harbor drove President Roosevelt to demand something be done, something big, something on Japanese soil that would show the enemy they might have struck first, but America would definitely strike back.

The "foolish idea" that would become a top-secret mission started with a question about an Army bomber flying off a Navy carrier and bombing Japan, perhaps even Tokyo. As the idea gained steam, chief of the Army Air Forces, Lieutenant General Henry "Hap" Arnold, joined in the planning. He ran the concept by Lieutenant Colonel Jimmy Doolittle, his staff troubleshooter. Doolittle was asked to look into the type of Army planes that could take off in 500 feet, carry a 2,000-pound bomb load, and fly 2,000 miles with a full crew. The other stipulation was that the wingspan of the plane could not exceed more than 75 feet.

Doolittle decided the B-25 Mitchell, a medium-sized bomber, could be modified to fit the specifications needed for the operation. In January, General Arnold requested Doolittle take over the mission.

At first glimpse, one might have questioned why Doolittle qualified to lead such an important undertaking. The man was just five feet four, but he was a fighter. From his early days in Alaska where he fought bullies to his years as a professional boxer, Doolittle could hold his own. He also was a man of intelligence and cunning, holding a degree from the University of California as well as a master's and Ph.D. in aeronautical engineering. Doolittle tested planes, pushing them to their limits, flying aerobatics that wowed crowds and gave him the ability to know what a plane could do.

While General Arnold set plans in motion with Doolittle, the Navy was finishing work on a new carrier named the *Hornet*. Before anything further transpired, it was decided a test run had to take place to see if a B-25 could lift off a carrier. General Arnold ordered three B-25s with the best combat crews available report to Norfolk where the planes and crews boarded the *Hornet*. On February 2, 1942, two bombers (a burned out engine grounded the third) took to the skies, zooming off the *Hornet's* deck.

Assured flying B-25s off a carrier was possible, Doolittle moved forward with plans. He needed aircrews with enough pilots, bombardiers, and gunners to operate two dozen planes. At that time, only a few outfits in the country flew the relatively new B-25. Doolittle was directed to the 17th Bombardment Group, comprised of the 34th, 37th, and 95th squadrons, as well as the associated 89th Reconnaissance Squadron, all based in Pendleton, Oregon. They had planes he could use and Doolittle decided to recruit his fliers from the same group.

Not a single airman in the group had flown in combat, few of the gunners had fired a machine gun from the plane, and many of the navigators had little practical experience, especially when it came to open water. Yet, orders rolled out on February 3, transferring all planes, aircrews, and ground personnel to Columbia Army Air Base in South Carolina.

Aware of the dangers of the mission, Doolittle only wanted volunteers. He assembled a group commander and squadron leaders, informing them he was in charge of a dangerous mission, one that would require the bombers to take off in just 500 feet. Unable to give them more details, he trusted them to select two dozen crews, made entirely of volunteers. In early March, the crews were moved from South Carolina to Eglin Field in Florida. Some of the men joked they volunteered just to get away from living in tents in the cold and mud of Columbia.

The crews trained in the modified B-25s, flying over the water, practicing bombing, navigating, and flying low. One of the men really did make a new bombsight out of scrap parts that cost mere pennies compared to the Norden bombsight's expensive price tag. He called it the Mark Twain in honor of the lead-line depth finders once used along the Mississippi River.

A few weeks later, Doolittle gave orders for the men to fly across the country to McClellan Airfield in Sacramento. Stories indicate many of the crews had quite a lively time on the flight from one coast to the other, flying low while scaring farmers, cattle, cars on the road, and others in their journey. From McClellan they went on to Alameda Naval Air Station where sixteen planes and all of the crews boarded the *Hornet*. Even though the crews still had no idea where they were heading (although many speculated the reason for the mission), Doolittle was afraid someone might leak information, so every man who had trained was taken along on the journey.

Once they were far out at sea, Doolittle gathered the men and told them of his plans to bomb Tokyo and a few other cities. The men knew their odds were slim of surviving the mission, but they didn't back out.

The morning of April 18, 1942, after spotting a Japanese ship, the decision was made for the Raiders to take to the air much earlier than planned. Hundreds of miles away from where they originally planned to leave the *Hornet*, they added extra cans of fuel and hoped for the best.

Of the eighty men who flew on that famous mission, 79 of them came from Pendleton Airfield. The only one who wasn't was Doolittle. Fifteen of the planes crashed in or near China. Three men died in the crash landings, and the Japanese captured eight others. Three of the eight prisoners of war were executed later in 1942, and one died of malnourishment. Miraculously, the other four survived the war in some of the most horrific conditions one can imagine.

The one plane that didn't make it to China landed in Russia where the crew was interned for fourteen months until they escaped and made it to safety.

The crew of plane number seven, piloted by Captain Ted W. Lawson crashed close to a beach when their engines failed. All but the gunner received severe injuries. This crew was the inspiration for the men with Klayne in the story.

Captain Lawson had to have a leg amputated in primitive conditions, but somehow survived. After he made it back to the States, he wrote a book called *Thirty Seconds Over Tokyo*. It was soon turned into a movie. I highly recommend both if you'd like a glimpse into the lives of what these unbelievably brave men went through on this mission. I also recommend *I Could Never Be So Lucky Again* by Gen. James H. "Jimmy" Doolittle and James M. Scott's *Target Tokyo*, an excellent, engaging book that takes you on the entire mission, right up through the release of the POWs and the reunion of the surviving Doolittle Raiders.

Although the raid on Tokyo didn't result in substantial damage to any of the cities bombed (in fact, Doolittle thought he'd be court-martialed when he returned to Washington D.C), it wreaked psychological havoc on the Japanese leaders who thought their country was untouchable. The raid also gave America a huge boost in morale that carried on through the coming dark days of the war.

As I read the stories of these men... men who volunteered with no idea where they were going or what they were doing, just that many of them most likely wouldn't survive, my heart swelled with admiration for each one of them. And not just them, but the families they left behind who had no idea of their fates for weeks (some for months and years) after the mission.

As you may have guessed, the reason for setting this story in Pendleton ties closely to the fact the Doolittle Raiders were based at the airfield there before Doolittle transferred them to South Carolina.

Those of you who are familiar with my _Pendleton Petticoats_ series may recognize some characters such as Kade Rawlings, Tony and Ilsa Campanelli, and Nik Nash, to name a few. It was fun to think about them in their "golden years," and what life might look like for them then.

Since there was a brothel involved in the story, I just had to make it Miss Clementine's place from the Pendleton Petticoat series. Miss Clementine is based on the historical figure of Stella Darby, a real-life madam who operated her bordello from the late 1920s until well into the 1960s in Pendleton. She supported any number of charities in town, often donating clothing, food and funds to the poor.

Pendleton is as unique and varied in its history as this story implies. The Umatilla Reservation really was located on one end of town while a hospital for the mentally ill resided on the other.

Wheat ranches were and are a vital part of the area's economy, with thousands and thousands of acres of golden, rolling hills visible in the summer months.

In fact, my Dad worked on wheat ranches in the area when he was a young man in the 1950s. He talks about roguing the wheat, along with many other fascinating stories of his days on the sprawling wheat ranches.

The magazine mentioned in the story that Delaney finds at the hospital with Klayne's picture inside is actually the June 1, 1942 issue of *Life* Magazine. One of the Raiders wrote that he came upon that issue of the magazine en route to the States from China and was quite shocked to see a photo of himself included. I had more fun than I should have thumbing through the pages of the copy I acquired, studying the advertisements even more than the stories.

In the course of writing this story, I've learned so much about World War II, about the courageous people who battled the enemy and those who triumphed on the home front. There were times Captain Cavedweller would come into my office and find me an emotional mess from reading what some of these people endured.

I am grateful every day for the sacrifices they made that created a better world for the next generation, and the next.

If you enjoyed this story, I hope you'll keep an eye out for the next book in the Hearts of the War series. Yes, there most definitely will be more. The characters awaiting their turn to have their stories told definitely wouldn't have it any other way.

Join Shanna Hatfield's mailing list and receive
a free short story!

Shanna's Newsletter

The newsletter comes out once a month with the
details about
new releases, sales, recipes, and more!
Sign up today!

ABOUT THE AUTHOR

SHANNA HATFIELD spent ten years as a newspaper journalist before moving into the field of marketing and public relations. Self-publishing the romantic stories she dreams up in her head is a perfect outlet for her lifelong love of writing, reading, and creativity. She and her husband, lovingly referred to as Captain Cavedweller, reside in the Pacific Northwest.

Shanna loves to hear from readers.
Connect with her online:
Blog: shannahatfield.com
Facebook: Shanna Hatfield
Pinterest: https://www.pinterest.com/shannahatfield/
Email: shanna@shannahatfield.com

If you'd like to know more about the characters in any of her books, visit the Book Characters page on her website or check out her Book Boards on Pinterest.